The Trasceran Chronicles

The
Kylgahran

Book One–The Kinsmen

Randy Ellena

The Kylgahran: Book One—The Kinsmen

Forest of Grativy Publications
Fresno, California

ISBN: 978-0-578-48301-6 (paperback)
ISBN: 978-0-578-48304-7 (ebook)

LCCN: 2019937457

rev202001

For Rebecca—
My joy and my solace
A bonnie if ever there was one

Contents

Preface

The Trasceran Chronicles is set in the lands surrounding the Middle Sea on the two-mooned world of Trascera. Magic, the mystic power of the Yir, stirs on Trascera, wondrous and ominous in equal measure.

The story opens in the Highlands of Kylgahra, a rugged green land of narrow valleys and tree-lined ridges wedged between the shores of a great ocean and the towering slopes of an inland mountain range. The Kylgahran are not so much one people as a loose confederation of clans, each ruled by an individual laird. Though bound by clan law and custom reaching back across generations, the Highlanders of Kylgahra are a raucous, fiercely independent lot. Ambitious lairds more often vie with one another than with any outside threat.

Book One of the Kylgahran focuses on the lives of two young Highlanders. The first is a sheriff who acquires a magic sword, which, some say, has a demon in the blade, as he contends with marauding borderland tribesmen and shifting clan politics. But these are the least of his worries, for he has women in his life.

The other is a headstrong youth living on the far eastern frontier, seeking to find his true purpose. He eagerly signs on with a trail crew and helps guide a herd of cattle across a trackless wilderness to a great city. Confronted by danger and tragedy during the drive, he encounters a raven-haired girl and an amber-eyed elf upon arrival. His courage is tested further as an improbable friendship grows. The erstwhile drover finds himself set to embark upon a quest destined to change his life forever.

The two Kylgahran share a common name, and though they do not know it, the bond between them runs deep. As their story unfolds, it will reflect watershed events, shaping a narrow window of time in a world swept up in rapid and widespread change. Choices matter amid the tumult, more than in less turbulent days, and some have hard edges, carving headlong into the most daunting of consequences.

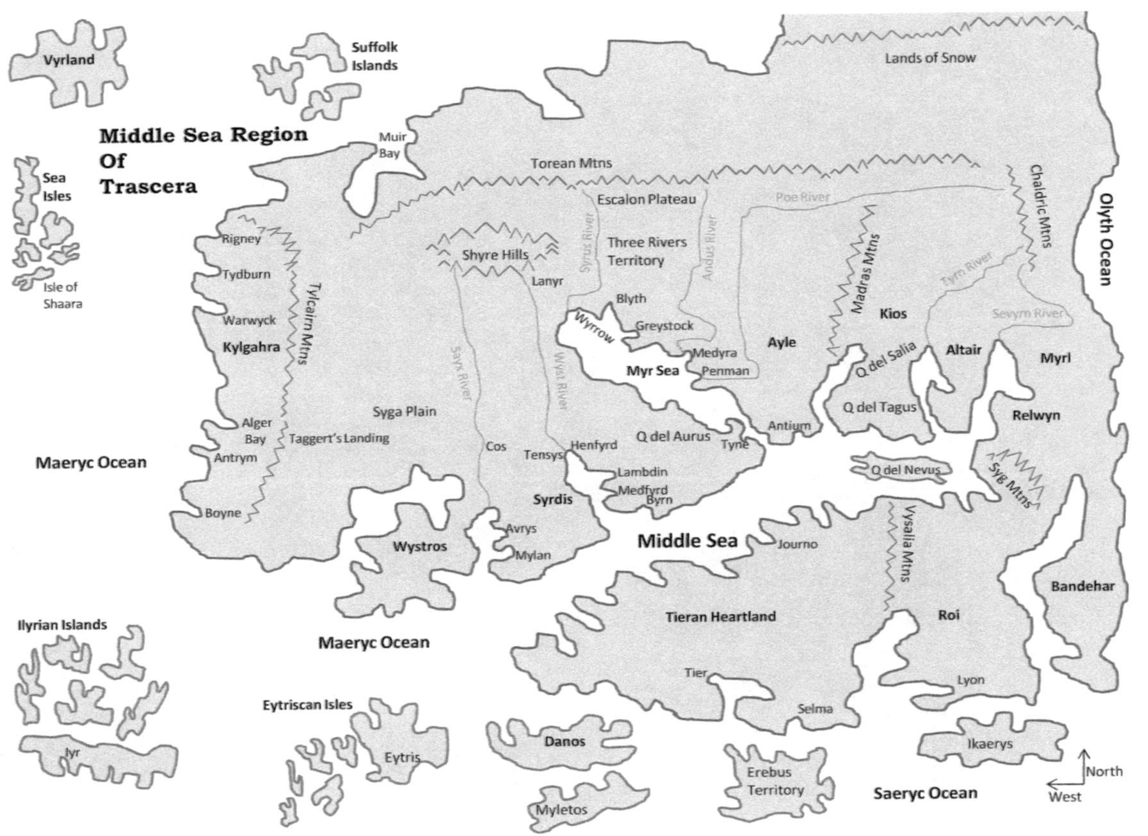

Middle Sea Region
Of
Trascera
Vyrland
Suffolk Islands
Lands of Snow
Sea Isles
Isle of Shaara
Muir Bay
Torean Mtns
Escalon Plateau
Poe River
Chaldric Mtns
Olyth Ocean
Rigney
Tydburn
Warwyck
Kylgahra
Tylcairn Mtns
Shyre Hills
Lanyr
Three Rivers Territory
Syrus River
Andus River
Madras Mtns
Tyrn River
Kios
Sevyrn River
Blyth
Wyrrow
Greystock
Medyra
Myr Sea
Penman
Ayle
Q del Salia
Altair
Myrl
Q del Tagus
Relwyn
Syga Plain
Savx River
Wyst River
Antium
Alger Bay
Taggert's Landing
Cos
Tensys
Henfyrd
Q del Aurus
Tyne
Antrym
Lambdin
Medfyrd
Byrn
Q del Nevus
Syg Mtns
Boyne
Syrdis
Avrys
Mylan
Middle Sea
Journo
Vysalia Mtns
Roi
Bandehar
Maeryc Ocean
Wystros
Maeryc Ocean
Tieran Heartland
Tier
Lyon
Ilyrian Islands
Selma
Iyr
Eytriscan Isles
Eytris
Danos
Erebus Territory
Ikaerys
Saeryc Ocean
Myletos
North
West

Kylgahra and Vicinity

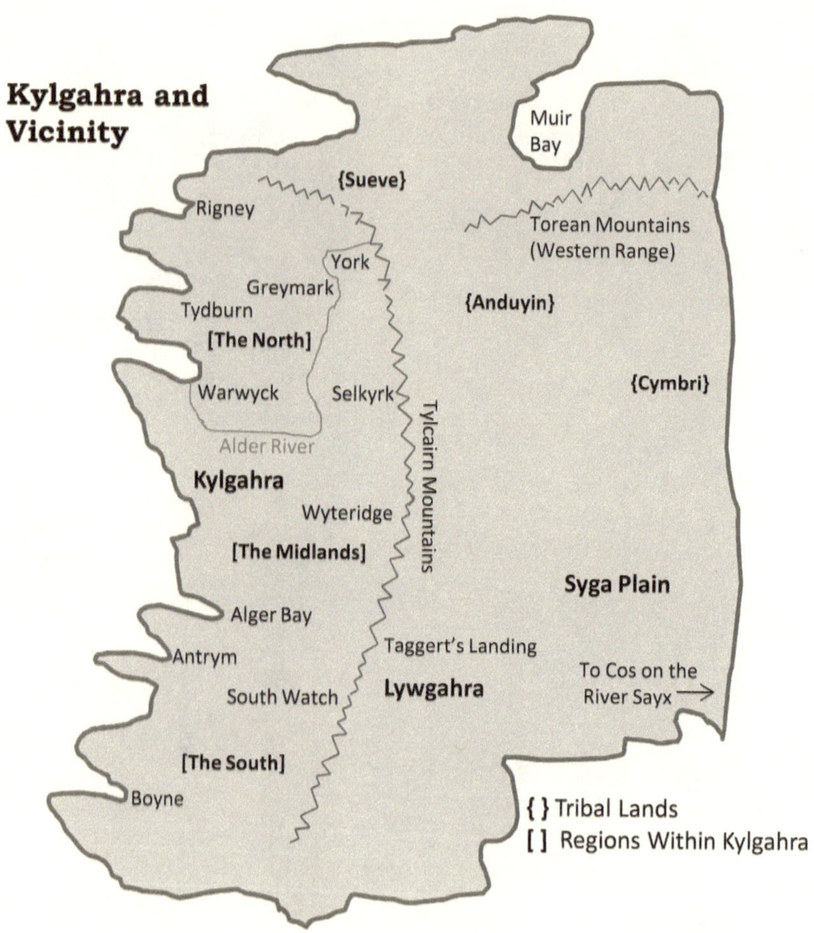

1

The Sheriff of Wyteridge

Dawn came softly to the Highlands of Kylgahra, as if the light of day waxed reluctant to intrude upon night's inky presence. The twin Trasceran moons had long since set when the first stir of waking rippled through a land still steeped in darkness. The night wind shifted and then faded as stillness descended. Furtively, the first tendrils of sunlight crept into the waiting silence. Having begun as a pale crescent, low along the eastern horizon, the gathering light surged like a slowly rising tide, gradually drowning out the stars until the deep velvety black of the nighttime sky gave way to the soft purple hue of early morning.

Two horsemen made their way into the rose-colored light, heading east, ever deeper into the borderland. They moved steadily, following the sign, but kept a sharp watch. Aware that little welcome awaited in the hardscrabble hill country through which they journeyed, the pair pressed on as morning waned, until a quick glance at the sky above showed the sun hanging high overhead.

Leaning forward in the saddle, Sheriff Ranyl Emyrt of Clan Ard Mourne eased his crotch and got a good whiff of himself in the pro-

1

cess. He smelled of wood smoke and leather and horse, with a touch of man stink. Ranyl noted an acrid tinge to the odor, the redolence of fear-sweat, he reckoned, or maybe just his imagination. He'd been scared right enough when the Guilleys jumped them three days ago, more so when one of the buggers managed to plant a spear in his thigh.

Ranyl had slipped and fallen after taking the spear thrust. The Guilley spearman, a tall, lanky boy with pimples on his face, yanked his weapon free of Ranyl's leg and stood gathering himself for a killing stroke when Kevyn slammed into him with his targe, the sturdy Kylgahran round shield. Ranyl's cousin, Kevyn Mourne of Clan Ard Mourne, knocked the young Guilley off-balance and then downed him with a well-placed sword thrust. Long limbed and rawboned, Kevyn handled a baelryc, the hand-and-a-half hilted bastard sword Highlanders favored, with both power and precision.

"This Guilley we're after is running like he owes us money," Ranyl remarked.

"He's limber; I'll give him that," Ranyl's companion, Ellis Tate, a ranger also of Clan Ard Mourne, acknowledged. "Knacky too, travelin' wherever he can over broken ground." Ellis indicated the way ahead. "A fit man afoot ain't at much disadvantage."

"You might have mentioned that yesterday," Ranyl challenged.

Intent on reading the trail before them, Ellis merely smiled. "Yesterday I wasn't so well acquainted." The ranger raised his eyes, squinting toward the horizon. "He's runnin' hard, this'n," Ellis continued, "but he ain't runnin' scared."

Ranyl smiled. "You can tell all that from a few scratches in the ground?"

"Scratches in the ground reflect a man's actions," Ellis explained. "His actions reveal his thoughts, kindly. There's no tellin' fer sure, but you get a feelin', ya know?"

"If he isn't running scared," Ranyl mused, "it could be we're headed in the wrong direction."

"Aye," the ranger allowed, "could be." Ellis stood as tall and as lithely muscled as Kevyn Mourne. There the similarity ended. Graced with wavy blond hair and sky-blue eyes, Kevyn's countenance more often than not garnered a second look from female passersby. Ellis's visage more closely resembled that of the dappled-grey Morgyn he rode. Half a head shorter but broader through the chest and shoulders, Ranyl, like Ellis, had hair of reddish-brown. They shared the same age, too—twenty and five. Ellis's green-eyed gaze settled upon the young sheriff. "You sure you ain't takin' this a little too personal?"

"I know of but one way to find out." Ranyl's eyes, charcoal grey, narrowed in response. He urged his mount onward. Their pursuit continued into early afternoon. The two Kylgahran reined to a halt alongside the bank of a shallow watercourse, about a stone's throw in width.

"How's yer leg holdin' up?" Ellis wanted to know.

"It only hurts when I'm awake," Ranyl replied shortly. Despite a series of thorough washings and repeated applications of a red bracken poultice in the days since, the wound in Ranyl's leg had begun to sour. It pained him some too, a dull, persistent ache.

"Are we closing on him?" Ranyl asked.

"The Guilley's slowin' down." Ellis spoke with quiet confidence. "I reckon we'll take him afore nightfall." The lanky ranger pointed. "He entered the creek just there. The track's right fresh."

Raising his eyes, Ranyl looked across the stream, staring intently into the dense brush and clusters of pine lining the far side. Seeing nothing, Ranyl squared his shoulders. "Best be about it, then."

Ellis shook his head. "Best you give that misery of yourn a good soakin' first."

"You sure we can afford the time?" Ranyl pressed.

"We can, milord sheriff, if you stop wastin' it," Ellis drawled. Tate's eyes lit with amusement as Ranyl climbed gingerly down from the saddle of his dun-colored mount, also a Morgyn, to gaze reluctantly at the swift flow of the brook. Even amid the midsummer warmth, the water coursing through the mountain-fed stream would be bitterly cold.

"Climbing in there is liable to shrivel my pod," Ranyl complained.

"Better that than letting your leg go to rot," Ellis observed matter-of-factly.

Ranyl unbuckled his sword belt, looping it over the pommel of his saddle. He left his dirk in place, attached to a second belt above his right hip. After pulling off his boots and carefully removing his buckskin trousers, he dropped them on the bank of the creek. Tugging his broad-brimmed grey felt hat firmly into place, he slowly waded into the frigid stream. Ranyl swore softly at the frosty bite of the water. He felt a sudden urge to urinate. Deciding that would have to wait a bit, Ranyl unwrapped the bandage about his right thigh and crouched to let the flow of water scour the wound.

As the sheriff of Wyteridge, Ranyl commanded a company of thirty-six rangers. Under Ranyl's direction, the rangers patrolled the region surrounding the town, keeping the peace, warding against outlaws and poachers, and fending off Guilley cattle raiders.

Guilleys were unaligned tribesmen, a mix of rogue, clanless Kylgahran and indigenous tribal folk, mostly Sueve with some Tuchyck, that dwelled in and among the windswept crags of the Tylcairn Mountains along the northern and eastern borders of Kylgahra, as far south as the Midlands. The distaff tribe folk called themselves the *Free People*. Kylgahran clansmen referred to them as Guilleys, a Guilley being a midsized scavenger bird renowned for its raucous call and ravenous appetite.

Three days prior, the day he'd taken the hurt, Ranyl had led a mixed force of rangers, Wyteridge townsmen, and Ard Mourne retainers—Kylgahran warriors directly in service to the laird of Clan Ard Mourne—in pursuit of about two dozen Guilleys, following a cattle raid the outlanders had staged on one of the laird's holdings just north of Wyteridge itself. Ranyl's company, thirty-eight strong, closed on the Guilleys at the southern edge of Ryeland Moor. The rangers, the Ard Mourne retainers, and even the townsmen were better armed and armored than the outlanders, and the brawl quickly turned in their favor. Without warning, a second group of Guilleys, about a dozen, came boiling out of the bog like so many angry hornets. Of a sudden, the Highlanders' advantage in numbers vanished, and the one-sided scrap looked like it might become a close-run affair.

Eventually, the Kylgahran prevailed. About two-thirds of the

Guilleys were killed or captured, but the rest scattered and fled into or around the moor. The next morning, Ranyl ordered the townsmen and Ard Mourne retainers, under the command of Kevyn Mourne, to return to Wyteridge, along with their wounded and the captured Guilleys and what cattle the Kylgahran had recovered.

Keeping to the saddle where he could favor his bandaged thigh, Ranyl led the twelve rangers that remained in pursuit of the marauders. On the following afternoon, Ranyl's men jumped a group of eight Guilley raiders. Only one managed to escape, a tall, lean fellow with long, fiery-red hair. The redhead proved to be the leader of the Guilley band, a man whose name, as Ranyl learned from the quartet of prisoners taken, was Verityx.

In the end, Ranyl chose to send his rangers and the four prisoners back and invest one more day to see if he and Ellis could catch the Guilley ringleader. They were into the afternoon of the second day and hadn't caught up yet.

"My leg is starting to sting worse than my pride." Ranyl tossed the words back over his shoulder.

"Pride has gotten more men killed than even stupidity," Ellis proclaimed. True enough, Ranyl supposed, except that he wanted this Verityx. The name was one Ranyl knew. The Guilley had successfully raided Ard Mourne lands, making off with goods and cattle, on at least three prior occasions.

"Sundown," Ranyl decided. "If we haven't caught up by then, we'll head back."

"All right enough," Ellis concurred.

Ranyl and Ellis each wore chain mail vests over padded leather jerkins. In addition to their baelrycs and targes, which they both carried, Ellis was equipped with a set of throwing darts, while Ranyl had a horse bow and a large quiver of arrows strapped to his saddle. Resembling oversized arrows—steel tipped and fletched with grey goose feathers—throwing darts served as the preferred missile weapon of the Kylgahran and their Guilley adversaries alike.

Moving slowly back toward the edge of the stream, Ranyl looked up to see that Ellis had swung down as well. Ellis had removed his chain mail armor and padded leather arming jacket. He stood clad only in a sweat-stained cotton shirt and buckskin trousers. The lean-ly muscled ranger had tethered both mounts to a deadfall a few steps upstream from where Ranyl had entered the brook.

Ellis pulled a spare shirt from his saddlebag, "Thought I'd scrub down some while you bandage up." Ellis had taken only a couple of steps in Ranyl's direction when the arrow struck him high in his abdomen. The shaft lodged deep, and Ellis crumpled to the ground without a sound.

Scrambling up the bank, Ranyl lost his footing and toppled to his knees. The fall saved him as a pair of throwing darts flashed by, whisker close. The first knocked his hat from his head, while the second scored his mail hauberk between his shoulder blades but failed to penetrate. Ranyl clawed his way up the gentle incline of the streambed and ran for the closest cover, a jumble of large boulders a few paces further upslope. The rocks offered the nearest shelter from more missiles he felt certain were headed his way but led away from the horses and the weapons they carried.

A second brace of darts whizzed overhead, near enough for him to hear the hum of the feathered shafts as they passed. They missed by finger widths when he was but a pace from the first large boulder. Just as he ducked behind the rock, an arrow skittered off the stone, so close to his face that the fletching brushed the bridge of his nose. Diving behind the boulder, Ranyl continued deeper into the rocks strewn up the gradual incline at the side of the creek. Scuttling as best he could on all fours, Ranyl desperately tried to open some distance between him and his assailants.

A few paces upslope, the sprawl of boulders merged with a much larger rock formation that towered far above his head. Thick brush ringed the rocky outcrop off to his left, leading to a stand of pines. Just to his right, he saw an opening between two house-sized rocks of mottled grey. Ranyl slipped into the split and kept climb-ing. Armed only with his dirk, he would stand no chance against missile-equipped adversaries unless he could draw them into close quarters. Though Ranyl still wore his chain mail vest over a stur-dy padded-leather arming jacket, he was bareheaded, barefoot, and bare-assed.

Not exactly dignified—and alone, too—Ellis looked to have been hit hard, and if not dead outright was certainly in no shape to fight. Ranyl found himself hoping Ellis was dead. Guilleys—Ranyl had no doubt that it was a group of outlanders who had ambushed them— were often cruel to prisoners.

Ranyl reckoned there must be three attackers or at least three carrying missile weapons. If they pursued him promptly, he was a dead man. Glancing down, Ranyl saw blood coursing from the wound in his thigh. His leg hadn't bothered him much during his mad dash into the rocks, and he'd forgotten all about having to pee. Removing his tartyn from about his neck, he bound the silk cloth tightly around his thigh. That would have to do.

Scared as he was, Ranyl knew he had to keep moving. If he was to survive, he would have to find an edge, some advantage he could exploit. The split in the rocks led upwards and widened. Ranyl soon realized he was traversing a man-made passage carved into the stone above the creek bed.

Ahead, the passage terminated in what appeared to be a small doorway cut into a sheer, vertical wall of rock. Bending down, Ranyl made his way through the opening and stepped into complete darkness. Keeping his right hand pressed against the wall of the entryway, Ranyl gingerly eased forward. A few steps only, and the narrow hallway turned sharply to the right, opening into a circular vault about six paces across. Amazingly, the chamber was well lit, sunlight having been routed in some manner through channels hewn in the domed roof of the enclosure. He could see shafts of light entering the room from a number of slits in the rock, with dust motes swirling in each.

Statues had been carved into the living rock walls of what Ranyl assumed must have been a tomb. A stag regarded him warily from the far side of the chamber, and to its side, a bull with a pair of wickedly curved, improbably long horns glared belligerently. Between them, two young men and a pair of similarly aged girls stood hand in hand. *A depiction of the Four Fates, perhaps?*

A large sarcophagus crafted not from the native granite of the enclosure but rather of pure white marble stood in the center of the circular vault. Despite the urgency of his situation, Ranyl found himself wondering how the sarcophagus had been placed in the tomb. He did not think it would fit through the door. The lid of the coffin had been thrown back. The body, if there was one, apparently had been removed. A set of shelves had been cut into the stone walls of the tomb as well. All stood empty. Either the tomb had never been occupied, or it had been thoroughly robbed, Ranyl suspected, long ago.

His eyes were drawn to a life-sized statue of a man positioned directly behind the sarcophagus. The figure depicted a warrior. Unlike the other statues in the tomb, the warrior was not carved from the granite walls of the chamber but stood separate and looked to be made of rare red marble. The warrior was helmeted. Full cheek guards disguised his features. A cuirass of some type girded his upper body; its skirts covered his loins. The warrior's well-formed legs were bare, while a pair of sandals covered his feet. Braced against his leg, a large round shield rested on the floor. In his right hand, he grasped a thrusting spear. A long-hafted sword was belted at his waist above his left hip.

Ranyl's eyes flicked back to the sword. The hand-and-a-half hilt ended in a large pommel with a wolf's head carved into it. Ranyl blinked; the pommel was fashioned of etched brass, and the simple, heavy, bar-shaped hand-guard appeared to be made of steel, not stone. Stepping across the enclosure Ranyl grasped the boar hide-wrapped handle of the sword. Ranyl felt a chill rush through his body. Difficult to describe, the sensation was something like a shiver, except he was certain it came from without. An instant only, and the feeling dissipated. Ranyl stood for a moment, gripping the sword hilt firmly in his right hand. A sense of calm washed over him.

Taking a breath, he pulled at the sword. The weapon slid easily from its red-marble sheath, and he swept it aloft, holding it into the light. About the same length as his baelryc, the blade in his hand was a true broadsword. Double edged its full length, the blue-grey steel of the sword tapered gracefully into an elegantly formed, perfectly symmetric point. The blade showed wider at the base than a baelryc, and Ranyl was surprised to discover it weighed about the same. He tested the edges of the sword with the thumb of his left hand and found them razor sharp.

He could await his enemies at the entrance of the tomb. They would have to enter one at a time. In the close confines of the passage, the Guilleys' missile weapons would avail them little. Reluctantly, Ranyl decided against the idea. If he stayed inside the tomb, he'd be trapped. With neither food nor water, he would not last long. Ranyl doubted the Guilleys would wait—they rarely did, this close to the border—but he didn't want to be stuck like a bug in a bottle either.

If he managed to work his way back into the brush alongside the jumble of rocks leading to the tomb entrance, he could combine good cover with mobility. With luck, he might be able to close with the Guilleys or hide until they lost interest. Pausing at the far end of the short entryway, Ranyl listened carefully. He could hear bees buzzing and the warbling cry of a thrush close by. If the Guilleys were right on top of him, there would be only silence.

Ranyl took a fresh grip on the broadsword with his right hand and stepped from the gloom of the passage into the bright sunlight that lanced down amid the rocks outside. Backtracking, he worked his way through the stones to the split boulders at the base. Crouched there, he heard the first scream, a man crying out in agony. Ellis Tate's luck had run dry. The Guilleys had taken him alive.

2

Meggie

Ranyl stole into the brush growing beside the rock formation and headed down slope toward the stream. Ellis screamed again, more faintly this time. *His strength must be failing*, Ranyl thought. Knowing he was likely crawling into a trap, Ranyl moved as quickly as he could. As he approached the jumble of boulders that had saved him from volleys of darts and arrows, Ranyl came upon one of the Guilleys' throwing spears embedded in the soft ground at the base of a large fern. Briefly, Ranyl examined the dart. The point appeared intact, and the shaft looked sound, even to the fletching.

Gathering up the dart, Ranyl crept to the verge of the brush and peered out. He saw three Guilleys ranged along the near side of the creek, a spear cast or so ahead of him and slightly to his right. The nearest, armed with a light bow, appeared to be a young girl. A slender redhead, she was, wearing a man's shirt of homespun wool, belted about the waist, a pair of ragged leather boots, and woolen leggings. She was bareheaded, with a canvas bag of arrows slung over her right hip and a long knife in a sheath attached to her belt on her left-hand side. A faded red woolen scarf wrapped loosely about her throat.

"Have done with him, Verityx," she called, looking about, "and let's be after the other one." The girl had an arrow fixed to her bow. A crude leather bracer was tied around her left forearm.

"Shut up, Meggie," the tall redhead replied, kneeling above the prostrate form of Ellis Tate. "This one's not through talkin' yet."

Verityx was clad in a dust-colored woolen shirt that fell to mid-thigh. A light woolen blanket, dull green in color, wrapped about his shoulders, and a broad leather belt encircled his lean middle. Verityx wore boots, while canvas leggings wound around his lower legs; his long, bright-red hair threaded into a thick braid that fell to the small of his back. Ranyl noticed a baelryc in a leather sheath affixed to his belt on Verityx's left side. A targe lay at his feet.

"All he's done is holler," Meggie protested, "and the other is liable to get clean away."

"The other has got no weapons and a hole in his thigh," Verityx opined. "We'll run him down easy enough." Pinning Ellis Tate's left hand against a melon-sized stone, Verityx used an already bloody knife to sever the ranger's middle finger. Ellis moaned in agony but weakly.

"You're just bein' mean the now," Meggie cried. "You didn't even ask him nothin'."

"I told you to shut up, Meggie," Verityx growled. "Say one more word, an' I'll be at you with more than just my prick tonight."

"There's a small threat," Meggie shot back.

"She's talkin' sense, Verityx," the remaining Guilley—a big, dark-haired lout dressed in the same manner as Verityx—drawled. "Why don't we go finish the other and get ourselves out of here?"

"You are even more of a woman than she is, Brohn," Verityx sneered. "All we got to show for this raid is a couple of horses an' a bunch of dead spear brothers. Their spirits call out fer blood."

Brohn shook his head but said nothing. Instead of a sword, this Brohn had an axe stuck through a loop in his belt. In addition, he was armed with a targe, carried on his left arm, and a quiver of throwing darts slung across his back. Ranyl saw a pair of feathered shafts protruding above the big man's right shoulder.

Ranyl could get no closer without breaking cover. Holding the throwing dart at the ready in his right hand, he gripped the broadsword in his left and stepped cautiously out of the brush, gliding silently toward the Guilleys. He'd closed the distance by three full strides before the girl, Meggie, turned in his direction. Shouting a cry of warning, she swung her bow up. Ranyl braced as she did so and hurled the throwing dart. The dart's steel tip tore into Meggie's middle just as she released her arrow. Her shot went wide, and Ranyl charged the two remaining Guilleys as young Meggie dropped to her knees, clutching at the haft of the throwing spear with both hands.

Instead of drawing his axe or a dart, Brohn rushed to Meggie's side, calling her name. Ranyl engaged him, swinging his broadsword down in a two-handed grip from the three-quarter position. Belatedly, Brohn reacted, raising his targe to fend off the blow. Ranyl's sword scored the leather-bound surface of Brohn's shield, and the force of the strike caused the Guilley to lose his balance. The large fellow stumbled and fell backward, sprawling. Ranyl slid forward and thrust his blade deep into Brohn's groin. The Guilley screamed. Blood spurted in a dark, heavy stream as Ranyl ripped the broadsword free.

Ranyl's eyes locked on to Verityx. The lanky Guilley had cast aside his targe but held his baelryc at the ready. Flourishing the blade, Verityx said, "I'm going to take yer head, Kylgahran, and piss down yer throat."

Saying nothing, Ranyl advanced with his broadsword held in the high-guard position. His arms raised, the blade canted backward above Ranyl's right shoulder while the fingers of both hands coiled round the hilt.

"Nice sword," Verityx commented. "I'll wear it well once I've done fer you."

Darting forward, Ranyl opened with an overhead strike. Verityx parried easily and drifted quickly to his left. "How's the leg, boyo?" the tall redhead taunted. "The damned thing must be achin' something fierce just the now."

Closing with him, Ranyl struck again from the three-quarter mark. Verityx warded the cut and countered with a thrust aimed at Ranyl's throat. Ranyl beat aside the Guilley's blade and launched a stab of his own. Verityx parried smartly and attacked, raining a series of short, hard slashes down upon the Kylgahran sheriff. Ranyl was in trouble, and he knew it. Verityx could handle a blade, and Ranyl's wounded leg was not going to hold up much longer.

Ranyl lunged at Verityx. Stepping effortlessly out of range, the tall Guilley's back foot came down upon a loose rock about the size of a small apple. The stone shifted, throwing Verityx momentarily off-balance. Seizing the opportunity, Ranyl pressed forward, switching to a one-handed grip and extending fully, driving his blade upward. The broadsword's finely hewn tip ripped into Verityx's lower jaw just behind his chin. Plunging further, the blade smashed through the Guilley's soft palate, lodging at the back of his throat.

Ranyl recovered, taking up the mid-guard stance, but he could see the fight was finished. Verityx dropped to his knees, his eyes a bright pale blue, wide with shock. Pressing both hands to the gaping wound beneath his chin, the tall Guilley toppled to his side and then rolled on to his back, uttering garbled, choking noises from his ravaged throat as blood coursed steadily between his fingers.

As he turned back, Ranyl saw Brohn curled into a fetal position, lying on his right side in a spreading pool of blood, making soft huffing sounds. Ranyl finished him by placing a hand's span of steel between the big Guilley's shoulder blades. Brohn shuddered and then lay still. Hurrying to Ellis Tate's side, Ranyl knelt beside the fallen ranger.

"Glad I lasted long enough to see that," Ellis whispered hoarsely.

"Sorry it took me so long to circle back," Ranyl said, his voice choked with emotion. Ellis's face looked deathly pale.

"Where did you find that?" Ellis's eyes flitted to the broadsword in Ranyl's right hand.

"You wouldn't believe it if I told you." Ranyl smiled at his friend. "Let's get you bandaged up."

"There's no need, boss," Ellis said calmly. "I'm about done. The redhead, he looped round somehow. Sorry I am about that. Don't know where the other two came from; plain bad luck that was."

"There's no accounting for chance," Ranyl assured the lean ranger. The Guilley Verityx had cut two fingers from Ellis's right hand

and one more from his left. Blood oozed from the stumps. Ranyl gripped Ellis's shoulder firmly. "You're still the best I've ever seen."

Ranyl slipped Ellis's tartyn from about his neck and tied the cloth tightly about the ranger's right hand. Ranyl cast about, looking for something to bind up the left, when Ellis smiled. "Tell Mae I love her." Mae was Ellis's woman, a pretty, full-figured blonde. "You'll look after her and the boys?" Ellis had two towheaded sons, four and six years of age. Fortunately for them, both boys looked like their mother.

"I will," Ranyl promised. "My word on it."

"You know it's funny," Ellis said—and died.

Gently pressing his friend's eyelids shut, Ranyl took up the broadsword and climbed to his feet. He stepped toward the girl. Somehow, she'd managed to extract the throwing dart from her abdomen. It lay on the ground at her right side. The Guilley lass was lying on her back, reclined at a slight angle by the slope of the streambed. She held both hands pressed firmly against the wound in her middle. She wasn't bleeding much, at least not that he could see. The sword seemed to quiver in his grasp, as if eager to strike.

The girl regarded him steadily with a pair of large grey eyes. Silver hued, her eyes shone, wide and wary. Ranyl drove the point of his blade into the soft sand at his feet and took his hand from the hilt. Startled at the effort required, Ranyl straightened, leaving the sword behind. "You must be Meggie," he said by way of greeting.

"Not fer much longer," Meggie responded evenly. "You kilt me all right enough, I reckon."

Approaching warily, Ranyl knelt by her right side, shoving the bloodied dart well away. He removed her knife, the blade longer than his forearm, and tossed it aside also. "That's a belly wound. If you're not bleeding too bad inside, you might last for days."

"You're a cheerful bastard, ain't ya?" Meggie groused.

"Time enough," Ranyl explained, "to get you to a healer."

"No healer," Meggie growled vehemently. "I don't want to wind up some Kylgahran's bed-warmer."

"There are worse fates," Ranyl said.

Meggie glared at him, flat-eyed. "Ever have some man you didn't want shove his cock into you?"

Taken aback, Ranyl ducked his head. "I'm sorry. Pay me no mind. I never have been able to talk to a girl, especially a pretty one."

"Pretty, is it?" Meggie regarded him carefully for a moment. She had a round face and a small, upturned nose with a smattering of freckles across it, framed by an unruly mop of red hair. Her body still evidenced the slim-hipped coltishness of youth. *She can't be more than fifteen or sixteen*, Ranyl thought sadly.

Meggie lifted her chin. "You're flirtin' with a corpse, mister; you must be real bad off."

Ranyl looked into her silvery eyes. "You'll be nobody's bed-warmer, Meggie. I promise."

"What's your name, anyway?" Meggie demanded. Ranyl told her, and she swore softly. "Shite, kilt by an Emyrt. My pap's shade will never let me live that down."

"You're a tough little cat, Meggie," Ranyl said. "Let's try for that healer." He eased his left arm behind Meggie's back and started to raise her up.

Meggie gasped with pain. "Don't move me, Ranyl; for Fates' sake, please."

Letting her back down as quickly and gently as he could, Ranyl took her right hand in his left. She squeezed his fingers with surprising strength until the spasm subsided. Looking at his face, Meggie smiled. "Don't take on so, Ranyl. I'd have done fer you happily enough."

"You came within an eyelash of doing just that," Ranyl remarked. "You're the best of this lot, that's for certain."

"I don't know," Meggie hedged. "Ol' Brohn, he wasn't much of a scrapper ... just big and strong and gentle. Verityx was meaner than a snake but right handy with a blade, and he weren't no fool. You must be pretty good with a sword."

"I got lucky," Ranyl acknowledged. "What are you doing with these two anyway?"

"Long story." Meggie's eyes drifted for a moment, someplace far away. She shrugged and smiled wryly. "Hard times; that's the short of it."

"At least Verityx won't be pestering you again," Ranyl asserted.

Meggie's smile warmed. "I hear there is a sheriff down Wyteridge way named Ranyl Emyrt."

"That would be me," Ranyl allowed.

"You're sweet, whoever you are." She squinted up at him. "And a damn liar, too. You're too young, and besides, everybody says that sheriff is canny. He wouldn't be stupid enough to go traipsin' 'round up here with but one ranger at his back."

"I won't do it again," Ranyl said fervently. "That I can assure you."

Meggie gave him a level look. "A sheriff, no foolin'," she murmured. "Ain't that somethin'. If my pap's fetch gives me any lip, I'll tell him ta stuff that in his hat." Another wave of pain washed over Meggie, and she clutched at Ranyl's hand, less strongly than before. "I'm awful scairt, Ranyl."

"You have nothing to be afraid of Meggie," Ranyl assured her, "nothing at all."

"I done some things, Ranyl," Meggie whispered, "things I oughtn't."

"We all have, Meggie," Ranyl told her firmly. "There's no need to dwell on that the now. Any fool could see that yours is a shining soul."

"Don't you worry none about talkin' to women," Meggie said on a breath. "I reckon you'll do just fine."

"That seems to depend almost entirely," Ranyl countered, "upon the woman I'm talking with."

"Bad luck this, then," Meggie concluded softly, "all 'round." Her gaze appeared to turn inward, and she fell silent, looking awfully young and terribly hurt.

"As if you'd have taken even a second look at the likes of me," Ranyl scoffed gently, trying to draw her back.

Meggie's luminous grey eyes again sought his. "I don't know," she mused. "You're a Kylgahran, of course, and a bloody Emyrt to boot, but ya have a nice heft to yer shoulders and pretty eyes."

"I don't think you are supposed to tell a man he has pretty eyes, Meggie," Ranyl admonished.

"Well, they are," Meggie retorted, unrepentant.

"They're not a patch on yours." Ranyl smiled at her. "Your eyes shine like moons' light, beaming down through a mist-shrouded dell. It's a beauty you are, Meggie."

"Stuff," Meggie exclaimed, her eyes swept downward behind impossibly long, lush lashes. "I know well enough what I look like, Ranyl Emyrt. My nose resembles nothin' sa much as a button, and I've got freckles."

"A few," Ranyl conceded, "just enough to give your face some character." Leaning forward, he kissed her gently upon the lips. Ranyl allowed the kiss to linger just long enough for him to taste the warm sweetness of her mouth.

As he pulled back away, Meggie tossed her head slightly. "Men," she chided him, "always takin' advantage." She didn't sound too displeased.

"Scoundrels and knaves all." Ranyl made no attempt at argument. "It's a wonder you women put up with us."

"It ain't like we got much choice in the matter," Meggie grumbled and then winced, her features tightening with pain. She inhaled sharply, and her eyes squeezed shut. Meggie's fingers closed upon his but weakly, her grip only a shadow of what it had been. A long moment passed. Ranyl's jaw knotted at the sight of her hurting so.

Finally, the paroxysm eased, and Meggie exhaled slowly. Her eyes opened. They shared a smile. "Since you done stole it already," she proffered, "I'll make ya a gift of my knife. A Hawken, it is called—good, heavy steel."

"I don't have anything to gift you with in return," Ranyl demurred.

Meggie's wide-set eyes narrowed slightly. "I'll strike ya a bargain instead. Bury me proper, and you can keep the knife with my blessin'."

"That's not much of a bargain, Meggie," Ranyl said softly.

Meggie shook her head; her eyes slid shut again. "Bury me deep,

Ranyl Emyrt, not too low down, mind. I don't want no water seepin' into my grave."

"I'll find you a hillside, Meggie," Ranyl pledged, "under a big white oak. I'll lay you next to Ellis Tate, over there."

"Your ranger?" Meggie asked suspiciously. "Why him?" She opened her eyes.

Ranyl found himself transfixed by her gaze. He nodded to where Ellis's body lay. "He was a good man, the best I ever knew."

"He walked you right into an ambush," Meggie protested.

"He made a mistake," Ranyl explained. "We all do, sooner or later."

"Won't he be mad at me fer killin' him like I done?" Meggie inquired.

"Ellis isn't one to hold a grudge." Ranyl squeezed her hand. "He'll take to you right off; you'll see."

Meggie's eyelids fluttered and then drooped once more. "Ranyl, don't leave me." For the first time she sounded really frightened.

"I'm right here, Meggie," Ranyl soothed, tightening his grip on her hand, "right here."

Meggie's eyes opened fully, focusing on his. "Did you mean it, what ya said 'bout my eyes and moons' light and all?"

"I've never said a truer thing," Ranyl affirmed, smiling at her.

Meggie's lips curved upward slightly. "When the day comes an' you make your mistake, I'll be waitin' fer ya on the other side."

"I'll be glad to see you again, Meggie," Ranyl proclaimed.

"That's what you think." Meggie's smile as she spoke twisted into a grimace of pain.

A spasm wracked her slender form. She could not bite back the low moan that escaped her lips. Her eyes shut, and her chin dipped as she contorted in agony. Ranyl unsheathed his Kylgahran dirk, intending to ram it into her heart. He hesitated. Meggie gasped and shuddered. Ranyl heard the breath rattle in her throat as she exhaled. Her eyes opened wide. An instant only, it took, but in that glimmer of time, Ranyl could see the light in them take flight. Meggie's body fell back against the sloping contour of the creek bed.

Ranyl set aside the long, triangular blade gripped in his right hand and placed his fingers lightly at the side of Meggie's throat, feeling for a pulse he knew he would not find. After a few moments, he reached out and gently closed her eyes. Only then did he release her hand. Wearily, Ranyl pushed himself to his feet. The ache in his wounded thigh felt as if it went clear to the bone.

Ranyl noticed that Verityx still lived. The tall Guilley lay stretched out on his back. His breathing rasped, labored, rapid, and shallow. Ranyl limped over to stand above him. Verityx's mouth stretched wide open in a rectus of pain as his body struggled for air. Barefoot, with his trousers off, it was a simple matter for Ranyl to lift the hem of his hauberk and the arming jacket beneath to piss in the Guilley's face. Aiming purposefully, Ranyl directed the flow of urine into Verityx's gaping maw. Verityx's eyes bulged, and he began to gurgle wetly.

Ranyl stared down at him. "Wait until Ellis's and Meggie's shades get hold of you, you bastard." The need to urinate had returned strongly, and Ranyl was able to maintain a steady stream until well after Verityx's tortured efforts to draw breath ceased all together.

3
Shadowed Homecoming

Six days it took for Sheriff Ranyl Emyrt to see again the crenellated walls of Wyteridge. Located upon a set of bluffs amid a deep horseshoe-shaped bend in the River Thadyck, the modern town of Wyteridge was built upon the ruins of an ancient city. Who the ancients were, no one knew. The ruins stood long abandoned when the first Kylgahran arrived generations ago. East across the river, the foothills of the Tylcairn Mountains crouched, as if in supplication to the jagged peaks towering just beyond.

Kylgahra proper lay wedged between the west coast of the vast Maeryc Ocean and the Tylcairn Mountains to the east. A narrow coastal plain ran north and south nearly the full length of Kylgahra. Inland, the Highlands rose above the plain, a tumbled patchwork of narrow valleys and forest-topped ridges—a green, if rugged, landscape, blessed with rich black soil along the valley floors and an abundance of water.

A good-sized town in the northern reaches of the Midlands, Wyteridge served as a key trading center. Further north, Kylgahra became truly wild country, home to fierce border lairds who claimed the land for the Ragged Harp, the battle standard of Kylgahra. Arrayed against them an ever-shifting alliance of Guilleys and tribal people, the most numerous—and therefore most formidable—of which were the dark-haired Sueve.

Ranyl was only twenty-one when he became sheriff four years ago. Sheriffs' postings generally went to older, more seasoned retainers—his father's influence and a bit of coin at work, no doubt. Esquire Stephyn Emyrt, Ranyl's sire, had become a wealthy man, and when gold talked, even lairds tended to listen.

However he'd attained the office, Ranyl had worked hard during his tenure as sheriff and felt he'd learned his trade well enough. Laird Daryn Mourne of Clan Ard Mourne said as much when he'd last visited Wyteridge, accompanying his second son, Kevyn. Kevyn, aged twenty-two, was to take up a commission in the Highland Guards stationed at Alger Castle later that year. Laird Daryn planned for Kevyn to spend a few months serving with Ard Mourne retainers on watch in Wyteridge for some seasoning, prior to joining the chieftain's elite force.

The young sheriff kept his promise to the Guilley lass Meggie, burying her alongside Ellis Tate on a hillock overlooking the stream by which she had died, at the base of a sturdy young oak. The tree, Ranyl reckoned, would grow to massive size over time and would stand for centuries. He hoped Meggie would be pleased. He doubted Ellis would care much, one way or the other.

Ranyl had wrapped Meggie in his plaid. She'd kick up a fuss over that, most likely, but it was damned good wool. Ranyl stowed Ellis's baelryc aboard the slain ranger's horse, figuring one of his friend's sons would want the blade. Ranyl secured his own baelryc and the sword Verityx had wielded to the saddle of Ellis's mount as well. He laid Brohn's axe and his own dirk in Ellis's grave. The dirk, in particular, was finely wrought. He placed Meggie's bow and what remained of her arrows in hers.

Ranyl wept as he finished the task. He had no words for his tall, quiet friend or his slim, talkative little foe. His choked silence seemed a poor tribute, and Ranyl could only hope his tears were enough. He'd prayed for their souls every evening since and knew he would continue to do so each night for so long as he lived. He kept Meggie's dying gift, a large, single-edged knife with a blade nearly three fingers wide at the hilt that the Guilley lass had called a Hawken and its plain leather sheath, attaching them to his belt on his right side.

Having no proper scabbard for the broadsword he'd found, Ranyl slipped the naked blade through a loop in his stirrup strap. He'd used the razor-like edge of the sword to severe the heads of Brohn and Verityx, wrapping the grisly trophies in the dirty green blanket the lanky redheaded Guilley leader had worn about his shoulders. Ranyl had a feeling he wasn't being fair to Brohn, but damn it, a man was known by those with whom he stood. He tied the blanket to the cantle of Ellis's saddle. Even wrapped securely in several folds of wool, the stench was becoming palpable by the time Ranyl crested the rise, from the summit of which he could see the walls of Wyteridge.

The pain in his right thigh had become a fierce and relentless companion. When he returned to Wyteridge, Ranyl would have Anharyd take a look at it. Anharyd had the healer's touch. A Guilley herself, Anharyd had been captured in a retaliatory raid when she was but a girl. Ranyl had inherited her, along with his posting, from the previous sheriff, a man named Guthbyrt Cutter of Clan Ard Mourne.

A hard man was Cutter. He'd kept a leather collar strung about Anharyd's slender throat, a reminder, he said, of who her betters were. Upon meeting her, Ranyl determined to treat Anharyd decently. His resolve lasted through the evening meal and his third cup of wine. He cut the collar off her then, just before bedding her. Anharyd was beautiful. Six years older than Ranyl, a small but voluptuous woman, her Tuchyck heritage clearly evidenced by lustrous blond hair and wide-set brown eyes. Anharyd had come into his bed willingly enough, as if she expected to be there.

Of course, all this was before Ranyl's betrothal to Helyn Chambers. Helyn was the daughter of Haskyr Chambers of Clan Ard Cullen, a commoner but the wealthiest merchant in Wyteridge. Chambers owned a general store and ran a freight business, hauling goods to and from Wyteridge in the interior and the city of Warwyck on the north central coast of Kylgahra. Kylgahra's largest seaport and capital, the city of Antrym lay far to the south.

Nineteen years of age the now, tall for a Kylgahran lass—his height exactly—Helyn had blond hair and sparkling blue eyes. Long legged and slender, Helyn had been a virgin the first time Ranyl had lain with her, nearly a year prior. He'd not been with Anharyd or anyone except Helyn since.

Long Reach, the main road leading down to Wyteridge from the north, forked three ways as it neared the town. The center path led to the main gate. The right-hand fork serviced a number of the local farms before looping back, ultimately terminating at one of the town's three lesser portals, while the left-most path wound along the banks of the river before rejoining the main road as it approached the town's front gate. A series of three artesian wells were situated between the left fork and the banks of the river. Ranyl and Helyn often visited the smallest of the wells to picnic or watch the sun set. It was by the side of the small well that she yielded her maidenhead to him.

The central path provided the most direct route. Despite the burning ache in his leg, he chose the left-hand fork. Ranyl could not have said why, except that at the end of this journey, he would have to share the news of Ellis's fate. Doing so would, in some way, be like losing his friend all over again. He was in no hurry to do that. The afternoon sun glinted, throwing sparkles off the blue river water as he rode along, but the day remained cool.

Ranyl neared the smallest of the artesian wells. He saw Helyn's horse, a docile little mare she had incongruously named Sprite, tethered to a juniper bush adjacent to the copse of cedar trees that surrounded the well, providing the privacy he and Helyn had made good use of on more than one occasion. Beside Sprite stood a tall roan gelding Ranyl recognized as Kevyn Mourne's usual mount. Curious, Ranyl halted and dismounted gingerly, tying both his and Ellis's horses' reins to the juniper branches as well.

Making his way through the trees, Ranyl saw Helyn and Kevyn together at the base of the well. Both were naked. Helyn was on her knees, her back to the tall Kylgahran. His betrothed's slender thighs were spread, her back arched, her golden-haired head flung back. Kevyn had mounted her from behind. His large, strong hands gripped her slim hips. Ranyl gaped in disbelief as their bodies moved together in passionate accord. Ranyl could see the expressions on their faces. Helyn's lips were parted, her eyes closed. Kevyn looked intent, as if he were concentrating. Again and again, his lean, well-muscled body thrust forward, riding her.

Ranyl turned away. His face flushed while his heart pounded. Shock gave way to rage, and he rushed to his horse. His hand closed on the hilt of the broadsword. An image of Kevyn standing above him at Ryeland Moor, a wry grin on his face, flashed into Ranyl's mind. He could hear Helyn's soft laugh, see the tender look in her light-blue eyes. He had no wish to see her harmed. Ranyl owed Kevyn his life. Kevyn was also the son of Ranyl's laird. How would Laird Daryn Mourne of Clan Ard Mourne react to the news that a sheriff of his had just slaughtered his second son for taking his ease with a commoner? Ranyl suspected the knowledge that the commoner was the sheriff's intended would not likely sway Laird Daryn from the path of swift and equally brutal retribution.

Anger waned, leaving a hollow ache in his chest to balance the fiery burn in his thigh. Painfully, Ranyl climbed back into the saddle. He could think of nothing to do but ride on, and so he did. A contingent of Laird Daryn's retainers garrisoned Wyteridge, serving alongside Ranyl's rangers in coordinated but separate commands. Ferguson Pawl—tough, sandy haired, and laconic, with a wry sense of humor—led the Clan Ard Mourne warriors. Ranyl liked him. A pair of Pawl's men stood sentry duty at the main gate. The town's security was Pawl's concern; the state of affairs in the surrounding countryside was Ranyl's.

Ranyl had cut and trimmed a pair of saplings into rough stakes on his final approach to the town gate. Swinging down he waved a casual salute to the sentries and drove one stake into the soft ground on either side of the road bed. Untying the green blanketed bundle from Ellis's saddle, he removed Verityx's decaying head and, carefully grasping it by long strands of red hair at the temples, impaled the nasty thing atop the right-hand stake. Just below the head, he tied Verityx's distinctive neck cloth about the wooden pole. Brohn's head and neck cloth went up next, adorning the left-hand stake.

One of the sentries, a pleasant-faced young Kylgahran, walked up to him at that point and said, "Sheriff Ranyl, it's good to see you. We'd about given up hope. What is it you're doing?"

"Sending a message," Ranyl replied shortly, "one even the Guilleys will understand. If Pawl has a problem with this, have him come see me."

Something about the sheriff's tone or maybe the look in his eyes gave the young Kylgahran pause. "Yes, sir," was all he said.

From the main gate, Ranyl went directly to his quarters. A two-story stone house, one of the oldest in the town, served as his personal lodgings and provided office space for administrative purposes. To one side of the house, a much newer wood-framed brick building functioned as a barracks for his rangers. On the other, a smaller stone-walled building housed a kitchen. While in service, rangers were not allowed to marry. By Kylgahran standards, rangers were well paid. A number of them, including Ellis Tate, kept women in the town. Across a small cobbled square from the stone house stood the stable for the rangers' mounts, and next to it, a blacksmith's shop doubled as an armory. To the rear was a pair of sturdily built stone storage barns.

Ranyl's steward, Cadigan Embry of Clan Ard Drew, a lean, wiry man of thirty-six years with dark hair and studious blue eyes, met him in the courtyard of the Sheriff's Station, as the collection of buildings had become known.

"Welcome back, sir," Cadigan called. "We're beginning to worry."

"Truth to tell, Cad," Ranyl admitted as he clambered wearily down off his horse, "I was a fair bit worried myself for a little while." Ranyl took a breath. "Ellis Tate is dead. Send word to Mae Hoskins. Tell her I'll come see her in the morning, if that is all right. Please have someone go to the Chambers' home and leave word for Mistress Helyn that I've returned and will see her tomorrow as well, in the afternoon sometime."

Cad nodded.

"Please send for Anharyd," Ranyl ordered. "I'm going to need some tending as soon as she can get to it. Oh, and have Fyrgus stop by my quarters straight away." Fyrgus Clyde of Clan Ard Mourne was the weaponsmith who serviced the Wyteridge ranger troop. "I'll be wanting a bath. Have someone bring in some water."

"Right away, sir," Cad replied, gathering the horses' reins. "I'll have the horses put up."

Sliding the broadsword free of the stirrup strap, Ranyl made his way to his quarters. Ranyl occupied a pair of rooms on the second floor. His thigh protested the climb with renewed vehemence. Ranyl had no sooner entered his bedroom than Tad Gyllis of Clan Ard Mourne, a groom, stepped tentatively through the still-open doorway bearing two large buckets of water.

"Afternoon, sir," Tad greeted him. "Mistress Kate said to tell you she'd be up in a moment with a kettle of hot water."

"Thanks, Tad," Ranyl said, slumping down on a wooden bench near the large copper-clad basin he used as a bathtub. Fyrgus Clyde stopped by next. Ranyl pointed to the broadsword he'd placed on top of a side table. "Take a look at that."

Fyrgus hefted the sword in one meaty hand. Like most smiths, Fyrgus was broad shouldered and deep chested. A man of middle years, he had iron-grey hair and thoughtful brown eyes.

"I've never seen the like, sir," the big smith commented. Slipping an iron file from a pocket in the black leather vest he wore over a homespun porridge-colored woolen shirt, Fyrgus carefully tested the edge of the sword. "It is fine steel, that's for certain—not water-marked, though. I'd stake my life on it. Don't ask me to make you one like it. I haven't a clue."

"I'll settle for a proper sheath by tomorrow morning, if you're able," Ranyl responded.

"That I can do," Fyrgus promised. "I'll have it back to you by first light." Ranyl nodded, and the smith left, taking the broadsword with him.

Ranyl hoped Anharyd's healing touch would leave him whole. *One lame brother in the family is enough.* Ranyl cringed at the thought. Haymish deserved better. Still, he hoped to escape his brother's fate.

Haymish stood thirteen months Ranyl's junior. Haymish appeared every bit as handsome as even the stalwart Kevyn Mourne, right down to the cleft chin and dimpled cheeks. Though he had the Emyrts' coloring—red-brown hair and grey eyes—somehow Haymish had managed to avoid the square build typical of his kin. Standing a full hand's span taller than his older brother, Haymish's body was lean and lithe, the type of man who looked good on a dance floor at a reel. Ranyl's stocky form and facial features were more usual for an Emyrt male. His jaw was firm enough, with a wide, well-formed mouth and a slightly aquiline nose. Not displeasing, really, but Ranyl knew he suffered by comparison to both his brother and his cousin.

Inseparable as children, an unshakable bond had formed between the two Emyrt siblings as they grew. Unshakable, that is—Ranyl recalled with some bitterness—until Elynor Childress of Clan Ard Mourne had come of age. Elynor was a raven-haired, grey-eyed beauty every bit as lovely as Anharyd. Ranyl loved Elynor with his whole heart. She chose Haymish. The day after she and Haymish married, Ranyl left his father's holdings in Shelby Township and began the seven-day ride north to Wyteridge to take up his posting as sheriff. His duties as sheriff and the distance between Wyteridge and Shelby provided just enough excuse to avoid visiting without being too obvious.

Haymish settled upon a naval career. This meant he was away from home a good bit. Elynor took up lodgings in a village just north of Antrym so she could be near when Haymish got shore leave. Haymish was at sea on the eve of his and Elynor's second wedding anniversary, when blackstrap fever struck her.

Called *blackstrap fever* because the stool of those afflicted often darkened with blood during the course of the illness, the disease routinely killed one-fourth of those who came down with it. About one in eight who survived the initial bout of fever succumbed slowly thereafter due to kidney failure. The breakout of fever that fall in the vicinity of Antrym proved to be especially virulent. Elynor died with the dawn on the morning of the third day after falling ill. Adding to the tragedy, Elynor had been four months pregnant at the time of her death.

In the spring of the following year, Haymish's left foot was crushed in a battle at sea with a Vyrlander corsair. The navy healer had little choice but to amputate Haymish's left leg at about mid-calf. One-legged sailors were not all that unusual, but Haymish had been commissioned an officer of the marines, seagoing infantry. Haymish retired his commission and returned home, then a twenty-two-year-old widower.

Elynor's death and Haymish's misfortune had shocked Ranyl and shamed him, too. Shamed him into recognizing his petulance for what it was. Neither Elynor nor Haymish had set out to hurt or deceive him. They had merely fallen in love. Ranyl had visited with Haymish twice since his brother's return from the sea. Haymish appeared much the same as always, joking easily about the advantages of a peg leg. Ranyl knew better than anyone, however, just how skilled Haymish was at hiding his true feelings.

True to her word, thirty-year-old Kate Wysset of Clan Ard Mourne knocked at Ranyl's door a short time later with a kettle of steaming hot water. Kate was buxom, brown haired, with a pert nose and merry green eyes. Wrinkling her nose, Kate declared, "Light, sir, what have you been about? You smell worse than a bear's behind."

"Nice to see you, too, Kate," Ranyl said wryly. "How do you fare?"

Kate was the chief cook—a good one—with a soft heart. Just about everyone's favorite, she was Emerson Hart's woman. Emerson served as Ranyl's lead ranger, effectively the sheriff's second in command.

"I heard about Ellis." Kate's voice lowered with concern. "Are you all right?"

"I will be," Ranyl responded, thinking, *Word does travel fast.* "I expect Mae will be needing some company for the next little while."

Kate laid a hand briefly on his arm. "We'll look after her, and don't you worry."

Ranyl nodded his thanks and began stripping down, even as Kate headed for the door. She closed it firmly behind her. Unsure if he should soak his thigh, Ranyl straddled the basin, naked, and had just about finished scrubbing himself clean when the door opened. Anharyd rushed in; she looked as if she'd been running.

The slender healer was clad in a high-waisted blue cotton frock. Her rich blond hair was swept back into a simple ponytail. Annie's luminous brown-eyed gaze, tight with worry, widened at the sight of him standing there wearing nothing but a bandage around his thigh.

Anharyd whirled about, and he found himself staring at her shapely back and round little bottom. She had a small leather satchel slung over one shoulder. "I'm sorry," she called out. "Cad said to hurry."

Ranyl smiled despite himself. "There's nothing here you haven't seen before, Annie."

"That's not the point, and well you know it, Ranyl Emyrt," Annie scolded him.

Ranyl wrapped a towel about his waist. "I'm decent the now."

Annie turned to face him. Ranyl saw she was blushing. "Well, you're covered anyhow," she allowed.

Ranyl gingerly sat back down upon the bench. "I'm glad to see you by any road."

Stepping quickly to his side, Annie pressed her hand lightly against his temple. "How badly are you hurt?"

"I thought the way this works, Healer, is that you are supposed to tell me," Ranyl commented.

"You're exhausted," Annie observed, "and in considerable pain."

"You have not even delved me yet," Ranyl protested.

"I have eyes, my lord sheriff," Annie told him sharply.

"You do, indeed," Ranyl murmured, "beautiful eyes, like a doe's."

"Hush," Annie ordered him, but she smiled when she said it. "May I?" she inquired.

At his nod, Anharyd's expression sobered, and she laid one hand on either side of his thigh wound. Instantly, Ranyl felt a slight warming and some easing of the pain. He could not have said whether that was due to a healing flow from Anharyd directed into his body or the mere touch of her hands.

"The wound is deep, dangerously so, and inflamed, but there is no rot." Extracting a small, sharp knife from her satchel, Anharyd deftly cut away the bandage, sniffing it briefly before casting it aside. "Red bracken," she noted, examining his wound, "and well moist. You are capable of learning a thing or two, it seems." Taking some fresh water, Anharyd wet down the bracken poultice before removing it.

"Of necessity," Ranyl replied. In spite of the aching throb in his thigh, he felt his body relax; Annie would look after him.

"Here we go," she warned him, laying one slim-fingered hand directly atop the open wound and taking his hand with the other.

Ranyl had experienced healing flows before but never so intensely. The sensation was akin to the tingling he felt after blood began circulating once again in a limb gone to sleep, except it wasn't that exactly; there was warmth too, but the heat seemed to come from within his own body, not exactly painful but distinctly uncomfortable. A thing of the Yir, it was; what sorcerers referred to as the Hidden Source—magic. Annie lacked the strength and breadth of ability required of a sorcerer, but her skill as a healer was highly refined.

Annie's eyes closed, her delicate features fixed in concentration. "There," she said at last. "I'm going to bandage this and let it drain a while. If you behave yourself, you'll be as good as new in a few days." She wouldn't look at him.

Gently, Ranyl extended his hand and slipped his fingers beneath her chin, tilting her face upwards so he could peer into her eyes. He saw tears in them. Ranyl was astonished. In all the time he'd known her, he'd never seen Annie cry.

"What's wrong?" Ranyl asked.

"I don't like to see you in such pain," she answered.

"The wound wasn't much," Ranyl said. "Doesn't hurt at all the now."

"I wasn't talking about your bloody leg," Annie replied softly.

She knows about Ellis, Ranyl thought. *Of course she does; by the now, everybody does.* Ranyl shook his head. "You know, women are complicated."

Tossing her golden mane in dispute, Annie glared at him. "Not so. Men are just bloody hopeless, most of them."

Gathering her, unresisting, into his arms, Ranyl said quietly, "Light, how I've missed you, Annie."

He told her, then, everything—their initial hunt for the Guilley cattle raiders, the sharp skirmish at Ryeland Moor, Kevyn's rescue of him, the continued pursuit that culminated in the ambush at the little stream, of his finding the broadsword, Ellis's death and Meggie's. He left out nothing except what he'd witnessed at the smallest of the artesian wells, just prior to his return to Wyteridge. He couldn't tell her about that yet. As he spoke, Ranyl felt Annie's slender form molding to his with the ease of long familiarity.

When he finished his tale, Annie surmised, "You are grieving for Ellis."

"Yes," Ranyl acknowledged, "and for Meggie, too." He leaned back a little so he could look into her eyes. "I wonder at the fascination I have for Guilley women."

Annie merely rolled her eyes at him.

Ranyl took note of the thin gold chain she wore about her neck. Soon after he'd removed the crude leather collar she'd been forced to wear when first he met her, Ranyl had replaced it with the gold chain now encircling her slender throat. A small medallion attached to the chain was emblazoned with the Ard Mourne Clan mark, a pair of crossed swords. Reaching behind her neck, Ranyl unfastened the chain. He removed it from about her neck. "No more collars for you, not ever again."

Her golden-brown eyes regarded his steadily. "Your collar ever seemed more gift than shackle. You showed me kindness when it would have been easy to be cruel."

"Small compensation," Ranyl averred. "Can you ever forgive me?"

"For taking me into your bed?" Annie's eyes warmed. "Yes, and gladly." Her eyes darkened, and her voice tightened. "For throwing me out of it, never."

"I was hoping we could be friends," Ranyl offered.

"Friends, you and me?" Annie hugged him tightly. "Light, you are thick, aren't you?"

"A little hopeful I'm being, maybe," Ranyl acknowledged, "and just a touch self-seeking." He brushed an errant strand of blond hair from her forehead. "Never did I mean to cause you pain."

"Aye, well, you did." Annie bit off the words as if speaking them caused her fresh hurt. Ranyl shut up. "Friends it's to be, is it?" Annie murmured.

"If you'll have me," Ranyl replied quietly.

"Is it because I cannot bear you a child?" Annie asked so quietly that at first he wasn't sure he'd heard her correctly.

"No, Annie," Ranyl assured her. He brushed her lips with his own and then looked directly into her eyes. "Sweet Annie, no it is not that." When he saw the relief in the liquid depths and knew that she believed him, he gathered Annie to his breast, once more cradling her as if she were a wee one. "I am bound to marry a woman of the clans."

"I would not have begrudged you such a wife," Annie told him matter-of-factly.

Ranyl laughed ruefully. "The problem with that is, no Kylgahran woman would have me without begrudging you—and for good reason."

"Kylgahran women make only little more sense than their men," Annie grumbled. She took a breath and then told him softly, "I am with Cadigan Embry the now." She went very still in his arms, as if she were afraid even to exhale.

Ranyl swallowed the lump suddenly formed in his throat. "I didn't know," he managed to say. "You never said anything."

"As if it was any of your business," Annie said tartly, her nostrils flared. She appeared to have no difficulty whatever with breathing the now.

He squeezed her gently. "He is a good man." Ranyl hesitated a moment and then asked, "Do you love him?"

"I like him," Annie replied. "He is kind, too, and gentle and understanding. We share a sense of humor. He has asked me to marry him."

"Cad is as smart as he looks," Ranyl said approvingly. "I wish you both joy."

She peered up into his face. "Truly, you do not mind?"

"I have not that right," Ranyl intoned. "I want you to be happy." The words were true but still seemed to him inadequate, poorly wrought.

"You are a good man, Ranyl Emyrt"—Annie looked deeply into his eyes for a long moment—"aside from your odd notions of honor. When you and Helyn are married—" Annie paused, her eyes narrowing. "What was that?"

"What do you mean?" Ranyl demurred, dropping his eyes.

"I saw a shadow steal across your face!" Annie exclaimed.

Annie was deeply intuitive. She saw glimpses of things, sometimes in a furtive glance or a flicker of moons' shadow or a wind-driven ripple running across still water—little pieces of what would soon be. Ranyl did not know if this was an aspect of her Yir-born healer's ability or something else, some vestige perhaps of Olde magic. When she saw a happening and understood its meaning, he never knew her to be wrong. Annie shook her head slowly from side to side, as if she could not believe what she had witnessed.

"You will not wed, not in this place. You are going away." Annie sounded alarmed, panicked even.

"I won't be leaving right away." Ranyl spoke soothingly, running a gentle hand down her back. "I don't even know for certain where I'll be bound."

"You won't take me with you?" Annie shook her head. "Us, I mean—Cadigan and me."

"Cadigan is a fine steward," Ranyl said with quiet conviction. "He knows the people here, and they trust him. He will be invaluable to whoever follows me as sheriff. I'll leave the decision to him. I suspect he'll want to stay. As his wife, your place will be by his side."

"I have not said I would marry him," Annie told him, "not yet." Her implication was clear. If Ranyl wanted her, she would follow.

"I think you should, don't you?" Ranyl kissed her as tenderly as he knew how.

Tears spilled openly onto Annie's finely formed cheeks. "How can I be your friend if I never see you?"

"Friendship has nothing to do with proximity," Ranyl proclaimed, sounding like a right fool, even in his own ears. "Besides," he hurried on, "you will never be further from me than this." Ranyl pressed a finger over his heart.

Annie began to weep openly, sobbing like a child. "I don't want you to go."

Ranyl held her close, saying nothing until she quieted. "I'll write to you," Ranyl said.

"You know I can scarcely read," Annie protested. "Writing—this scribbling of yours—is vexing beyond belief." Most Guilleys were illiterate. However much she decried it, Ranyl knew Annie had learned to both read and write.

"Cad can help you with that," Ranyl cajoled. "Together we can gossip shamelessly, and once you are a safely married woman, perhaps we can visit on occasion."

She took his hand in both of hers, gently prying open his fingers to touch the chain he'd removed from her neck. "May I keep this?"

He passed the chain over to her. They sat together for a time after that, beneath a window built into the outer wall of his chamber, watching the sun set, sharing the silence.

4

Natural Enemies

Ranyl awoke the next morning with a ravenous appetite. After Anharyd left the evening before, she had ordered food prepared. Once she'd gone, he had slept for a little while, no more than an hour or so, and had awakened hungry. Upon eating his fill, he truly slept for the first time in days, free of pain. When Ranyl woke in the morning, he finished what was left of the previous evening's victuals before going down to breakfast.

Dressed in a white cotton shirt and tan woolen breeches, with an Ard Mourne plaid draped over his shoulders and a matching tartyn about his neck, Ranyl spent a few moments at table speaking with Emerson Hart of Clan Ard Mourne about changing the rangers' patrol schedule. They settled quickly on a reduced number of sweeps employing larger units. Ranyl's next stop was his office, located in a back corner of the first floor. He found Cad Embry waiting.

"Hart was looking for you," Embry informed him. "And Fyrgus stopped by to deliver this." Cad proffered the broadsword Ranyl had taken from the outland tomb, encased in a finely crafted leather scabbard.

"I saw Emerson at breakfast," Ranyl replied, thanking Cad as he took possession of the sword. "Have you ever seen its like?"

"No," Cad shook his head. "Fyrgus seemed mightily impressed with the quality of the steel. The thing is lighter than it looks. Fyrgus thinks it might be of Elven manufacture."

"I understand you and Anharyd are to be married," Ranyl stated, watching Cad's eyes.

Cad met his gaze without wavering. "I've asked her. She has not said yes."

Ranyl smiled. "I think she will. Be good to her."

"I love her," Cad declared.

"That is not the same thing," Ranyl replied with a harsher tone in his voice than he intended. He instantly regretted it.

Cad took his meaning, though, without offense, saying, "I'll be good to her. I promise."

Moments later, a light knock sounded upon the door, and Anharyd stepped into the room. She wore a dark-green cotton frock with a modest neckline. Her silky blond hair fell loose, held back off her forehead by a matching green cotton ribbon.

"Kate is overjoyed," Anharyd announced. "She seems to think you have finally developed a true appreciation for her cooking."

"I could have eaten my boots for breakfast this morning." Ranyl grinned. "Come to think of it, Kate's stew was pretty good." Grasping the scabbard with his left hand, Ranyl partially drew the entombed sword with his right, uncovering about one third of the blade. "This is the sword I told you about yesterday. There are some markings on the blade. Do they mean anything to you?"

"I know nothing about swords, Ranyl Emyrt," Anharyd informed him briskly. "I came to examine your leg, not your new toy."

"Hardly a toy, this thing is," Ranyl commented dryly. "You can delve my wound to your heart's content in a moment, but first take a look at these markings."

Anharyd stepped close, brown eyes narrowing in concentration as she gazed at the sword. Slowly, she extended her left hand. Her fingers hovered just above the surface of the blade, not quite touching the steel. Anharyd shivered.

"There is something," she murmured absently, sounding as if she was talking only to herself, "disquieting here."

She ran the fingers of her left hand along the edge of the blade, drawing blood. Ranyl pulled the sword away and sheathed it fully. Doing so seemed to break Anharyd's reverie. She stood staring at her hand. Three of her fingers were bleeding steadily.

Setting the sheathed sword down upon the office writing table, Ranyl removed the tartyn from about his throat and wrapped it around her hand. "That was a little careless of you, Healer." He kept his voice casual but looked carefully into her eyes.

Anharyd met his gaze. "I don't like weapons, swords in particular." She spoke softly. "I think that one"—Anharyd pointed at the broadsword—"feels exactly the same way about me." Her eyes widened, imploringly. "I know not what the markings mean, Ranyl, but there was something of the Yir involved in the making of that blade. It hungers, Ranyl, and it is dangerous, for you as well as your enemies, but somehow I think it was meant for you to wield." She raised her bandaged hand to her temple and swayed slightly.

Taking a firm grip on her upper arms to steady her, Ranyl asked anxiously, "Annie, are you all right?"

She glanced up at him for a moment and then looked to Cadigan. "You must think me foolish." Ranyl released her and swallowed hard as she stepped quickly into Cad's arms.

Embracing her, Cad joked, "Healers and swords would seem to be natural enemies."

Not knowing what to make of her reaction or her assessment, Ranyl fastened the scabbard to his belt. Another knock sounded at the door. Ranyl turned to see Ferguson Pawl, of Clan Ard Mourne, standing at the threshold. Ranyl waved him into the room. Tall, blond, and green eyed, Ferguson moved with the ease of a well-trained swordsman. Nodding to Ranyl, the Kylgahran warrior cast a somewhat disdainful look at Cad and Anharyd. Stewards were, of course, necessary but little more than that, and however lovely, Anharyd Swallow was a Guilley.

"Heads on stakes, old son." Ferguson directed his remarks to Ranyl. "A bit much, don't you think?"

"Those two staged an ambush that cost Ellis Tate his life." Ranyl spoke calmly, as he usually did, but there was something different, something the other three in the room, who all knew him well, had not heard before in his tone, as hard the now as the steel on his hip. "I'll send someone to dispose of them at sunset."

"My boys will see to it," Ferguson offered.

"Not before sundown," Ranyl growled, looking Pawl straight in the eye.

"Full dark it will be; my word on it," Ferguson promised, wondering what had happened to Ranyl Emyrt on his last patrol. Though they'd only exchanged a few words, it showed clearly to Pawl that the young sheriff who had embarked upon it was no longer the man who had returned.

5

The Widow's Boy

Aeryk Emyrt of Clan Ard Mourne could not have said what woke him. He opened his eyes to find the rain had ceased, but the night air clung still, heavy with damp. Aeryk lay on his side, wrapped in his plaid and an oiled canvas ground sheet. Overhead, the clouds had broken, and the light of two full moons filtered through, bright enough to cast shadows amid the surrounding pine wood. There, he heard the muted sound of a hoof fall and a nervous jostling among the horses a stone's throw away, along the tether line. Aeryk started to rise.

"Easy, lad," Danyl's gravelly voice whispered from behind as he placed a big, broken-knuckled hand on Aeryk's arm. "We've got company, the uninvited kind."

Aeryk felt the first spurt of alarm course through him. "Who are they?" he asked, matching Danyl's soft tone.

"Can't tell," Danyl answered. "I think there are two of the buggers down by the creek and at least one in among the horses."

"Where's Jervis," Aeryk inquired, referring to the third member of their trading party.

"Creek side, over yonder a bit." Danyl pointed to the northwest. "Take up yer weapons and follow me."

Clad all in woolens and leather, with a broad-brimmed black-felt trail hat set firmly atop his head, Danyl crouched low and stepped to Aeryk's right, heading away from the creek. Slab-shouldered and powerfully muscled, Danyl was built like a block of granite. Despite this, and the streaks of grey liberally threaded through his rust-colored hair, Danyl Trask of Clan Ard Drew moved easily, silently, staying just outside the ring of light thrown by the low-burning campfire.

Slipping his baelryc from its worked leather scabbard, Aeryk crouched beside his bedroll long enough to slide his dirk, still sheathed, into place at the small of his back. His pulse racing, Aeryk tugged his own battered trail hat into place and followed Danyl into the trees. At nineteen, Aeryk stood a hand's span taller than Danyl, with shoulders just as wide if not so thick. Danyl swung further to his right so that he could approach the horse line from the east, moving down slope toward the creek.

The night breeze freshened, rushing through the pine boughs above. Clouds aloft shifted, dissipating further, bathing the forest in a burst of moons' light so intense Aeryk could make out the green of the pine needles. A figure rose up to Danyl's left. A man, armed with a wooden round shield and a single-handed axe, closed swiftly. His axe swung up and back.

"Danyl, your left!" Aeryk cried, his voice sounding high and thin in his own ears.

Danyl pivoted smoothly, taking up a mid-guard stance. The axe descended; Danyl's baelryc swept up to meet it. Out of the corner of his eye, Aeryk spotted movement to his right. He turned his head to see a spearman approaching Danyl from behind.

Aeryk darted forward. "Here," he called. *Not much of a battle cry—* the thought flashed into Aeryk's mind as he drew near—but enough to catch the spearman's attention. Planting his right foot, the spearman veered toward Aeryk. Once in range, the stranger aimed his weapon at Aeryk's throat and launched a determined thrust.

Aeryk had trained for years with the baelryc, and he reacted instinctively. Setting his feet, both hands positioned on the long hilt of his sword, Aeryk parried, intercepting the spearhead at its base. Shifting to his left, Aeryk drove the spear point down and away. His foeman was slightly built, and Aeryk registered surprise at how easily he'd thwarted his adversary's strike. Reversing the sweep of his weapon, Aeryk lunged forward in a controlled movement that drew its power from the full weight of his body, and he plunged his blade into his assailant's breast, just below the heart.

The spearman collapsed immediately, dropping straight down onto the carpet of pine needles at his feet. Aeryk yanked his sword free, astonished at the fountain of blood spurting from his enemy's chest. Aeryk whirled round to his left in time to see Danyl's baelryc take the axe man in the throat.

From down near the creek, the high, keening screech that was the Clan Ard Drew battle cry rang in the darkness—*Jervis*. A moment later, his heart pounding, Aeryk stood over the crumpled form of the unknown spearman. The bloodied sword suddenly heavy in his hand, Aeryk heard more shouting, followed by the sound of horses—not theirs—galloping away. *It's over.* Aeryk tried to swallow. His throat muscles convulsed to little purpose as he found his mouth as dry as old bones.

"Are you hurt?" Danyl inquired. Aeryk looked over to find the burly Highlander's gaze steady upon him.

"No," Aeryk managed. He scrounged up a paltry sort of smile. "I may have to change my britches."

Danyl grinned like the curly wolf he was. "C'mon." The two of them found Jervis, a distant cousin of Danyl's, aged thirty years, sitting on the creek bank nursing a gash to his sword arm.

Jervis appeared as lean as Danyl did bulky, but he shared his older cousin's blue eyes and red hair. Jervis's face showed regular features, pleasing if not quite handsome. Danyl's battered visage looked as if it had been slapped together by accident, nothing quite fit, except for the cut of his jaw and the twinkle in his eye. Danyl claimed not to know his actual age. Aeryk had known him all his life, and reckoned Danyl to be somewhere in his middle years.

"Two of the bastards," Jervis reported without being prompted, "they were on top of me afore I knew it. I stuck the one what cut me. The pair of them cleared out. You two look hale enough."

"Two more tried to work their way in among the horses," Danyl recounted. "We shorted them both, one apiece."

Jervis directed a smile at Aeryk. "You're a blooded warrior the now."

"Better that," Aeryk responded, speaking in what sounded to him like a normal tone of voice for the first time since waking, "than the other way around."

Making his way to Jervis's side, Aeryk knelt. "Let me have a look at that arm." The cut, about halfway between elbow and shoulder joint, did not look too bad. Blood seeped from the wound but slowly. Aeryk bound up the injury using Jervis's tartyn. "We'll make up a poultice once it's light."

Danyl glanced at the sky. "Two hours until dawn, I reckon. You two better try to get some rest."

"What about you?" Aeryk asked.

Danyl's mouth twisted into a wry smile. "I won't be able to so much as close my eyes, lad; never can after a killin'." Danyl's weathered features relaxed, and his smile broadened. "You did well tonight, Aeryk. Be sure to wipe the blood free of yer blade afore ye put it up."

Aeryk nodded, glad of the gloom that hid the blush suddenly mounting his cheeks. Aeryk scrubbed his baelryc free of gore using the damp sand at creek side. A simple task, except of a sudden, Aeryk found his hands would not stop shaking. Aeryk returned to his blankets and dried the blade carefully before sliding it back into its oiled leather scabbard.

Like most Kylgahran, Aeryk was fair skinned. Like many, his hair showed reddish brown. Aeryk succeeded in closing his eyes— light green in the center, banded around the edge of the iris with a darker grey, a color combination Kylgahran referred to as Highland Blue—but sleep proved elusive.

Danyl's admission earlier took the sting out of that. Danyl seemed to have made a habit of it, easing the stings out of Aeryk's life. Aeryk could not remember a day Danyl had not been part of his world—gruff, plainspoken, but always easy to talk with.

The three of them—Danyl, Jervis, and Aeryk—had left the steading, or small ranch, Danyl half owned with Basyl Conroy of Clan Ard Owen with the spring thaw some weeks ago, headed north to Anduyin country to trade. Basyl and Danyl's steading was situated in the southern reaches of the Lywgahra. In Glaylic, the Kylgahran language, the term *Lywgahra* meant Lowlands.

Dryer than the Highlands on the western seaward slopes, the Lowland country east of the Tylcairn Mountains stretched out into a vast wilderness. Composed of gently rolling hills and broad, grass-covered valleys more suited to grazing horses, sheep, and cattle than growing barley or wheat, the eastern Lowlands attracted ranchers and farmers alike seeking free land outside the traditional boundaries of Kylgahra. Lywgahra had come to symbolize freedom in other respects as well. No particular clan—and therefore, no clan laird—held sway in the Lowlands out east. The Lywgahran were a mix of clans. While old clan loyalties and rivalries held, there existed little in the way of direct authority. Life lived less rigidly in the Lowlands.

"A man can breathe out east," Basyl often said.

"Aye," came Danyl's sardonic rejoinder, "but just you try finding a decent tailor."

A tribal people, the Anduyin occupied a large swath of land northeast of the Tylcairn Mountains. The Anduyin were a settled tribe; their metalsmiths were as good as you'd find anywhere. They farmed and raised cattle and goats. They did not run sheep, however, and cotton was unknown to them. Wool, cotton cloth, and, for some reason, copper pots and all manner of shiny trinkets, no matter how cheaply cast, were much in demand among the northerners. Fur, beaver pelts, and horses composed the main trade items in return.

The Anduyin were the real power east of the Tylcairn Mountains. Even the fierce Cymbri had found that out, with graves aplenty to mark the lesson. The Cymbri were a warlike, nomadic tribe from the far north. They crossed over the Torean Mountain range and had pressed steadily south and west, until running afoul the Anduyin. The Cymbri had settled more or less in recent times, claiming territory east and south of Anduyin lands.

Trading with the Anduyin had gone well. The three Kylgahran

were about half the way home, bringing with them seven good horses and a load of fine-grade furs to show for it. They'd had no trouble, until last night.

Aeryk must have dozed just before first light, as he woke with a start to discover the sun well up. The smell of bacon frying wafted through the air. The morning sky showed blue above, promising a fine spring day with no sign of the rain that had pelted them the previous afternoon.

"You'll have to settle for flapjacks this mornin'," Danyl called from where he knelt beside the campfire. "Don't want ta take the time fer biscuits."

Aeryk climbed out of his bedroll and took a closer look at Jervis's arm. He saw no signs of bleeding or swelling. Aeryk applied a red-bracken poultice before tying the bandage back into place, just to be sure.

After breakfast Danyl, accompanied by Aeryk and Jervis, examined the bodies of the two intruders slain the night before. Both were blond and fair skinned. The axe man appeared to be in his thirties, with a missing front tooth and a scraggly beard.

The spearman Aeryk had downed turned out to be more boy than man, lacking, Danyl estimated, a couple of years of Aeryk's own age. Clad in rags, he looked dirty and gaunt with none of the distinct coloring of the Anduyin or the Tuchycks or the tribal markings of the Cymbri.

"They're Guilleys, most likely," Danyl concluded. Aeryk thought he sounded relieved.

Danyl looked skyward and raised his hands, palms up, in the gesture of prayer. "Wise Fates, we beseech thee to seek mercy for the souls of these miscreants. We know not their lot in the world or under what circumstances they came into this life. We know they left it as would-be thieves and murderers. We commit their souls to your keeping and their bodies to the jackals."

The Kylgahran rode off, leaving the Guilleys' corpses where they lay. Danyl kept the three of them in the saddle, pushing steadily south, until near sundown. Settling round the campfire that night, Aeryk guessed they'd covered half again the distance of a normal day's ride. Jervis had last watch and so was first to take to his blankets.

"I want to thank ye," Danyl proffered, adding a couple of dry sticks to the fire. "I did not see the Guilley with the spear. If you had not been there, it would likely have been me trying to talk my way past the Fates this morning instead of them."

"If that's true, the reverse must be also." Aeryk smiled. "I reckon we're even."

Danyl shook his craggy boulder of a head while the corners of his mouth quirked. "You sound like Basyl the now."

Sinewy lean, a head taller than Danyl but with the same blue eyes and grey-streaked red hair, Basyl Conroy of Clan Ard Owen stood the only father Aeryk had ever known. And Basyl's wife, Lara, was as near to a mother, Aeryk reckoned, as he would have in this life. It was Basyl who first told Aeryk of his true mother's fate. Already a young widow, Aeryk's mother had died, taken by a Cymbri war arrow, while trekking over the Tylcairn Mountains to the Lowlands out east.

Aeryk had but little knowledge of his mother—her name, Joslyn Emyrt of Clan Ard Mourne, and her age at the time of her death, nineteen. Aeryk understood he had some relations—cousins and such—back west in the Midlands of Kylgahra. Emyrt was a common name among the Kylgahran. Of his sire, Aeryk knew nothing.

When asked, Basyl would say only, "I did not know him."

"I wish I could tell ye, lad," was always Danyl's response.

While Jervis snored steadily, Danyl and Aeryk sat by the fire. A silence sprang up between them, stretching into the night. The moons had set, enveloping the surrounding woods in darkness as deep as forever. Danyl slipped a leather-bound flask from a pocket woven into the plaid he wore. Opening the stopper, he took a short pull.

Danyl tossed his head, "That's good wysoi, all right enough." Wysoi, distilled from fermented corn, was the preferred liquor among the Kylgahran and a potent one. "Would ye care fer a wee nip?"

Aeryk shook his head. "That Guilley boy with the spear was unskilled. I could have disarmed him."

"In the dark, caught up by the rush of the moment ... just how is it ye were to be knowin' that, I wonder?" Danyl rumbled gently, putting away his flask. Aeryk said nothing, and Danyl continued, "Man or boy, when you level a spear, you had better do so in earnest."

"I reckon." Aeryk let go the breath he'd been holding.

"Killing a man, robbing him of all his tomorrows, is a terrible thing," Danyl observed, "terrible and profound because it can never be undone. It is also sometimes necessary." Reaching out, Danyl gripped Aeryk's shoulder firmly. "We're none of us perfect, lad, but you've done nothing for which ye need feel ashamed. Let that bit go, and the rest will drift away, little by little. I promise ye."

Aeryk climbed into his bedroll shortly thereafter. Grateful for Danyl's counsel and the reassurance it provided, Aeryk managed to find sleep. Even as he drifted off, the image of the dead Guilley boy filled Aeryk's mind. The youth had toppled into a heap at the base of a pine sapling, his head cocked at an odd angle. Aeryk knew for as long as he lived, he would remember the pinched features of the young thief, especially his eyes, frozen in death, as they stared, unseeing, into the bright morning sun.

6
Steading

Summer 1357
Near Taggert's Landing,
Lywgahra

Lara Conroy of Clan Ard Owen loved eating asparagus harvested from the patch growing at the edge of her vegetable garden; weeding the beds, less so. On her knees, Lara worked the short-handled hoe in her right hand through a particularly stubborn patch of crabgrass. Delivering a final determined whack, she straightened, arching her back to ease the ache that seemed to creep up her spine from the top of her hips more and more readily these days.

"I'm getting old," she'd complained to her husband, Basyl, the other night.

Basyl embraced her, saying, "You'll always look nineteen to me, lass." His voice took on the growly tone she heard in it only when the two of them were alone. She'd been nineteen the first time they met. Of course, he was quite a bit older, and she had married young Roger Dunn of Clan Ard Fraiser.

Sturdily made, standing to medium height, Roger had curly blond hair and eyes of blue. Lara, tall for a Kylgahran woman, could look him right in the eye. Well laced with grey the now, her hair on the day she'd wed Roger Dunn showed raven's wing black. Most often then, as today, she dressed her hair in a thick single braid that trailed to the small of her back. Skinny as a child, Lara had remained slim as an adult. Lara's eyes were grey, a shade darker than the faded cotton frock she wore beneath a forest-green apron.

A good man, Roger, when he was sober, and a generally happy drunk otherwise. Toward the end of his life, Roger spent more and more time otherwise. His drinking got worse, Lara guessed, when Roger came to the realization that the life he led was never going to match the one he'd dreamed. Roger perished trying to save a neighbor's two sons from a burning building. The boys managed to make their way out using a second-story window. Roger had not been so lucky.

He'd given her a daughter, Roger had—Brianne, a sweet child who had grown into a kind and clever woman. Brianne and her husband, Tomas, ran the inn that Lara and Roger had started some twenty-five years ago. The Wandering Heart was the most successful such establishment in the village of Taggert's Landing. Truth to tell, though four taverns dotted its streets, the village featured only two inns. The proprietor, Jemy Duggins, of the second, called the Willow, was thick as porridge, not exactly formidable as a competitor, but still, the Wandering Heart returned a steady profit.

Lara did not spend much time at the inn any longer. She would help out during the busy stretches, after the fall harvest or during the winter solstice season, but the Wandering Heart was Brianne and Tom's place the now. The steading had long since become Lara's home.

Basyl and his partner, Danyl Trask, ran several dozen head of cattle and a slightly smaller horse herd, fine saddle mounts all. The horses were mostly Danyl's concern; Basyl ever seemed more at ease among his herbs and potions and his books, and neither had done more than he had to with respect to the cattle before Aeryk came of age. Until Aeryk took an interest, actually making a go of their steading seemed only a secondary consideration, as far as Basyl and Danyl were concerned. Try as she might, Lara would never understand men.

Basyl was a healer, touched by the Yir. His skills were highly regarded throughout the Elkhorn Valley they called home and beyond. Basyl never charged for his services. That was but one of the things Lara loved about him. He liked her. They got on well enough.

Lara had taken Basyl into her bed a couple of years following Roger's death but had put off marriage until after Brianne and Tomas were wed. Lara's somewhat scandalous relationship with Basyl had not stopped her from mothering Aeryk from the moment Basyl had returned, a year or so after the close of the Eldyr rebellion, with the babe in his arms. Aeryk was twelve years of age when she finally became Basyl's wife.

"Even the longest human life amounts to little more than a few breaths of air," Lara's grandmother had told her. Youth being an effective barrier against mortality, such sentiment, however true, had made little impression at the time. The once-sturdy barricade was fair tottering the now. She and Basyl looked to be of an age these days. She could not help wondering how long that would last.

"Hullo, Mum." At the sound of Aeryk's voice behind her, Lara felt her pulse throb. She closed her eyes for one sweet moment to let the secret dread shrouding her heart fall away. *Blessed Fates, thank ye.*

Climbing to her feet, she turned to find him standing before her. He'd been gone a week less than two months. *Not of my blood but rather of my heart.* Basyl had expressed that thought once with reference to Aeryk. *How true it is for me as well.* Lara fancied she could see him with a woman's eyes, not only with a mother's. Average height for a son of the clans; wide shouldered and muscular; handsome, not just good-looking; with a square-jawed countenance, a well-formed mouth, auburn hair, and wide-set grey-green eyes.

In three quick steps she was in his arms. Aeryk lifted Lara easily from the ground to whirl her about.

"Aeryk," Lara cried, laughing. "Put me down. You'll crack my ribs."

"Can't have that." Easing her to the ground, Aeryk smiled. "If I damage you, there will be nothing for it except to eat more of Danyl's cooking."

Pushing him away, she took a step back. "It doesn't appear to have hurt you any. You look fine."

"A testament to my fortitude, Mum"—Aeryk's smile stretched to a grin—"not Danyl's vittles, I assure you." A pure fib that, Lara reckoned; Danyl was a rare talent with a skillet.

"Where is the old reprobate?" she inquired.

"Out back somewhere," Aeryk replied, "trying to sneak up on Basyl, I imagine."

Lara embraced him a second time. "It's so good to have you home."

"Aye." Aeryk's arms tightened about her, and his voice softened. "Missed you, Mum." Her sob took Lara by surprise, filling her eyes with tears. "Let's have none of that," Aeryk chided her gently, "silly woman."

"Silly, is it?" Lara sniffed. "What a thing to say. I ought to box your ears."

"You're too tender-hearted for such as that," Aeryk opined fondly. "If you aren't careful, you're liable to spoil me something awful."

Lara stepped away and used her apron to wipe her eyes. "Are you hungry, truly?"

Aeryk's grin returned. "I'm awake, aren't I?"

"Come along, then," Lara smiled. "There's fresh bread, some fine yellow cheese, and a bit of ham."

"Sounds good." Aeryk offered her his arm. "Although truth to tell, I stopped by mostly for the company."

Arm in arm, they walked toward the house. "You made good time," Lara remarked. "Did you have any trouble along the way?" She saw the shadow flicker across his face.

"None to speak of," Aeryk told her.

In the hour after sundown, three days hence, Lara and Basyl, along with Aeryk and Danyl, sat at table, finishing supper. Though he took his meals with the rest of the family in the "big house," Danyl lived in what he referred to as the "little house," a cabin located across the yard that had served as the original dwelling on the place. Lara, with Danyl helping, started to clear away the dishes.

She'd reached the washbasin atop the kitchen counter when Aeryk said, "I hear they're forming a herd under Samwell Austyn. The plan is to trail them east to Cos city."

"There's a bold notion," Danyl scoffed, placing a handful of plates on the counter beside the basin. "Cos is on the far side of the Syga Plain."

"Aye," Basyl commented, "it is one of King Dardan's so-called new cities." The planes and hollows of Basyl's leanly contoured face reflected a muscular sort of scholarship, not hard so much as pared down, as if nothing unessential remained.

Dardan, first of his name, ruled the kingdom of Syrdis. The Syrdisian monarch had devoted much of the early part of his long reign to expanding the borders of his realm northward, pushing back the tribal folk, mostly Tuchyck and Chyrchroni, who occupied the region. The city of Cos stood beside the River Sayx on land once claimed by the Tuchycks.

"Word is," Aeryk reported, "Syrdisian merchants are willing to pay top money for cattle on the hoof."

"Assuming any cattle are left alive at the end of the trip," Danyl retorted. "Anybody making that drive is as likely to run afoul a Cymbri war band as they are to find enough water to keep the poor beasties going."

"Samwell Austyn is nobody's fool," Basyl remarked. "Are you certain Sam has signed on as trail boss?" Basyl directed his question to Aeryk.

"Caleb Edger says so," Aeryk answered. "I saw Caleb just this afternoon. He was headed over to Sam's place to sign up. Caleb told me half a dozen of the local ranchers are supporting the drive, putting up cattle and coin for wages. Caleb heard the pay is a talent a day, Tieran-weight silver."

"That's good money," Danyl allowed.

Lara turned her back to the washbasin. Her eyes sought Aeryk's. "You just got home," she blurted, more loudly than she'd intended.

Aeryk met her gaze and smiled. "The drive won't start for weeks yet. The round-up is not yet underway. I reckon plenty more will want to sign on than Sam will need. Like as not, his roster is already full."

Lara tore her eyes away and pivoted back 'round to face the washbasin.

"There will be plenty to do around here this summer," Basyl noted.

"Not for a silver talent a day," Aeryk countered. "For that kind of money, we could buy some new breed stock."

"I'll bet you my best bottle of wysoi," Danyl proclaimed, "that them fancy wages are contingent upon delivery of the cattle to Cos. You could spend nigh on to three months eating dust and dodging Cymbri war arrows and wind up with nothin' more to show fer it than a bloody sunburn." Danyl cast a quick glance Lara's way. "Beg pardon, Mum."

"That's true enough, I reckon," Aeryk acknowledged. His gaze settled on Basyl. "In the morning I thought I'd ride over to Sam's and find out if he is still hiring."

"You are nineteen, son," Basyl said evenly. "The choice is yours to make."

Upon hearing this, Lara slammed a cast-iron roasting pan into the washbasin hard enough to rattle the crockery.

Aeryk climbed to his feet. "I'm going to take a quick look at the yard stock before turning in." He started for the front door.

"I'll come along with ye," Danyl proffered. "Looks like it might be a wee bit chilly tonight." Danyl winked at Basyl before following Aeryk out the door.

Basyl rose from his chair and stepped across the kitchen to stand at Lara's back, not quite touching but close enough for him to feel the warmth of her body.

"I don't want him to go," Lara said in a soft, plaintive tone. Her hands clasped the edges of the washbasin in a white-knuckled grip.

Basyl smiled. "As indicated by the dent you put in that cast-iron pot."

Lara spun about and glared up at him. "I ought to bend it over your bloody head."

"Why, I am wondering," Basyl inquired mildly, "is this suddenly all my fault?"

"*You are nineteen, son*," Lara mimicked him, dropping her voice an octave. "*The choice is yours to make.*" She jabbed a slender forefinger into his chest. "You might just as well have shoved him out the ruddy door."

"We cannot live his life for him, Lara," Basyl intoned. "Was it not you who said this to me, time and time again, over the years."

Lara dropped her eyes. "That was before."

"Before what?" Basyl queried.

"Before he started to bloody do it," Lara cried.

Basyl put his arms around her. "You have already given him a lifetime's worth of loving, my beauty, the most precious gift anyone can give a child. One far too few receive. Aeryk will have to find his way from here. He'll have a better chance than most, thanks to you." Slipping his hand beneath her chin, Basyl tilted Lara's head back so that he could kiss her.

A long moment slipped by. Lara finally broke off the kiss to rest her head on Basyl's shoulder. "This is all happening too fast, Basyl."

"Aye," Basyl sighed. "I'll speak to him." Lara reared back in his embrace; an eager light sparked to life in her eyes. She was about to speak when Basyl forestalled her. "Not tonight," he said firmly. "There's naught to be gained by badgering the lad. In the morning, I'll ask a few questions before he rides over to Sam's place."

Lara smiled, relief written large on her face. "You are a dear."

Basyl waggled a finger under her nose. "I've promised only to put the questions, not that you would like the answers."

7

On the Syga Plain

Aeryk wondered how long it had been since he bathed last. He supposed you really couldn't count river crossings. A good dousing, they were, but not a proper bath. The drive began in midsummer, according to his reckoning, five weeks and three days ago.

A Tieran week measured eight days. As despised as the Tierans were out west, you had to give the scralyngs credit. They had a knack for organization. In the Highlands of Kylgahra, the term *scralyng* referred to a person of low regard and questionable heritage. A good idea, however, remained a good idea, wherever it came from. Most folk seemed to agree. The Tieran calendar had been adopted by friend and foe alike in lands all around the Middle Sea.

Aeryk twisted in the saddle and surveyed the column of cattle stretched out behind him. Well used to the trail the now, the beasties moved along readily enough. No wind to speak of, and he saw a pall of dust hanging in the air like a shroud over the rear of the herd. "Luck's leaning our way, old son," he said with a smile to Wyli, his horse. "We could be back there pushin' 'em." Wyli tossed his head—in equine agreement, Aeryk assumed. Aeryk reckoned

Wyli, being a reasonable critter, didn't fancy eating dust any more than he did.

This day Aeryk rode point, ahead and to the right of the herd—"on the starboard bow," Cable Dowd of Clan Ard Cullen called it. Cable assumed the role of senior cook for the drive and had been a sailor in his youth. No longer young, Cable had lost most of his hair and a few of his teeth but none of his grit. This was according to Samwell Austyn of Clan Ard Gregyr, the trail boss, who praised sparingly.

At the outset, Sam had ridden point most days himself. Every day over the last two weeks, he had assigned Aeryk to the position. Riding point entailed a good deal of responsibility. Aeryk figured either he'd managed to earn Sam's trust, or the trail boss had decided they were on safe ground the now, and any bloody fool could head them out. He wasn't about to ask. By any road, Aeryk liked the freedom that went along with riding up front.

Settling back into the saddle, Aeryk reached forward to pat Wyli on the neck. His mount descended from the Morgyn breed, a dappled grey with mane and tail the color of summer wheat. Mountain bred, Morgyns were medium sized, swift, and sure-footed. Not as fast as the elegant Enduyi horses favored by the Elves of Ilyria or as powerful as the Panyir chargers of Roi, Morgyns combined a good turn of speed with incredible endurance. They made excellent cow horses.

Aeryk had named his gelding Wyli after the sly fairy creature so prominently featured in the story of *Pigdyn A-Wandering*. How many times had he badgered Basyl or Danyl to recite that particular tale to him throughout his boyhood? Dozens, certainly; hundreds seemed more likely.

Aeryk wore buckskin trousers, sturdy leather boots, and a blue cotton shirt so faded by the sun it was almost the color of pearl. About his throat lay a loosely tied tartyn. Most drovers wore one to keep the sun off their necks or the dust out of their mouths and noses. Atop his head perched a sturdy but misshapen, broad-brimmed trail hat that looked as if Wyli had sat on it.

Aeryk's hand brushed the hilt of the baelryc sheathed at his left hip. *"Kylgahran are raised to the sword."* Danyl's gravelly voice echoed in Aeryk's memory. *"A baelryc is the mark of a man, lad; its use his measure."*

Most of what Aeryk knew of the sword he'd learned from Basyl and Danyl. Lessons had come daily most times, starting at age nine, and usually employed the stryath, or wooden practice sword. His two teachers contrasted as much in approach as they did in appearance. Basyl favored a graceful, flowing style of fighting that featured a counter strike, while Danyl fought in a blunt, aggressive manner.

"Rain comin'," Caleb Edger, a drover, also of Clan Ard Mourne, called out as he and young Daymen Reed of Clan Ard Drew, one of the wranglers, rode over, joining Aeryk on the side of a low hill overlooking the leading edge of the herd.

Aeryk looked skyward. The sun approached its zenith. He saw what might have been a hint of cloud skirting the northern horizon. "If you say so," Aeryk replied.

Recent neighbors, Aeryk and the green-eyed, black-haired Caleb had become friends. Most of the drovers were young. Caleb had a year on Aeryk, and only a handful of the other cowhands were older than he. Daymen Reed couldn't have been a day over eighteen. A hand's width taller than Aeryk, lean, lithely muscled, and handsome, with curly brown hair and laughing blue eyes, Daymen rode as if he'd been born in the saddle.

Aeryk had known Daymen for years and didn't like him much. *Jealous of his good looks*, Aeryk reckoned. Well, maybe, but in Daymen's presence, Aeryk couldn't help thinking of something Basyl once said: "A friend to all is a friend to none."

"Aren't you supposed to be with the horses?" Aeryk greeted him.

Young Daymen smiled, bringing dimples to his cheeks. "Had to bring a remount up fer one of the Conor boys," he explained. "Thought I'd be neighborly and say how do afore headin' back."

"Skylarking is more like it," Caleb observed.

"I notice you rode along with him," Aeryk pointed out.

Daymen's smile broadened and his eyes settled upon Aeryk's baelryc. "The boys say you stuck a Guilley up north a while back."

Aeryk's features tightened. He nodded. "Not much to it."

"A bit more than that, though, I reckon," Caleb said.

Aeryk exchanged glances with both Caleb and Daymen. "You two want to hear about that right the now?"

"Just the bloody bits," Daymen enthused.

Aeryk recounted the events of that damp night on the edge of Anduyin country the previous spring. "He wasn't much good," Aeryk concluded, thumbing the brim of his battered trail hat a little further up his forehead. "I knocked his spear aside and shorted him in the first pass. A Guilley most likely, Danyl said."

Flicking the tag ends of his reins at a fly that settled on the neck of his horse, a roan-colored Morgyn, Daymen surmised, "Sounds as if you regret the deed."

"I do," Aeryk acknowledged. "I figure I could have disarmed or disabled him without killing. In the press of the moment"—Aeryk shrugged—"well, I just reacted without thinking."

"Anyone who levels a spear had better mean it," Caleb observed, echoing Danyl's words the night after the incident. "You had a right to defend yourself."

Aeryk looked Caleb in the eye. "I said I regretted the killing, Caleb," he said evenly, "not that I was ashamed of it."

"My grandpa says," Daymen proclaimed, "that killin' Guilleys is akin to stompin' gophers."

"Your grandpa has queer notions," Caleb scoffed, "especially after taking that mule kick to his noggin."

Daymen's perpetual smile blossomed into a grin. "Truth to tell, that mule straightened ol' Grandpa out some. He actually makes sense every once in a while the now."

"If Sam catches the three of us loafing," Aeryk said, "he's liable to do some straightening out of his own. I'll see you boys." So saying, Aeryk nudged Wyli into motion, riding down the hill.

After Aeryk rode out of earshot, Daymen remarked, "Talks kindly fancy, don't he?"

"Compared to some, mebbe," Caleb allowed. "At least he don't talk too much."

"An orphan, they say." Daymen pursed his lips. "I wonder who his people were?"

Caleb shrugged. "Back in Kylgahra proper, there are Emyrts all over the Midlands."

Daymen smiled. "Do you think that's his papa's name or his mama's?"

Caleb's brows drew down; being bastard born was no great stigma to the Kylgahran, so long as a clan would have you, but still. He raised his eyes to Daymen's. "I'd be careful about that if I was you; 'tis none of his doin' either way."

Ignoring the look Caleb cast in his direction, Daymen spat between his teeth. "Blooded or no, I ain't sure I trust a fella what works harder than he has to fer nothin' but wages."

Time rolled by, the day eventually succumbing, as so many before, to the steady rhythm of the moving herd. Late in the afternoon, Aeryk eased Wyli to a halt, lifted the dust-covered felt trail hat from his head, held it aloft as a shade, and took a quick squint at the sun. A couple of hours remained until sunset. Caleb's weather sense appeared to have rung true; clouds were rolling in from out of the northwest, a mottled grey-blue in color, and to Aeryk, it smelled like rain. *Another soaking that won't count as a bath,* he thought.

Samwell Austyn estimated they were about two-thirds of the way to the Syrdisian city of Cos; another three or four weeks would see them there. Sam, as he preferred to be called, owned a good-sized ranch across the valley from the steading maintained by Basyl Conroy and Danyl Trask. About five hundred of the well over three thousand head of cattle in the herd belonged to Austyn. Sam, therefore, had a vested interest, more than most, in seeing to the success of the venture.

Aeryk had known Sam since the black-haired, grey-eyed Highlander had settled with his young wife in the Elkhorn Valley across Bright Water Creek six summers ago. Tall for a Kylgahran and spare of flesh, Austyn moved with a warrior's sinewy ease. Danyl said once that Sam's features, especially his eyes, tended to spark women's interest and give knowing men pause. Sam's wife was with child when they arrived. A pretty woman, blond of hair, Aeryk remembered, with a laugh that made even old Danyl smile. She gave birth to a fine healthy girl. The following spring, both mother and daughter succumbed to a fever that swept through Lywgahra.

Basyl had been away at the time. A shame that, as he had a healer's uncanny knack for helping anyone sick or injured. Sam never spoke of his loss. Nor had he remarried.

"We, each of us, grieve in our own way and in our own time," was all Basyl had to say about it.

Altogether, twenty cowhands, two cooks who doubled as wagon drivers, a third full-time wagon driver, six wranglers, and one Tuchyck scout had signed on for the drive. The Tuchycks were an indigenous nomadic people who roamed over much of the Westlands. Harried for generations by the expanding kingdoms of the west, most prominently Syrdis, and the incursion of fierce northern tribes like the Cymbri, the Tuchycks stood few in number the now. Their scout was a slender, blond-haired, brown-eyed man a few years older than Aeryk, with skin the color of tanned leather. Named Wyatt, the Tuchyck moved like a shadow and seemed to know every pace of ground they had so far traveled. Unlike the drovers, Wyatt armed himself with a bow and a short-hafted thrusting spear with a broad, leaf-shaped point.

Wyatt rode a hammer-headed piebald horse that most of the drovers scoffed at. Handsome he wasn't, but Aeryk had noticed the deep chest and easy gait of the rangy piebald and couldn't help wondering if Wyatt knew something they didn't. Wyatt scouted ahead of the herd, returning usually in time for the evening meal and to report to Austyn. Aeryk knew the trail boss trusted the wiry Tuchyck implicitly.

Around sundown on the night before the start of the cattle drive, Sam came calling, bringing with him a bottle of light, dry Elven wine. He and Aeryk sat on the porch that fronted the ranch house, sipping the vintage from a pair of matching ceramic cups.

"We're friends, lad, you and I, as well as neighbors," Sam said, peering over the rim of his cup at Aeryk. "Tomorrow we start a long, hard trip, with me as trail boss. Do ya ken what that means?"

Aeryk smiled into the fading light. "If I step wide, you'll rein me in as sharp as anybody else."

"I will that," Sam affirmed. His eyes glinted, set wide in a face that seemed to have been carved not from stone but life lived just as hard.

"I'll do my best for you, Sam," Aeryk promised.

"I know that, Aeryk," Sam replied. "I want no hard feelings between us when it's done, is all."

"Do you reckon we can stay clear of the Cymbri?" Aeryk asked. More than a few Kylgahran frontiersmen had met their ends at the hands of a Cymbri war band. The Cymbri didn't seem to get along with much of anyone, not even themselves.

"Our route will take us south of the Cymbri's usual range," Sam replied. "We'll swing as wide as we can without running the herd short of water and hope our luck holds." Sam took a last swallow of his wine and held his empty cup aloft. "That's to a dull trudge, sweet Fates allow, and a profit at journey's end."

They'd been lucky so far, and with Wyatt ranging ahead like some wary, leather-clad ghost to give them warning, Aeryk liked their chances. In the distance, thunder growled, bringing Aeryk back to the present. Rain, then, for certain, Aeryk figured, before sundown, most likely.

"Hoi, the point!" a shout from behind rang out. Turning in the saddle, Aeryk saw Samwell Austyn galloping toward him. Austyn rode a splendid bay stallion that had to have some Enduyi blood in him. Sam sat his horse as if he was part of the animal. As he drew near, Sam said, "Let's bed 'em down early today, in those trees yonder."

Reining up, Sam pointed to a copse of elm trees a short distance ahead. "Maybe we can get them settled in time for some hot food before the weather catches us."

Aeryk smiled. "Sounds good to me."

"Thought it might; doing nothing comes natural to you," Sam retorted but with an answering smile. "I blame Basyl for your shoddy upbringing."

"That's a sure bet," Aeryk responded, his smile stretching into a grin. "So long as it's Danyl you ask." Gigging Wyli forward, Aeryk rode toward the stand of trees. Caleb Edger manned what drovers called the offset position, riding slightly behind Aeryk on the opposite side of the herd. Once he reached the trees, Aeryk brought Wyli to a halt and stood in the stirrups. Raising his hat high above his head, Aeryk swept it 'round in a wide circle, signaling Caleb to head them up.

Weather, especially thunderstorms, could spook cattle, but this time 'round the herd settled down without any fuss. While they saw lightning flashing along the horizon, it never drew near, and the thunder remained a distant rumble, at first ominous but over time less and less threatening. Supper consisted of boiled beans flavored with black pepper and dried onions, goodly strips of fried bacon and flatbread. A large mug of hot tea with a dollop of honey stirred in rounded off the meal. Plain fare as evening meals went, but the portions were generous, and the food had indeed been served hot.

The rain held off until they were pretty much done eating. When it came, it manifested as a soft, soaking rain. "A farmer's rain," the cowhands called it, enough to wet the ground thoroughly without coming down so hard as to damage tender shoots or ripening crops.

In the days prior to his departure, Lara had gifted Aeryk with a new plaid. The Kylgahran plaid was fashioned from three rectangular pieces of wool, a back piece and two roughly half-sized front pieces stitched together, with the seam running along the top of the wearer's shoulders. The front pieces were also tacked to the back piece about a third of the way down the garment, forming a pair of loose-fitting arm holes. Worn like an oversized vest, with the hem falling usually to mid-thigh, the plaid could be belted in place or simply left open in front. Warm and lightweight, the tightly woven plaid offered stout protection against wind and rain alike.

Wrapped in Lara's plaid and an extra blanket and covered overall by a waxed canvas ground sheet, Aeryk tugged his hat down over his eyes, leaned back against his saddle, and listened to the rain. He lay stretched out near a campfire in the lee of one of the supply wagons. If the Fates were even-handed, he'd wake up dry in the morning. Everyone took turns riding night guard—everyone, that is, except Sam. The trail boss rode out each night. Aeryk was off this evening with nothing to do but look forward to breakfast. Aeryk lay still, awaiting sleep, and let his mind wander.

Lara had wanted Aeryk to take no part in what she described as "Sam Austyn's bloody adventuring."

Once it became clear Aeryk had decided to go, Danyl had initially wanted to accompany him on the drive to Cos. Ultimately, Basyl talked Danyl out of it by telling him Aeryk deserved the chance to stand on his own feet without one or the pair of them staring over his shoulder. At the time, Aeryk was glad of Basyl's decision and Danyl's acquiescence.

Basyl had presented Aeryk with a medallion affixed to a slender chain that might have been silver. The medal itself, forged from what appeared to be black iron, had embossed upon it the Elven runic symbol Fey. Basyl said the Fey rune stood for freedom and something more. Specifically, the symbol represented the freedom and dignity of the human spirit.

"This was my father's and his before him. It is a powerful shield against evil and adverse magic of all kinds. It is not a trinket to be bartered away for a night in the arms of some female."

Eyeing the medallion and chain, Aeryk found them to be decidedly ordinary. *An entire night, was it?* Though he had no direct experience, Aeryk suspected prices had likely gone up some since Basyl's day.

Danyl's gift proved to be a throwing dart. Instead of the hand-and-fingers span of razor-sharp steel that usually tipped the weapon, Aeryk found the point of this particular dart crafted of heartstone. Heartstone was a grey, glasslike rock, capable of being crafted into spear points or arrowheads. Hard to find, heartstone could be knapped in a manner similar to flint and would hold a very sharp edge.

"And," Danyl told him, "even the most powerful of sorcerers cannot ward against it."

On the last morning, just before he headed out, Lara hugged and kissed him. "May the Fates smile upon you, Aeryk," she whispered. "Come back to us."

"I will, Mother." Aeryk had to push the words past the lump in his throat.

"Don't forget to duck," Danyl admonished, clasping Aeryk's hand in his own bear-sized paw.

And then it was time to say good-bye to Basyl. "Any last-moment advice?" Aeryk asked.

"Anyone who actually needs last-moment advice," Basyl replied sagely, "is probably buggered for fair."

Aeryk smiled. "That's encouraging."

"All right." Basyl relented with a smile of his own. "How about this: pilfer, then despoil."

Aeryk blinked. "What?"

"Something to ponder." Basyl's deep-set blue eyes glinted, and his smile broadened. He put his arms around Aeryk. Aeryk returned his father's embrace. *Basyl is my father, no matter what.* The thought both warmed and strengthened Aeryk.

"I'll see you," Aeryk vowed.

"I'm counting on it," Basyl said.

Lara's gift had been practical and thoughtful, much like the woman herself. And while in his wildest imaginings, Aeryk could not conjure up a reason why he would be chucking throwing darts at a sorcerer, he was happy enough to accept Danyl's. At first, for some reason, he felt a little uneasy about wearing Basyl's gift. During the long weeks of the drive, however, the chain and the medal suspended from it seemed to become a part of him.

Though he could not be certain of its potency against evil or magic, the medallion did help to keep loneliness at bay. Aeryk had never been parted from all his loved ones for this long before. However unseemly it must be for a blooded Kylgahran clansman to become homesick, Aeryk could not deny that he was. Sleep embraced him finally as he lay beneath scudding clouds and the gentle patter of the rain, thinking of home.

8

Other Considerations

Anharyd delved Ranyl Emyrt's thigh and decided he was fit enough to walk about. With the sheathed broadsword fastened to his belt over Ranyl's left hip, he made his way out of the sheriff's station into the town. Ranyl did so reluctantly. His first stop would be at Mae Hoskins's small house. He was obliged to speak with Mae about the death of her man, Ranger Ellis Tate—a man she loved dearly, the father of her two boys. Mae had been informed of Ellis's fate the day before, but that would spare neither of them the need to prod a wound so deep and still too fresh.

Before departing Ranyl asked Cadigan Embry to contact Kevyn Mourne. Ranyl instructed Cad to arrange a meeting with Kevyn in the sheriff's office at noon that day. The meeting with Kevyn would entail another conversation Ranyl would rather not have but one he also knew he could neither put off nor avoid.

Only a short walk from the sheriff's station, Mae's house, a modest single-story, wood-framed building with a thatched roof and a red brick chimney, appeared tidy and sound. Ranyl knocked, and

Mae's mother, Delcia Hoskins, of Clan Ard Mourne, opened the door. Mother and daughter shared a strong physical resemblance, comely the both of them, blessed with generous curves, light blond hair, and lively blue-green eyes. Delcia's figure had become somewhat more matronly over the years but not much.

Delcia had not approved of her only daughter's union with the lanky, soft-spoken Tate. By direct inference, neither did she care for the ranger's commander, Sheriff Ranyl Emyrt. That the policy against rangers marrying was widespread throughout Kylgahra and imposed by the clan lairds, not the sheriffs themselves, apparently had little if any mitigating influence. A deeply religious woman, Delcia was not prepared to be reconciled with her daughter's being dragged into a sinful relation with and throwing bastards for a man who stood, in the eyes of some, little more than a trumped-up game warden.

"Good morning, ma'am." Ranyl removed his broad-brimmed trail hat made of grey felt. "I'd like to speak with Mae, if I could."

Giving him a level look, Delcia stepped to one side. "Come in, Sheriff."

The house that Ellis Tate and Mae Hoskins had shared looked as clean and neat inside as it had from without. Ellis was good with his hands, and Ranyl suspected the tall ranger had made most of the furniture in the sitting room. The smell of fresh baked goods wafted from the kitchen adjacent to the sitting room. Two bedrooms, one for the boys and one for their parents, were located down a hallway just to the left of the kitchen. A privy stood out back in a yard dominated by a large vegetable garden.

Mae stepped out of the kitchen wearing a conservatively cut grey cotton frock. Upon seeing him, she quickly removed the white apron tied about her waist and smoothed her hair, tied into a bun at the nape of her neck.

"Sheriff Emyrt." She curtsied. "It is good of you to come."

Crossing to her, Ranyl clasped Mae's hands in his own. He'd been rehearsing something to say to her on the walk over. The words fled, and he blurted, "I'm sorry, Mae, so damned sorry."

Mae's face crumpled at the sound of that, and tears filled her eyes. Ranyl embraced her and found he could not hold back his own.

"He died as well as he lived, Mae"—Ranyl's voice sounded thick with grief—"with courage and honor. His last thoughts were of you and your boys."

"I'm sorry," Mae sobbed. "I can't. I'm sorry."

"It's all right, lass," Ranyl said gently, struggling to control his own emotions. "If ever a man deserved a woman's tears, it was Ellis Tate."

"How did he die?" Mae asked.

"An arrow took him," Ranyl told her, which was true enough. "There was some pain at the end, but he did not suffer long." A lie, that was, but he could see no harm in it.

"You were with him when he died?" she wanted to know.

"I was," Ranyl said simply.

"Then he did not die alone," Mae concluded. "The Guilleys who struck him down—what happened to them?"

"With his help," Ranyl informed her, "I killed them."

"They say"—Mae swallowed—"you put their heads on stakes outside the main gate."

Ashamed suddenly of his actions, Ranyl said, "Ellis was my friend, Mae, the best I ever knew."

"I'm glad," Mae said softly, fiercely. "I hope the Fates shun the headless sons of bitches."

Ranyl released her and stepped back. Mae looked into his face. Ignoring her own tears, she reached up to gently wipe away the tears mantling his cheeks.

"You loved him, too." Mae spoke the words as if she dared not believe them.

At the look of raw pain in her eyes, Ranyl's throat closed up tightly, and he could only nod.

"Ellis thought the world of you, you know," she said. "He would have followed you anywhere."

"I buried him on a hill overlooking a little stream," Ranyl told her, "underneath a great white oak. I thought it a good place." It was

Mae's turn to nod. "I promised him I would look after you and his sons. This should help keep you a while." From his belt he pulled a small leather purse.

Mae shook her head. "You don't have to do that."

Pressing the purse into her hand, Ranyl insisted, "You must let me, Mae, please, to honor him."

Slowly, reluctantly, Mae closed her fingers around the purse.

"When the boys are of age, I'll take them into my service," Ranyl continued. "I know the sword, Mae, so that's what I'll teach them. They'll learn to read and to write, too. That I promise, and when their training is done, it will be their choice what path to follow." He paused to make sure she understood him.

After a moment she nodded. "I think Ellis would want that. Thank you."

"We'll talk again soon," Ranyl promised.

Hugging her briefly, he turned and left. Cut and run is what he did, and he knew it. Mae's grief was too strong a reflection of his own for him to bear it long. Perhaps in time they could be a comfort to one another. He hoped so.

Upon returning to his office, Cad informed Ranyl that Kevyn Mourne of Clan Ard Mourne would stop by, as requested, at the noon hour that day. Cad also let him know that the Chamberses had sent word, expecting him for dinner that evening at their home in the hour before sunset. Ranyl walked to the cabinet placed against the far wall of his office that contained his strongbox. Opening the locked box with a brass key, Ranyl extracted a canvas bag that held what he'd taken to thinking of as his marriage fund.

Ranyl opened the drawer built into the base of his writing table and dropped the bag inside. Removing his sword belt, Ranyl laid the sheathed broadsword atop the writing desk. Taking a seat in the large overstuffed leather chair that sat behind the writing table, Ranyl found himself staring absently out the window.

Emerson Hart stuck his head into the opened doorway of Ranyl's office to inquire if he should begin recruiting ranger replacements. Ranyl told him to go ahead, and plan on increasing the size of the ranger contingent to an even forty. Ranyl would need his clan laird's approval for that and, deciding he might as well try to get some work done, was sitting, pen in hand, trying to compose a letter to Laird Daryn, when that worthy's second son, Kevyn Mourne, knocked lightly upon the doorframe, calling Ranyl's name.

"Come in, Lord Kevyn," Ranyl invited, "and close the door, please."

Kevyn Mourne stepped into the room, moving, as always, with the effortless grace of a natural athlete. Tall, wide shouldered, and leanly muscled, Kevyn had dark blond hair and vivid blue eyes that ever seemed to regard the world with wry amusement. Clad simply in a dark-blue cotton shirt and brown woolen trousers fitted into soft, calf-high leather boots, Kevyn took a seat opposite Ranyl. A grey silk tartyn wound about Kevyn's neck, adorned by Ard Mourne clan markings—a pair of crossed swords—embroidered on it. Ranyl's third cousin wore both baelryc and dirk sheathed at his belt.

Ranyl had to admit by any standard, Kevyn Mourne was handsome, with a strong jaw, cleft chin, and dimples in his cheeks when he smiled, which he did often. Kevyn was smiling the now.

"Guilley heads topping stakes." Kevyn's expression stretched into a grin. "Finally pissed you off, did they, cousin?"

Ranyl spoke frankly. "I managed to get Ellis Tate killed. It was easier to blame them than myself, I suppose."

Sprawled in the simple wooden chair on the far side of Ranyl's writing table, Kevyn observed, "You led, and Ellis followed. He died because his time ran out. Not your fault, Ranyl."

Ranyl shrugged and looked his cousin in the eye. "When you leave to take up your commission at Alger Castle, do you plan on taking Helyn with you?"

Kevyn didn't even blink. "Your betrothed? Why would I do that?"

"Then yours was only a recreational form of fornication?" Ranyl replied evenly.

"Mostly." Kevyn made no attempt at denial.

"Does she know that?" Ranyl pressed.

"Who knows what a woman truly believes." Kevyn shrugged eloquently. "Her actions often belie her true feelings."

"You made Helyn no promises?" Ranyl inquired, dropping his eyes momentarily to the table top. Seemingly without thought, Ranyl's fingers closed upon the hilt of his broadsword. If Kevyn noticed, he gave no outward sign; his body remained relaxed, his eyes calm and watchful.

"No," Kevyn asserted. He regarded Ranyl carefully for a moment. "Is this going to lead to difficulty between us, cousin, of the bared steel variety?"

Ranyl relaxed his hold on the sword that lay atop his writing table; his fingers drummed absently on the boar hide grip. "I shouldn't think so." He raised his eyes once again to meet Kevyn's directly. "I owe you my life, for one thing, and for another, I suspect you are better than I am with one of these." Raising his hand free of the sword hilt, Ranyl waved at the blade. "You are going to be leaving Wyteridge a little ahead of schedule."

"Why would I be doing that?" Kevyn's tone took on a slight edge.

Opening the drawer in his writing desk, Ranyl extracted the canvas purse. Holding it aloft, he gave the bag a shake. "There are lots of ways, cousin, to have you killed," Ranyl said conversationally, "for this, with a bit of coin left over."

Kevyn smiled slowly, and Ranyl tossed him the coin purse. Hefting it, Kevyn took a quick look inside and nodded. "I've always wanted to see Antrym around this time of year. When do I depart?"

"We'll hold a memorial service two days hence. I'd like to take the opportunity to thank you publicly for your service and your courage." Ranyl leaned back in his chair. "A reel is already planned for the day after, any time the week following will suffice."

"No unseemly haste, is that it?" Kevyn surmised. Ranyl nodded. Kevyn rose smoothly to his feet. "If there is nothing further, I'll take my leave."

He started to turn toward the door when Ranyl observed quietly, "You said *mostly*."

Kevyn stopped, appearing for the first time slightly uncomfortable. "Perhaps you should speak with your father about that."

Ranyl smiled a brief, bleak expression that never touched his eyes. "So that's it. Tell me, Lord Kevyn, have you ever had any luck speaking *with* Stephyn Emyrt?"

Kevyn's smile matched Ranyl's, and they shared a glance that spoke of understanding, "Farewell, cousin," Kevyn said.

"And you," Ranyl responded. He turned again to the window and stared without seeing at a bright blue sky overhead as Kevyn's footsteps faded down the hall.

Ranyl's father, Stephyn Emyrt, and Kevyn's, who ruled as laird of Clan Ard Mourne, were second cousins. Emyrt was a common name—literally, as it claimed no clan designation. A characteristic shared by most Kylgahran surnames, only one in ten bore any direct affiliation with the nobility. Esquires like his father and him, because he was his father's son, were of the lesser nobility. "Lesser by comparison, I suppose, to the greater nobility, those with blood ties to the lairds," Ranyl had offered in explanation to Anharyd some while ago.

"But your father is related by blood to the laird," Annie protested.

"A second cousin," Ranyl expounded. "Only first cousins and closer count. Pap used to say he finished out of the running by a great-grandparent."

"Blood is blood," Annie maintained.

"Power must be concentrated, Annie," Ranyl contended, "lest it lose its potency. Of course, too much power in one place or one person is a dangerous thing. Some say that explains, at least in part, why esquires exist."

Annie's golden brows drew down. "I don't understand."

"Unlike a patent of nobility, which may be attained only through birthright or decree," Ranyl answered, "a Writ of Esquire can be purchased. It is available to anyone born of the clans with coin enough, and once acquired, the rank of esquire may be handed down like any other bit of property."

"Sounds to me like just another way for the lairds to collect money," Annie opined.

Ranyl smiled. "True enough. Of course, the Council of Lairds frowns on overuse of the writ."

Annie snorted. "If wealth is the true measure, and you become wealthy enough to buy the rank, why bother?"

Ranyl grinned. "An excellent question. When I asked my father, he said most times you do what you must. At others, if you are worth a damn, you do what you should. If you are fortunate, every now and again, you have the luxury of doing something simply because you can." Ranyl's expression sobered. "I suspect closer to the truth, my father purchased a Writ of Esquire as an investment, a means of providing leverage, a way of making more money." Ranyl had received a letter two months earlier from his father, who'd written to say he had entered into a marriage negotiation on Haymish's behalf with a northern border laird named Ryan.

"Kylgahra is not a nation so much as a gaggle of clans"—another of Stephyn Emyrt's favorite observations. Accurate enough, Ranyl reckoned. Generations ago Kylgahran established a Confederation of Clans governed by a ruling body known as the Council of Lairds. At the head of the council stood the chieftain, chosen by vote among its members for a term of six years. Principally a battle leader, the chieftain wielded considerable authority in time of war or emergency.

Real power, however, remained vested in the lairds themselves. Generally, a laird's title was inherited. Per Kylgahran clan law, inheritance went to the eldest child, regardless of sex. About half of the Kylgahran lairds were, as a result, women. Ryan's heir was an eighteen-year-old daughter named Tessymir. Her inheritance would include lairdship of Clan Ard Ryan.

In need of coin, Owain Ryan would offer land and title to secure a rich husband's portion. Esquire rank, while perhaps not first choice among prospective suitors, appeared to be no impediment. When Ryan heard that his potential son-in-law had been maimed, however, he apparently lost interest. Stephyn had hinted broadly that as Ranyl was not yet wed, he might be wise to consider a marriage contract with the Ryan heiress. With Ranyl settled in the north as the future Laird Tessymir's consort, Haymish would be free to inherit the remainder of Stephyn's estate, a significantly larger endowment for him than would otherwise be possible. *I should have torn that bloody letter to shreds.* Ranyl had not.

His interest in completing the correspondence to Laird Daryn waning, Ranyl fetched his horse bow from his quarters above stairs and made his way to the target range at the rear of the ranger station. The bow was of composite construction, patterned after an Elven design. Short enough to be handled readily from horseback, the deeply recurved shape of the weapon allowed for considerable draw length. Though not as powerful as some longbows, the wood and horn laminate generated plenty of punch over ranges out to two hundred paces, the distance over which combat normally took place. Launching a sheaf of arrows at a straw-stuffed target some seventy-five paces down range would give Ranyl time to think.

9

Little Forgiveness

Helyn Chambers stood gazing out the back window of the sitting room in her parents' home, waiting, her large blue eyes drawn with worry. She'd asked her parents to leave the house to Ranyl and her for dinner this evening. She had not told them why. Her mother, Rachel, saw the look in Helyn's eyes and lost no time deciding she and Haskyr, her husband and Helyn's father, should stop in to visit her sister across town. Her mother, Helyn knew, would later want an explanation. Helyn did not know yet what she would tell her.

Haskyr, of course, was disappointed; he wanted to hear directly from Ranyl of the pursuit and what rumor said was a desperate little fight along a streambed someplace deep in the outlands. Haskyr was wise enough to see that mother and daughter united formed a force he didn't want to tangle with and instead chose to be mollified by the promise of fresh baked pie upon arrival at Rachel's sister's place. Rachel planned to bring along some pie fresh from her own oven, just in case.

A young man in Ard Mourne livery whom Helyn recognized as Kevyn's manservant had arrived a couple of hours ago, bearing a note from the young nobleman. The servant handed Helyn the note, sealed in wax, and left immediately, not waiting for any reply. Brief, the missive read:

H,
He knows. I know not how.
I am leaving next week.
Take care of yourself.
K

Helyn felt as if icy fingers were coiling about her heart as she read the note over again and again. They'd been careful. She and Kevyn had only ridden out twice together; both times had been during those long days after Ranyl had sent the major portion of the patrol force back to Wyteridge under Kevyn's charge. *"He knows"*—the words flayed her.

Helyn dressed carefully. Paying close attention to small things helped calm her. She wore her new dress, a light-grey, high-waisted cotton frock with a slightly daring neckline. She'd wound her long blond hair into a bun at the nape of her neck. She was careful to wear the ear fobs, sapphire inlaid on gold, Ranyl had given her at the close of the winter solstice celebrations at the start of the year. Her hands felt cold and were clammy with sweat. She held a handkerchief wadded tightly in her left hand. She'd been passing it from palm to palm to prevent wiping her hands on the front of her dress.

Ranyl was slow to anger, to the point of being too placid, in her opinion. They had squabbled from time to time, as all couples did, but he had never raised his hand to her. She would not fear him. The knock at the front door came at the appointed time. Ranyl was ever punctual. Lannie, the Chamberses' housekeeper, let him in, and the sheriff walked directly into the sitting room.

"Ranyl," Helyn called from across the room, "how are you?"

"I'm well enough, Helyn, thank you," Ranyl replied. He sounded the same. On the surface, he looked the same also. Clad in a white cotton shirt and tan woolen breeches with an Ard Mourne plaid draped about his shoulders, his demeanor appeared calm. She noticed he had a sword belted about his waist. He'd never come calling upon her armed before.

Her father had told her when first she started walking out with Ranyl that most Emyrts were built like tree stumps and tended to be just as stubborn. Helyn had learned quickly that the young sheriff's easygoing air masked a surprisingly strong will. Once his mind was made up, he was not readily swayed. Solidly made, perhaps a finger width or two short of medium height, with broad shoulders and heavily muscled arms and thighs, Ranyl's features were more pleasing than handsome. Ranyl had a strong jaw, a slightly hooked nose, and wide-set dark-grey eyes.

His eyes drew hers like a magnet. Something was wrong with them—not wrong, exactly, but different. Ranyl's eyes appeared darker somehow and more intent, harder than when last she'd seen him. She'd intended to embrace him, regardless of what he knew or thought he knew about her and Kevyn, but his eyes—the stark expression in them—froze her in place. She could only stand watching him. Ranyl's left hand gripped his sword hilt. She could see his knuckles going white.

"Ellis Tate is dead," he said quietly. "My fault, that."

Grief; that's what it was. She'd never seen him grieving before. Helyn rushed across the room to fling her arms about his neck. They were very nearly the same height.

"Beloved," she cried, "I'm so sorry. I heard you were injured. Are you all right?"

"A scratch," Ranyl told her. "It's been tended to."

"By that Guilley woman of yours," Helyn said in a sharper tone than she intended.

"She's not mine any longer," Ranyl said quietly. Slowly, he raised his arms, encircling her back; he held her gently. "Ellis and I were chasing the Guilley leader. The outlander could sure run, I'll give him that, and he knew the ground better than we did. We got him but at the cost of Ellis's life. I let the chase go on too long. I knew it. I just ..." He sighed. "How many times, I wonder, have I heard my father or someone say some choices come with sharp edges?"

Holding her a little closer, Ranyl continued. "On the road back, coming down from the north yesterday, I took the left fork for some reason." Helyn stiffened, dreading the words that followed. "I saw Sprite tied to some junipers near the small well. I was curious. I saw you and Kevyn." He paused a moment. "I didn't know what to say or do, so I just rode on home." Ranyl didn't sound angry, only confused and hurt.

"I never meant to cause you pain," she whispered urgently, "never."

"I know that," he said quietly. "Are you in love with him?"

"No," Helyn replied quickly. "I loved the attention he paid me, I suppose."

"I don't think"—Ranyl spoke hesitantly, as if not certain what words to use—"Kevyn intends to take you with him when he goes."

"I never expected that of him, Ranyl," Helyn explained. "Kevyn Mourne made it very clear from the outset just exactly what he wanted of me. One of the things I found most attractive was that I knew pleasing him would be easy, and it was."

"Whereas pleasing me is difficult?" Ranyl inquired.

"I didn't say that," Helyn responded.

"Something is wrong between us," Ranyl stated. Loosening his grip upon her, Ranyl leaned back so he could look into her eyes. "If you loved me, you would not have lain with him."

"How could you possibly know that?" Helyn's eyes sparked with anger.

"I'll not apply for a second term as sheriff," Ranyl said, his charcoal eyes steady on hers. "I'll be leaving Wyteridge in the fall."

"*I*, you say," Helyn met his gaze, "not *we*. So I'm to be given no second chance?"

"Why would you want one?" Ranyl asked frankly.

"Because I am in love with you," Helyn told him. "If you give me the chance, I'll prove it. I promise."

"Men are simple creatures, Helyn," Ranyl said. "We mix pride and self-esteem together, even knowing we should not. But a man who lets go of the one soon loses the other and becomes a sorry sort of thing."

"I'm to be cast aside for an afternoon's folly?" Helyn could not quite keep the tremor out of her voice.

"No." Ranyl's tone firmed, and his eyes hardened. "You are being cast aside for a title and my brother's inheritance."

Helyn shook her head. "I don't understand."

"Kevyn is leaving for Alger Castle next week." Ranyl confirmed the content of Kevyn's note. "There will be no scandal. Things between us simply didn't work out. I will arrange a stipend for you, twelve hundred silver talents per annum."

"The price of my maidenhead, is that it?" Helyn questioned bitterly.

"Balm to my conscience for not marrying you last year as I should have," Ranyl admitted. "The stipend is all I have to give you that is truly my own."

"I don't want it, not without you," Helyn cried.

"I will not leave you with nothing, Helyn," Ranyl insisted. "You may do with the money what you like, but have it you will."

"What do you mean by title and inheritance?" Helyn asked softly. Her eyes begged him for understanding, for just a little forgiveness.

"I don't know exactly," Ranyl replied evenly. "Arrangements will be made."

Helyn's sky-blue eyes widened with shock and outrage. "You're doing this to please your father, not because I made love to Kevyn Mourne."

"By taking Kevyn Mourne to your thighs"—Ranyl's voice hardened to match his eyes—"you removed the last, best reason I had to deny my father's wishes."

Helyn slapped him hard across the face. "You never loved me," she accused.

Ranyl made no attempt to block or evade the blow, and his cheek stung sharply. "No, Helyn, that is not so." His eyes held hers remorselessly. "I just never loved you enough."

Ranyl did not return directly to his quarters, going instead to his office. Full dark cloaked the town by the time he walked into the sheriff's station. A ranger was on duty in the front office, should an emergency arise. Rangers called the front office the lobby.

The curly-haired young man whose name was Shamus Todd of Clan Ard Cullen stood warming his hands over embers glowing in the fireplace built into the far wall. In response to Ranyl's inquiry, Shamus told him that so far it had been a quiet night. Ranyl's office was dark. He lit an oil lamp on a side table near the door using a taper he'd set alight from a lamp glowing on the counter in the lobby.

Carrying the lamp to his writing table, Ranyl sat down and completed the letter to Laird Daryn Mourne, putting forth his argument for further augmentation of the ranger company stationed at Wyteridge. When finished, he set what he'd written aside for posting in the morning. From the drawer in his desk, he removed his father's letter that spoke of a potential marriage contract between Ranyl and eighteen-year-old Tessymir Ryan, heir to the lairdship of Clan Ard Ryan. Ranyl reread the missive slowly and carefully and then took up a fresh vellum sheet.

He wrote:

> Father,
> I remain unwed and will not marry in Wyteridge.
> If Laird Ryan is amenable to a marriage contract, pursue its negotiation.
> If he is not favorably disposed, then seek a similar arrangement elsewhere.
> Your son,
> Ranyl

"If she truly loved me, she would not have lain with Kevyn Mourne." Staring at the letter he'd just written, that is what Ranyl told himself. He wondered how many times he would have to repeat the litany before he believed it.

10

Broken Hub

Aeryk made his way cautiously to the crest of a small rise. He reined Wyli to a halt amid a stand of scrub oak. Behind him, to the northwest, the herd ambled along. The air smelled sweet but dry. Overhead, warmed by the sun, the vault of the sky showed cobalt blue.

To his front a familiar figure on horseback appeared. Moving at a canter, Wyatt pushed his big piebald up the opposite slope of the ridge, heading straight for Aeryk. *So much for my stealthy approach to the top*, Aeryk thought as he waited for the Tuchyck to close the distance between them.

"A wagon broke down yonder." Wyatt jerked a thumb over his left shoulder. "Farmers, I think." The Tuchyck spoke the word *farmers* the same way most folks said *snakes*.

"All by their lonesome, are they?" Aeryk inquired.

Wyatt nodded. The wiry Tuchyck spent words about as freely as bankers lent coin.

"Sam's off northeast a-ways, looking for water," Aeryk reported.

"Good water"—Wyatt pointed—"half day's drive toward morning sky."

79

Due east, then, Aeryk thought, and close enough to ease the worry Aeryk fancied he could see just starting to crease Sam's brow.

"C'mon," Aeryk said. Together he and Wyatt rode across the front of the herd. Reining in beside Caleb Edger, Aeryk called, "There's good water due east of here, about half a day's push. Keep 'em moving until you get there."

"That's good news," Caleb enthused. "While I'm moving 'em, just what is it you'll be doing?"

"Wyatt spotted a settler's wagon," Aeryk replied, "southeast of here a-ways. They look to be broke down. I thought Wyatt and I should stop by and be neighborly."

"Are there any females alongside that wagon?" Caleb wanted to know.

Aeryk glanced expectantly at Wyatt, who held up two fingers. Aeryk grinned. "I promise you first call on the other one."

Caleb tossed his head. "You're a little on the sly side; do you know that, Aeryk Emyrt?"

"Have Dustyn take offset, while you ride point," Aeryk directed in a more serious vein. He took a quick squint at the sky. "Send word to Cable so he'll know what we're about. Sam should be back by midafternoon."

"Will do," Caleb replied. Aeryk and Wyatt turned their horses away. "Serves you right if they both look like Cable's mules," Caleb called after them.

As they neared the vehicle, Aeryk saw the wagon was a large freighter with an arched canvas cover. Four mules stood in harness, with two more on tethers attached to the tailgate. Three men gathered 'round the left front wheel. A young woman, with medium-blond hair bound in a long single braid reaching nearly to the tops of her slender hips, tended to a large kettle suspended over a cook fire. An even younger girl, also blonde, her hair dressed in a similar braid, sat perched on the front seat.

The girl on the wagon seat took note of Aeryk and Wyatt's approach. She pointed and called something down to the men by the wheel. Clad in work clothes, plain woolen shirts and trousers, with broad-brimmed leather hats crowning their heads, all three showed stocky, wide-shouldered builds. A father and two sons, Aeryk reckoned. *Farmers, all right enough.* Each of the three took up a charged crossbow. They held the weapons across the fronts of their bodies, at the ready but not aimed.

Aeryk brought Wyli to a halt about ten paces shy of the campfire. "How do you fare?" He proffered speaking Aylitic, the language of Ayle. Aylitic was ancient, predating the kingdom of Ayle itself, and competed with Lynium, the Tieran tongue, as the most commonly used throughout the lands surrounding the Middle Sea. Though Glaylic served as the native speech of the Kylgahran, most clansmen spoke Aylitic, Aeryk included.

"Been better," the fellow in the middle replied. "Left front wheel has worked loose." A man of middle years, Aeryk guessed, judging by the lines in his face, with deep-set brown eyes and grey-flecked brown hair.

"My name's Carter Birdwell. These here"—Birdwell lifted one hand free of the crossbow to point left, then right—"are my sons, Jeb and Lewyn. The pretty ones are my daughters: Inez tending the soup and young Estyr on the wagon."

Birdwell's two sons shared their father's square-shaped face and brown hair and eyes. The older one, Jeb, looked to be around Aeryk's age, the younger about fifteen or sixteen. Inez and Estyr must have taken after their mother. In Aeryk's estimation, describing them as merely pretty qualified as an injustice.

Both were delicately featured, with small straight noses and high cheekbones just pronounced enough to accentuate large, wide-set eyes—robin's-egg blue in Inez's case, and emerald green for Estyr. Aeryk estimated Inez's age to be somewhere between those of her two brothers. Estyr couldn't have been more than twelve. Estyr peered at him inquisitively, while Inez flashed a brief smile and proceeded to add a large pot's worth of chopped cabbage to the kettle on the fire.

"I'm Aeryk Emyrt of Clan Ard Mourne," Aeryk responded. He nodded toward the Tuchyck scout at his side. "This is Wyatt. We're part of a trail crew, working a herd east to Cos. Wyatt spotted your wagon. Thought we'd stop by and say hullo."

"Hullo," Estyr piped up from her seat atop the wagon. "That sure is an ugly hat you're wearin'."

Aeryk met the girl's green-eyed gaze and couldn't help but smile. "Wyli sat on it the other day."

"Who is Wyli?" Estyr demanded.

"This fella." Aeryk leaned forward to pat Wyli on the shoulder. The gelding tossed his head in response.

Estyr smiled back. "Well, *he's* good-lookin' anyway."

"Estyr." Inez leveled a firm look at her younger sister. Turning her attention to Aeryk, she continued. "Thank you for stopping by, Master Emyrt. Judging from your accent and your name, you must be Kylgahran."

"Our mother was Kylgahran," Estyr announced.

Aeryk grinned. "That explains the pretty."

Inez smiled. Estyr hooted.

Jeb Birdwell thrust his chin Wyatt's way. "What's he?"

"Wyatt's Tuchyck," Aeryk answered.

Jeb spat into the prairie grass at his feet.

"Do you folks mind if I step down?" Aeryk requested.

"We don't need help," Jeb declared, "from you or your savage."

Aeryk fixed his eyes on Jeb's. "I'd say that's a little high-toned for someone who is about to have cabbage soup for supper."

"You have not yet tasted my cabbage soup, sir," Inez chided him.

Smiling despite himself, Aeryk conceded, "True enough, ma'am; my apologies." Aeryk's gaze settled again on Jeb Birdwell. "Wyatt is his own man and my friend." Aeryk then directed his question to Carter Birdwell. "Do you mind if I take a look at that wheel?"

The settler shrugged. "Climb down, if you are of a mind to."

Handing Wyli's reins to Wyatt, Aeryk dismounted, walked to the wagon, and knelt beside the left front wheel.

"We've heard tell of a trading post, supposed to be a couple of days' ride north of here called Sutter's," Birdwell recounted. "Do you know anything about that?"

"I can't say that I do," Aeryk allowed. He looked over his shoulder at Wyatt. The Tuchyck shook his head. "Sorry." The problem with the wheel turned out to be obvious. "The hub's cracked all the way to the seat," Aeryk noted. "You'll need a wheelwright to repair or replace it."

"Tell us something we don't know," Jeb commented.

"Are you a wheelwright?" Estyr inquired.

"No," Aeryk answered.

Little Estyr put her hands on her hips. "You're not good for much, are ya?"

Aeryk winked at her. "Not so far."

Thumbing back his trail hat, Aeryk thought for a moment. "Samwell Austyn is our trail boss. We have some wagons along. Sam's provisioned for spare parts—wheels and hubs, too. Some fitting up will likely be required. A couple of the fellas can help with that." Aeryk turned to Carter Birdwell. "I'll ask Sam to ride over. We may be able to help you out."

"At what price?" Carter asked warily.

Aeryk shrugged. "That will be up to you and Sam." Aeryk glanced Inez's way. "I hear Sam is partial to cabbage soup."

Inez straightened. Aeryk saw the corners of her mouth curve upward slowly, as her eyes found his. He felt the pull of that blue-eyed look. "It's about done. Why not stay awhile?"

"I really ought to be getting back to the herd." Aeryk felt his face warming. "The boys will be jealous enough as it is." Returning to Wyli's side, Aeryk swung back into the saddle. "I hope to be able to visit again."

"Thanks fer the warnin'," Estyr cried with a grin. "And see if you cain't do somethin' 'bout that hat."

Sweeping the garment referenced from his head, Aeryk emulated a seated bow he'd seen Basyl render to Lara a time or two. Putting Wyli into motion, Aeryk set out, with Wyatt riding at his side.

No sooner were they out of earshot than Wyatt growled, "Farmers." Ringing with wry emphasis, the Tuchyck's one-word assessment managed to speak volumes.

"Best you take a look 'round," Aeryk decided. "I'll ride back to the herd."

Without so much as a word, Wyatt turned away, heading east.

Sam proved less than enthusiastic about coming to the Birdwells' aid. "We've got more than enough to handle without wet nursing some know-nothing plow pusher." Sam fumed upon hearing Aeryk's report.

"A know-nothing plow pusher with a couple of mighty fine-looking daughters." Aeryk attempted to sweeten the pot. "Well, one at least; Estyr is a bit young."

"I don't know about you, Sam," Cable Dowd put in, "but I *am* partial to cabbage soup."

"I know exactly what you're partial to, you old geezer," Sam grumbled. "You're liable to hurt yourself."

"I've risked my neck fer lesser causes." Cable grinned.

"We do need to water the cattle," Aeryk suggested carefully. "That likely means an early stop today and a late start tomorrow."

"Refitting a wheel could take all morning, replacing a hub even longer." Sam launched the toe of his boot at a clump of grass. He looked at Aeryk. "You say the wagon is too heavy for the team."

"Aye," Aeryk affirmed. "Their mules look tuckered. Two more, they'll be needing, I reckon."

"So we're supposed to hand over spare parts and a pair of prime mules?" Sam fairly snarled at him.

"Seems like Birdwell was expecting to pay," Aeryk proffered.

"With what?" Sam retorted. "More cabbage soup?" He sighed and thrust his chin at Cable. "You think you can actually fix a wagon wheel?"

Cable's grin returned. "I was six years a carpenter's mate."

Sam tossed his head. "The cattle are pretty thirsty." He said to Aeryk, "Once watered, they ought to settle down easy enough. Keep 'em on this side of the creek. We'll worry about crossing tomorrow."

"I'm to stay with the herd?" Aeryk tried to hide his disappointment. "I thought maybe you'd like me to guide you over and introduce you to the Birdwells."

"I can say howdy as well as the next fella," Sam countered with a knowing smile. "And Cable, here, has a nose for soup and blondes both. I doubt we'll get lost."

A spare wheel turned out to be a good fit for the Birdwell wagon and a straight-up swap the simplest repair option. After taking a meal with the farm family, Sam decided to sell them a pair of mules. The price settled upon amounted to twelve silver talents in coin, a large crock of honey, and two bottles of brandy wine.

Cable gleefully related details of the transaction to Aeryk while they sat with Sam at breakfast the following day. "When we get to Cos, Samwell," Cable chortled, "you'd better let me do the dickering. At the prices you sell stock, the ranchers off home are liable to lynch you once we get back to Taggert's Landing."

"Shut up, the both of ye," Sam barked.

"I didn't say anything," Aeryk protested.

"No," Sam acknowledged, "but you're grinning loud enough to wake the dead."

Sam ordered Aeryk to take the two mules to the Birdwell campsite. The trail boss had agreed to return the settler's coin if the mules didn't meet with Birdwell's approval. Carter Birdwell looked them over carefully when Aeryk arrived.

"These are fine-looking animals," Birdwell concluded grudgingly.

"You don't sound best pleased," Aeryk commented.

"They're worth a lot more than I paid," Birdwell stated. He frowned. "I didn't ask fer charity."

"They're for your girls and our pleasure," Aeryk said quietly.

"Thank Austyn fer me." Birdwell extended his hand. "I'm in his debt, and yours too, youngster."

"Hoi," Estyr bubbled, appearing, as if conjured, at Aeryk's side. "It don't seem possible, but that hat of yours is even uglier than when last I saw ya."

Aeryk smiled down at her. "While somehow you've managed to get even prettier. Life is a wonder, ain't it?"

"C'mon." Estyr grabbed Aeryk's arm with both hands. "You're expected. Inez set aside some sausage fer ya. You can have breakfast twice in one day."

With their wagon repaired and their team augmented, the Birdwells had little trouble keeping pace with the Kylgahran's cattle herd over the next few days. For added security, the farm family took to pitching their camp within sight of the trail crew's night fires. It didn't take long for off-duty drovers to start visiting. One evening, Aeryk spruced up a bit and determined to gather a spray of wildflowers for Inez before heading over to the Birdwells' camp.

This late in the season, it took a while longer than Aeryk had anticipated to find anything in bloom. By the time he swung down beside the Birdwell wagon, Aeryk saw that both Caleb Edger and Daymen Reed had preceded him. Daymen held his lyre in his lap, as both he and Caleb serenaded Inez. Daymen sounded a natural tenor, and Caleb a fine baritone. Between the two of them, Inez seemed well and truly occupied. She didn't so much as cast a glance Aeryk's way when he stepped into the ring of light thrown by the campfire.

Estyr greeted him with a mischievous grin. "Too slow."

"Seems like," Aeryk acknowledged, venturing a rueful smile of his own.

"You could pretend like you was courtin' me," Estyr offered. "We could both of us use the practice, I reckon."

Aeryk bowed formally. "For you, Bones, with my compliments."

"Them's weeds, mostly," Estyr observed, accepting the flowers. "Bones, you say."

"Aye," Aeryk enthused. "It seems a likely nickname for you."

"Why?" Estyr demanded, brandishing her flowers. "And if you tell me it's 'cause I got boney knees or somethin', I'll smack ya."

"It is in honor of your perfectly sculpted cheekbones," Aeryk told her, "that look especially lovely in the moons' light." Estyr really was a pretty little thing, her cheekbones indeed high and fine.

"You're teasin'," she scoffed.

"I am in earnest, Bones," Aeryk said sincerely. "My word on it."

Estyr stared at him suspiciously for a full breath. "Mebbe you don't need quite sa much practice as I thought."

Three days later, as soon as the herd had been settled down for the evening, Aeryk rode over. Dismounting, he noted the Birdwells were still in the process of setting up camp. No sooner had he tied off Wyli, looping the reins through the spokes of one of the wagon's rear wheels, than Estyr hurried up. She barreled into him, wrapping her arms tightly about Aeryk's middle.

"Whoa," Aeryk exclaimed. "Easy, Bones. What is it?"

"We're leavin'," Estyr cried, all in a rush. "We got to go north tomorrow or the next day, Papa says."

"Did he say why?" Aeryk asked, embracing her.

"The colony is north of here, mostly, Papa said," Estyr recounted. "If we trail along with you boys, we'll wind up goin' too far east. Papa says we cain't afford to take so long gettin' there, as all the good parcels will be took." *Colony* was the term Syrdisians used to describe new settlements being established on what once were tribal lands.

"I see," Aeryk soothed. "Well, I reckon your papa knows what he is about."

"Mr. Sam said it weren't safe," Estyr half sobbed. "He said the country was wild, and that there were Cymbri and bandits and such, and that no piece of land was worth the risk."

"Sam said that," Aeryk questioned, "in front of you?"

"I heard 'em talkin'. They was pretty loud," Estyr confessed. "I walked up kindly soft and hunkered down. I don't think they saw me, but I could hear them." There was no mistaking the hushed dread in her voice.

"Come on," Aeryk suggested, lifting Estyr bodily into the saddle. Freeing the reins, he clambered up behind her. "Let's you, me, and Wyli go for a little walk."

Estyr settled against him. "Papa said we'd have just this one chance to make good. Mr. Sam was dead set again' it." She took a breath and blurted, "Papa is just so stubborn." Estyr's voice quavered, on the verge of tears.

"It takes a lot of stubborn to open up new country," Aeryk told her. Estyr was flat out sobbing the now. Aeryk brought Wyli to a halt and held her, silently cursing both Carter Birdwell and Sam too, for not paying closer attention.

"Fat lot, you know," Estyr cried, "you and your ugly hat."

"Listen to me, Bones," Aeryk urged. "It's true you're heading into wild country, but it is also big and mostly empty. Like as not, you won't see another soul until you roll up on this colony you're headed for."

Estyr sniffed. "But Mr. Sam said—"

"Sam's mighty cautious," Aeryk interrupted gently. "He gets paid to be that way. The Cymbri generally stay north and west of here; you'll be heading northeast. Bandits are bad men, but they're some short on courage, usually. Your papa and your brothers ain't."

Estyr quieted. "Do you ..." She swallowed. "Do you think it will be all right?"

"I know it will be all right," Aeryk assured her. "I promise. Here." He slipped a bracelet off his left wrist. A simple thing, fashioned of braided leather, Aeryk had made it himself years ago. "This is a talisman of sorts. It has brought me good luck." He slipped it onto her wrist, adjusting the strap to tighten it. "It will bring you good luck the now, too."

Estyr shook her head. "I don't want to take your luck, Aeryk."

"I have another," Aeryk hastened to tell her, "from my mum. Don't you worry about me."

"I know I shouldn't be so scared," Estyr whispered, as if owning up to some wrongdoing, "but I wish we could go on along with you boys."

"I wish you could, too," Aeryk allowed. "Once past the ornery"—he hugged her close—"you're not bad company."

With the sun hanging low in the western sky the following day, Aeryk made his way to the Birdwell campsite for one last visit. He secured Wyli to the end of the tether line that held the Birdwells' mules. Aeryk found Inez busy, as usual, 'round the cook fire.

He greeted her, whipping his hat from his head. "I stopped by to say my farewells and wish you luck."

Inez wiped her hands on the apron tied about her slender waist and tossed her golden braid back over one shoulder. She regarded him in silence for a moment. In the fading light, amid the soft glow of the campfire, her blue eyes looked black and bottomless. "You've never tried my soup."

Aeryk felt a smile tug into place. "I'll have something to look forward to, then."

"The colony is not that far off, Papa says," Inez remarked. "You could visit on your way home from Cos."

To his right, Aeryk heard the sound of horses approaching. A quick glance over his shoulder revealed both Caleb Edger and Daymen Reed, hauling their mounts to a stop. Aeryk saw Daymen's lyre, strapped to his back in a worked leather case. "I may have to wait until the traffic dies down."

Inez flashed a smile as warm as the embers glowing at her feet. "Afraid of a little competition, are you?"

"I don't play," Aeryk confided, "and I sing like something dying."

Inez's smile took on a mysterious cast. "Perhaps we could find some other way to pass the time."

"Perhaps." Aeryk felt glad of the soft light, as it hid the blush burning its way into his cheeks. "Have a safe journey, Inez, and all the best."

"Thank you." It might have been his imagination, but Aeryk thought he heard a wistful note thread its way through Inez's voice. She extended her hand. Aeryk was surprised at how small and soft it felt nestled within his own.

"I hope the same for you," Inez said in parting.

Aeryk could not find Estyr. Growing concerned, he returned to the tether line. He saw her, then, standing at Wyli's head, the fingers of one hand curled round a leather strap of the gelding's bridle, while the other gently stroked his muzzle.

"I meant to warn you about, Inez," Estyr stated quietly as he approached. "She's my sister, and I love her." Slipping her hand free of Wyli's bridle, Estyr turned to face him. "There's no meanness in her, none at all, but she is inconstant. Any breeze will shift her; every smile turns her head."

Aeryk stopped and gazed down at her. In the gloaming, he could not discern the color of her eyes. They appeared as two dark pools. "How old are you, Bones?" he asked.

"Thirteen." Estyr ducked her chin. "I'm small for my age."

"And wise beyond your years, it seems," Aeryk observed.

Estyr tossed her head. "Just a little jealous, I reckon."

"In a couple of years," Aeryk told her, "wherever you are, you'll be the prettiest girl there. Young men will be lined up halfway 'round the barn, all trying to catch your eye."

Even amid the growing dark, Aeryk saw her eyes flash as Estyr smiled. "Only halfway?"

Aeryk smiled in return. "You're going to have lots of choices, Bones. Pick a good'n. Promise me."

Her eyes softened. "I'm never going to see you again, am I?"

"I wouldn't say that," Aeryk hedged. "Kylgahran and bad pennies—we're liable to turn up anywhere." He took her hand. "I won't say good-bye to you, only farewell, my bonnie."

"Bonnie," Estyr echoed, sounding puzzled.

"In the Highlands," Aeryk explained, "a bonnie is a lass who is beautiful and steadfast. The winds of fate may blow a gale and never budge her."

"A bonnie," Estyr repeated softly. "I won't forget." Her fingers closed on his, squeezing tight. "And I'll remember you, always."

"Well"—Aeryk grinned—"naturally."

Estyr stepped into his arms, pressing her cheek to his chest. "Don't worry," she assured him, "I won't cry until you've gone."

He held her for a little while. Estyr felt small and warm in his arms. She trusted him. Aeryk's throat tightened. "Take care," he said, finally.

"I will," Estyr promised. "Aeryk, when you get to Cos ..." She hesitated.

"Yes," Aeryk prompted.

"Be sure and buy a new hat."

11
A Lot of Stubborn

At dawn the day following, Aeryk watched as the Birdwell wagon trundled off to the northeast. Knowing it was bad luck to see them out of sight, he turned away at the last. Cantering around the leading edge of the herd, Aeryk resumed his post at the point.

He was riding point a few hours after sunrise two days later when Sam, accompanied by Wyatt, Caleb Edger, and Dustyn Claire of Clan Ard Drew caught up to him. Aeryk noticed that both Sam and Caleb had short-handled spades lashed to the cantles of their saddles.

Sam came right to the point. "Wyatt decided to circle round. Off to the north a-ways he spotted the Birdwell wagon. Looks like bandits hit 'em."

Aeryk felt as if his heart had turned to ice. "Is it bad?"

Sam nodded. He turned to Dustyn. "Take the point." Sam's eyes settled upon Aeryk. "Let's go," he said evenly. "We've got some burying to do."

The four of them—Sam, Wyatt, Caleb, and Aeryk—moved north at a canter. Sam slowed them to a trot, then a walk, and back to a canter, covering the ground swiftly and efficiently, while sparing the horses as best he could. Just before noon Aeryk caught sight of the wagon.

As they approached, Aeryk saw the bodies of Jeb and Lewyn sprawled on either side of the fire pit. Both had been stripped of their clothing. Carter Birdwell was tied to a rear wheel of the wagon, naked to the waist. His left ankle had been fastened with a leather thong to a wooden stake driven into the ground. The farmer's bare left foot looked like a piece of undercooked meat, red and swollen. His throat had been cut.

The drovers dismounted. On the far side of the wagon, Inez's body lay sprawled, nude, atop a rough woolen blanket. Caleb made his way over to kneel by her side. Aeryk did not draw near. Even from where he stood, beside the tailgate of the wagon, the expression on Caleb's face told Aeryk more than he wanted to know about Inez's last moments. Gently, Caleb pulled one end of the blanket up to cover her.

Dreading what he might find, Aeryk lifted the canvas flap that covered the opening at the rear of the vehicle and peered within. The interior showed signs of thorough rifling—foodstuffs and some articles of clothing scattered about—but no sign of Estyr.

Sam's face looked as if it had been carved from marble. "Bandits, you reckon, not Cymbri?" he said to Wyatt.

The Tuchyck nodded. "Shod horses, not Cymbri. Renegades, I think, mebbe."

Aeryk pointed to Carter Birdwell's corpse. The mostly white hair mantling the dead farmer's broad chest was matted with blood, dried but still sticky-looking.

"Why would they torture him?" Aeryk asked.

"Sometimes people hide coin or things of gold or silver inside." Wyatt raised his chin in the direction of the wagon.

Aeryk steeled himself. "What do you think happened to Estyr?"

"They take," Wyatt answered.

Caleb Edger stepped up beside Aeryk. "Why would they carry Estyr off and"—he swallowed—"murder Inez?"

"Better for trade." Wyatt spoke matter-of-factly. "Young one not known to man. Good price. Everybody knows this, so no fighting over her before trading is done."

"How long ago?" Sam inquired.

"A day and a night, mebbe," Wyatt responded. "They go north-west," the Tuchyck added without being prompted, "six of them."

"Do you think they spotted the herd?" Sam asked next.

Wyatt shook his head. "They come from the north and go away again. Too far to see."

"The bastards have got at least a full day's ride on us." Sam's jaw knotted. "They're headed straight for Cymbri country. And we've got a herd of cattle to look after."

"She's just a child, Sam." The words were out before Aeryk could call them back. Sam faced him. The tall Highlander's eyes appeared frozen, still as a winter dawn. Aeryk squared his shoulders. "I told her everything would be all right. I promised her."

"That was a damn fool thing to do." Sam bit off the words. "And it changes nothing."

"I had to say something," Aeryk insisted. "Estyr was frightened. She heard you and Birdwell arguing."

Something flickered in the ice-grey depths. Sam said nothing.

His heart throbbing, Aeryk pressed. "I have to try, Sam."

"You're like to die, boy," Sam ground out, "and they'll probably make her watch."

Aeryk flared. "At least she'll know she wasn't abandoned."

Sam turned away, looking to the north.

"Leave me an extra horse," Aeryk requested. The words seem to come from far away, as if someone else was speaking. "I'll go alone."

"Not alone," Wyatt said firmly. "You get lost, mebbe. I go with you."

Sam glared at the Tuchyck for a moment and then rounded on Caleb Edger. "I suppose you want to play hero, too."

"I'll do whatever you say, boss," Caleb replied steadily.

"Goddammit," Sam cursed. To Aeryk's ears he sounded more resigned than angry—relieved, even. "Get back to the herd," Sam directed Caleb. "Pick up a fresh horse for yourself and four remounts. We'll need a packhorse, food for a week, and our bedrolls. Have

Cable keep 'em moving, due east. With luck, we'll catch up in four or five days." Sam stepped up and unlashed the spade from the back of Caleb's saddle. "I want no more heroes. Too many people back home are counting on us to get the cattle through to Cos. Tell Cable to make that stick, or I will."

"Aye, sir." Caleb said.

"You're sure you can find your way back here?" Sam queried.

Caleb nodded. "I can."

"All right enough," Sam told him. "Quick as you're able, get moving."

Caleb mounted and galloped south.

"Wyatt," Sam said next, "see if you can figure out where they're headed and how fast they're moving. We'll follow along as best we can. Look for us in the morning."

Without a word, Wyatt urged his piebald into motion, heading northwest.

Sam removed the second spade from his own saddle and stood facing Aeryk.

"Thank you, Sam," Aeryk proffered, trying as best he could to keep his voice steady.

Sam nodded. Taking a couple of steps closer, he tossed the shovel in his right hand to Aeryk. "Let's get these folks planted."

Sometime later, Sam and Aeryk stood beside four freshly dug graves, each marked by a rough-hewn Kylgahran cross, a symbol of the Four Fates. Neither Sam nor Aeryk knew what religion the Birdwells practiced. Most Syrdisians were Penitents, but Birdwell had wed a Kylgahran woman, who was likely of the Brynnai faith. The crosses would have to do.

Sam removed his hat. Aeryk did also. "Kind Fates," Sam prayed, his voice firm and clear, "we ask you to welcome the souls of these departed." He paused a moment, as if gathering his thoughts. "Bad things happen sometimes to good people," Sam went on, "to innocents, to brash youths, to young women, and stubborn-assed hayseeds. It is hard for us who remain to figure why. Amid the mystery that is life and your many lessons, one thing seems certain. To live well it is necessary to choose well. At least these folks here chose bravely. Sweet Fates, give their souls rest; grant them peace. We ask this in God's name." Sam clapped his hat back onto his head and turned away. "Best we get some rest," He advised. "It's going to be a long night."

Caleb returned a couple of hours before sunset, leading a well-laden packhorse and four remounts.

"Any trouble with the crew?" Sam inquired.

"Not much," Caleb told him. "Dustyn Claire had to knock Daymen Reed down, but that was about it."

"A good man, Dustyn," Sam commented.

The three of them set out immediately, following the bandits' trail north by west. Just why the outlaws would be traveling in the direction of Cymbri territory posed a question. Cymbri tended toward the irascible in the best of times. Sam had heard tell of small groups of renegades who managed to trade with the Cymbri. Maybe the six they pursued were of that stripe. Wyatt seemed to think so. If the renegades managed to reach the lodges of the Cymbri, any hope of recovering Estyr would likely be dashed.

Night fell, but Sam kept on, using a torch he'd fashioned from soaking a strip cut from the canvas cover of the Birdwell wagon in lamp oil. "This light can be seen from a long way off," Sam noted, "but the trail is plain enough, and we need to close in a hurry." They alternated, leading their horses for a time and then remounting. When one strip of canvas burned through, Sam replaced it with another, keeping the torch lit. The ground fell away behind them.

A couple of hours before sunup, Sam called a halt. He doused the torch. "Get some sleep," Sam ordered, the first words he'd uttered in hours. "I'll take the watch."

Caleb and Aeryk hunkered down, wrapped in their plaids. "I wouldn't want Sam chasin' me," Caleb muttered.

"Sam can be a hard case when he puts his mind to it," Aeryk agreed. "Lucky for us."

"Would you have really gone alone?" Caleb wondered.

"I don't know," Aeryk answered, the words sounding hollow in his own ears.

"I think you do," Caleb asserted. "You hide it well, but I reckon there is some hard case in you, too." Tugging his hat down over his eyes, Caleb gathered his plaid closer about him and rolled on to his side. In moments, the young drover was sound asleep.

Aeryk lay on his back, gazing up at the stars twinkling in a sky already beginning to pale. *Would I have gone on alone?* Aeryk could be certain of only one thing: the relief he felt at having been spared that choice.

Wyatt caught up with them early the following morning. "They go slow," the Tuchyck reported. "Many mules and some horses, too. Three captives, I think, mebbe."

"How long to run 'em down?" Sam asked.

"Tomorrow," Wyatt estimated, "before the sun sets."

They closed on the bandit camp the next day with about an hour of sunlight remaining. Observing from the crest of a small rise to the southwest, Aeryk counted eight men and three smaller figures with their wrists bound behind their backs. One of the three had long blond hair.

"They have a cook fire started," Sam observed quietly. "We'll wait until the sun is just going and take them with the light at our backs."

"Where'd the other two come from?" Caleb wondered.

"Doesn't matter." Sam's terse whisper sounded hard as steel. "They're dead men the now. Aeryk, you and Wyatt work your way round to the left. Caleb and I will make our way down the ridge from here. When you hear me holler, jump 'em."

"Right," Aeryk responded, glad of the need to whisper, as his mouth tasted as dry as desert sand.

"When I yell, boys," Sam directed, "move fast and hit hard. Show them no mercy, as ye will receive none."

Sam nodded at Wyatt, who briefly touched Aeryk's arm. "Come. We move as when stalking elk," the Tuchyck murmured.

Aeryk followed Wyatt into the gathering dusk. Crouched low, the Tuchyck made no noise that Aeryk could discern, none at all. Shifting the targe affixed to his left arm, Aeryk hefted the two throwing darts held in his right hand and tried to match Wyatt's silent progress. Wyatt finished by crawling on his belly through knee-high prairie grass, browned by the sun. Positioned at Wyatt's side, Aeryk reckoned they were little more than a dart's throw from the nearest renegade, a tall, lean-looking man clad in loose-fitting woolen trousers. He was shirtless but wearing a sheepskin vest. The man carried a steel-tipped spear, and Aeryk saw a light axe resting in a loop in the leather belt at his waist.

Aeryk shifted one dart to his left hand, simultaneously holding it and the handle of his targe. His pulse surging, Aeryk readied the dart clasped in his right hand. He started at the fierce roar of Sam's battle cry. Aeryk leapt to his feet and rushed toward the man with the spear. The bandit turned toward the sound of Sam's shout and stood in a fighting-man's crouch, with his back toward Aeryk. Aeryk skidded to a halt, braced, and hurled his dart. He missed. The dart flashed past the tall man's shoulder.

The stranger whirled about. Aeryk launched his second missile. The finely wrought steel tip of the dart tore into the renegade's chest, and the man dropped. Wyatt loosed an arrow and then another, grunting softly with each shot. Aeryk drew his sword, grateful for the familiar feel of the baelryc in his grasp.

Aeryk hurried onward. A man appeared before him, swinging a light axe in an overhead strike. Reacting as he'd been trained, Aeryk darted toward him, raised his targe to fend off the blow, and stabbed with his baelryc beneath his shield. The axe slammed into Aeryk's targe, becoming fouled in the wicker core. Aeryk felt his sword bite. The man grunted; Aeryk twisted the blade, stepped quickly to his left, and jerked the weapon free. His foe, a stocky middle-aged man with a pock-marked face, let go of his axe and reached for a long knife in his belt.

Aeryk launched a second thrust aimed at his enemy's throat. The baelryc struck home, blood fountained, and the bandit collapsed. Aeryk recovered, dropping into a mid-guard stance, his foeman's axe still embedded in his targe. He caught sight of a tall man with a shaved head standing a few paces away.

The stranger held a long, wickedly curved knife in his right hand, the blade pressed lightly to the base of Estyr Birdwell's throat. The tall bandit's left arm wrapped firmly about Estyr's body; her wrists were still tied at the small of her back. He smiled, flashing white, evenly spaced teeth. The dimming light hid the color of the bandit's eyes, but there was no mistaking their intensity.

"You look a little ridiculous, standing there with that axe stuck in your shield," the bandit commented. He spoke in the well-rounded tones of an educated man. Estyr's eyes showed wide with terror.

"The fella what put it there looks a little dead just the now," Aeryk replied. Aeryk shifted his weight.

"One step closer," the shaved-headed man warned, "and I'll cut her."

Aeryk's mind raced. He shrugged. "We're here for the mules."

The renegade's smile faded. "Too bad, darlin'," he said to Estyr.

"Let her go," Aeryk bargained, "and you can walk away."

"It is a long walk to anywhere," the bandit remarked, never taking his eyes from Aeryk's.

"Any two horses from your lot you want," Aeryk offered, "and all the gear you can carry; my word on it."

The outlaw tossed his head. "Not that I doubt your veracity, but recent experience has taught me to be wary. Two horses and the girl to ensure my safe conduct and a night's head start. I'll go due west. If I see no one following at first light, I'll let the lass go. You'll have no trouble finding her."

Aeryk shook his head. "She'll not leave here with you."

The bandit's smile returned, devoid of mirth, "Then she'll not leave here at all. What a shame that would be. She's such a pretty little thing. You know I—"

The tall man's eyes bulged with surprise as Wyatt's arrow drove deep into the base of his skull. The heavy-bladed knife tumbled from his fingertips as the renegade crumpled to the ground. Tossing aside his targe, Aeryk sprang forward to clasp his left arm about Estyr's waist. "Are you all right?" Aeryk asked urgently.

"I think so." Estyr's response sounded eerily calm, stripped of emotion.

Wyatt emerged from the shadows. An arrow fixed to the bow in his hand. "They're done," the Tuchyck stated. Wyatt spoke with no more emotion than Estyr had, but his dark eyes shone; his arrows had brought down three of the bandit crew.

Looking across to the other side of the campsite, Aeryk saw Sam gazing back. Even amid the gloaming, Aeryk could see the blood staining the trail boss's sword.

"How do you fare?" Sam called out.

"We're all right," Aeryk answered, relief pulsing through his veins, "and so is Estyr."

"All eight of the bastards are down," Sam reported. "Caleb took a sword thrust to the thigh. He'll need tending."

"C'mon," Aeryk said to Estyr, "let's sit you down by the fire, and see if we can't get Caleb doctored up."

The other two captives, a boy and a girl, years younger than Estyr, were dead. One of the renegades had slit their throats before Sam put him down. Sam stood over the small bodies, redheads both, brother and sister most likely. "Pure meanness," Sam grated. He spat into the face of the dead renegade. "Scralyng bastard."

It took some doing—the wound was dangerously deep—but they managed to stop the bleeding in Caleb's left thigh. Estyr did not know the names of the other two captives. While Caleb and Estyr rested by the fire, and Wyatt prepared a simple meal, Sam and Aeryk scooped out shallow graves for the two children. Once they'd covered the still forms with sod, the two Kylgahran returned to the campfire.

As Aeryk approached, Estyr climbed to her feet. "You said everything would be all right." She hurled the words at Aeryk like a stone. "You promised." Estyr tore the leather bracelet from her left wrist and threw it on the ground at his feet. "Liar!" she cried, in a voice ragged and torn. "I hate you!"

"I'm sorry," Aeryk managed. "Bones, I'm sorry."

Estyr turned away and flung herself down by the fire. Her shoulders shook as she wept. Aeryk knelt by her side. "Bones, please," Aeryk entreated, "I didn't mean to." He reached out to gently touch her arm.

Estyr recoiled, snatching her arm away. "Leave me alone," she sobbed. "Leave me alone."

Aeryk felt a strong hand on his shoulder. "Best let her be, lad," Sam said quietly.

Aeryk walked to the other side of the campfire, hunkering down at the edge of darkness. Wyatt brought him a plate. Aeryk's stomach roiled, but he forced himself to eat. The food, flatbread and bacon, tasted like ashes.

Dawn came. They rigged a drag for Caleb. The morning brought no signs of further bleeding, but Sam thought it best to be cautious. Traveling slowly, the long poles of the drag would act as springs, easier on Caleb's wounded leg than riding would have been. The five of them headed out, leaving the bodies of the eight bandits where they lay.

The renegades' riding stock proved to be poor. Sam decided to turn them loose. The outlaws had stolen sixteen mules, all of whom were in better shape than the horses. The Kylgahran also gathered whatever coin and silver the bandits had on them, figuring Estyr had as much claim to the money—roughly three hundred talents' worth—as any. Proceeds from the sale of eight of the mules would also go to Estyr. Not much for a thirteen-year-old with no family left but better than nothing.

Aeryk made no attempt to speak with Estyr during breakfast before they started or through the long day that followed. Sam kept them moving, slowly but steadily, until sundown. Caleb appeared to have weathered the journey well; his color had improved by day's end. Aeryk tethered the mules and their horses. He lingered awhile with Wyli. The gelding butted his head into Aeryk's chest. Aeryk gave him a good scratching behind the ears, grateful for Wyli's unwavering companionship.

When he returned to camp, Estyr wouldn't so much as look at him. The young girl's estrangement hurt, filling him first with resentment and then with sorrow. *She's safe; nothing else matters*, he told himself, except, of course, it did matter.

At the close of their second day on the trail back, Sam selected the mouth of a shallow draw as a campsite. The banks of the draw offered shelter for the animals and shielded their campfire from view on three of four sides. As usual, Aeryk saw to the tethering of the stock for the night. On his way back into camp, he saw Wyatt speaking in low, fierce tones to Estyr. The girl said nothing in response; her expression looked fixed, determined.

Aeryk drew first watch. He settled himself near the crest of the bank on the southern face of the draw. A brisk, raw wind, hinting of the cold weather to come, had blown most of the day, leaving the night air clear as crystal. As the moons set, Aeryk thought he'd never seen the stars shine so bright.

He sensed movement to his right and turned to see Estyr standing a few paces away. She was wrapped in his spare plaid. Aeryk had passed the garment on to Sam, fearing the girl would not accept it from his hands. She looked tiny, swathed in the oversized folds of wool, her face a pale oval. She said nothing.

"Can't sleep?" Aeryk prompted.

Estyr shook her head.

"Bad dreams?" Aeryk guessed. Estyr ducked her chin. "Dreams are scary sometimes because they are shadows of what we fear. They are not real, Bones; they can't touch you." With continued silence from Estyr, Aeryk found himself not knowing what to say or do.

"Wyatt says if it weren't for you and the promise you made, no one would have come for me," Estyr burst out. "He says I'm a stupid girl, not fit even for the gathering of firewood, and that if I had any honor, I would apologize."

"You don't have anything to apologize for, Bones," Aeryk told her, as relief and a touch of hope coursed through him. "You should know it was Sam who came after you and Wyatt who showed us the way. Caleb and I mostly did what we were told."

Estyr's eyes bored into his. Aeryk could not have looked away if he'd wanted to.

"I lied to you, Bones. I made you a promise I couldn't keep. I did it because I couldn't stand to see you frightened. I shouldn't have. It was wrong of me, and I'm sorry." Aeryk's voice strained at the last.

"I didn't mean it"—Aeryk heard the quiver in Estyr's tone—"when I said I hated you. I didn't mean it." Her face crumpled, and she dropped to her knees, sobbing.

Aeryk rushed to her side and went to his knees as well. He hesitated and then slowly put his arms around her. Estyr made no protest, and Aeryk hugged her close. "It's all right, Bones." He heard his voice shaking. "It's all right." Estyr clung to him. "Can you forgive me, Bones? Please?"

She grew still in his embrace. "I reckon I'm gonna have to," Estyr answered, her voice twisted and bleak. "You're about the only friend I've got left."

"You'll make plenty more," Aeryk assured her.

Estyr pressed closer. Neither of them said anything for some time. Finally, Estyr whispered, "Those men, when they came, they shot arrows into Jeb and Lewyn." Estyr spoke so softly that even amid the still of the night, Aeryk had to strain to hear. "I tried to run, but they caught me and tied my hands and blindfolded me so I could not see." Her voice broke, and she swallowed hard before continuing. "I heard ... what they did. Inez screamed and screamed, and Papa, he begged for them to stop hurting her, and then ... and then ..." She couldn't go on; Estyr buried her face in the front of his plaid.

"They are safe the now, Bones." Aeryk spoke gently but as firmly as he dared. "Your father, your sister, and your brothers—they are with your mother, in the arms of the Creator, free from want or pain or regret. And one day you'll see them again, in the spirit realm."

Estyr sniffed. "Papa said that men most likely made the gods, not the other way around."

"There are some who believe that," Aeryk acknowledged. He tucked his hand beneath her chin and tilted Estyr's head back. "Look up, Bones, at the stars." She complied, her eyes searching. "Do you think anything so beautiful, so vast, so perfect is some kind of accident?"

Slowly, Estyr shook her head.

"Aye, well, me neither." Aeryk's voice deepened; he'd never before tried to express such thoughts. "He's there, Bones; the Creator's hand is in all things, and this life, no matter how long, no matter how hard, is only a beginning."

"Is that what you believe?" Estyr murmured.

"I do." As he spoke the words, Aeryk realized that he did. He briefly tightened his hold upon her. "I'm done with promises I can't keep. I'll make you a new one, Bones—to be your friend, a true friend, until my last breath."

She considered what he'd said for a moment or two. "And I'll be yours." Estyr's voice gained strength and purpose as she responded. "A true friend, forever."

12
Odd One In

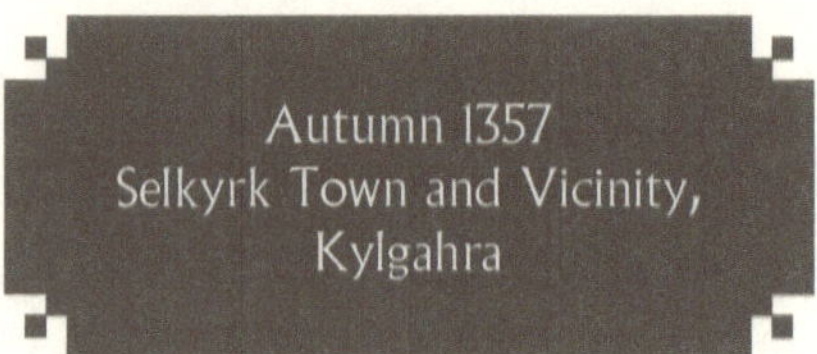

Ranyl Emyrt of Clan Ard Mourne sat his new horse, a grey-coated Morgyn, he'd taken to calling Stepper. Stepper was even tempered for a stallion and longer of leg than typical of his breed—two marks in his favor, as far as Ranyl was concerned. Stepper exhibited the vaunted endurance of the mountain-bred Morgyns and a better turn of speed than most. Reaching forward, Ranyl patted Stepper on the shoulder. The stallion whickered lightly in response, tossing his head. A quick glance at the autumn sky overhead showed only a couple of hours remained until sunset. They'd be stopping soon. Turning in the saddle, Ranyl looked back down the road that Kylgahran referred to as Long Reach, gazing upon his retinue.

Ranyl smiled wryly. *Retinue, indeed.* If he wasn't careful, he'd be putting on airs. Eighteen of his rangers had elected to accompany him north. Of course, his men, a round dozen of them anyway, had also elected to bring along their women and children. As ex-rangers, the ban on marriage no longer applied. Before their departure from Wyteridge, a flurry of weddings had taken place. In other instances, secret marriages, some concealed for years, were suddenly made public.

The short of it was that in addition to the men who were once his rangers, twelve wives, three of them pregnant, and fourteen children, ranging in age from thirteen years to ten months, had joined him on his trek north. This wasn't counting the smith, Fyrgus Clyde; his wife, Emma; and his three sons, Emmyt, Byli, and Thadius, aged sixteen, fourteen, and twelve, respectively; and the youthful apothecary, Waltyr Boone of Clan Ard Owen. Mae Hoskins and her two sons by Ellis Tate had also joined the company.

Ranyl had promised Mae's boys, a pair of green-eyed towheads, a place in service with him when they came of age. He would have been willing to fetch them from Wyteridge, but Mae wanted a new start, someplace free of memories and perhaps fewer stares and whispers directed at an unwed mother, now without a man. Ranyl could not bring himself to say no. Consequently, Mae and her two sons, Rafe and Bowen, shared his wagon.

Young Tad Gyllis, a groom from the sheriff's station at Wyteridge, had cast his lot with Ranyl as well. Tad drove Ranyl's wagon. At seventeen years of age, Tad was still a touch too young to have become a ranger. Apparently, the whippet-lean, dark-haired youth had set that long-held dream aside in favor of becoming one of Ranyl's retainers. Mae and the boys slept in the wagon, while Ranyl and Tad stretched out on their bedrolls underneath the vehicle. Not exactly the accommodations Ranyl had planned on, but he really couldn't complain. The boys were easy enough to get along with, and Mae was a fine cook. The way north had been good for her. Though sorrow still shadowed her wide-set, blue-green eyes, grief's merciless grip seemed to loosen a bit each day upon the trail.

Altogether, forty-three people accompanied him north toward York, the village at the center of Clan Ard Ryan, holdings. Owain Ryan was a border laird. His lands rested amid the northernmost reaches of Kylgahra, some four hundred kylos north of Wyteridge. Ranyl's party had been on the road for two weeks less a day and was due to reach the halfway point in their journey, a village called Selkyrk, sometime the next day.

Ranyl had not pushed the pace. Eight sturdy freight wagons equipped with canvas covers they had in the van, one lighter day wagon, and two smaller carts, plus a dozen well-laden pack mules. Every step took them deeper into less-settled country. Including the smith and Ranyl himself, twenty well-armed and well-mounted men accompanied the wagons and carts and their improvised mule train—enough, Ranyl reckoned, to discourage all but the most determined of bandits and Guilley raiders. Travel to this point in their journey had proceeded smoothly enough. Thanks to Fyrgus and his sons, the wagons were in good repair, and the weather had been fine, with naught but an occasional rain to mar their progress.

Ranyl was more than a little concerned about what would transpire upon their arrival. The marriage contract agreed upon by Ranyl's father, Esquire Stephyn Emyrt of Clan Ard Mourne, and Laird Owain Ryan had been a little vague with respect to the number of retainers Ranyl would bring with him when he wed into Clan Ard Ryan. Tessymir, Laird Owain's eighteen-year-old daughter and sole heir, would one day inherit lairdship of her clan. As her husband, Ranyl would become the laird's consort and would ascend to the nobility, assuming the mantle of a lord. Ranyl would retain his name—an Emyrt he was and would remain—but his children were to be Ryans. His retainers would also join Clan Ard Ryan.

At least this was the Kylgahran custom. Forty-three additional mouths to feed was no small obligation. Perhaps he worried for nothing. Eighteen trained warriors as well versed in the ways of the wild as they were skilled in arms would have been a welcome addition to most any laird's war band. Family men, as most of Ranyl's one-time rangers were, brought stability and a sense of purpose to the clan, as well as their prowess as fighting men. Fyrgus was a highly skilled smith, capable of turning out fine metal work of all types. Smiths of Fyrgus's ability were welcome virtually anywhere. Even young Mae, with her winning smile, the fulsome curve of her bosom, and coolly challenging blue-green eyes, would be sought after.

Ranyl's smile twisted. In truth, his retainers would likely be more welcome than he. Though a member of the lesser nobility only, Stephyn Emyrt, Ranyl's father, stood a wealthy man, even by a laird's standards. No doubt his husband's portion formed Ranyl's primary attraction as a prospective son-in-law in Laird Owain's eyes. Ranyl had never met Laird Owain or his daughter. His father had, however, and appeared suitably impressed.

That was encouraging—or would have been, except that Ranyl knew full well his father's main interest in the marriage was to secure a laird's title for his grandchildren. As he would not be bedding her, Ranyl suspected his father would have been just as enthusiastic about his soon-to-be daughter-in-law, even if she resembled nothing so much as a walrus. Stephyn's eyes glinted slyly when Ranyl had asked about young Tessymir. Stephyn had said only that Ranyl would find her "pleasing enough."

Ranyl knew little about Clan Ard Ryan, aside from his father's description. "Theirs is an ancient clan," Stephyn Emyrt had said, "one of a handful of northern clans to remain loyal to the Confederation during the Eldyr rebellion."

Though conflict stirred regularly among the clans, the last serious threat to the overall unity of the Confederation came some twenty years in the past, when a majority of northern clans rose united in open rebellion. The insurrection became known as the Eldyr rebellion, as the northerners were led in battle by Magnus Eldyr, laird of Clan Ard Eldyr. For two years the rebels rampaged, winning victory after victory. In the end, they could not prevail against the combined strength of the Confederation of Clans and were crushed at the climactic battle of Wurland Moor.

Stephyn Emyrt recounted, "Orrick Ryan, then Eron's heir, famously defied his father and rode with a picked band of retainers to fight under the rebel banner. There are those who say wily old Laird Eron Ryan actually sent his son to fight with the rebels, thereby planting a Ryan boot on both sides of the rift. Orrick was killed, so who can say? His younger brother Owain became laird upon Eron's death.

"A hard choice was Eron's either way, amid a time of hard choices. The north paid a heavy price for its failed rebellion. Magnus Eldyr and both his sons fell at Wurland Moor. Lachlan Clyre, the Confederation chieftain, did not stop there. The Eldyr clan was broken, disbanded entirely—the first time that's happened in centuries—its retainers scattered. Though no other clans were broken, in all nine northern lairds were either killed in battle or executed in retribution. Life has not been easy in the north these last twenty years. Clan Ard Ryan has seen its share of troubles. But in difficulty there is also opportunity, for those canny enough to take advantage."

Marriage as opportunity, a means to prosper—a view Ranyl found consistent with his father's ever-pragmatic turn of mind. The thought occurred to Ranyl that his younger brother, Haymish, had been his father's original choice for marriage into the Ryan clan. Ranyl had been put forward only as an acceptable alternative once his betrothal to Helyn Chambers unraveled. Ranyl could not think of Helyn without wincing.

"She betrayed you," his inner voice murmured scathingly. She had, and the hurt of it still burned. *All right enough,* but Ranyl still couldn't help believing Helyn's affair had been at least as much his doing as hers. Had he married Helyn last year, as they had originally planned, Ranyl felt certain there would have been no dalliance with Kevyn, despite his cousin's height and his laughing blue eyes and the dimple in his chin.

Maybe he should have just bundled Annie up and headed out east. If he'd asked her properly, Ranyl had no doubt Anharyd Swallow would have accompanied him to the Lowlands. In the east, Ranyl had heard, a man was free to follow his heart, less burdened by custom and clan than anywhere in Kylgahra. He had not, and Annie wed Cadigan Embry of Clan Ard Drew. Cad was a good man. He'd look after Annie and make a home for her back in Wyteridge. At least Ranyl could rest easy on that score.

"What do you want?" The voice in his head fair shouted at him. Deep within his heart, an answer rang, clear as a temple bell: *a life of mine own.* A life that mattered to him, Ranyl Emyrt, born of his will and shaped by his hands. *"Good luck with that,"* the bastard between his ears scoffed.

Ranyl tightened his grip upon the reins. He doubted it was possible for a man to simply walk away from his past. Ranyl could also see no reason to stay mired in it either. Maybe there was no such thing as a fresh start, but a man could learn what his mistakes had to teach him and move beyond them. Offering a brief prayer for guidance to the Four Fates, Ranyl vowed to do so.

What if Tessymir Ryan has the physique of a blacksmith and the face of a mule? If she's easy to get on with, would that be so bad? What if she can't abide me? Pushing any thought of his future bride aside, Ranyl tugged his broad-brimmed, grey-felt trail hat squarely into place atop his head. Standing in his stirrups, he gazed carefully up the trail. They'd seen little traffic during the previous two days. As far as he could see, the way ahead lay empty.

Ranyl wore an Ard Mourne plaid over a forest-green woolen shirt and grey woolen trousers, while a pair of well-worn leather boots covered his feet. His reddish-brown hair had grown out a bit longer than was his custom, and Mae had offered to cut it for him. He reckoned he'd take her up on it in a day or two. She cut her boys' hair, and the pair of them looked trim and neat.

The broadsword he'd found in the tomb the day Ellis had been killed was attached to the wide leather belt about his waist on his left side. Meggie's knife he carried in a sheath over his right hip. Across his shoulders slung a full quiver of arrows fletched with white swans' feathers. A powerful, recurved horse bow rested in a leather case strapped to the left side of his saddle, and a Kylgahran targe fastened into place on the right.

Ranyl's grey eyes narrowed at the sound of a horse approaching. Instinctively, his hand curled around the haft of his broadsword. He felt a moment of anticipation, bordering on exhilaration. Peering up the road, he recognized Lukas Holt of Clan Ard Cullen returning. According to Ellis Tate, Luke Holt was mighty handy working a trail. High praise, this; Ranyl had never known a better tracker and scout than Ellis. Luke was as tall as Ellis had been, with the same lean, ropey build, perhaps a little wider through the shoulders.

Ellis had not been much to look at. "I'm at least as good-looking as my horse," Tate had often joked. Luke Holt, on the other end, appeared darkly handsome, with wavy brown hair and piercing blue eyes. A couple of years Ranyl's senior, Holt was another of those fellows with a dimple in his chin. Ranyl didn't know Luke all that well. He'd been a member of the Wyteridge Rangers for only a year or so. Ranyl had patrolled with him only two or three times. The man's quiet competence was irrefutable. Luke Holt never said much but seemed to be well liked by his fellow rangers. Ranyl had been a little surprised when the tall, taciturn ranger had asked to join his retinue. During the ride north, Luke had stepped seamlessly into the role of lead scout.

With a salute as formal as any ranger would proffer to his sheriff, Luke reined in a few paces away. "I spotted the temple spire and a few chimney tops from a ridge about five kylos to the north, sir," the ranger reported. Armed with baelryc and dirk, Luke sat astride a deep-chested bay-colored Morgyn. A targe slung from his saddle on his left, while a half dozen throwing darts rested in a leather quiver strapped in place on the right. Clad in a buckskin shirt and brown woolen trousers, the leanly built scout wore a wide-brimmed, black-felt trail hat. An unadorned plaid draped about his shoulders.

"Selkyrk, is it?" Ranyl asked, knowing it could be none other.

Luke nodded. "We should reach the village itself by noon tomorrow. Plan on stopping, do you, sir?"

"Don't dare not to," Ranyl declared. "If we bypass the place, Kate will be badgering me for fresh eggs or milk or some damn something for the kids or the pregnant lasses or both before we're more than a stone's throw beyond."

Luke grinned but said nothing. Kate Wysset of Clan Ard Mourne, a buxom, brown-haired woman with a slightly turned-up nose and lively green eyes, had become something of an unofficial quartermaster. Kate was one of those ranger women secretly married for years, in her case to Emerson Hart. Harry, as Kate called him, had been Ranyl's lead ranger and second in command of the Wyteridge station. Harry and Kate, very publicly wed the now, had been the first to join Ranyl's retinue.

"A meadow, there is," Luke told him, "'round a bend in the road no more than a kylo off. Should do for a campsite."

"Good and all," Ranyl concurred. "Let's pull up there."

Supper that night consisted of fried bacon, sliced thick, on freshly made flatbread with a tangy sourdough taste; a helping of parched corn; and dried peas, boiled and flavored with salt, black pepper, and pearl onions and a healthy dollop of bacon grease. For dessert, baked apples, sweetened by molasses and sprinkled with cinnamon and crushed walnuts. Mae Hoskins did the cooking. As usual, the food was delicious.

After eating, Ranyl helped Mae with the dishes. *Woman's work.* The thought brought a smile to Ranyl's face. *My father would be astonished.* Still, Ranyl found he did not mind the small chore, providing, as it did, the opportunity to speak privately with Mae. Ranyl had discovered she was a good listener. Mae washed while Ranyl dried. The two of them worked by the light of an oil lamp placed on top of the folded-down tailboard of Ranyl's canvas-covered wagon.

Tad read aloud to the boys by firelight. From the sound of it, Ranyl thought he recognized a tale from *Pigdyn A-Wandering* concerning Wyli, the slyest of fairy folk. "They're growing like weeds," Ranyl observed, nodding toward Rafe and Bowen.

"Aye, they'll be tall ones, the pair of them," Mae said, smiling gently. Mae's long blond hair was twined into a thick single braid, trailing nearly to her hips. She looked a little tired and a bit sad, her grief still fresh, but pretty for all that. Ranyl didn't know Mae's exact age. A couple of years shy of his own twenty and five, he reckoned. "I'm sorry we are such a burden."

"Don't be silly," Ranyl responded, meaning it. "You're good company, and so are the boys. Besides which"—Ranyl dropped his voice to a conspiratorial whisper—"you are the best cook in the van." He paused a moment to peer furtively about. "Don't tell Kate I said that."

"Coward," Mae teased.

"Prudent, lass," Ranyl proclaimed. "The word is prudent."

Placing the last of the dishes atop a folding table for him to dry, Mae wiped her hands on the apron tied about her slender waist. "You must be looking forward to starting your new life in the north."

"Must I?" Ranyl replied. "I suppose I am at that."

"Becoming a laird's consort," Mae asserted, "sounds mighty fine."

"Consort to a laird apparent," Ranyl corrected her gently. *Laird apparent* was the formal title of the heir to the lairdship of a Kylgahran clan. "A fine thing it is, too," Ranyl went on, "until comes the time some other clan rises in dispute over water rights, or the Guilleys come calling or maybe, this far north, the Sueve." The Sueve were a fierce tribal people whose homeland lay just north of the Highlands. Traditional foes, the Sueve, and over generations the tribesmen had mixed with the ragged array of clanless Kylgahran that formed the bulk of the wild Guilley population. While the Guilleys were a nuisance, often a deadly one, the more populous and perennially belligerent Sueve tribesmen formed a truly dire threat, at least within the northern reaches of Kylgahra.

"Ellis always said you worried enough for the lot of us." A shadow flickered for a moment, deep within her blue-green eyes, eyes that looked grey in the lamplight. "He meant it kindly. You were a fine sheriff," Mae continued staunchly. "I am sure you will do well as consort."

A breeze had kicked up by the time Ranyl unfurled his bedroll beneath the wagon. He'd placed his saddle at the head of the roll, anchoring the oiled canvas ground sheet. The night wind hinted of rain. Ranyl had positioned himself upwind of young Tad. The youth was a loyal retainer and a fine hand with horses. The boy spent a little too much time caring for them and not enough with a bar of soap. Ranyl determined to have a quiet word with young Tad come morning. Glancing over, Ranyl could see his youthful companion slept already, rolled warmly in his blankets and a spare plaid Ranyl had given him. The lad was never without the bloody thing.

Tugging loose the buckle, Ranyl slipped his sword belt from about his waist, carefully laying the hilt within easy reach. The weapon fit Ranyl's hand as well as if it had been crafted for him alone, and he found its balance perfect. However splendidly made, Ranyl was always a little relieved to set the sword aside at the end of day. He found himself sitting cross-legged atop his blanket, holding Meggie's knife in his hand. Meggie had called the weapon a Hawken.

"Good, honest steel," Fyrgus said of Meggie's knife, likely of Tieran manufacture. Ranyl smiled; he wasn't any too certain of the *honest* part. She'd likely stolen the thing. *Funny, Ranyl thought, I only talked to her the one time while she lay dying, but for as long as I live, I will nay forget her face.* As much as he loved his mother, dead some six years the now, Ranyl could not envision her features. Helyn's countenance had begun to dim, and he'd been parted from her only a few weeks. Meggie's visage was forever emblazoned in his memory. He could vividly recall her small upturned nose with its smattering of freckles, her wild mass of bright-red hair, and her eyes. Mist grey, they were, truly beautiful, wide and wary and wise beyond her years.

As had become his custom, Ranyl breathed a prayer to the Four Fates in honor of Meggie's soul and that of his friend Ellis Tate before sliding into his own blankets. He sheathed Meggie's knife but kept a firm hold on the hilt. By now he supposed Meggie would have amassed some influence with the Fates. Knowing Meggie, the Fates would have to at least occasionally acquiesce to her desires or have their legs talked off. Ranyl smiled into the darkness. He could feel her presence, warm and bright, somewhere deep in the heart of him. *"Meggie, if you could see your way clear,"* he implored silently, *"to help me not make a fool of myself in the north, I'd appreciate it. I ask not so much for my sake as for Emerson and Kate and Mae and all the rest who have cast their lots with mine."*

Just after noon on the following day, the wagon train from Wyteridge pulled up about a kylo west of Selkyrk village, stopping in a copse of oak trees. A light rain had been falling most of the morning. Slacking just as they halted, the drizzle ceased. The day was mild; damp but not chilly. Filling his lungs, Ranyl savored the sweet scent of the air washed clean by the rain. Ranyl had decided to take Kate and Mae with him into the village, accompanied by six rangers. The women would know best which supplies were needed, and Ranyl suspected they were sharper bargainers than he or any of his men. Emerson, of course, would come along as well. The burly lead ranger would not want to be parted from his wife while she went among strangers.

Five others Ranyl singled out, including young Watt Quigley. Watt looked scrawny, with long blond hair, lively green eyes, and a carefree gap-toothed grin. For all that, Ranyl knew him to be level-headed and cool in tight spots. The youngster was also a wizard with the powerful horse bow he carried, the finest archer Ranyl had ever seen. The rest of the men selected were all steady, not the type to cause a ruckus. Ranyl left Luke Holt in charge of the train.

Selkyrk proved to be middling sized, warded by a sturdy wooden palisade. As it was just past midday, the gates of the village stood open. Four Kylgahran, armed with baelrycs and targes and wearing Ard Fraiser colors, held the watch. They straightened as six mounted, well-armed warriors approached. The sight of two women seated alongside a freshly scrubbed Tad Gyllis, driving a day wagon among the horsemen, seemed to give the quartet some ease. Ranyl identified himself and his people, and after assuring the head guardsman their purpose involved only the procurement of supplies, they were waved through with no fuss at all.

To Ranyl's eyes, Selkyrks' layout appeared typical of a Kylgahran village or small town. Two cobblestoned thoroughfares, wide enough so that a large wagon and a team of six could turn about, ran arrow-straight, connecting all four of the gates. An open-air market stood at the intersection of the two main streets. Off the principal roads, buildings were arrayed higgledy fashion, connected by a warren of narrow stone-surfaced streets and walkways. The buildings themselves were typically fashioned of stone or brick, featuring a mix of mostly slate or wood-shingled roofs.

Though it was not market day in Selkyrk, goods there were in plenty. Kate and Mae took turns being outraged at the prices, sharing secret smiles between them as the haggling progressed. About finished with the shopping, they were, Ranyl reckoned, when he heard a commotion off to one side of the square, where he stood beside the now well-laden day wagon with young Tad.

A pair of young men was being dragged into the square. The two had been bound, wrists tied behind their backs. A cursory examination from across the market yard revealed the two of them had also been beaten. The larger of the two, a dark-haired teenager, slumped over; his left shoulder looked as if it had been dislocated. The second boy, who appeared even younger than the first, was slightly built with long blond hair. Ranyl could see streaks of blood marring the left side of the young man's face. The taller youth was clad in a tousled white cotton shirt and baggy brown woolen trousers, while his blonde companion was more finely attired in what appeared to be a pearl-grey silk shirt and close-fitting leather breeches. Both boys were barefoot.

Herding the bound pair into the square were four sturdy-looking fellows in work clothes, bearing stout wooden truncheons and long-bladed dirks in their belts. They were led, it appeared, by a fifth man, tall and wide shouldered, with a wide-brimmed leather hat atop his head and a baelryc belted at his waist.

"Tie the buggers to the crosstrees," the big man shouted, "and fetch the magistrate."

"Straight away, Darl," one of the truncheon-armed quartet replied, hurrying toward a nearby side street.

The crosstrees were two stout wooden stanchions fashioned from squared-off posts at least a third of a span thick. Reaching about to chest height, a vertical member of the crosstree jutted from its mooring in the packed earthen floor of the market square. Centered atop it, a horizontal post had been bolted into place. The dark-haired youth screamed as his left hand was bound to the horizontal post.

"His shoulder has been dislocated," the fair-haired lad cried.

"Shut your gob, sodomite," Darl, the man in the leather hat, barked, cuffing the slightly built blond across his mouth. A sixth man appeared, even larger than the fellow giving the orders, wearing a blacksmith's vest and carrying a thickly coiled leather whip. Without comment, the smith handed the lash to Darl. In short order, both youths' wrists were tied firmly to the horizontal posts of the crosstrees.

"Please," the blond youth tried again, "you'll maim him." For this he received a knee between his legs from the tall man holding the whip. The boy sagged in agony against the crosstree, crying out softly.

Ranyl found himself striding to the far side of the square. Stopping a few paces short of the nearest crosstree, he asked, "With what are they charged?"

Darl had close-set pale-blue eyes. They settled on Ranyl. "Who are you?"

"Ranyl Emyrt of Clan Ard Mourne," Ranyl answered.

"You are a stranger here," Darl said brusquely. "What business is it of yours?"

Ranyl shrugged. "I was sheriff, down Wyteridge way, until a few weeks ago; just curious is all."

"We caught the two of them," a skinny fellow, with a truncheon in his left hand and a prodigious eagle's beak of a nose, supplied, "buggerin' away like a pair of stouts."

"Which one was being mounted?" Ranyl asked matter-of-factly.

"The little one there." The buck-toothed truncheon-bearer pointed to the blonde.

Stepping closer, Ranyl knelt in front of the blond youth. Despite the battering he'd taken, Ranyl could see the boy was handsome, his features finely wrought. The youth had laurel-green eyes. His left was nearly swollen shut, and the soft flesh just beneath the eye socket had already gone purple. His lower lip was split, and blood from a cut above his left eye streaked the cheek below.

"What is your name?" Ranyl asked of him.

"Tuan," the boy replied, speaking through teeth still gritted in pain from being kneed in the balls. "Tuan Marques is my name."

"Was it consensual?" Ranyl queried. The boy merely looked at him, green eyes unblinking. "Were you forced?"

"No," Tuan Marques responded, "the act was born of mutual desire." Tuan spoke in round, cultured tones. His voice sounded light but evocatively rich.

"So the little Odd offered his bum up willingly," Darl observed. "What difference does that make?"

"Consensual coupling is not a crime in Kylgahra," Ranyl stated.

"Perverts of the Odd Persuasion ain't wanted here," Darl declared. "We got the right to punish them."

"What is this?" a fulsome baritone voice inquired. Turning in the direction of the speaker, Ranyl saw an owlish little man wearing a magistrate's register step into the square. Common throughout Kylgahra, the magistrate's register was a pendant worn on a silver chain depicting a four-leaf clover. A symbol of the Four Fates, the clover, it represented Tal, in particular—the fate who championed justice. Aside from his badge of office, the Selkyrk magistrate appeared plainly dressed in a brown cotton shirt and coat with dark-blue woolen trousers.

"Afternoon, Master Haupt." Darl spoke respectfully. "We caught these two in Braylin's barn, humping away, unnatural like. We done brung 'em along for a public scourging."

"Without so much as a hearing, Darl Croker?" Of middle years, Magistrate Haupt stood short of stature and slight of build, with smallish brown eyes and thick grey hair. The man's deep, authoritative voice appeared to be at odds with the rest of him.

"We caught the buggers plain as day," Darl reiterated forcefully, glancing at his foursome of truncheon-wielders for confirmation. They four nodded vigorously.

Haupt glared at the two accused; his eyes glowed like small dark beads beneath bushy grey brows. "I might have expected as much from an itinerant minstrel." He thrust a bony chin at the young blonde and then turned his attention to the larger, dark-haired youth. "I thought better of you, Davyd Walker."

"This stranger says such perversion ain't against the law." Darl nodded at Ranyl. "Claims he used to be the sheriff of Wyteridge."

"My name is Jonas Haupt of Clan Ard Fraiser," the magistrate informed Ranyl. "Are you Ranyl Emyrt of Clan Ard Mourne?"

"I am," Ranyl said.

"I expected an older man." Haupt peered carefully at Ranyl for a moment. "We have a local ordinance that prohibits sodomy."

"I'm no student of the law," Ranyl acknowledged. "I was a sheriff only. My understanding is that a local ordinance may never contradict any law passed by the Council of Lairds."

"The Laird's Law is silent on this point," Haupt stipulated.

"Is it?" Ranyl questioned, "The magistrate in Wyteridge seemed to think the law was quite clear." Ranyl paused; his men, all six, had fanned out on either side of him, weapons at the ready. Out of the corner of his eye, he could see young Watt, poised with an arrow set to his bow. "You can hump anyone you want in the Highlands"—Ranyl quoted Mervys Trane of Clan Ard Mourne—"provided your partner is willing and human and at least sixteen years of age."

"Our intent is to discourage such unseemly behavior." Haupt's baritone sounded a little less confident. His small bird's eyes danced intently, taking in the dangerous posture of Ranyl's rangers.

Glancing at the two youths, Ranyl smiled wryly. "I'd say these two have been discouraged sufficiently for one day, don't you think?"

"I hear tell," Magistrate Haupt ruminated, "of a Ranyl Emyrt, once sheriff of Wyteridge, bound to marry the Ryan heiress up north a-ways. That would be you, eh?"

"It would," Ranyl confirmed.

Haupt smiled, beady eyes aglow. "Ryans are hardheaded. Anybody ever tell you that?"

"Some," Ranyl countered, "have said the same about us Emyrts."

Haupt's knowing smile broadened. "We'll see." Turning to Darl Croker, the magistrate directed, "Cut those two rascals down."

Darl hesitated a moment, as if on the edge of protest, but then did as he was told. Their bonds were severed; both lads sagged to their knees at the base of the crosstrees.

"If you darken our streets again, minstrel," Haupt informed the slender, blond-haired Tuan Marques, "you'll rue the day."

"I shall be happy to put your picturesque little village behind me forever, sir," the youth replied, sounding like a lecture on perfect grammar. "Davyd is badly injured. If you will allow, I may be of assistance to him."

"You done enough harm to Davy Walker as things stand, boy," Darl growled, the menace ringing clear in his tone.

"How can you be of help to him?" Ranyl inquired.

"I have some skill with the healing art," the youth replied, "and some formal training as well."

Ranyl took a long look at Davyd Walker and then spoke quietly to Magistrate Haupt. "I take it you know the dark-haired lad?"

Haupt nodded. "He's apprenticed to Mattrim Killig, a blacksmith here in town." Ranyl's eyes flicked to the big man in the smith's vest. "Not him; that's Berton Wode of Clan Ard Fraiser, the *other* blacksmith in Selkyrk."

"The lad's shoulder is in bad shape," Ranyl observed. "He won't be of much use to his master or anyone else without care. Why not let the minstrel try his hand?"

"You like sticking your nose in where it don't belong, don't you, little man?" Darl took a step in Ranyl's direction.

Without thinking, Ranyl's hand dropped to the hilt of his broadsword. He felt something hot and fierce pulse through his veins. "Speak to me again, and we'll see which one of us is the littler man."

Belying his years Haupt darted between Coker and the grey-eyed young sheriff that was. "My lord, please; there is no need for that."

"I'm a squire only, magistrate," Ranyl said automatically, never taking his eyes from those of Darl Croker.

"Lord-to-be, then," Haupt offered, raising both hands in a pacifying manner. "Clear out of here, Croker," Haupt ordered, his deep voice firming.

Without further comment, Darl turned on his heel and strode away. Reluctantly, with an almost visible force of will, Ranyl took his hand from about his sword hilt and let it drop to his side.

"All right, boy," Haupt commanded impatiently, waving at Tuan Marques, "get on with it."

Marques stepped a little unsteadily to Walker's side. Kneeling, he helped the larger youth to straighten his back. Taking a firm but gentle grip on Walker's left arm, the green-eyed Marques positioned it carefully, bending the elbow.

"Steady the now you must be, Davyd," Marques murmured, his voice gentle and soothing. Walker nodded, his jaw tightened in anticipation. Marques tugged and lifted in one smooth motion. Walker gasped as his shoulder shifted back into place with a barely audible pop. "There now," Marques continued, "the worst is over; only a few moments more."

Placing one hand on either side of Walker's head the young healer closed his eyes. Walker stiffened, fists clenching. Nearly as soon as he'd begun, Marques lowered his hands.

Free of pain, Walker's expression took on a look of wonder. A handsome lad, young Davy, Ranyl noted, nearly as fine featured as the youthful healer kneeling before him. "Thank you," Walker intoned.

"My pleasure." Marques kissed the dark-haired Walker lightly on the cheek. Turning to Ranyl, the young healer implored, "My lord, Davyd wishes to return to his father's farm."

"The sheep will be glad to see him, no doubt," one of Darl's truncheon bearers said with a grin.

Ignoring the laughter that ensued, Tuan Marques spoke again to Ranyl. "If you would be willing to purchase his apprenticeship, I will offer myself in bond to you in return."

"No," Davyd protested, "Tuan, you can't."

"Because of me," Tuan responded, speaking softly but urgently, "any life you may have had here will be ruined the now. You must allow me this." Marques evidently interpreted the silence that followed as acquiescence on Walker's part. "What do you say?" he asked of Ranyl.

"Can you stand?" Ranyl directed his question to Davyd Walker. "How is your shoulder?"

The young man climbed to his feet. Slowly he raised his left arm above his head. "There is no pain," Walker announced, "but it feels funny."

"Your body is still responding to the healing flow," Tuan explained. Still on his knees, the youthful healer looked up at the apprentice smith. "Your shoulder is free of damage but not yet at full strength. You should rest it as much as you can for the next ten days."

"How much to buy you free of apprenticeship?" Ranyl asked next.

"Four hundred silver talents, my lord," Davyd Walker replied without hesitation.

Ranyl nodded. Pursing his lips, the young esquire let his gaze settle on Tuan Marques. "Three years' bond."

Tuan's back straightened; his undamaged right eye blazed emerald fire. "That is outrageous." The youth swayed slightly as he spoke.

Ranyl smiled. "I doubt you'll get a better offer."

Tuan hesitated only a moment. "Done," he spat and fainted dead away.

13

Cos

By actual tally, Samwell Austyn and his drovers delivered 3,316 head of cattle to the city of Cos, eight weeks and seven days after leaving Taggert's Landing. The city nestled amid a series of bluffs just west of the River Sayx, in the northern reaches of the kingdom of Syrdis. The course of the River Sayx marked the traditional western boundary of Syrdis. Navigable by large ships from just north of Cos all the way to the river's estuary on the Maeryc coast, the Sayx flowed generally south from its headwaters in the Shyre Hills to the north.

Over the course of the final three weeks of the drive, Sam, Cable, and Aeryk had spent some time trying to determine what might be best for Estyr.

"She's been raised as a Syrdisian," Sam pointed out one evening while the three of them gathered about a low-burning campfire. "No clan will have her."

"One look at Estyr," Aeryk countered, "and a small horde of bright-eyed Kylgahran will. She'll enter a clan through marriage as soon as she is of age. Our problem will be fending off the churls and bleaters among 'em."

"All I'm saying," Sam argued, "is that she might feel more at home in a place like Cos."

"Surrounded by strangers," Aeryk protested.

"Cos has become a big city," Cable noted. "There's like to be an orphanage, run by the Reverent Sisters. They are tough old gals, them Sisters, strict as Tieran generals, but they take good care of their charges." The Reverent Sisters were a female religious order sanctioned by the Penitent Church.

"Combined with the silver we recovered," Sam added, "and the sale of the mules, Estyr will have more than enough coin to pay for room and board with the Sisters. They will look to her safety and her education, too."

"Syrdisian girls marry early, most of 'em," Cable put in. "Like you say, after a year or two with the Sisters, Estyr will have her pick of suitors and enough coin left over for a tidy little dowry to sweeten the pot."

Aeryk shook his head. "She'll think we're trying to get rid of her."

"Not if you explain things right," Sam charged him.

"Me?" Aeryk exclaimed. "Why me? It's not my idea."

"You take responsibility for a child." Sam's tone left no space for argument. "You do what is right for that child, not what's easy for you." One glance at the firm look in Cable's eyes convinced Aeryk he'd find no wiggle room there either.

Aeryk tried, but Estyr would have none of it. "I want to go with you," she insisted.

"It is a big decision, Bones," Aeryk cajoled. "Maybe it would be a good idea for you to look things over, talk with the Sisters, before you decide."

The shadow of dread suddenly clouding Estyr's big green eyes nearly cracked his heart. "I don't need to visit some musty old orphanage to know what I want," Estyr declared.

"Sometimes what's easiest isn't what's best," Aeryk contended. Looking into her eyes, he saw the dread swirling in those emerald depths transform into terror, and his resolve shattered. Aeryk took one quick step forward and pulled her into his arms. Her body felt tense, wound tight. "The decision is yours, Bones," he assured her. "We just want what's best for you."

"You're what's best for me," Estyr proclaimed. "You're my family the now, you and Mr. Sam and Caleb and Cable. Even Wyatt likes me some better. Just the other day, he said I might be fit to cook a meal."

"Did he?" Aeryk teased. "That's high praise from a Tuchyck." Her slim little form still felt taut as a bowstring.

"I won't be no trouble," Estyr averred.

"You're nothing but trouble." Aeryk laughed softly. "We wouldn't want you any other way." He felt her body soften, tension draining away.

"I can come with you, then?" she implored.

"Aye," Aeryk relented, "as long as you are sure it is what you want."

She hugged him. "Tell me again," Estyr entreated, "about the Elkhorn Valley, and Bright Water Creek, and how the pines stand tall along the ridge lines."

"You've heard that a dozen times," Aeryk demurred.

"I want to know it," Estyr replied, "in my heart when I see it."

Cos had expanded considerably in size over the past ten years, and much of the recent sprawl was evident. Cos looked new, its outer walls fashioned of raw timber, not stone. Aeryk felt a twinge of disappointment. He'd yet to see a stone-walled city. Compared with the villages and towns of the Lowlands, he had to admit, Cos appeared enormous.

At first, the citizens of Cos—and especially their sheriff, a hard-eyed nobleman—seemed uncertain just what to do with such a large gathering of beasties all in one bunch. Finally, one enterprising merchant by the name of Boswell Canty suggested they drive the herd through the north end of the city into a box canyon between two bluffs, just outside the walls. A large spring-fed pool of water occupied the back of the canyon, and only a short distance remained between it and the city docks. Negotiations came to a quick conclusion.

The sheriff scowled, less than enthusiastic about pushing three thousand-odd cows through his city's streets, but the city council, merchants all, thought it a fine idea. The cattle had been well watered the day before, and grazing on the approach to Cos was plentiful. They went docilely enough, and it wasn't long before the cowhands had the herd safely "boxed in," as Caleb Edger described it. Aeryk saw no significant damage as a result of the herd's passage through the city; no sign at all, really, if you took no reckoning of the cow flops and the occasional splash of urine.

Their progress resulted in at least one broken water jug, however. The incident occurred as they entered one of the many squares, or plazas, as they were known in Cos. The squares were actually nothing more than widened areas at selected street intersections, usually with a fountain or water well in the center. Street vendors, he'd been told, would occupy the square during daylight hours, plying their various trades. The wells and fountains provided fresh water for public use, and the locals would often gather there to discuss the day's events. This day, plazas along the route the cattle were to take through the city were supposed to be vacant.

Riding into the square near the head of the herd, Aeryk noticed what he thought at first was a crippled child standing alongside a fountain, clutching a clay water jar in one hand and her crutch in the other. At the sight of the cattle jostling toward her, the girl dropped the water jug and hobbled as quickly as she could behind the fountain. The clay jug shattered as it struck the cobbled stones of the street, and water spewed forth. Urging Wyli forward, Aeryk rode to her side.

"Here, lass, we'll not hurt you," he said in Aylitic. The girl wore a dark-red woolen shawl wrapped about her head and shoulders, clad beneath in a pale-blue dress—cotton, he thought—belted at the waist, with a sash that matched her shawl. When she looked up at him, her shawl fell away. Open at the throat, the cut of her dress revealed the upper contours of two full, firm young breasts. Hastily averting his gaze, Aeryk realized it was no child he was addressing.

When he looked back, he found himself gazing into a pair of large golden-brown eyes, the color of pine sap in spring. Her hair, he saw where it tumbled free of the shawl, shone jet black like a raven's wing. Her face was oval shaped; her features delicately formed. To keep from staring, Aeryk eased Wyli up beside her and then leaned down out of the saddle, extending his hand.

"Turn 'round," he instructed, "and we'll get you up out of this."

The girl complied, turning away from him, and Aeryk slipped both hands into her armpits from behind, very gingerly, so as not to touch anything he wasn't supposed to be touching. Straightening, he lifted her into the saddle in front of him. Though sweetly made, her body graced with a woman's curves, the raven-haired lass was tiny. He settled her sideways across the saddle in front of him with surprisingly little effort. She managed to hang on to her crutch—carved from an odd golden-colored wood splashed here and there with dark, nearly black whorls—and cling to him at the same time. He marveled at the feel of her in his arms. He wouldn't have believed human flesh could seem so soft and light, as if she was made of air.

"Where away is home?" Aeryk asked. Releasing him just long enough to point at a side street, she tucked back into his arms in an instant.

It took only moments to enter the street where she'd pointed, riding clear of the cattle trundling by through the square. "I'm sorry." She spoke Aylitic with a lilting accent he couldn't place, releasing him as he reined Wyli to a stop. "I've never been up on a horse like this." Her voice had a soft, smoky timbre to it that set the hair at the nape of his neck to tingling.

"I should say not," Aeryk replied, reaching around her to pat his gelding on the shoulder. "A rare gentleman, Wyli is."

"Wyli." The girl spoke again, brown eyes widening. "A fairy, he is, then?"

"Well, no, actually," Aeryk responded, delighted that she recognized the inspiration for Wyli's naming. "Some days he's very nearly as much trouble, though." The girl smiled, lighting her eyes with a mischievous glint. Reluctantly, he shifted back in the saddle, saying, "Let's get you down." Gently lowering the girl to her feet, he found himself once again looking into her eyes.

"Besides Wyli, who am I to thank for helping me?" she asked.

Smiling despite himself, Aeryk said, "Aeryk Emyrt of Clan Ard Mourne."

"That's a lot of name," she commented while returning his smile. "Mine is Tierza."

"Tierza," he repeated. "That's all?"

"Tierza of Barber Street," she said with a touch of pride in that throaty voice of hers.

"Are you a barber?" Aeryk asked.

"Aye, well, an apprentice still," Tierza admitted, "but I also sew, and sing and play the lyre. I don't dance too well." She raised her crutch.

Aeryk saw no obvious deformity and was not comfortable asking. Instead, he said, "Neither do I."

Settling her gaze on Wyli, she laid a hand gently on the horse's muzzle. "Thank you, sir. It is not every day that I meet such a fine gentleman." Looking back up at Aeryk, she continued. "And thank you, too, Aeryk Emyrt of Clan Ard Mourne. You'll find a welcome here on Barber Street, should ever you wish it."

Somewhat at a loss, Aeryk tugged his hat brim in farewell. Backing Wyli up a step or two, Aeryk turned him smartly and rode back to the square. The first person he ran into when he emerged from Barber Street was Samwell Austyn, astride his fine bay.

"What have you been playing at?" Sam growled by way of greeting.

"Well," Aeryk stammered a little, caught off guard, "there was this girl ..."

Sam waved away the rest of Aeryk's explanation, pointing to the rear of the herd. "Get back there and do some good." Aeryk supposed finishing the drive riding drag should have been a disappointment. Thinking of Tierza's bright smile and flashing brown eyes, it seemed a small enough price to pay.

Bidding for the cattle turned out to be crisp, with Boswell Canty purchasing the largest share of the stock, over one thousand head himself. The entire herd sold on the spot, and the total seemed like a staggering amount to Aeryk. With the price settled and responsibility for the cattle transferred to the good citizens of Cos, the drive came to its end, more successful than they had dared hope. Even Sam seemed satisfied.

Austyn arranged for accommodations at a large inn called the Rising Star on Copper Street, near the eastern gate of the city. After putting up their horses in an adjacent stable, Aeryk and Cable walked with Sam to the main entrance of the inn. The three of them were standing atop the front steps when Aeryk heard the unmistakable clatter of horses' hooves approaching at the trot.

Peering up the street, Aeryk saw a small troop of cavalry, about twenty, riding toward the inn in a precise column of twos. Polished steel helmets with full face guards glinted in the soft afternoon sun. Each rider appeared identically equipped, wearing white-and-green-colored surcoats over long-sleeved chain-mail armor, with round shields that reminded Aeryk of Highland targes slung across their backs. Gracefully curved long swords in worked leather scabbards swung from their belts, and Aeryk noticed large quivers of white-fletched arrows strapped to the sides of their saddles, opposite what looked to be deeply recurved bows.

Aeryk knew Syrdisian horsemen were renowned by friend and foe alike. He turned to Sam. "Is that cavalry Syrdisian?"

"They ride for the Leopard Throne all right enough," Sam answered. Aeryk noted the tall Highlander's gaze also fixed upon the troopers. "But they aren't Syrdisians; they're Elves."

"Ilyrian Elves," Aeryk exclaimed, "from the island realm?"

Sam smiled. "Do you know of any other kind?"

The Elven nation, composed of an island chain collectively known as Ilyria, was located in the Maeryc Ocean, a few weeks' sail southwest of the Kylgahran coast. In addition to their home islands, the Elves maintained a series of trading centers spread all throughout the Middle Sea region. Typically, seacoast settlements built around natural harbors, a number of the Elven trading centers had grown into good-sized towns and some into cities, the largest of which, located on the southwestern coast of the Cambrian Peninsula, amid the very heart of the kingdom of Syrdis, was named Mylan.

"Mercenaries." Cable spat into the street below.

"How do you know?" Aeryk wondered.

"The green piping on their surcoats marks them as such," Cable answered.

Basyl had taught Aeryk that Elves flourished a breed apart, differing from the other peoples of the Middle Sea by more than language and customs alone. Elven skin tones varied from light brown to the color of aged mahogany. This, coupled with large, almond-shaped eyes and four fingered hands, rendered them physically distinct. Female Elves, called Elfin, stood to a near uniform height, matching that of the Elfan, or male Elves, a stature roughly the same as an average-sized Kylgahran man. Elfan gonads apparently did not dangle in a sack like human males but instead were internal organs. Aeryk had yet to meet an elf.

"I've heard Elves include females among the ranks of their warriors," Aeryk remarked.

"The Elven warrior class," Sam supplied, "has long been divided into different societies, or orders, as the Elves refer to them. Some orders, such as Castellan, are wholly Elfin. Elfan make up most of the Elven orders, though, four-fifths or thereabouts." The cavalry contingent swept by, apparently headed for the city's eastern portal.

"Do you think there are any Elfin among that bunch?" Aeryk queried.

"Elven mercenary companies tend to be a mixed lot," Sam replied. "Hard to tell from here with the helmets and chain mail, but I wouldn't be surprised to find an Elfin or three among 'em."

"Are they good fighters, the Elfin?" Aeryk inquired.

"Elfin deploy as light troops usually, skirmishers," Sam explained. "The Castellan are horse archers, like them what just rode by. I doubt the Elfin of Order Castellan would win many arm-wrestling contests against the likes of us, but they're more than capable of putting an arrow into your eye at a hundred paces. Brave as terriers, they are, and if used right, bloody effective."

"Order Baralein," Cable noted, "are Elfan melee fighters, heavy infantry, nasty buggers, a match even fer Tieran foot."

"The largest and most famous of the Elven military orders is the Aquastani, or Rowers," Sam commented. The Elven navy compared favorably in size and striking power to even that of the vaunted Tieran battle fleets. Elven crews, especially the Aquastani, who manned the warships' rowing benches, were renowned for their stamina and disciplined courage.

"What are they like? Elves, I mean," Aeryk asked next.

"Well, fer a start," Cable stated, "ye cain't hardly tell one from the other, all blond, brown skinned, and big eyed—blue or grey, usually—standing to within a hand's span of each other in height, male and female alike, and lean as whippets. I ain't never seen a fat elf. That makes me kindly nervous."

"Theirs is a matriarchal society. Queens rule in Ilyria and inheritance flows strictly through the mother's line," Sam related, leaning against a wooden column at the top of the stairs. "In their homeland, Elfin wield more power and influence than even the female lairds of Kylgahra aspire to. For all that, I reckon Elves are mostly just people, Aeryk. They live and work and fight and die and love a little, if they're lucky, in between, just like us."

"Not like us," Cable interjected. "Elves don't act natural, forever bowing and such, polite as all get out, right up until they open yer gullet, likely still a smilin' like Aunt Ellah at a bake sale while they're about it."

"You're gettin' cranky in your dotage, Cable," Sam accused lightly. In a more serious tone, he said, "Elves place great importance on self-control. Comportment matters to an elf, so manners do, too."

Cable snorted, "Touchy as highborns, Elves are, the lot of them."

Choosing to ignore Cable's outburst, Sam continued. "Theirs is an ancient race, Aeryk, a race of warriors, proud and cultured and tough as old boots. Elves have filled many a grave with those foolish enough to underestimate them."

"Best avoided, if you ask me," Cable asserted.

"Basyl told me Elves and ... well, non-Elves can procreate," Aeryk recounted.

"Procreate." Cable flashed a gap-toothed grin. "Old Danyl is always tellin' me you read too many books. I reckon that there is proof."

"Elves and humans can have children together," Sam affirmed.

"Elfan don't seem to mind making babies with our women

folk," Cable retorted, "and while Elfin ain't averse to a little push and pull every now and again, some of 'em, Elves generally don't take too kindly to one bearing a tersyan child."

"Tersyan is the Ilyrian word for us, someone not an elf, I mean," Aeryk ventured.

"The polite form, anyway," Sam stipulated. "They sometimes call us *theyan*, a contumelious term for which there is no direct translation."

"Contumelious, is it?" Cable squinted Sam's way. "Done some reading yourself lately, have ye, Sam?"

"Means scornful insult," Sam expounded.

Cable tugged at an ear. "And just how, I'm wondering, do you insult without scorn?"

Sam smiled wryly. "Suffice to say, *theyan* is less than complimentary. If an elf says it to your face, you're in for a fight."

"As far as I know, we Kylgahran have never warred with the Elves." Aeryk recalled Basyl having said something along those lines.

"We've squabbled often enough with the Syrdisians, though, and on occasion that has led to crossing swords with Elven mercenaries," Cable responded.

"Relations have been a little testy of late," Sam allowed. He nodded Cable's way. "As much as I hate to admit this ornery geezer might be right, best avoided is likely the wisest course."

Aeryk couldn't help thinking he heard a tinge of regret in Sam's voice.

14
Root of All Wisdom

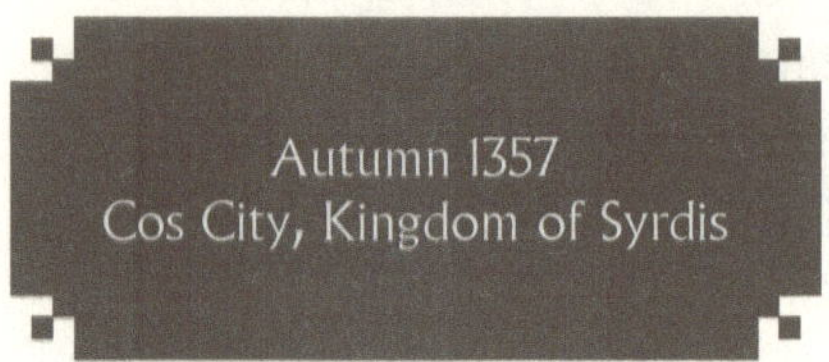

It had turned into a long day by the time the crew settled into the Rising Star, one that led to an even longer night. Sam prudently passed out only a portion of the drovers' wages. *Walking-around money,* he called it. Each cowman could pick up the rest of his pay at sundown on the following day. No one complained. The drovers all trusted Sam, and most could see the wisdom in it.

The walking-around money flowed freely enough, and the proprietress of the Rising Star, one Elsbeth Canty, appeared delighted with their patronage. A woman of middle years, Boswell's shrewd, statuesque sister seemed to be everywhere at once, gracious and sharp eyed all at the same time. Sam had spoken with his drovers, short and firm, before handing out the coin. Though boisterous after the long drive, the cowhands, cooks, and wranglers generally behaved themselves. Wyatt had refused to enter the city. He would wait, he said, for sign of their return.

Mistress Canty appeared only too happy to take charge of Estyr. For what she referred to as a nominal fee only, Elsbeth suggested a private room. Somewhat to Aeryk's surprise, Estyr went along peacefully enough. As she proceeded upstairs, Mistress Canty's arm about her, Estyr tossed a brief smile back over her shoulder at Aeryk. Estyr's spirits had recovered steadily in the time since her rescue, but she remained far more subdued than before the tragedy that had struck down her family.

Having managed to avoid infection, Caleb had also recovered well during the final stage of the drive into Cos. Sam arranged for a healer to examine Caleb. No sooner had the healer departed than Caleb came cavorting downstairs, claiming his leg felt good as new.

Aeryk invested some of his wages in a bath and a new shirt. Made of cotton, it was, the same shade of blue as the prairie sage flowers they'd passed on the way into the city. The garment buttoned down the front, all the way, so he didn't have to pull it on over his head. Sam offered to share a meal and a bottle of wine. Deeply honored, Aeryk joined him for supper, although he didn't much care for the fish—a Sayx perch, the buxom serving girl called it—which served as the main course.

After the meal, Sam excused himself and headed upstairs with his arm around the blue-eyed young serving girl. A number of other women, in an array of sizes and shapes, some not directly affiliated with the Rising Star, kept company with the drovers as well. Mistress Canty offered to make arrangements for Aeryk, but he declined. Aeryk had never been with a woman and was suddenly embarrassed by the prospect. Elsbeth Canty seemed to understand and proffered a quick, motherly smile and a pat on his arm. Though he remained oblivious to it, Elsbeth's expression was indeed motherly, her brown-eyed gaze lacking the degree of calculation that usually accompanied a smile she directed at a customer.

Aeryk slept in until midmorning the next day before he ventured downstairs to the main room for breakfast, wearing his new shirt and the cleanest pair of trousers left to him. He needed to have the rest of his stuff washed and get some mending done, too. He supposed Mistress Canty could give him directions back to Barber Street. His room was equipped with a washbasin and a polished steel mirror. After some thought, he decided to shave before donning his shirt, using an ivory-handled razor Danyl had given him.

An apprentice still, Tierza had said. Safer, he thought, to stick with the sewing. Whether he really needed to shave or not was debatable. Running his fingers over his chin, he concluded that at least he hadn't done any serious damage. In the reflection of the mirror, he caught sight of the medallion hanging about his neck. Briefly grasping the Fey symbol, he thought of Basyl and Lara and home. *We'll be headed back soon*, he reckoned. His sword he left in his room. Sitting at table, even with his dirk belted at his waist, he felt the absence of the baelryc.

Thatch, Mistress Canty's barman, brought Aeryk his food. Thatch sported a chest the size of a wine barrel, with arms to match. Aeryk asked him if he had seen Sam so far this morning. Thatch replied that Master Austyn had not come down yet, nor, for that matter, had young Estyr. Thatch commented that the same held true of about half the serving girls. While that must have meant some extra work for him, Thatch didn't appear to mind. Like many big men, Thatch seemed to be naturally easygoing.

Breakfast consisted of roast chicken, honey oat bread with fresh butter, and porridge made of oats mixed with peas, bits of ham, and pearl onions. He had just about finished eating when Cable Dowd stepped in, saying Aeryk had better come out front straightaway. Elves, Cable said. Looking for Sam, they were.

What Elves might want with Samwell Austyn, Aeryk had no idea. Aeryk pushed aside his plate and climbed to his feet. Following Cable toward the front door of the inn, Aeryk felt suddenly, keenly aware that he wore no sword on his left hip.

The main double-wide entryway of the Rising Star opened on to a veranda that ran the entire length of the building. Customers of the inn could take a meal on the veranda, if they were so inclined, or simply sit and enjoy the cool of an evening. Exiting the inn with Cable at his heels, Aeryk saw several cowhands gathered there, Caleb included. They looked tense. All were armed with swords. Wishing yet again that he was, Aeryk took note of five Elves standing at the head of the stairs leading up from the street.

The Elves were all clad in armor, long-sleeved chain mail that fell to mid-thigh. Like the cavalry troops Aeryk had seen the day before, each wore a sleeveless cloth surcoat over their coats of mail, white with green trim.

Aeryk knew the subtly curved long swords Elves carried were called johtens. Elven weaponsmiths were highly regarded; the remarkably tough, lightweight steel they produced was known for its slightly blue coloring. The group standing at the head of the stairs before him all bore johtens in sheaths attached to wide leather belts, positioned so that the swords rested on their left hips. Aeryk noted long-bladed daggers carried in belt sheaths on their right sides. Close-fitting leather trousers, knee-length leather boots, and helmets with full face guards completed the Elves' attire.

The head gear was finely wrought and included a sturdy central boss, fitted with fasteners to hold plumes or other decorations. Their helmets this day were free of any such embellishments. Aeryk did not know if there was any significance to that or not.

The face masks featured a center bar, protecting the wearer's nose, that extended the full length of the guard. A series of crossbars radiated from the lower half of the center bar to protect the Elves' cheeks and jaws, leaving fairly wide openings about the eyes. Made of steel, like the helmets themselves, the face guards were crafted separately, designed to bolt onto the helmet fronts. Four of the five Elves wore their helmets. The fifth stood with helmet tucked under one arm.

The bareheaded elf was about Aeryk's height, he figured. The elf's features were finely formed—a small, straight nose and a delicately shaped, full-lipped mouth. *She's an Elfin*, Aeryk thought. *She must be; nothing male could look like that.* Aeryk realized he had no notion of how to gauge how old an elf was, but the one standing before him appeared young, Aeryk's own age, certainly not much older. The Elfin had white-blond hair gathered into a braid stuffed between the back of her surcoat and the underlying chain mail. Aeryk glanced at the Elfin's hands and saw three fingers and a thumb on each. Well proportioned, the shape of the Elfin's hands appeared long and slim.

Judging from her face, the elf's skin showed the color of wild honey. The Elfin's eyes were striking, large, almond shaped, and of a tawny, amber hue. *Aren't Elves all supposed to have blue eyes or something?* Aeryk thought. *This one has cat's eyes.* He wondered how well Elves could see in the dark.

Exotic, even alien in appearance, Aeryk still thought her beautiful. Uncertain as to whether or not the elf would find that assessment complimentary or insulting, Aeryk concluded he didn't know shite about Elves. He took a breath.

Before Aeryk could speak, the elf with her helmet under her arm bowed at the waist, managing to transform the simple movement into a sleek, graceful gesture. Returning to full height in an equally elegant manner, the elf said, "Good morning."

The Elfin spoke precise Aylitic in a pleasingly feminine voice, lighter in tone than Tierza's but not by much. Again, before Aeryk could respond, the door of the inn burst open, and the young wrangler, Daymen Reed of Clan Ard Drew, rushed out. Crossing to the front railing, Daymen bent over it and vomited profusely. Aeryk looked back in time to see the helmeted Elves relaxing, four-fingered hands sliding away from their sword hilts. The bareheaded Elfin was struggling to keep her expression neutral. The four wearing helmets were openly amused.

Unable to keep a smile from his own face, Aeryk shook his head. "Better for some than others, it appears." Turning to Cable, he jerked his head in Daymen's direction and continued. "Might be a good idea to put something into his stomach that doesn't contain alcohol."

Nodding, Cable strode quickly to Daymen's side and unceremoniously grabbed the younger man's arm, saying, "Come on, you idiot." The cook half dragged the young wrangler to the door, and the two disappeared back inside the inn.

"We've had a long trip," Aeryk said by way of explanation, "and have been making rather merry."

"You are not Samwell Austyn." The cat-eyed Elfin arched one delicately curved eyebrow, transforming her statement into a question.

"No," Aeryk confirmed. "I am one of his drovers. My name is

Aeryk Emyrt." Remembering Tierza's reaction yesterday, he left out his clan affiliation.

"Of what clan are you?" the elf inquired immediately.

Chagrined, Aeryk said, "Clan Ard Mourne."

"I am Jyn-Ael-Tor," the Elfin responded, bowing once more. "I serve as an aide to Captain Aya-Bal-Mar of Order Castellan. I bear a message from my captain for Samwell Austyn of Clan Ard Gregyr."

"Sam has been making merrier than most, I hear," Aeryk said carefully. "He hasn't come down for breakfast yet. If you like, I can pass the message along when he does."

Jyn-Ael-Tor shook her head. "My orders are to deliver the message in person and await a reply. My captain was specific about this. When my captain is specific, anything short of full compliance tends to invoke a certain degree of displeasure. You are understanding this?" The young elf's Aylitic slipped just a little at the last.

"Aye," Aeryk affirmed. "Sam's a little like that himself." *The bastard did set me on drag yesterday for doing nothing wrong, and then more or less tricked me into eating fish for supper,* Aeryk thought and made a decision. "Why don't you follow me? I'll take you to him. Your four compatriots are welcome to a table and a bottle of whatever they prefer." Only after making the offer did it occur to Aeryk that he might have to make good on the bottle out of his own pocket.

Turning to her companions, Jyn-Ael-Tor tossed her helmet to the nearest and spoke briefly in what Aeryk assumed must be Ilyrian. "Thank you, but the bottle will not be necessary. I will follow you," she said to Aeryk.

"Dymena," the elf who had caught Jyn-Ael-Tor's helmet called in a firm baritone, the sound of warning ringing clear in his one-word utterance. Jyn-Ael-Tor merely smiled and said something in Ilyrian that caused the Elfan holding her helmet to duck his head while the other three chuckled.

"Mornin', boys." Aeryk pitched his voice to carry to the drovers assembled on the veranda. Looking Caleb in the eye, he continued. "You fellas take it easy. We'll be back in a little while." Caleb nodded, and Aeryk thought he could feel tension easing.

"This might get a little interesting," Aeryk warned on the way up the stairs.

"My captain said exactly the same thing before sending me over here," Jyn-Ael-Tor informed him.

Knocking on Sam's door, Aeryk said, "Sam, it's Aeryk." He heard no response. He tried a second time, speaking louder. By the third go, he was fairly shouting.

"Is the inn on fire?" Sam's voice drifted through the door.

"No," Aeryk said.

"Has anyone died or been arrested?" Sam queried. Aeryk thought he heard muffled female laughter coming from the other side of the door.

"No," Aeryk said again.

"Then go away," Sam directed. The trail boss's statement was accompanied by laughter from within, definitely female.

"I have an Elfin with me named Jyn-Ael-Tor," Aeryk told the door, "bearing a message for you from Captain Aya-Bal-Mar of Order Castellan, requesting an immediate response." *That will teach the wise ass,* Aeryk thought, *or put mine in a sling.*

"Is she good-looking?" Sam asked, speaking Glaylic. "The Elfin with you, that is."

Feeling a fool, conversing through the closed door, Aeryk couldn't help a quick glance at Jyn-Ael-Tor before responding, also in Glaylic, "Yes, very is the answer to your question. What has that got to do with anything?"

"Merely curious," Sam said, opening the door, speaking Aylitic. Unarmed, naked to the waist, his hair rumpled, Sam still managed to look dangerous. Peering at Jyn-Ael-Tor, Sam observed, "I see what you mean." Bowing at the waist to the young elf, he announced, "I am Samwell Austyn."

Returning the bow, Jyn-Ael-Tor introduced herself and handed Sam a folded piece of paper. "My captain instructed me to wait for your answer."

After reading the message, Sam stood thoughtfully for a moment or two, tapping his fingers on the piece of paper. "Tell Aya the answer is yes. We'll meet with her, as requested, at midday today."

"When you say *we*, what do you mean?" Jyn-Ael-Tor asked.

"Me and this fellow here," Sam answered, pointing at Aeryk. "He's more useful than he looks. Fair enough?"

"Yes," Jyn-Ael-Tor said, looking, Aeryk thought, relieved.

Shifting his gaze to Aeryk, Sam said, "We'll need to leave about half an hour before noon. Bring your hanger." He closed the door, ending the conversation.

"I should have bowed," Aeryk said to Jyn-Ael-Tor on their way back downstairs. "When we exchanged names, that is. I'm sorry."

"You did not know. I took no offense," Jyn-Ael-Tor told him.

"It appears there is a great deal I do not know," Aeryk admitted ruefully.

"My people say that realization is the root of all wisdom." Jyn-Ael-Tor smiled at him.

By the Fates, Aeryk thought, *she is beautiful, chain mail, johten, and all.*

"Hanger?" Jyn-Ael-Tor questioned as they neared the door.

"Hanger is Kylgahran slang for a baelryc, a sword," Aeryk explained.

"Baelryc," Jyn-Ael-Tor stated, as if reciting from some text. "Actually a hand-and-a-half hilted bastard sword with a typical blade length of two and a half span, for most men about the same distance as from shoulder joint to fingertip with hand and arm fully extended." Jyn-Ael-Tor spoke in crisply accented Glaylic.

"A straight-bladed weapon, the tip of the baelryc forms a symmetric, double-edged point," she went on. "The leading edge of the sword is razor sharp over its full length. About a span from the point, the backside of the baelryc blade gradually thickens to a blunt, rounded edge that extends back to the hilt."

She smiled, looking very like a contented tabby about to tuck in to a bowl of cream. "I know what a baelryc is, Aeryk Emyrt of Clan Ard Mourne."

15

A Promise Kept

"Just exactly how much trouble are we in?" Aeryk asked Sam an hour or so later as they made their way across town to the villa—Aeryk thought that was what it was called—where the Elves were quartered.

"Don't know," Sam answered. "With Elves, it is hard to tell."

"What are Elven mercenaries doing in Cos?" Aeryk knew from Basyl's teaching that Elves had served in Syrdis as mercenaries for generations.

"That will depend on their charter, whatever deal they worked with King Dardan back in Avrys," Sam replied. "Elven horse archers are bloody expensive. I doubt old Dardan has them sitting up here just for show."

Avrys, located on the west coast of the Cambrian Peninsula, well south of Cos, had long served as the capital city of Syrdis, home of the Syrdisian royal family, descendants of Balan Kinslayer, first of the so-called new kings. Despite substantive religious and cultural differences, the Elves of Ilyria and the kingdom of Syrdis honored still a treaty of alliance initiated hundreds of years in the past.

"You know, Jyn-Ael-Tor speaks Glaylic," Aeryk commented. "Her accent is better than yours."

"Does she the now?" Sam seemed impressed. "Most Elves don't. Did she smile at you in parting?"

"Aye," Aeryk recollected. "Come to think of it, she did; said something like, 'Know ye peace, Aeryk Emyrt.'"

"No worries, then," Sam said, clapping him on the arm. "If that young elf had been offended by your opinion of her looks, she would have left without a smile or any expression of good wishes. Elves only challenge you upon meeting. To offer challenge when departing is considered very bad manners. If an elf ever walks away without saying something pleasant, you might be in for a scrap the next time you meet. In future, you might want to be a bit more careful about voicing your opinion on such matters. Elves, especially Elfin, can be a little touchy about their appearance. "

"You're the one who asked," Aeryk protested.

"Aye, well," Sam explained, "Elves figure anyone can ask pretty much anything. It's answers that sometimes get you into trouble."

"Do you have any Ilyrian, Sam?" Aeryk inquired.

Sam glanced at him. "Some. Why do you ask?"

"What does *dymena* mean?" Aeryk queried.

"It's a title," Sam replied, "the proper feminine form of address for one of the vyldeen, the Elven nobility, roughly equivalent to saying *my lady*. A noble Elfan is called dymenu, or *my lord*."

"One of the Elfan escorting Jyn-Ael-Tor called her that," Aeryk reported. "At least, I think he did."

"Makes sense," Sam commented. "Aides to senior officers are often drawn from the ranks of the nobility. That's true of armies the world over."

In addition to everything else, Jyn-Ael-Tor is a bloody noble, Aeryk thought. *Well, shite.*

The villa turned out to be a large rectangular building complex. Their destination, the central annex, was a three-story building made of whitewashed brick. An exterior wall, about twice the height of a tall man, surrounded the villa.

A pair of Elven sentries guarded the primary gate. For all the decorative carving engraved upon the two oak doors of the entry-way, Aeryk estimated that once closed and latched, nothing short of a battering ram would breach the thing. The main gateway opened onto a spacious inner courtyard. A fountain babbled pleasantly, and fruit trees of various types provided shade.

From where she stood just inside the main door of the central annex lobby, Jyn-Ael-Tor noticed something different about Aeryk Emyrt as he and Samwell Austyn strode across the courtyard. It took only a moment for Jyn to realize the difference was the sword riding at his left hip. With training, most could become competent with a blade. Some, Jyn knew, seemed born to bear a sword. For such, the weapon soon became more an extension of their bodies than some external accoutrement. The baelryc fit Aeryk Emyrt like wings on a falcon. *Perhaps*, Jyn thought, *the young drover who appears to be Samwell Austyn's favorite hound has some wolf in him.* Stepping through the door, Jyn approached the two Kylgahran.

At first glance, Aeryk did not recognize the young Elfin striding toward them. Pale blond hair, parted down the middle, fell loosely about her shoulders. Clad in a simple tunic made of white silk that fell to mid-thigh and belted around her slender waist with a green sash, also of silk, the elf seemed to glide toward them, moving with a natural grace. The silk garment clung to her body, accentuating the curve of her breasts. A pair of leather sandals covered her feet. The Elfin's legs and arms were bare revealing light honey-toned skin flowing over long, smooth muscles that rippled easily as she walked.

Bowing to each of them in turn, Jyn-Ael-Tor said, "Welcome, Samwell Austyn of Clan Ard Gregyr, and welcome to you, Aeryk Emyrt of Clan Ard Mourne."

Returning her bow, Sam said, "Peace walk with you, Jyn-Ael-Tor."

Though remembering to bow, the best Aeryk could manage was to say, "Hullo."

"Please follow me," Jyn-Ael-Tor said, turning on her heel and walking back toward the door through which she had entered the courtyard.

Jyn's unbound hair fell to the small of her back. Aeryk's eyes were drawn irresistibly to the supple movement of the young elf's hips as she walked away from them. Sam saw the nonplussed expression on his young companion's face and recalled his own reaction the first time he'd seen an Elfin wearing the silk tunic they called a sulsah; Sam allowed himself a brief smile.

The captain's quarters were located at the back of the central annex on the third floor. Jyn-Ael-Tor paused at the door long enough to knock briefly, but then pushed the portal open without waiting for a reply. Stepping to one side, Jyn waved Sam through and then motioned for Aeryk to follow.

Aeryk paused as he drew abreast of the amber-eyed elf. "If I make a fool of myself, will it reflect poorly on you?"

"No, why should it?" Jyn-Ael-Tor said, a note of amusement in her voice.

Feeling a fool, Aeryk nodded and started to step past her. He stopped when the elf placed a hand on his arm.

"Thank you for your concern," Jyn said quietly. "Follow your companion's lead, and all will be well."

Aya-Bal-Mar appeared to be somewhat older and a touch shorter and slimmer than young Jyn. Not old, certainly. *Sam's age, maybe,* Aeryk thought. Aya's hair showed a darker shade than Jyn's, more of a medium blond. Her skin was about the same tone as that of the younger elf. The elder Elfin's eyes, however, were a deep blue. Aya-Bal-Mar also wore a silk tunic and sash of the same design as the younger elf.

Stepping around a large writing table with a map atop it, Aya-Bal-Mar bowed briefly, saying to Sam, "I see thee, Sam." The warmth in the Elfin's voice and in her smile was unmistakable.

"And I see thee, Aya," Sam replied, returning the bow and the smile. With a sweep of his hand, the tall Highlander acknowledged Aeryk. "May I present Aeryk Emyrt of Clan Ard Mourne?"

Aya then looked at Aeryk. He could feel the weight of that sapphire gaze.

The elf bowed at the waist and said, "I bid thee welcome, Aeryk Emyrt of Clan Ard Mourne."

Aeryk had never been called a *thee* before. Bowing, he responded, "I am honored, Aya-Bal-Mar."

Jyn appeared at Aeryk's side, carrying a silver platter heaped with small pastries. Jyn presented the platter to the young Kylgahran. Neither he nor Sam took note of the slight rise of Aya's right eyebrow at this breach of manners. As Sam was the principal guest, Jyn should have offered the platter to him first. Aeryk lifted one of the pastries, a doughy little thing that looked like it was covered in honey and walnuts, from the platter and took a bite.

"Hoi," he exclaimed, "this is good."

"Why, thank you, Aeryk," Jyn said, smiling. Stepping by him, Jyn extended the tray to Sam, who also took a pastry, nodding his thanks. Aya declined with a brief shake of her head. Jyn set the tray down upon a side table and turned back toward Aeryk. The young elf positioned herself slightly behind and to one side of her captain, within Aeryk's line of sight.

Aya directed her comment to Sam. "It was good of thee to come."

Swallowing what remained of his pastry, Sam said, "Promised I would."

What's that about? Aeryk wondered but kept silent.

"Thy promise was made long ago," Aya observed quietly, a shadow crossing her finely chiseled features. "Circumstances have changed much since then."

"A promise is a promise." The intensity of Sam's voice surprised Aeryk. Sam and the elder Elfin locked eyes. For a moment, Aeryk thought the air between them might crackle into flame.

Finally, Aya nodded. Looking again at Aeryk, she asked, "Why is he here?"

Thee was now *he*; Aeryk couldn't help feeling that was probably not a good thing. Sam spoke evenly, without hesitation. "I trust him. He's smarter than I am. And he's honest. I figured it might do thee some good, Aya, meeting an honest man."

Aya tossed her golden-haired head. "I doubt that."

"Can I go, then?" Aeryk asked before thinking better of it. "Could I take a couple of those with me?" He pointed to the pastry tray.

Jyn laughed outright, delighted. A moment passed, and though he might have imagined it, Aeryk thought he saw the corners of Aya's mouth tilt upwards. "There may come a day, young Aeryk, when thou will wish thee had."

Striding briskly to the writing table, Aya looked down at the map. "We have a journey to make, north of the Toreans, somewhere about here." The elf laid a slim finger on to the map. "We are hoping you will be able to guide us."

Apparently, the thees and thous stopped, Aeryk noted, once Elves got down to business. Sam took a look and then motioned for Aeryk to join him. The Toreans were the tallest mountains in the known world, majestic and forbidding. Aya's finger pointed to a spot on the northern slopes of the Torean range, south of Muir Bay, some six hundred kylos west of the Syrus River.

The kylo, a standard Tieran measure of distance, comprised sixteen hundred paces. Each pace, the length of an ordinary stride, consisted of three span. A Tieran span approximated the distance between the crease in an average-sized man's elbow to the base of his middle finger.

"What do you think?" Sam asked, directing his question to Aeryk.

"There will already be snow in the high passes," Aeryk stated.

"We'll never make it before winter closes in, Aya," Sam agreed.

Aya nodded. "Our intent is to wait until the spring thaw."

"You'll wait until summer," Sam said flatly. "I wouldn't want to try a crossing until the solstice at least."

"The mountain passes we'll need to use lie within Anduyin lands," Aeryk said carefully. "It wouldn't hurt to carry a passel of trade goods. With a little luck, we can just about stay clear of Cymbri territory."

"Will you guide us?" Aya asked. "We will pay one thousand silver talents to each of you." A sum of one thousand talents of silver equated to nearly three years' wages for a top hand.

Sam looked to Aeryk. "It's going to be a hard trip, lad. Not what I expected. You are under no obligation."

"You got lost twice on the walk over here," Aeryk said, grinning.

"I reckon I ought to tag along." Seeing the expression on Sam's face, Aeryk continued, speaking earnestly. "I'd like to see the country, Sam. You could use a hand, and a thousand talents is a lot more than I stand to earn in one season pushin' somebody else's cows."

Sam glanced at Aya. "I told you he was honest." He returned his attention to Aeryk. "Going north of the Torean Mountains"—Sam shook his head, the warning clear in his voice—"is liable to be the last trip you make."

"Wyli could step in a hole a stone's throw from Taggert's Landing and do for the both of us, too," Aeryk said. "It's bound to be country worth the seein', Sam. With any luck, we'll be back before the Fates know we've gone."

"Why do you want to make this trip?" Sam queried the Elven mercenary captain.

A brief silence greeted his question. "We too have a promise to keep." Aya spoke softly in answer. "I will tell thee when I can. Until then, neither thee nor thou should speak of this to anyone." Aya glanced at Aeryk.

Absorbing the intensity of that brief look Aeryk thought, *Back to thee and thou again.* He felt lost.

Straightening, Aya looked Sam in the eyes, "I'll have thy word on that, Samwell."

"You have it," Sam said.

Looking at Aeryk in turn, Aya said, "I'll have thine as well, Aeryk."

With a feeling that his life was about to change forever, Aeryk said, "I promise."

16
Finding a Home

Tuan Marques regained consciousness lying reclined against a large sack of beans in the back of a small wagon. They were moving; that is, the wagon moved—Tuan could sense that, as something deliciously cool and wet pressed gently to the swollen, throbbing ruin that was the left side of his face. The damp cloth lifted away. He heard it being dipped again into what he imagined was a bucket of cold water. The swelling in his left eye was such that he could barely open it enough to see. At least he could see, although he suspected the swelling might well get worse before it improved.

"How do you feel?" The voice sounded soft and feminine, laced with the lazy drawl typical of the Kylgahran.

"Well enough, considering," Tuan replied. Opening his good eye, Tuan saw a young woman kneeling beside him.

"Sheriff Ranyl says your ribs are bruised, but he does not think any are broken. You are battered and bruised all over. He was some concerned about internal bleeding but said only time would tell," she informed him.

"Examined me carefully, did he, the good lord ruffian?" Tuan asked absently, not caring over much, until a thought suddenly occurred. "Where are my harp"—Tuan's voice tightened with concern—"and my horse?"

"Your harp is right beside you, along with the rest of your baggage. Sheriff Ranyl saw to that," the woman assured him kindly, "and young Tad is riding your horse. Tad says your mount is a lot of animal."

"Tad has a good eye, for horses at any rate," Tuan muttered, "and my lord ruffian would appear to be very thorough when it comes to looking after what I suppose are his possessions the now."

"Sheriff Ranyl is nothing if not thorough, and he is a good man." The woman smiled; she was pretty, blond, with bright blue-green eyes and the kind of bosom most men fawned over. "I'd watch my mouth around him if I were you. He's just ruffian enough to box your ears."

"A minor offense compared to the robbery he has already committed," Tuan decried. "Three years' bond to clear a paltry four-hundred-talent debt. If there was a proper lordly court in this wilderness, I could earn that much in a month."

"Sounds like a mighty *if* to me," the young woman chided him. "And just how would you be earning such a sum?"

"Why as a jongleur, my darling," Tuan declared, "a singer and a musician. I also compose."

"And a healer, too." The blonde smiled, a mischievous glint lighting her eyes. "You appear to be a man of many talents."

"Wasted in this backwater." Tuan sighed and then winced. His ribs were indeed bruised and rather badly, and his balls hurt fiercely; they'd kicked him there more than once. "Peopled by savages and rogues." He sighed again as the woman pressed the cold compress once more against the side of his face. "Present company excepted. May I ask what your name is?"

"Mae Hoskins is my name."

"A pleasure to make your acquaintance, Mae," Tuan stated grandly. "You are quite lovely, and that dress you are wearing is most appealing; the color suits you perfectly." In truth, the dress the woman wore was a rather ordinary cotton frock, light blue in color. The shade favored her eyes, however, and while the cut of the garment was as plain as unsalted porridge, it fit well enough.

"Why thank you, young sir." Mae smiled. "I sewed the dress myself, you know. The cloth was a gift."

The wagon stopped. A moment later, Ranyl Emyrt swung up into the back of it to kneel at Mae's side. Nodding at Tuan, the esquire asked, "How's he doing?"

"He came to a little while ago," Mae answered. "Since then he's been about equal parts charming and aggrieved."

Ranyl grinned. *He's not bad looking*, Tuan thought, *rather heavily muscled for my taste but with a good firm jaw and intriguing grey eyes the color of thunderheads.*

"I hear healers make the worst patients," Ranyl said.

"He claims to be a jongleur, a musician of some sort," Mae reported. "Healing is apparently only a pastime."

Ranyl looked directly into the young man's eyes—eye, actually, as the youngster's left orbit was so swollen he could see nothing of the eyeball itself. "Mighty rough country for a jongleur," Ranyl observed.

"So I have discovered," Tuan concurred sourly, "much to my chagrin."

"Can you be moved safely, Healer?" Ranyl inquired. "Our camp is not far, and we have an apothecary among us. He can administer something for your pain."

"Your concern is touching, my lord ruffian," Tuan remarked, "but a trifle belated, don't you think?" He waved a languid hand about the back of the wagon.

"We'd about worn out our welcome in Selkyrk." Ranyl smiled, apparently taking no offense at being referred to as a ruffian. "Moving you was necessary. That said, I'd hate to kill you off accidently. Should you expire immediately, I'm out four hundred silver."

Tuan snorted delicately "My falchions alone are worth more coin than that."

A falchion was a double-edged dagger featuring a gracefully waisted blade about a span and a half in length. The blades usually came in pairs and were favored as dueling weapons among the Sea

Isle folk to the west. Ranyl had looked over Tuan's weapons carefully and had to admit they were finely crafted.

"Our bargain was for three years' bond," Ranyl reminded him. "You've not answered my question."

Tuan thought the great lout sounded rather smug. "Extortion." Tuan sighed bitterly, looking a little forlorn. "I suppose I'll survive to reach the dubious comforts of your campsite."

"You intend to complain the entire time, do you?" Ranyl smiled. Tuan merely glared at him. Ranyl's smile stretched to a grin. "Cheer up. I'll give you credit for a full day today, which leaves you only two years and 382 days to go."

"Two years and 381 days," Tuan corrected him, "as 1360 is a short year."

"Even so"—Ranyl winked at Mae—"keep a good thought; we'll be there in no time."

Tuan Marques took no time at all to become infamous among Ranyl's retainers.

"I've met Odds before," Fyrgus Clyde noted, his astonishment etched clearly onto his craggy face, "but by the Fates, never one quite so ..." The big smith hesitated, searching for the right word.

"Flamboyant," Ranyl supplied, sipping his tea.

"What does flamboyant mean?" young Tad Gyllis wanted to know.

Ranyl tossed his head and extended an arm in an elegant fashion, holding his cup imperiously out toward Mae Hoskins. "A splash more of your impeccably well-boiled weeds, if you please, my girl." Ranyl spoke in a precisely clipped tone.

Mae blinked and then laughed, placing both hands on her well-rounded hips. "I ought to dump the bloody pot on your head."

Ranyl chuckled and turned to Tad. "That's being flamboyant."

"Flamboyant means being a pain in the ass, then?" Tad ventured.

"Yes, generally," Ranyl allowed, "but with a distinctly colorful sense of style."

Tad tugged at an ear, looking a little dubious.

"He's as prissy a girl most times," Emerson Hart put in and received a flat-eyed stare from his wife while she stirred the stew in a large cast-iron pot, suspended by a portable wrought-iron stanchion over the campfire.

"I've yet to meet a Kylgahran lass who was the least bit prissy, Harry. I take your point, though," Ranyl said diplomatically, which earned him an even sterner glare from Kate and another from Mae as well for his pains.

"Women are soft as rose petals," Ranyl's father, Stephyn, had told him once. *"The trick is staying free of the thorns."*

Ranyl took a judicious sip of his tea. The six of them were gathered round Mae's cook fire at the close of their sixth day out of Selkyrk. Mae and Kate were sharing the chore of preparing the evening meal, something they did often, as much for a chance to visit, Ranyl suspected, as to save labor.

Oblivious, Hart pressed on. "You'd think one of the Odd Persuasion would learn to be a little more circumspect. This little blighter acts like he's got no shame at all."

"I think, Harry," Ranyl theorized, "young Tuan is determined to be who he is. Living without shame is, I reckon, the whole point. The boy's got plenty of sand; I'll give him that."

"Maybe," Harry acknowledged. "Even so, a little discretion wouldn't do him any harm. He wouldn't last a month on his own, acting the way he does."

"He ain't on his own," Ranyl said firmly, "not anymore, so there's one problem solved." Ranyl glanced up to find Mae smiling at him, and Kate, too. *Women.* Ranyl could only shake his head.

The next morning, a mule shied and managed to knock nine-year-old Darius Ward, the eldest son of Glynnis and Jon Ward, both of Clan Ard Mourne, into a thicket. The boy's fall disturbed a nest of yellow-backed wasps. Before his folks could extricate the lad, he'd been stung multiple times. Though painful a yellow-back's sting was usually not life-threatening. Young Darius, however, showed immediate signs of distress. His tongue began to swell, and the lad went pale, lapsing quickly into unconsciousness.

Scooping the boy up into his arms, Ranyl sprinted to his wagon, calling for Tuan. Though still hobbled by the beating he'd taken in Selkyrk, the young healer clambered down from the vehicle. Ranyl laid the stricken child upon the ground. Kneeling, Tuan grasped Darius by the hand and then placed the fingers of his other hand on the side of the boy's now badly swollen face. Tuan closed his eyes. Ranyl could see Darius's body stiffen and then writhe slightly, weakly. Moments dragged by. Ranyl became aware of Jon and Glynnis standing anxiously by his side. Mae and Kate both appeared, as if conjured, waiting silently, as did Waltyr Boone, the apothecary, medicine bag in hand.

"That's done it, I think," Tuan murmured.

Looking down, Ranyl saw that Darius's color had already improved. The boy seemed to be breathing easily, and the grotesque swelling of his features was all but gone.

The boy's gaze rested momentarily on the young healer kneeling by his side and then swept the ring of adults standing around him. "Hullo, Mum," he said calmly to his mother.

"Darius, oh, thank the Fates," Glynnis Ward cried, dropping to her knees to gather her son into a loving embrace, all of which embarrassed young Darius to no end. "Thank you, Healer," Glynnis said to Tuan.

Tuan merely nodded and stood a little unsteadily. "If you will excuse me." The blond-haired youth turned away, took two steps, and dropped to his knees, vomiting. Ranyl knelt at the young man's side.

"I'm sorry," Tuan managed, his normally precise manner of speech slurred slightly. "I'm ... this is rather ..." Before he could finish the thought, another wave of nausea struck, and the youthful healer vomited again.

Removing his tartyn, Ranyl slipped his arm about the slender green-eyed youth. "Take it easy." Gently wiping spittle from Tuan's mouth, Ranyl said, "Let's get you back into the wagon."

"The boy," Tuan protested softly, "he is not out of danger. He must have rest and nourishment. For the next few days, he will be susceptible to the slightest ailment."

Ranyl glanced at Glynnis and dark-haired Waltyr Boone. Glynnis nodded her understanding. Waltyr followed suit, a look of wonder on his leanly contoured face. "He's in good hands," Ranyl assured Tuan. "Can you stand?"

"Of course," Tuan snapped. The youth's first effort barely got him off his knees before his legs gave way. Tuan was as slender as a reed. The boy's flesh was firm but supple. He felt more like a child than a man. Taking a firmer grip, Ranyl leveraged Tuan to his feet, easily bearing most of the young man's slight weight.

"Light," Tuan muttered, "this is humiliating."

"That's what you get for indulging in heroics," Ranyl informed him matter-of-factly. With the youth leaning heavily upon him, Ranyl guided Tuan back to the wagon, lifting him bodily inside.

"You're quite strong, my lord," Tuan observed as Ranyl helped him on to a pallet in the rear of the wagon.

"You're just a skinny little critter," Ranyl countered with a smile. "Can I get you anything?"

"Some decent wine would be nice," Tuan suggested.

Pouring a cup of water from a clay pitcher suspended from the ridgepole of the wagon cover by a length of twine, Ranyl replied, "See if you can keep this down first."

Wrinkling his nose, Tuan took a tentative swallow. "Sweet Light, what a barbarian you are."

"I think we've established that. I'm also a fair reach larger and stronger than you, healer, so behave yourself," Ranyl told him.

Muttering something unintelligible, Tuan drained the cup and lay down. Returning the vessel to Ranyl with a flourish, Tuan proclaimed, "As you command, my lord."

Accepting the cup, Ranyl grinned.

After a moment, Tuan arched a single golden eyebrow and said with a flounce, "What?"

"You say *my lord* as if it was something you found stuck to the bottom of your boots," Ranyl remarked.

Tuan merely sniffed.

Wetting a rag he found lying alongside the pallet, Ranyl began to bathe Tuan's still-battered countenance. Tuan was healing well, but his face remained discolored by bruises, his left eye blackened.

"Stop that," Tuan protested, raising his left hand to ward off Ranyl's ministrations.

Taking a firm grip on the youth's slender wrist, Ranyl admonished, "You're still feverish. Simmer down, or I'll sit on you. I don't imagine that will do those ribs of yours much good."

"Feckless brute," Tuan growled at him.

Ranyl's smile returned. "You must get beat up a lot."

Tuan shrugged slightly in acknowledgement. "Of late"—he hesitated a moment—"I seem to be out of place."

"How old are you, really?" Ranyl inquired.

"I told you," Tuan replied shortly.

"You don't lie worth a damn," Ranyl stated, waiting.

"I'm nearly seventeen," Tuan allowed.

"Which would make you sixteen," Ranyl concluded.

Tuan fixed him with a glare most sixteen-year-olds reserved for their parents. "I owe you a life," Ranyl remarked. "While I live, you will not be harmed for being who you are. Nor will you be taken from us against your will. You may speak your mind, but should you play the churl before me or mine, I'll tan your bottom."

"In other words," Tuan said tartly, "I can speak my mind so long as I say nothing that offends you."

Ranyl nodded with a grin. "Some advantage, it seems, there is to being lordly after all."

"So you are my protector the now," Tuan surmised, ignoring Ranyl's contention. "Simple as that, is it?"

"Simple or no," Ranyl affirmed, "that's the way things are. Anything or anyone I should know about?"

Tuan lay quiet as Ranyl finished bathing his face. Ranyl dampened the cloth once more and placed it across Tuan's forehead.

"My father's holdings"—Tuan spoke in a tone just above a whisper—"are on the Isle of Shaara."

That explains your accent, Ranyl thought.

"I was the youngest of three sons. My older brothers were like you, strong and handsome and oh so masculine. I was tolerated, you see, the clever child who liked music and cooking and other things." Tuan's soft uttering faded to silence. "Last winter," he began again, "my elder brother was killed in a duel. In the spring, my eldest brother, my father's heir, was lost at sea, two weeks before he was to wed. When my father and I last spoke, he said he'd rather have no sons than"—Tuan swallowed—"a perverted little weakling. I left the next day. That was some months ago, the now." Tuan raised his eyes to Ranyl's. "You needn't worry. I don't think anyone will come looking."

"Sometimes," Ranyl spoke quietly, "those closest to us say things that hurt beyond all reason, beyond intent."

"My father," Tuan asserted, "is the type of man who says what he means and means what he says."

"Like his youngest in that regard, then," Ranyl declared. He gently grasped Tuan's right hand with his own.

"Are you trying to seduce me, my lord?" Tuan murmured.

Ranyl merely shook his head. "I'm not made that way, Tuan."

"How do you know?" Tuan objected. "I'm not exactly at my best right at the moment. Fully recovered, I can be likeable enough."

"I like you right well as is," Ranyl professed. "As to knowing"—he shrugged—"I suppose it's a matter of fish and fowl. I think you understand that better than I."

"That being the case," Tuan said with a sigh, "why don't you go away and stop wasting my time?"

Ranyl tightened his hold upon Tuan's right hand, squeezing firmly. "Thank you for your courage, Healer, and your skill. You've earned your place here among us, and no one will question it. Welcome home."

Tuan nodded briefly but said nothing. Releasing the youth's hand, Ranyl slipped out of the wagon and then paused, listening. He tarried only a moment before striding briskly away. Ranyl didn't reckon Tuan would appreciate his hanging about while the young lad wept.

17

Decisions

The morning after Sam and Aeryk's first visit to the Elven villa, a party of four Elves arrived at the Rising Star, bearing a message. The Elves were led by a scar-faced syr-sah, an Elfan named Tyk-Ban-Gyl. With features pleasing enough despite the thin white scar mantling his left cheek, Tyk's eyes showed sky blue; his medium-blond hair was worn long and tied into a queue at the nape of his neck. His skin appeared a shade darker than that of Jyn-Ael-Tor, typical coloring for one of Elven kind.

The Elven word for warrior was syr, which literally meant one who bears a sword. A syr-sah, Aeryk understood, was a sort of non-commissioned officer. Aya's title of captain served, apparently, as an informal designation, assigned to the commander of a mercenary company. Within the Castellan Order, Aya bore the rank of syr-tan, a step below that of general.

Tyk-Ban-Gyl introduced himself with a brief but formal bow. "Good day to you, Aeryk Emyrt."

"Do I know you?" Aeryk inquired, returning the bow.

"I was among those escorting the syr-ryx yesterday," Tyk informed him.

The one Jyn tossed her helmet to, Aeryk recalled. "Syr-ryx is a junior officer?"

"Yes," Tyk confirmed, "that is Dymena Jyn-Ael-Tor's military rank."

The message, addressed to Sam from Aya-Bal-Mar, indicated something unexpected had arisen, and the meeting planned for noon that day would need to be delayed. Aya closed the message by saying she would send word as to their next meeting as soon as she could be certain of a day and time.

"Would you mind waiting in case Sam wants to send a return message?" Aeryk requested.

"It would be my pleasure." Tyk bowed informally. Aeryk was struck by how the elf could impart such distinction into so similar a movement, a slight bend at the waist, by comparison to the more formal bow rendered in greeting a few moments before. Sam had nothing to say with respect to Aya's message, except a brief acknowledgement.

Aeryk nodded and turned to leave Sam's room. Sam stopped him, saying, "As our noon meeting with Aya has been canceled, you should have plenty of time to visit the orphanage."

Cable had been correct; a group of Reverent Sisters staffed and administered an orphanage known as Hope Manor in Cos city.

"The only way Estyr is going to set foot in that place," Aeryk declared, "is if we hog-tie her and toss her over the threshold."

"All of which is no reason for you not to visit," Sam replied, unperturbed. "Speak with the Sisters, find out if they would even accept Estyr, how much they charge—get a feel for what life might be like there for her."

After seeing Tyk off, Aeryk belted on his sword and dirk and left the inn, heading for the stables across the yard. Sam had provided directions to the orphanage. As Aeryk and Wyli made their way to Hope Manor, his thoughts turned to the young girl the Fates had placed in his charge. He'd taken breakfast with Estyr that morning, showing off his new shirt. A couple of nights and a day under Mistress Canty's wing appeared to have been good for her. She seemed a touch more her old self.

As he rose from his chair to leave, Estyr smiled at him. "Done any hat shoppin' yet?"

Aeryk grinned and clapped his dilapidated headgear into place. "I reckon this 'un has a bit of wear left in it."

Hope Manor turned out to be a large slate-roofed building with walls constructed of painted brick—a great, grey rectangular box, about as cheery as a tomb. Aeryk nearly reined Wyli about on the spot. He would have, except the front door of the place swung open, and Jyn-Ael-Tor stepped through, exiting the building.

Bareheaded, her silver-blond hair wound into an elaborate single braid, the young Elfin wore a grey-silk riding dress with a divided skirt. A broad leather belt wound about her slender waist. Suspended from the belt, Aeryk saw a long-bladed dagger but no johten. Dismounting, Aeryk intercepted her at the base of a flight of stone steps leading up to the entry door of the orphanage.

"Good morning, dymena." Aeryk bowed in the manner Basyl had taught him was appropriate for introducing oneself to a lady.

Jyn's amber-eyed gaze fixed upon him. The look of Jyn's irises and pupils appeared the same as any human's would, perhaps a touch larger than most, but the overall contour of her eyes was distinct, more of an ovoid shape.

"Aeryk Emyrt." Jyn bowed briefly, a quick graceful motion. "What are you doing here?"

"I need to speak with the Sisters about a child," Aeryk answered. "May I ask why you were here, dymena?"

Jyn hesitated for a moment, as if considering whether or not to answer his query. "I am a patron. The Sisters do good works here. Theirs is one of the few orphanages in Syrdis that will accept Halflings, the offspring of Elves and tersyans. Occasionally, I bring a bit of coin, some small gifts for the children, and I read to them."

Aeryk noticed the book tucked under her arm, a copy of *Pigdyn A-Wandering*. "That's my favorite," he enthused, "as a child, I mean."

A slight smile played with the corners of Jyn-Ael-Tor's mouth.

"Somehow, I am not surprised." Her expression sobered. "You mentioned you were here about a child."

"On the drive east we came across a settler's daughter; thirteen, she is," Aeryk replied. "Estyr is her name. She saw her family murdered by bandits. They carried her off. We managed to get her away from them."

"How, exactly?" Jyn-Ael-Tor inquired.

"We tracked the bastards down and killed them," Aeryk said evenly. He glanced at Jyn. "Your pardon, my lady. We brought Estyr with us to Cos."

"And you'd like to be rid of her the now?" Jyn's amber eyes narrowed as she spoke.

"No," Aeryk asserted, "it's just … well Estyr's mum was Kylgahran, her da Syrdisian. Her mother died early, and Estyr was raised in Syrdis. Syrdisian ways and beliefs are what she knows. Sam says when you take responsibility for a child, you do what's best for that child, not what's easiest for you."

"And you think a Syrdisian orphanage is what's best for her?" Jyn wondered.

"I don't know," Aeryk allowed. He found himself staring at his boot tops. "Back home, my mum—my stepmother, that is; her name is Lara—she's good with children, and good for 'em too, I know. Lara has a big heart. She'll take one peek at wee Estyr and that will be that. And when it comes to my father … well, you'll look a long time to find a better man." Aeryk peered over his shoulder at the grey edifice looming above. "But here, in Syrdis, with the Sisters and all they know, maybe …"

"Have you spoken with Estyr?" Jyn interjected.

Aeryk straightened. "Aye, the little mort is bound and determined to stick with me—with us, I mean. She's been through a lot, and she trusts us, ramshackle bunch that we are."

"The Sisters here are a wonder," Jyn told him, "selfless and devoted, wise and kind, highly skilled and determined. But they will never be able to give Estyr what your mother and father can—a home of her own. See she has that, Aeryk Emyrt, and you need never doubt you've done the right thing."

Aeryk peered for a long moment into the tawny depths of Jyn's eyes. Her gaze never wavered. Finally, he nodded. "Looks as if I've no business here, then." Aeryk brightened. "Which means I'm free to escort you back to the villa, my lady."

"My thanks, Aeryk Emyrt," Jyn said crisply, looking away at last, "but no such service is required."

"You might need someone to open a door for you," Aeryk contended, "or fend off a pickpocket or something. Besides, you haven't met Wyli yet." Aeryk pointed to his gelding, standing patiently at a hitching rail nearby. Hearing the sound of his name, Wyli's ears perked up. "Everyone likes Wyli."

"Wyli," Jyn mused. "Is he named after the fairy in *Pigdyn A-Wandering?*"

Aeryk grinned. "The very one."

Jyn-Ael-Tor tossed her head, not quite able to keep the smile from her face. "All right, you may ride along. Feel free to thwart any cutpurse we encounter, but be warned. If you try to open a door for me, I'll brain you."

A short time later, Jyn and Aeryk rode through the main gate of the Elven villa and dismounted. A young syr, an Elfan, trotted up.

"Greetings, dymena." The syr bowed respectfully. "The captain sent me to find you. She requests you attend her directly. She's in her quarters." The young syr smiled. "Luck is with me this day, as I have also been directed to make the same request of you, Aeryk Emyrt."

"Are you sure about that?" Aeryk more or less blurted.

The Elfan's smile broadened. "It is not as bad as all that," he said reassuringly. "The captain isn't angry or anything, at least not with you."

Jyn handed the reins of her mount, a clean-lined Enduyi mare, to the syr. "Angry or no, we'll not improve the captain's mood any by keeping her waiting," Jyn said, sounding to Aeryk as prim as a school marm. "Come along, Aeryk Emyrt."

Aeryk had little choice but to pass Wyli's reins to the syr and follow in Jyn's wake as she strode briskly toward the front door of the central annex. As they stepped into the captain's quarters on the third floor, Captain Aya-Bal-Mar glanced up from her seat behind a small writing table, placed beneath a large window overlooking the courtyard below.

Jyn-Ael-Tor bowed briefly, respectfully. Aeryk did his best to emulate her. Aya returned their gestures by executing a brief but elegant seated bow.

"That was quick, syr-ryx," the captain commented, "and with Aeryk Emyrt in tow, I see."

"Aeryk Emyrt intercepted me as I was leaving Hope Manor earlier this morning, Captain," Jyn explained. "He insisted upon escorting me back to the villa"—Jyn tossed a brief, undecipherable glance Aeryk's way—"to ward off ruffians, cutpurses, and any other undesirables we might encounter along the way."

"Successfully, it would appear." Aya smiled. "What were you doing at an orphanage, Aeryk Emyrt?"

"Bit of a long story, Captain," Aeryk replied. "I've become somewhat responsible for a young orphan girl. My intent was to speak with the Sisters—"

"Estyr, of course," Aya exclaimed. "Samwell so informed me."

Had he, the now? Aeryk thought. *And just when did he do that? Come to think of it, I didn't see Sam at supper last night or at breakfast this morning.*

The Elven captain went on. "It would appear you are taking your responsibility seriously."

"Trying to, Captain," Aeryk said.

"Have you made a decision?" Aya inquired.

"Aye, with the dymena's help." Aeryk looked to Jyn, who appeared, for some reason, slightly less self-assured than usual. "The orphanage is no place for Estyr."

Aya smiled. "Samwell seemed confident that would be your choice."

Did he? Then why did the bugger insist I go visit the bloody place? To see for myself, of course. The answer blossomed, self-evident the now, in Aeryk's mind. *That canny bastard.*

"This"—the captain lifted a vellum sheet from the surface of the table before glaring at the piece of paper, as if it had called her a dirty name—"states that the consignment of household goods slated for delivery to Lord Martyn Clearview is delayed—a river barge incident, apparently—for perhaps a week."

"He won't be happy to hear that, Captain," Jyn opined.

"You have a gift for understatement, Jyn-Ael-Tor," Aya remarked, a hint of sarcasm laced through her tone. "Tomorrow at dawn you will ride to the Greenwood estate. Lord Martyn and his retinue are visiting there—a cousin, I believe. Please inform His Grace of the delay, and assure him that as soon as the shipment arrives, I will personally see to its safe delivery to his new holding, Balmuir, at no expense to him."

"Why are Elven mercenaries delivering household goods?" Aeryk asked.

Aya's eyes fixed upon him. "We are not delivering household goods, Aeryk Emyrt, merely assuring their safe arrival."

"None of my business, in other words," Aeryk surmised. "My apologies, Captain."

Aya smiled. Aeryk could read nothing in her expression.

"It is only a few hours' ride to Greenwood, Captain," Jyn pointed out. "I could leave immediately."

Aya shook her head. "We are expecting further, relevant correspondence this afternoon that will also warrant prompt delivery. Dawn tomorrow will be soon enough."

Aya's sapphire-blue eyes settled once again upon Aeryk. "I would like you to accompany Jyn-Ael-Tor on this errand, Aeryk Emyrt."

"That is not necessary, Captain," Jyn asserted immediately.

"Obviously," Aya said evenly, never breaking eye contact with Aeryk, "but prudent, I think. We'll pay three silver talents for a day's effort. I have no authority to command you, Aeryk. This is a request, not an order. What say you?"

"I'll be glad of the opportunity to accompany the dymena, Captain," Aeryk answered with a smile.

Jyn flared. "That makes one of us."

"You have your orders, Syr-ryx," Aya said firmly.

Jyn ducked her chin slightly. "Yes, Captain."

"Plan to leave at first light," Aya directed. "See me here before you go."

"Yes, Captain," Jyn said again.

Aya turned to Aeryk. "My thanks, Aeryk Emyrt."

"You're welcome, Captain." Aeryk's smile stretched a tad. "Any chance I could get paid in advance?"

Aya's smile matched Aeryk's own. "None whatsoever." She straightened in her chair, "That will be all."

On the way back down the hall, Aeryk said, "This seems like a lot of fuss, assigning the captain's personal aide and all. Why not just send a galloper after breakfast tomorrow?"

Jyn stared at him as if he'd suddenly sprouted horns. "Martyn Clearview is the Duke of Highgarden." Jyn spoke as if that revelation should have provided Aeryk with all he needed to know.

"Aye." Aeryk shrugged. "And so?"

"Highgarden is the most prominent duchy in all of Syrdis," Jyn said, astonished at Aeryk's lack of acumen. "Duke Martyn is fourth in line to the Leopard Throne and almost certainly the richest man in the kingdom, including his uncle, the king."

18
Invitation

Evening had drawn near to full dark by the time Samwell Austyn and Aeryk Emyrt returned to the inn on Copper Street. They'd taken supper at a small eatery a few blocks down. As he and Sam stepped on to the veranda of the Rising Star, Aeryk heard a familiar, smoky voice singing "Little Lamb Lost," a ballad about a mother searching for her missing child.

Entering the main room of the inn, Aeryk saw Tierza seated at the edge of the bar, her fingers strumming a stringed instrument held in her lap. Her crutch leaned against the bar, close to hand. A number of patrons sat at the array of tables spread throughout the room; all seemed to be listening intently. The song was an old one, and he had heard it sung often. Something about Tierza's rendition, though, spoke to him of true heartache and longing. Aeryk felt as if he was hearing the ballad for the first time.

"She's good," Sam noted.

"Aye," Aeryk agreed. "Her name is Tierza."

"How do you know that?" Sam asked.

"Ran into her on the day we drove the cattle through town,"

Aeryk explained. "Nearly ran over her, actually. I hauled her out of the way. That's what I was doing down that side street when you booted me back to drag."

"Sounds like she might well have been worth it," Sam observed.

"I reckon," Aeryk said, seemingly unable to take his eyes off the girl with the lyre.

"I'm headed up to my room," Sam informed him. "Would you like to share a bottle? Maybe play some cards?"

"Ah, no thanks," Aeryk responded a little absently. "I think I'll just sit here awhile." Smiling and wondering where the young got all the energy, Sam bid him a good night and made his way upstairs.

An empty table and a set of chairs stood near where Tierza played. Aeryk tossed his hat on the table.

While Aeryk settled in, Thatch walked over, asking in a bass whisper, "Some ale, lad, and maybe a bit of bread and cheese?" Thatch's voice was as deep as his chest. The burly barkeep had light brown hair, thinning on top, and guileless brown eyes.

"The ale will do, Thatch, thanks," Aeryk said quietly, and the barman stepped away to fetch it. For a big man, Thatch was light on his feet. Looking up, Aeryk saw that Tierza had noticed his arrival. She favored him with a quick smile.

Thatch returned promptly with Aeryk's drink. Tierza asked the crowd if anyone had a favorite tune. In response to a couple of shouted requests, Tierza's next song was a hymn called "The Shining Soul." By the last chorus, Aeryk had tears in his eyes. Glancing surreptitiously about the room, he reckoned he was not the only one. Thatch stood unabashedly wiping his eyes with a bar towel. Tierza changed the mood and finished her performance with a breezy little love song about an amorous fishmonger that Aeryk had never heard before.

After bowing at the waist to the smattering of applause that rippled through the main room of the inn after she finished singing, Tierza slipped nimbly off the bar and slid her lyre into a leather carrying case.

"Hear now," Thatch called, banging a large wooden mug on the bar to catch the attention of the customers, "for the little lass."

Thatch tossed a coin into the mug and then passed it to a well-dressed fellow standing nearest. Under Thatch's watchful gaze, the man dropped a pair of coins into the cup before hastily passing it on.

Sipping his ale, Aeryk was startled by the sound of Tierza's voice. "Thatch is handy to have around," she said, standing nearly at his elbow. "Good for revenue, I mean."

Before Aeryk could conjure a response, a lanky young fellow, who had obviously been drinking, stepped up to Tierza. "That was some singin' you done," he said. "You know, my pa is a fishmonger." The fellow smiled sloppily, weaving just a little. "My name's Buel. Why don't you come with me?" He pointed to a table across the room where a couple of other young men sat, looking distinctly uncomfortable. "We'll buy you a drink."

"No, thanks," Tierza replied, smiling. "I hear alcohol is liable to stunt my growth."

The tall fishmonger's son blinked and then took a step closer. "That's not being very friendly."

"She said no," Aeryk heard himself saying as he climbed to his feet.

Buel took a look at the young man standing beside the crippled little singer and noted his wide shoulders, the sword at his hip, and his eyes. Buel had a long knife in the back of his belt, and he was good with his fists. Despite the drink, he couldn't help noticing there was something about how the stranger stood, his eyes watchful and ready.

"Well, piss on you," Buel sputtered finally, backing up a step. "And you, too," he put in for good measure, glaring at Tierza. Turning, he made his way, a little unsteadily, back across the room. "C'mon," Buel called to his friends, and the three of them left the inn.

"And so goes a trio of satisfied customers," Tierza said flatly. "Thank you ever so kindly." Something flickered in her eyes, something Aeryk couldn't read.

Feeling two kinds of fool, Aeryk was uncertain how to respond. Burn him if he'd apologize. Instead, he said, "I must have heard

'Little Lamb Lost' sung a hundred times before, but I never felt its meaning until I came upon you singing it this evening." She said nothing, her eyes a mystery. *Bloody female.* "Sorry. I didn't mean to step on your trade." Reaching into his wallet, Aeryk grabbed the first coin his fingers came in contact with, a silver talent. He stepped across to the bar and laid the coin down next to her crutch.

Aeryk started to walk back, intent upon retrieving his hat, but had to stop when Tierza pushed a chair into his path. "First you cost me money, and now you're turning tail," she said, a dangerous tone slipping into the honey-sweet sound of her voice.

Glaring at her in return, Aeryk pointed to the bar top and growled, "That's a day's pay, girl, for a top hand."

She placed both hands on the back of the chair and pushed off with her good leg, swinging over to the bar. Picking up the coin, she turned to Aeryk and smiled. "I know." Not taking her eyes off his, she slipped the coin into her bodice. The dress she wore was green, he noticed, and cut just low enough to accentuate the lush swell of her breasts. Picking up her crutch, she slid it under her left arm. "If you stay," she said, looking up at him through long dark eyelashes, "I'll buy you a drink."

"I thought you didn't like alcohol," Aeryk said pointedly.

"I said it wasn't good for me. Sometimes, though, I feel like celebrating." Her eyes warmed. "Depends a lot on the company I'm with."

"Don't reckon I could refuse an offer like that," Aeryk said as dryly as he could.

"Especially not so long as you are within reach of my stick." Tierza took a seat at the table and tapped the chair she'd pushed into Aeryk's way with her crutch. "Please, won't you sit down?" Positioning the chair, he sat. No sooner had his bottom lit than she continued. "You know you deserve a good thumping."

"How's that?" Aeryk asked.

"Your home is on the far side of the Syga Plain, is it not?" Tierza queried.

"Aye," Aeryk responded, not knowing where this was going.

"A very long way and much of it uncharted, yes?"

"It is," he said.

"So you managed to guide three thousand head of cattle—"

"I had a little help," he interrupted.

Tierza scooted her chair closer to his. Aeryk had left the top button of his new blue shirt undone. Reaching up, Tierza slipped a slender finger into the buttonhole, twisted gently, and purred, "It is not polite to interrupt." She was looking into his eyes. Hers were a rich golden brown, buttery soft in the candlelight of the Rising Star's main room. He was sitting close enough to easily catch her scent, warm and soapy with just a hint of flowers—roses, he thought. He kept quiet. She smiled a slow, sweet smile, nodding her approval.

"As I was saying, thousands of cattle across hundreds of kylos of uncharted wilderness, and yet you can't seem to find your way back to Barber Street."

"I've been meaning to ..." he started but fell silent as she gently pressed her finger against his lips, arching an eyebrow. Elves, apparently, weren't the only ones who had mastered the art of eyebrow arching.

"Your absence has forced me to come here to sing before strangers, for money, just so that I could properly thank my rescuer." She straightened, removing her finger from his mouth, and then asked, "How is Wyli, by the way?"

"He's fine," Aeryk said, grinning like a fool and not caring. "Eating more oats just the now than is good for him. Had he known we were going to cause you such hardship, I'm sure we would have visited much sooner."

"There." Tierza sighed, sitting back in her chair. "I knew a true gentleman would not ignore a sincere invitation. So the delay is entirely your fault." Her eyes again latched onto his. "Too busy consorting with Elves, or so I hear," she surmised, golden-brown orbs narrowing just enough to make him squirm.

"Sam knows some of them, from way back, apparently," Aeryk hedged. "Takes a while to be properly polite in the Elvish manner where old friends are concerned. Turns out they—the Elves, I mean—want us, Sam and me, to find them some horses." If asked, this was the tale Sam had instructed Aeryk to tell in relation to their Elven association.

"Horses," Tierza's tone sounded incredulous.

Safe harbor, Aeryk thought, *at least for the now.*

"Anduyin horses, out west a-ways," he added for good measure, completing the story.

"What would Elves want with Anduyin horses?" Tierza seemed dubious.

"I don't know. Sam says it'd be impolite to ask. Apparently, it's not healthy, being impolite around Elves. The pay is pretty good, though."

"When do you leave?" Tierza sounded concerned.

"Don't know that either. Elves eat a lot of fish, you know. I'm probably going to have to down some more of the damn things before I find out." He spoke in as mournful a manner as he was able.

"You do not care for fish?" Tierza asked.

"I like fish just fine." Aeryk leapt at his chance. "Were it up to me, I'd leave the buggers alone. No harm would come to them by my hand." He waited expectantly. She just looked at him, no smile, no nothing. *Bloody women.*

Reaching up, she ran her fingers lightly through his hair. "You are in need of a haircut, unless you intend to wear yours long in the Elven fashion."

"A haircut sounds like a fine idea. I'm a little nervous about apprentice barbers, though, sharp objects, scissors," Aeryk said carefully, "not to mention razors."

She smiled at that, eyes aglow. "Tomorrow, Aeryk Emyrt, Barber Street, in the hour before sunset, or you and Wyli are both in for a good talking to." Tracing her fingers along his jawline, her lips pursed slightly. "I don't think you'll need to worry much about razors, unless you're late, that is."

"Could we settle on the day after?" Aeryk proffered, unable to take his eyes from hers. "Tomorrow I have to run an errand for Captain Aya."

"An errand," Tierza said ruefully. "What kind of errand?"

"The captain asked me to escort a dispatch rider," Aeryk explained, "bearing a message to whatever lord owns the Greenwood estate north of the city. Apparently, the lord or one of his relations is waiting on a consignment of household goods the Elves are transporting. The shipment has been delayed, and we are to convey the captain's regrets and assurances."

"Hmm." Tierza did not sound mollified. "So you prefer serving as an Elven errand boy to my company?" A dangerous undertone definitely threaded through that silky voice of hers the now.

"I have three perfectly good reasons for making the trip," Aeryk demurred, "silver talents all."

"Three silver talents for what? Less than a day's ride?" Tierza exclaimed. At his nod, she continued. "Tell me, Aeryk Emyrt, how do I become an Elven errand boy?"

Aeryk smiled. "Transforming you into anything remotely boyish would be impossible on one end and pure travesty on the other." He saw the candlelight dance in the maple depths of her eyes as Tierza answered his smile with one of her own.

"The day after, then," she agreed. "Don't be late."

Thatch appeared, looming over the table—the big man loomed very effectively, Aeryk thought.

Plunking down the wooden mug, Thatch declared, "Stingy guts."

Glancing at the few coins gathered at the bottom of the mug, Tierza looked up at the burly barman, shrugged, and smiled. "It's all right, Master Thatch. I've run into a windfall." Handing him a silver talent, she ordered, "We'll have a bottle of your finest—something dark, I think, and sweet—and some bread and cheese and a little beef."

Aeryk couldn't help wondering how she'd managed to pull the coin, assuming it was the coin, out from between ... well, out of her bodice anyway without him noticing.

Pocketing the silver piece, Thatch said, "Right away, lass."

As he turned to go, Tierza called out, "Oh, Master Thatch ..." The barman paused, looking at her inquisitively. "No fish, if you please."

Perplexed, the barrel-chested barkeep nodded. "Right you are, lass, no fish indeed."

Giggling like a little girl, Tierza slipped her hand into Aeryk's. "You don't mind?"

So it had been his coin. *How in the name of all the Fates had she done it?* "Money well spent," he said, "two times over." Her smile this time was both warm and bright.

Thatch brought no change with the meal. Apparently, dark, sweet wine—Valerian, Thatch called it—was expensive. Aeryk found the wine too sweet, actually; cloying, almost. Having already eaten, Aeryk wasn't particularly hungry, but the beef tasted good, the bread even better, and the cheese had a smoky flavor he especially liked. They talked about small things while they ate. After the meal, Tierza straightened, pushing full back in her chair.

"Time to go," she announced.

"I'll walk you home," he offered.

"If you walk me home, you will have no excuse whatever for being late for our appointment, and that could lead to tragic consequences," Tierza said, and her tone brooked no nonsense. "Thatch will see me home. He always does. He has a daughter"—her voice softened—"like me." She indicated her left leg. "Except that Sylva was born lame. When I was a little girl, my foot caught under the wheel of a cart. The bones in my ankle were crushed. An infection set in. I was near death when the healer came. It was a miracle, really. Healers didn't often come to"—she paused a moment—"to where I grew up." Tierza's eyes were far away. "At first, the healer wanted to take my foot off. My mother wouldn't hear of it. Said she'd rather see me dead. Girl children aren't worth all that much, where I'm from, and maimed ones even less."

"Time heals wounds," Basyl once told him, *"but some scars never fade."*

"The healer was able to ward off the infection," Tierza went on. Aeryk could not be sure if she was still talking to him or not. "He saved my life, my leg, and my foot. But he could not correct all the damage. Too much time had passed since the injury. So I was left a cripple. My mother was very disappointed." Not knowing what to say, Aeryk kept silent. After a moment, Tierza took his left hand in both of hers and squeezed. "Do you like to dance, Aeryk?"

"It's all right for some, I reckon. Not me. Bloody waste of time, as far as I'm concerned. I'd much rather sit and listen to a lyre and a song well sung."

Leaning forward, she stretched up and kissed him on the cheek. "Come to Barber Street when you can, Aeryk Emyrt," Tierza murmured. "You will always find welcome there."

19

Precipitous Action

Jyn-Ael-Tor had insisted Aeryk meet her at the main gate of the Elven villa. Knowing the ride to the Greenwood estate, north of the city, and back would take the better part of a day, Aeryk had strapped his spare plaid and an oiled canvas groundsheet to the cantle of his saddle and packed rations for two days on the trail, just in case. Aeryk decided to leave his targe behind but filled his saddle quiver with six throwing darts—five standard plus the heartstone-tipped weapon Danyl had gifted him.

Further armed, as usual, with baelryc and dirk, Aeryk dismounted a few paces outside the gate and tugged his battered, broad-brimmed trail hat a touch further down across his brow to shield against the glare of the rising sun. Jyn appeared just as the blazing orb broke above the horizon.

Resplendent in a cream-colored silk blouse tucked neatly into snug-fitting brown-leather breeches and a pair of finely crafted knee-high calfskin boots, Jyn also wore a lightweight pearl-grey woolen cloak about her shoulders. A johten hung in a richly worked leather scabbard over her left hip, and a long-bladed dagger, sheathed, was attached to the wide leather belt wound about her narrow waist above her right hip. A deeply recurved bow rested in a case strapped to the left side of her saddle, while a large quiver of white goose-feather-fletched arrows angled downward, back to front, on the right.

Jyn sat astride the same Enduyi mare she'd ridden the day before. Clean lined, the roan appeared nearly as sleek and graceful as the elf herself. With her light-blond hair bound up in a single braid looped over one shoulder, Jyn had also donned a grey-felt hat called a fore-and-aft cap. Though the felt looked sturdy enough, the fore-and-aft cap lacked a brim and, to Aeryk's eyes, did not appear to be a very practical piece of headgear.

"Good morning, Aeryk Emyrt," Jyn greeted him in the crisp tone he'd become accustomed to hearing from her. She executed a brief, seated bow from the saddle.

Aeryk bowed and smiled up at her. "No complaints so far."

"Shall we go?" Without waiting for a response from him, Jyn urged her horse to a trot, heading down the street toward the river. Clambering quickly onto Wyli's back, Aeryk followed.

As they passed through the city gate, Aeryk guided Wyli up to the side of Jyn-Ael-Tor's mare. "Have I worn out my welcome, dymena?" Aeryk asked.

"It is not that I find your company objectionable, Aeryk Emyrt." Jyn looked his way. He could read nothing in the honeyed recesses of her eyes. "Merely unwarranted."

"Indifference, then." Aeryk sighed. "Familiar ground, at least."

Jyn flashed a smile and then tossed her head. She set a brisk pace, traveling north out of the city along a dirt road that paralleled the River Sayx. After a couple of hours, Jyn reined to a halt beside a narrow stream.

"Let's water the horses and let them blow awhile," Jyn directed.

Swinging down, Jyn led her mare to the water's edge. Aeryk watched with approval as the elf carefully monitored the amount her horse drank. Aeryk allowed Wyli his turn and then emulated Jyn, tying the gelding's reins to a low-hanging bough beside the Elfin's Enduyi mare.

"We should be there in less than an hour," Jyn estimated.

Searching for something to break the ensuing silence, Aeryk said, "Dymena, I've heard Captain Aya sometimes address Sam and me using *thee* or *thou*."

Jyn nodded. "Such usage is what Elven kind refer to as familiar speech. It is often employed ceremonially or upon first meeting, but more generally, the familiar is used when speaking to friends and family, and among lovers, of course."

"Is there any particular significance?" Aeryk inquired.

"Familiar use is merely an alternative form of address," Jyn informed him with an inscrutable gleam in her luminous, almond-shaped eyes. "This is so, unless one speaks of love. *I love thee*, spoken four times, is, with the barest nod of acceptance, a marriage, an oath that binds two as one for life." Jyn took a seat on the trunk of a toppled cottonwood close to hand.

"Four times," Aeryk exclaimed. "Doesn't that seem a little redundant?" Aeryk found a spot to sit at a fork in the deadfall a couple of paces from where Jyn sat.

"Anything may be said once," Jyn replied, amber eyes aglow, "and once said repeated. Saying it a third time means the speaker is in earnest, and the fourth utterance is a promise, the life-mate's oath, made for all Providence to hear. Be careful of the fourth *thee*, Aeryk."

"I will that," Aeryk agreed, thinking that perhaps he had strayed into dangerous territory. To those of the Brynnai faith, as most Kylgahran, including Aeryk, were, four was a sacred number. Perhaps this stood true of the Elves as well.

Aeryk shifted his weight and then yelped. "Ow, bloody damn, that hurt." He leapt to his feet.

"What happened?" Jyn rose and crossed quickly to his side.

"I don't know." Aeryk clapped his hand to the back of his right thigh, just below his buttock. "It feels like the mother of all bee stings."

Jyn knelt, peering carefully at the bough upon which Aeryk had been sitting, "A Jacken wasp," she exclaimed, pointing at a large winged insect, with a deep-green body nearly two finger widths in length. "You've crushed the poor thing."

"Serves the bugger right," Aeryk proclaimed. "That critter stung me clear through my bloody trousers."

"The sting of a Jacken is memorable," Jyn allowed, "but not venomous, at least not enough so to do any harm to a creature as large as yourself, Aeryk Emyrt. Aside from the pain, a single sting is not serious." She pointed to the insect. "The wasp's stinger is still intact. A welt is likely to form soon, and it will no doubt be a bit sore and perhaps itchy for the next couple of days but should do you no lasting harm."

"You seem to know a good deal about Jacken wasps, dymena," Aeryk noted. "I've never heard of them."

"They are native to Ilyria," Jyn told him. He caught the glint in her eye. "It is widely believed that Jackens were introduced to these shores from the holds of our ships."

"Remind me to thank you properly for that when I get the chance, dymena," Aeryk said wryly. With an effort, he managed, barely, to keep his hand off his bum. *That bloody hurt.*

"The oil of the chola plant is an effective treatment for the itch and soreness," Jyn proffered, as a hint of a smile touched her lips. "If we see any along the way, I'll make you a poultice."

Jyn eased the pace for the remainder of the ride to the Greenwood estate. Whether in deference to his damaged backside or not, Aeryk could not have said. An hour and a half more it took before the estate's lodgings came into view. Located on a small hill overlooking the River Sayx, the manor house stood surrounded by a number of outbuildings. The complex, as a whole, was encompassed by a wooden palisade. A large courtyard lined with young apple trees fronted the manor. Beyond the palisade, Aeryk saw large tracts of land under cultivation, well-ripened corn and wheat, mostly.

Jyn, with Aeryk riding at her side, approached the main gate, a double-wide postern large enough to readily accommodate passage of six horses riding abreast. A half dozen guards in chain mail armed with round shields and spears manned the front gate. When challenged, Jyn informed the sentries that she bore a message for Duke Highgarden from the commander of the Elven contingent in

Cos. The lead sentry passed Jyn and Aeryk through without further questioning.

Upon entering the compound, Aeryk saw a large gathering on the front lawn. Tables had been set, it appeared, in preparation for a meal to be taken out of doors. Aeryk glanced at the sky and noted at least a couple of hours remained before noon.

"A midday feast," Jyn informed him without his having to ask, "in honor of Lord Felix Clearview's birthday. Felix Clearview is the duke's cousin, and master of this estate. The duke is visiting in preparation for occupying his new holdings at Balmuir, a long day's ride to the northwest."

"It is barely mid-morning, dymena," Aeryk pointed out.

"Proper Syrdisian midday feasts begin in the middle of the morning," Jyn informed him, "and continue well into the afternoon."

A pair of grooms appeared, offering to look after their horses. Dismounting, Jyn removed her cloak, draping it across her saddle bow, and passed along the reins of her mount to the first groom. Shrugging free of his plaid, Aeryk stepped from the saddle and handed Wyli's reins to the second groom. Jyn led Aeryk toward a pavilion erected at one end of the long line of tables. A small group of men in silk coats milled about near the entrance. A guard, bareheaded but wearing mail, armed with broadsword and a light axe thrust through his belt, intercepted Jyn as she neared the tent.

"What is your business here?" the guard inquired, speaking in a neutral tone of voice. Green-eyed with blond hair, the man stood a full head taller than Aeryk, with massive shoulders and a chest to match.

"I am Dymena Jyn-Ael-Tor, an Ilyrian representative," Jyn responded. "I bear a message for Duke Highgarden from the commander of the Elven mercenary contingent in Cos."

"Follow me." The guard walked to a small table standing to one side of the pavilion. Aeryk saw the table was lined with food—baked goods, it looked like; an assortment of wine bottles, a number already decanted; and an array of goblets, plates, and trays. "Wait here if you please, my lady," the guard directed. "Help yourself to the refreshments." Saluting, the guard strode to the tent and spoke briefly to a man wearing a dark-green waistcoat and trousers.

Aeryk's eyes went immediately to the pastry dishes. "Don't you dare," Jyn whispered.

Aeryk noticed some stirring among the men in silk coats. A young man emerged, clad in a richly embroidered dark-blue waistcoat and tan trousers, both crafted of silk. Mid-twenties, Aeryk guessed, medium height and build, the man already showed a paunch at his middle. He wore an elaborately hilted straight sword at his waist.

Flanked by a pair of guards dressed in black-leather cuirasses and armed with broadswords and trailed by a trio of middle-aged fellows in various shades of silk, the young man strolled toward Jyn. The elf closed the distance between them by taking two quick steps; she bowed, formally. The young man stopped and smiled. He was good-looking, if not quite handsome, tending to jowl, Aeryk saw, with brown hair and eyes.

"Welcome to Greenwood, dymena," he announced, speaking in the crisp, rounded tones of the well-educated. "I am Felix Clearview, High Lord of Syrdis and master of this estate."

"Thank you, my lord," Jyn replied evenly. "I am Dymena Jyn-Ael-Tor of the House of Tor. Congratulations on your birthday."

Felix Clearview smiled, flashing white, evenly spaced teeth. "You appear to be out of uniform, my dear."

"I am not here in a military capacity, my lord," Jyn stated.

Clearview's eyes roamed languidly over the young Elfin standing before him, at her close-fitting silk blouse and leather trousers. His smile broadened. "I'm not complaining, dymena; your attire is as appealing as it is provocative."

"I find it utilitarian, my lord," Jyn said matter-of-factly. Aeryk eyed Lord Felix's guards. Both stood half a head taller than he and every bit as wide across the shoulders.

"Indeed." Lord Clearview stared openly at Jyn's bosom for a moment.

Having spent some time in Jyn's presence resisting the very same temptation, Aeryk had to allow some sympathy, but he quickly came to the conclusion he didn't like the fancy bugger. *He's wearing a silk shirt with ruffles at the sleeves, for Fates' sake.*

"My cousin Duke Martyn went hunting early this morning," Felix Clearview went on. "He is expected back shortly. In the interim, I offer you the hospitality of my home."

"You are very kind, my lord," Jyn asserted.

"And quite curious," Lord Felix pronounced. "To date, I've experienced only limited close association with Elven kind."

"It is a pleasure to make your acquaintance, my lord," Jyn assured him.

"Excellent," Felix Clearview proclaimed. "I always strive for mutual pleasure when dealing with female acquaintances."

Aeryk walked up to the side table. He noted a pair of goblets already filled with wine, set upon a sturdy metal tray. Aeryk folded a serving towel over his left arm and took up the tray.

"You are truly lovely, dymena," Lord Felix was saying, "in an odd sort of way; quite exotic, really, like a rare species of bird or fish."

You scralyng, Aeryk thought.

"No more exotic than your birthday feast, my lord," Jyn proffered smoothly.

Lord Felix's smile returned. "You really must try the blue perch, my lady, as is it native to the River Sayx."

"I shall make a point of it, my lord," Jyn told him.

"The sigil engraved upon the hilt of your sword is that of Order Castellan," Lord Felix observed.

"I'm gratified you noticed, my lord," Jyn said dryly.

"You've taken the Castellan oaths, then, never to wed and the like," Lord Felix prompted.

"And the like, my lord," Jyn affirmed.

"Your oaths do not preclude the taking of lovers, I understand," Lord Felix remarked.

"That is one interpretation, my lord," Jyn acknowledged.

"Have you taken many lovers, my lady?" Lord Felix inquired. Aeryk took a step nearer.

"I am not at liberty to say, my lord," Jyn demurred. Aeryk saw Jyn's chin lift and her shoulders square up.

"Ah, but you see, dear lady, I am not nearly as interested in what people say as in what they do." Lord Felix took a step closer and leaned in. "You must tell me, my lady, before I perish of curiosity: what color are your nipples?"

Jyn didn't so much as blink. "Nearly a match for my lips, your lordship."

"Intriguing," Lord Felix enthused. "The imagination reels." He winked. "Forgive me, my dear," Lord Felix entreated, "but I really must insist upon closer examination." The Syrdisian noble extended his right hand, reaching for Jyn's left breast.

Jyn pivoted effortlessly, turning her torso away, thereby avoiding his touch. Lord Felix's left hand shot out, clasping Jyn about her right wrist. Jyn stiffened.

Aeryk quickly closed the distance separating them. "Your wine, dymena," he said. He saw Jyn glance toward him.

"Aah," Aeryk cried, clapping his right hand to the base of his buttock. As he did so, Aeryk's left arm shot forward, depositing both goblets of wine all over the front of Lord Felix's fancy silk coat. "I've been stung," Aeryk moaned.

"You idiot!" Lord Felix exclaimed. Releasing Jyn's wrist, Lord Felix looked down, aghast at the ruin Aeryk had made of his raiment.

"Terribly sorry, your honor," Aeryk professed. "Let me help you." Transferring the towel to his right hand while holding on to the tray with his left, Aeryk hurried forward and began to wipe down the front of Lord Felix's coat. Stepping close, Aeryk managed to trod heavily on his lordship's instep.

Lord Felix howled. "Get away from me, you clumsy lout." He pushed at Aeryk, who simultaneously lowered his shoulder. Lord Felix staggered backwards, nearly losing his balance.

"All right, you," the guard nearest Aeryk cried, closing quickly. The guard tried to grab hold of Aeryk's shirt front. Using the serving tray, Aeryk swatted his hand away.

"Easy, boyo," Aeryk warned, sidestepping to his left.

"Easy this," the guard snarled, snapping an overhand right at Aeryk's face. Aeryk again raised the tray as a shield. The tray was fashioned of heavy brass. The guard grimaced as his fist thunked solidly into it. Aeryk darted close, bringing his right knee up into the guardsman's groin. The guard grunted, and Aeryk slammed the heel of his right hand into the base of the guard's jaw. Slipping his left foot behind the larger man's right, Aeryk shoved. The guard toppled onto the lawn.

The first guard's companion squared off in front of Aeryk, dropping his hand to the grip of his broadsword. Aeryk turned to face him, the fingers of his right hand coiling about the hilt of his dirk.

"Hold, the both of you!" Jyn-Ael-Tor shouted in a voice that expected to be obeyed. Aeryk froze. The guard hesitated. Jyn stepped adroitly between them.

"What is going on here?" a deep, masculine voice, fairly ringing with authority, called out. The second guard snapped to attention, while the first climbed somewhat painfully to his feet and followed suit. Aeryk took a step back and turned to his left.

He saw a man, clad in a brown-leather jacket worn over a cream-colored silk shirt and grey woolen trousers approaching. The stranger looked to be about thirty years of age. Family resemblance to Lord Felix showed unmistakably in the shape of his face and the color of his hair. About the same height as Felix, the newcomer's build was leaner, more muscular. The sword he wore over his left hip featured a plain workman-like hilt, clearly a fighting weapon. A single guard, the largest Aeryk had yet seen, dressed in mail with broadsword and axe in his belt, strode easily, two steps behind and slightly to the left.

"Your Grace," one of the middle-aged fellows in silk hastened, speaking to the man in the brown jacket. "I'm afraid we've experienced a bit of an altercation."

"Apparently," Martyn Clearview, Duke of Highgarden, observed wryly. The duke's eyes, an icy shade of blue, settled upon Jyn. "You are the Elven emissary?"

"I am, Your Grace." Jyn bowed formally. "Dymena Jyn-Ael-Tor of the House of Tor."

The duke nodded. "Explain," he commanded.

"Lord Felix and I were conversing, in anticipation of your arrival," Jyn began. "My man"—she nodded at Aeryk—"attempted to serve some wine. Startled by an apparent wasp sting, he managed to spill wine all over Lord Felix's coat. My man then compounded his error by rather clumsily attempting to wipe down his lordship's attire. Lord Felix's guards took exception, and precipitous action ensued."

"You don't look like the type that startles easily." Duke Martyn's ice-blue eyes rested upon Aeryk. "A Jacken, was it?"

"I reckon, Your Grace," Aeryk said.

"A Jacken sting will get your attention." The Duke's gaze never wavered. "Leaves quite a welt, usually. Did you know it takes a few hours for the weal to form? A fresh bite will show only a mild discoloration."

"I was not aware of that, Your Grace," Aeryk allowed. Aeryk's pulse began to pound under the weight of Martyn Clearview's frosty regard.

"What would you have done if Charl, here"—the duke indicated the second guard—"had drawn his sword?"

The duke's a scrapper, not like that turd of a cousin of his—the thought calmed Aeryk. "I'd have taken him with my dirk, Your Grace."

"A knife against a broadsword," Duke Martyn questioned.

"Close quarters, Your Grace," Aeryk replied steadily, indicating Felix's two guards with a nod of his head. "Those two are sturdy enough but none too quick."

Duke Martyn's smile never touched his wintry eyes. "A Kylgahran all right enough." He shook his head. "I could have you flogged, boy, whether you've got a fresh wasp sting on your bum or not."

"Your Grace," Jyn intervened, her voice calm but emphatic, "my man's behavior was inexcusable, and he deserves to be chastised thoroughly. But as he is my man, that responsibility falls to me."

"A fine point, dymena," Duke Martyn countered, "but then I'd expect no less of an elf." The duke turned to Lord Felix. "The next time you feel inclined to grab some Elfin's tit, cousin, I suggest you do so in a less public environ, without her Kylgahran watchdog standing close to hand."

Felix flushed but said nothing.

The duke returned his attention to Jyn-Ael-Tor. "You have a message for me, dymena?"

"We received word the consignment of goods scheduled for delivery here in two days has been delayed—a river barge incident—for perhaps as long as a week, Your Grace," Jyn expounded.

"Goddammit," Duke Martyn growled, "that bloody shipment is a week late as it is."

"My commander assures that as soon as the consignment arrives, she will see personally to its safe delivery to Balmuir at no further expense to you, Your Grace."

"No further expense, my ass," Duke Martyn fumed. "You tell your commander that if my household goods don't arrive intact in ten days' time, her bloody order will recompense me entirely, plus two thousand talents silver for my pains. Do ya hear?"

"I shall relay your message, Your Grace," Jyn averred. "If it pleases Your Grace, there is a final matter, one I was instructed to convey to you only in private."

The Duke sighed. "Bloody Elves."

"Aye," Aeryk commiserated without thinking.

Duke Martyn barked a laugh. He pointed at Jyn and Aeryk. "Come along, you two." He turned away. "And you also, cousin." With the big guardsman trailing along, Jyn, Aeryk, and Lord Felix followed the duke to the nearest outbuilding, a storehouse constructed of stone with a wood shingle roof.

The duke opened the door and spoke to his guard. "See we are not disturbed, Gill." The big man's eyes flicked to Aeryk. Duke Martyn smiled. "Don't fret; the lad's a hound, not a wolf. I won't be long."

The guard nodded, saying not a word, and took up station beside the door. Entering the storeroom, the duke waited until the rest preceded him and then closed the door. Light spilled in from a pair of windows set high in adjacent walls, illuminating the chamber.

"All right, what is it?" Duke Martyn demanded.

Jyn extracted a heavy piece of folded vellum from a pouch attached to the back of her belt and silently handed it over to the duke. Aeryk noticed the blue wax seal on the document, an impression showing a cross embedded in the base of a triangle. The duke stared at the sealed vellum sheet for a moment and slipped it into the inside pocket of his jacket.

"Shall we leave you to examine the contents, Your Grace?" Jyn inquired.

Duke Martyn shook his head. "That will not be necessary, dymena, nor will I require you to wait upon a reply. If such is warranted, I will see to it myself." The duke looked again at Aeryk. "What is your name, boy?"

"Aeryk Emyrt of Clan Ard Mourne, Your Grace."

"Should you ever grow weary of safeguarding Elves, Aeryk Emyrt," Duke Martyn offered, "come see me. I'll find something for you to do."

Aeryk bowed in the manner Basyl had taught him was appropriate in the presence of a laird. "Your Grace," he said.

Jyn and Aeryk departed as soon as their brief interview with the duke concluded. She maintained a dignified silence until the two of them were well clear of the estate. Jyn then rounded on Aeryk. "What in the name of all Providence were you thinking?"

Aeryk resisted, barely, a sudden urge to hunch his shoulders. "I was thinking the paunchy toad had no right to lay his hands on you."

Jyn flared. "Do you think me so feeble, Aeryk Emyrt, as to be unable to defend myself?"

"When I think of you, dymena," Aeryk confessed, "the term feeble does nay come to mind." He saw her amber eyes widen slightly at that, and something he could not read swirled briefly within, replaced a moment later by a flash all too easy to interpret.

"Felix Clearview is a Syrdisian noble," Jyn fairly spat at him.

"Lord Paunchy Toad, then," Aeryk shot back. "He still had no right to paw at you. Besides ... well ... you looked distressed."

"I was startled," Jyn contended, vexed. "I didn't ..." She took a breath. "In future, Aeryk Emyrt, you are not to come to my aid unless I ask for help."

"Oh, aye," Aeryk groused, "we should have a system of signals. One finger, and I'm to allow whoever it is to fondle ye some more; two fingers and I take off his arm. Bloody elf."

Jyn laughed, the sound pure and musical.

Aeryk ducked his head. "I didn't mean to embarrass you, dymena. I'm sorry if I did."

Jyn drew rein. Aeryk brought Wyli to a halt beside her. Jyn's features sobered. "You could have been flogged, or worse."

"Comes to that," Aeryk allowed, "I reckoned you'd protect me, seeing as you are a dymena and all." He looked at her. "You did, too. And I thank you for it."

Jyn's tawny gaze softened. "Turn your shoulder away," she instructed. He complied, and Jyn brought the tag ends of her reins down across his back, just firmly enough for him to feel it. "If anyone asks," Jyn said primly, "we can both attest that you've been lashed for your behavior earlier today. We'll speak no more about it."

Aeryk looked again into her eyes. "As you say, dymena."

20

Friends

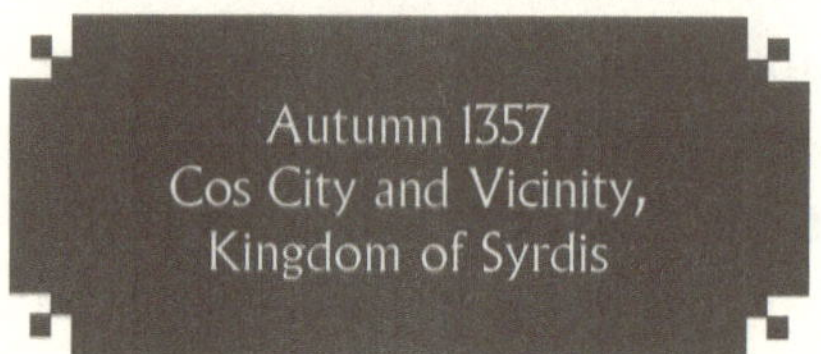

Jyn-Ael-Tor kept to a steady pace on the return trip. An hour's ride south of the estate, she stopped to rest the horses and partake of a brief meal. Aeryk sat cross-legged beside her beneath the spreading branches of a large oak trailside while the horses grazed nearby.

"All that fancy fare," Aeryk lamented, gnawing on a strip of jerked beef, "and nary a bite for either of us."

Jyn leveled a direct look his way. "And whose fault is that?" she inquired pointedly before biting into a dried apricot.

Despite his best effort, Aeryk couldn't quite banish the sheepish cast from his smile as he answered. "I thought we agreed to speak no more of it."

Jyn merely arched an elegantly curved eyebrow at him, saying nothing as she daintily finished off the apricot.

"The food here is nay so grand, nor the gathering so well attended," Aeryk proclaimed, "but I much prefer the company."

"I'm gratified to hear it," Jyn noted. "For someone who agreed to speak naught of it, you seem determined to return to the topic." That shut him up.

A couple of hours further on, the two of them approached a fork in the road. Aeryk saw they didn't have much further to go—the wooden walls of Cos rose above the plain, visible to the south.

Jyn brought her mare to a halt. "Have you ever seen the Stair Step Falls?"

"No, dymena," Aeryk confessed. "I can't say that I have."

Jyn hesitated for a moment, glancing at him and then lowering her eyes. "Would you care for a brief excursion? We have made good time, and I have no further duties assigned this day."

Aeryk smiled. "And will incur none until after our return."

Jyn smiled back, and her chin dipped, indicating the accuracy of his observation. "A brief excursion on horseback sounds a fine idea to me, dymena," Aeryk professed.

Jyn led him down the left-hand fork toward the river, where the Sayx split into a narrow side channel. While only a small portion of the mighty river's water flowed through the cut, it did so in a torrent, tumbling and frothing over a series of large, rectangular slabs of rock that did indeed resemble a set of steps carved into the riverbed and over a corresponding set of waterfalls, the highest of which easily encompassed the height of a tall man. Reining in along the riverbank downstream of the falls, Jyn informed Aeryk that the Ilyrian Islands were a land of waterfalls and white-water rapids.

Some distance upstream from where their horses stood, Aeryk spotted a light wagon hitched to a team of two horses, parked on the same side of the river as they were. Long training under Danyl and later under Sam and Wyatt's watchful eyes had taught him to look closely. A man and a woman he saw, and four children—a family they were, most likely. They had a cook fire burning. He caught sight of a kettle suspended above it from a black iron stanchion. The wagon looked pretty beat up. He hoped, for their sake, they were coming, not going.

"What are rivers like in Kylgahra?" Jyn wondered.

"Wet, I imagine," Aeryk quipped and then added more seriously, "Having never been there, I'm only guessing, dymena." Jyn cocked her head to one side, the question written large in the golden whorls of her eyes. "I was born and raised out east in the Lywgahra," Aeryk explained. "I'm something of a back-door Highlander. I've yet to actually set foot in Kylgahra proper." He could tell by the slight widening of her eyes more questions were headed his way. The next thing he heard, though, was a scream coming from upstream.

Looking in that direction, he saw the woman from the group gathered at the wagon, pointing to something in the river and shouting for the man to come quick.

"I see a child in the river," Jyn cried, dismounting and unbuckling the belt holding her sword and dagger. Looping the weapons belt over her saddle bow, the elf glanced back at Aeryk. "Look for us downstream. I may need help getting out of the river."

"Jyn, wait!" Aeryk shouted. "The water's moving too fast. You'll both drown."

Jyn wasn't listening. The young Elfin sprinted to the water's edge. Tossing aside her cap, Jyn pulled off her boots and, looking carefully into the water to make certain she had the child in sight, dove in head first. The elf's slim body sliced cleanly into the torrent, and moments later, he saw her swimming strongly, angling toward the boy, who seemed to be bobbing helplessly in the current.

"Shite," Aeryk swore. "Bloody elf."

Aeryk turned Wyli about, and they pounded downstream, pulling Jyn's mare along behind. Despite peering constantly over his left shoulder in an attempt to keep Jyn in sight, he could see neither the elf nor the boy she was attempting to rescue. Aeryk noticed a flat spot in the bank a short distance ahead. He urged Wyli down to it, praying for all he was worth. *"Fates, be kind."* Scanning the river upstream, he caught sight of them. Jyn had reached the boy, for all the good it was likely to do either of them. Apparently a very strong swimmer, the Elfin had managed to steer toward the near bank. Despite Jyn's heroics, Aeryk realized that in a few moments, the current would carry them past the point where he and Wyli stood.

Dropping the reins to Jyn's Enduyi, Aeryk gigged his horse forward. Most horses didn't like water all that much, especially fast-moving water, but the sturdy Morgyn never hesitated. Wyli pushed into the river; the footing seemed sure enough, and Wyli stood steady against the current. The water rose quickly, though, and soon Aeryk dared go no further.

Loosening his ryatta, Aeryk looped one end 'round his saddle horn and made ready to cast the rope. "Jyn!" he shouted, holding the rope above his head. The Elfin saw him and somehow managed a quick wave. Promising himself he was going to throttle the elf if the river didn't get them all first, Aeryk cast his rope. A good toss—*Thank the Fates*—and Jyn grabbed hold. Moments later, the rope went taught. Aeryk could feel Wyli's muscles bunch beneath him, taking the strain.

"Back, boy, easy back," Aeryk called hauling gently on the reins. Wyli dug in and backed them out of the river. Dismounting, Aeryk caught hold of the rope and pulled hand over hand, dragging Jyn and the boy through the shallows to the bank. "Are you all right?" Aeryk called.

Exhausted, Jyn nodded. "Take the boy, Aeryk. Take the boy."

Lifting the child—about nine or ten, Aeryk estimated—into his arms, he carried the youth a few steps up the riverbank and laid him down. The boy's face was pale and a bluish tinge clung to his lips. He did not think the child was breathing. Casting aside his trail hat, Aeryk remembered something Danyl had taught him.

Aeryk tilted the child's head back, pinched his nose shut, and breathed into the boy's mouth. Nothing happened. Not knowing what else to do, he tried again and again. Suddenly, the youngster began to cough, and water spewed from his mouth. Turning the boy onto his side, Aeryk rubbed his shoulders and scarcely dared to hope. The child took a ragged breath and continued to cough. Already Aeryk saw the boy's color looked better.

He felt a hand on his shoulder. "How did you know to do that?" Jyn asked, amazed.

Grinning, Aeryk said, "An old trick that sometimes works." *Fates bless you, Danyl Trask, you old badger,* Aeryk thought. He noticed the child shivering. Aeryk's shirt was mostly dry. Pulling it off, he wrapped it about the lad's shoulders. Standing, he turned to look at Jyn. The elf stood soaking wet, and her lips seemed drained of color. Moving quickly to his horse, Aeryk untied his plaid from its usual spot. Returning to the elf's side, he reached out to wrap the woolen garment about her.

Jyn protested weakly, saying, "The boy ..."

"He'll be all right," Aeryk insisted. As he placed the plaid about Jyn's shoulders, he saw blood coursing down her left arm. "You're bleeding," he said.

Jyn nodded. "A snag in the river. I don't think it is too bad."

Untying the tartyn about his throat, he started to wrap it about the young elf's upper arm. Jyn stayed him by placing a hand on his. "You'll ruin that," she said, indicating the silk neckerchief.

Leaning back just enough so that he could look Jyn directly in the eyes, Aeryk growled, "You know you're going the right way for a good thumping."

Jyn smiled at that and made no further protest as he wrapped and tied the tartyn over the cut in her arm and then finished pulling his plaid about her shoulders. Kneeling again at the boy's side, he helped the youngster to a sitting position. He was a skinny, hawk-nosed little fellow, with a mass of light brown hair. "Are you all right?" Aeryk asked, speaking Aylitic.

"Thank ... thank you," the boy stammered.

"Thank the Elfin," Aeryk said, jerking his thumb in Jyn's direction. "She is the one what fetched you out of the river."

The boy looked past Aeryk's shoulder at Jyn, blue eyes widening in recognition. "Elves are spawn of the Tainted One!" he cried, loudly enough, Aeryk was certain, that Jyn could hear.

Genuinely angry the now, Aeryk said, "I don't know who this Tainted One is, boy, but that elf sure enough just saved your scrawny hide."

"Jervis!" The man from the wagon rushed up, breathing hard. "Oh, thank God." Wrapping the youth in his arms, the stranger hugged him tightly. The man looked like an older, larger version of the boy, brown haired, blue eyed, with a hawk's beak of a nose. Raising his eyes to Aeryk, he said. "Thank you. Thank you for my boy's life. We don't have much. How can we ever repay you?"

"Tell you what," Aeryk said, trying to keep the anger out of his voice. "Thank my friend, here, who risked her life in the river for your boy's sake, and we'll call it even."

The man looked at Jyn. Aeryk saw his features tighten. He glanced back at Aeryk and then spoke, stiffly, to the air somewhere above Jyn's head. "Thank you for my boy's life." Lifting the child into his arms, the man pulled Aeryk's shirt free and dropped the garment into the dirt at his feet. Without another word, he turned and walked away, carrying the child in his arms.

Embarrassed the now, as well as angry, Aeryk bent down, retrieved his shirt, and walked back to the elf's side. "Sorry, Jyn; that is, dymena," he said, shaking his head before donning the garment. "I just ... some people, I can't figure."

"Every now and then," Jyn said mildly, her amber-eyed gaze fixed upon him, "you meet someone who surprises you."

Aeryk heard a tremor in the elf's voice. Drawing close, he noticed that Jyn was trembling. Jyn's face looked drawn and a grey cast had enveloped her mouth. She swayed slightly. Instinctively wrapping his arms about the slender elf, he gasped, "Light, Jyn, you're freezing."

Jyn sagged against him, shivering violently. "The water was so cold, Aeryk, so cold."

Easing Jyn to a sitting position on the ground, he said, "Hang on." Loosening the girth, Aeryk pulled Wyli's belly strap free and hauled his saddle down. Laying the saddle on the ground next to Jyn, he removed the saddle blanket from Wyli's back and placed it in front of his saddle. Helping Jyn on to the blanket, he rested her back against the warm underside of the saddle. Aeryk untied Jyn's blanket roll and spread the grey woolen cloth over her. He next tugged his spare plaid and groundsheet free from his saddle and added them to the coverings over Jyn's still quaking form. After unsaddling Jyn's Enduyi mare, Aeryk took a close look about.

"Rest a bit the now," he enjoined. "I'll be right back."

The Fates were kind as he hurried along the riverbank; a deadfall lay close by. Drawing his baelryc, he slashed a few dead branches free and stripped some bark as well. Not bothering to sheath his sword, he gathered the kindling into his arms and rushed back to where Jyn lay. Dropping the pile nearby, he pulled flint and steel from his saddle bag to start a fire.

"That is poor use of good steel, Aeryk." Jyn said, indicating the tangle of firewood and his sword where it lay in the dirt.

"Next time I go for a brief excursion with you, Jyn," Aeryk said evenly, "I'll know to bring an axe, some extra blankets, and a bloody rowboat. This being my first trip, I was a little unprepared." The elf laughed softly at that, which would have cheered him, except her laughter ended in a ragged cough. With the fire going, Aeryk turned his attention once again to the young elf. Kneeling at her side, he noted Jyn was still shivering. "Jyn, your clothes are soaked. We need to get you out of your blouse, at least." With a nod, Jyn reached for the top of her blouse with her uninjured arm, fumbling at the laces fastening the garment.

Helping Jyn to sit up, Aeryk gently pushed her hand aside and undid the stays. He turned away as Jyn wriggled free of her blouse and trousers as well. She passed the sodden garments to him. Aeryk took up the clothes and laid them on top of Jyn's saddle. Fishing out his dirk, he cut a couple of supple branches from what looked to him to be a poplar tree close to hand. Driving the ends of the branches into the ground on the far side of the fire, he bent them toward one another and entwined the leaf laden tips. He then draped Jyn's clothing over the lashed-together branches to dry.

Retrieving his sword, he sheathed the weapon. Rummaging again through his saddlebag, Aeryk removed a leather-bound flask and a small waxed canvas bag. He took a seat at the side of the Elfin's blanket-shrouded form and gently grasped her left arm, careful not to touch the wound.

"Dymena," he said quietly, "I need to have a look at that cut." Jyn responded with a vague nod of her head. "Come on," he encouraged. "You need to sit up again, just for a little while."

Gingerly unwrapping the tartyn from about Jyn's upper arm, he briefly examined the wound. The cut did not look too deep, a ragged tear in the flesh about two finger widths in length. He pulled the stopper from the flask with his teeth, speaking round the cork with a hint of satisfaction in his voice. "This is going to sting some."

"What is that?" Jyn asked, indicating the flask with a thrust of her chin. The elf seemed to be more alert, for which he thanked the Fates.

"Wysoi," Aeryk said, spitting out the cork. "Highland nectar, good for what ails you, inside and out." Voicing no further warning, he poured a liberal dose on to the cut. Jyn hissed in pain as the alcohol soaked into the torn flesh of her arm. "Here"—he extended the flask to the elf—"it feels better inside; trust me." The elf hesitated. "Go on," Aeryk urged. "It will warm you up."

Jyn took a swallow and then gasped, coughing. "Nectar?" she exclaimed after taking a couple of breaths. "It tastes more like liquid fire."

"Swallowing it is the tricky bit. Bide a minute and get acquainted," Aeryk advised. "Take another; you'll be glad you did." Jyn complied, somewhat reluctantly, and then handed him back the flask. Downing a quick draught himself, just to be polite, Aeryk grimaced and gave his head a shake. "That will get your attention, all right enough."

Setting aside the flask, he extracted a small enameled clay jar from the canvas bag. Freeing the cork from the opening of the jar, Aeryk dipped his fingers into the mixture inside.

"Now what?" Jyn asked, a little apprehensively.

"This is a salve. It helps to relieve pain and ward off infection," Aeryk explained. "It is made from the oil of the umbar plant, juniper berries, and other goodly stuff." Noting the look on Jyn's face, he smiled. "Don't worry; the salve is for external use only."

He rubbed a healthy dollop into the wound and took note of Jyn's reaction.

The elf arched one pale blond eyebrow and said, "That actually seems to help." After a moment, the elf exclaimed, laying a hand on her belly, "Oh! That nectar of yours is warming."

With a nod of his head, Aeryk observed, "It's good medicine, Jyn. You'll be right as rain soon enough." After rebandaging her arm, Aeryk examined the elf's face closely. Jyn's delicately shaped features seemed wan, and the grey cast still mantled her lips. Jyn's efforts in the river had amazed him. He knew he could never have made such a swim. Aeryk had no idea how such exertion might affect an elf.

He was startled as her fingers closed lightly about his. "You should not worry so much," Jyn chided him gently. "I will be fine."

Shifting so that he could look directly into her eyes, Aeryk said, a little more forcefully than he intended, "Dymena, you scared the shite out of me."

"If it is any consolation, I frightened myself rather thoroughly about halfway along. If you had not been able to reach me with the rope ..." Jyn's voice trailed off into silence. Her eyes found his. "Twice today you have come to my rescue. I did not thank you earlier. I should have. I do so the now. Thank you."

"Aye, well, you're welcome, then and the now," Aeryk relented. "Happy as I am to take the credit, Wyli there did most of the work this time round." He nodded toward his gelding, standing patiently a short distance away. "Speaking of which, I'd better see to them." Rising, he recovered his hat and led the horses a little further into the trees, tying their reins to a pair of low hanging boughs. Aeryk hobbled Jyn's Enduyi mare. He would put no hobble on Wyli. Aeryk scratched the gelding's ears, saying, "Here's my brave lad. Thank ye, fella." Wyli tossed his head, whether in reproach or acknowledgement, Aeryk couldn't say.

Stepping back to Jyn's side, he could see that the elf still shivered, battling the chill. Doffing his trail hat once again, Aeryk unbuckled his belt. Carefully leaning his sword and dirk against his saddle within easy reach, he sat and kicked off his boots. "Shove over," he directed and then lay down beside her as she complied. "No offense," Aeryk hastened to add, slipping his arm around her, "this is only to warm you."

"The warming will be much more effective if we share the blankets," Jyn remarked. Lifting the folds of the coverings, Jyn draped them over Aeryk. Beneath, Aeryk discovered Jyn wore—he knew not what to call it. A camisole, maybe. Thin and wet, whatever it was clung to Jyn's lithe form, leaving little to the imagination. Aeryk quickly looked away. Without hesitation, Jyn settled against him, laying her head on his shoulder.

"Be assured, Aeryk Emyrt," Jyn announced, "should you ever succeed in offending me"—she hiccupped—"you will know it."

He couldn't help smiling at the sound of the hiccup, and it occurred to Aeryk that wysoi might affect Elves a little more strongly than … well, non-Elves. After a few moments, Jyn murmured, "I much prefer this"—she hiccupped—"to drinking wysoi." The elf snuggled just a little. "Very warming, with no unpleasant"—she hiccupped again—"aftertaste."

"Aye, well, as to that, wait until you get to know me a little better," Aeryk said, achingly aware of Jyn's slender body pressed in close contact with his. However alluring the Elfin might be under normal circumstances, Aeryk found that with a case of wysoi-induced hiccups and wearing only her underthings, Jyn was downright enchanting.

A little while later, Jyn spoke tentatively but with no further sign of hiccups. "To the man from the wagon, you said I was your friend."

"Aye," Aeryk confirmed.

"You were angry when you said it." Jyn lifted her head free of his shoulder. "Sometimes, words spoken in anger have no meaning." Beneath the weight of his arm, he could feel the Elfin's muscles tense.

"I'm your friend, Jyn," Aeryk said simply.

"How do you know?" Jyn queried immediately. "We've only just met."

"I don't know how I know; I just do," he mused. The Elfin remained silent. "You stood up to a bloody duke to spare me a flogging; you give of your time to read books to orphans, humans and Halflings," he elaborated, "and it isn't every day I meet someone who bakes as well as you do." With continued silence from the elf, Aeryk felt as if he had his arm around a coiled spring. Speaking from the heart, he went on, "I can't explain it, Jyn, but I know it to be true. I am your friend, and I'd be honored if you will consent to be mine. I'm sorry if I spoke out of turn."

"I'm glad," Jyn said softly. Aeryk felt her relax, her head lowered, resting once more on his shoulder. Jyn's body lay fast against his—supple, firmly muscled in most places, enticingly soft in others. Aeryk's pulse quickened.

"You'll have to be patient with me. I don't have many friends," Jyn said quietly.

"Don't feel bad," Aeryk said lightly. "Aside from you, the best friend I have has four legs." Smiling, he jerked his thumb in Wyli's direction. His smile faded as he realized he spoke the truth. If he didn't count Basyl and Danyl, Fates affirm, it was the truth. Sam would look after him all right enough, and he would follow wherever the tall warrior led, but that was different. He thought of little Estyr, but that was different, too. *Wasn't it?*

"I understand the now, a little. Thank you," Jyn murmured. "We shall help one another, as friends do." He did not know what the elf meant and didn't know how to go about asking without sounding like a child.

A moment passed, and then another. Aeryk was about to speak, intending to change the subject, but when he turned his head, he discovered that Jyn had fallen asleep. The young Elfin breathed easily, and at least she was no longer shivering.

Aeryk must have dozed a little himself. Upon coming fully awake, he saw that the afternoon shadows had lengthened. They were going to have to get moving in order to make it back to the Elven villa by nightfall. Jyn still rested comfortably against him, sound asleep. He tried to slip carefully away. Jyn roused a little in drowsy protest and clung to him. As gently as he could, he disentangled himself and climbed to his feet.

After saddling Jyn's mare, there was no help for it. He had to wake the elf. A firm grip of her shoulder was all it took.

"You must have a clear conscience," Aeryk remarked as Jyn awoke to regard him with those remarkable eyes of hers. Cat-eyed, she was. He decided there was something catlike about her, a kind of tawny grace and self-assurance. Her color had returned.

"How is that?" Jyn asked, stretching like a cat.

The plaid fell away, showing Jyn's sleek young body to full effect.

Dry, the camisole or whatever it was properly called appeared very nearly as revealing as when wet. Burn him if he'd look away this time. Smiling, he said, "You sleep like a sack of cornmeal."

However well spoken, Elves tended toward the literal. "That statement makes no sense," Jyn said as he handed over her blouse. "Cornmeal can neither sleep nor wake," Jyn pointed out, donning the silk garment. "It is inert. Like a log or a rock, or is that the point?"

Aeryk smiled.

"You find that amusing?" Jyn sounded perplexed.

"You don't?" was his rejoinder.

Saddling Wyli with familiar ease took only a few moments. Cinching down his saddle girth, Aeryk looked back over his shoulder. Fully dressed, wrapped in his spare plaid, Jyn stood there, holding the reins to her mount. She cocked her head slightly in the Elven manner and gazed at him intently.

"I suppose it is not necessary that I understand you," Jyn said, as if trying the words on for size. Taking note of the expression on his face, Jyn laughed. "I just realized every road runs two ways."

And just where might this particular path lead? Aeryk wondered. Taking a second look at his companion, Aeryk swore. "Burn me, I forgot about your boots. They must be back upstream a-ways."

Jyn stepped close. "A pair of boots is a small price to pay to discover a friend such as thee, Aeryk Emyrt." The elf climbed into her saddle, moving gracefully despite the injury to her arm. Mounted, Jyn sighed. "I am going to miss my fore-and-aft cap, however."

A fine pair of boots, the elf cares nothing about, but sighs over the loss of a silly hat. Aeryk thought. *Two ways, indeed.*

21

The Courting Road

Two weeks after departing Selkyrk, just before they broke camp for
the morning, Lukas Holt reported to Ranyl that a horse had been
stolen.

"You're certain?" Ranyl inquired.

Luke's response was that he'd seen the tracks himself. The animal stolen was a clean-limbed little sorrel. As best Luke could reckon, the theft happened just before sunrise.

"Take four men," Ranyl instructed, "and give it a full day. If you
haven't run him down by then, head back to the Long Reach. You
should catch up to us before we cross into Clan Ard Ryan territory."
The rawboned scout nodded, chose four rangers—all single men,
Ranyl noted—and took up the pursuit.

In Kylgahra, when a prospective groom or a bride was to travel
to meet their intended, it was said they journeyed along the courting
road. Often, the bride and groom would meet at some point along
the way, and the courting would begin in earnest. Sometimes, in
lieu of nuptials, the courting road would in end with a parting of

198

ways. Ranyl didn't expect to meet Tessymir Ryan until reaching her father's hold.

A signed marriage contract effectively rendered traveling the courting road together superfluous. Still, Ranyl couldn't help wishing he could meet Tessymir privately before the two of them were caught up in the ritual that would culminate in their wedding. About all he knew of his intended was her name, her age—eighteen—and that she was dark of hair with a countenance his father had described as "pleasing enough." Ranyl couldn't help wondering exactly what that meant.

A problem for another day, Ranyl figured. *One not far off,* the voice in his head reminded him. Absently, Ranyl ran his hand along his jaw. He had not shaved for a couple of days. A bad habit, that, he supposed. Plugging along somewhere in the back of beyond, the effort seemed more of a bother than usual. If he got too scruffy-looking, he reckoned Kate or Mae would put a bug in his ear.

Rains had soaked the Long Reach Road off and on for several days past. In the hour after midday, one of the wagons bogged down in a soft spot. By now, Ranyl and his companions had accrued considerable experience with similar occurrences. Familiarity, Ranyl had discovered, didn't make the process of digging the flaming vehicle out any less onerous. Stripping down, Ranyl removed his hat, sword belt, and plaid. Taking up a shovel, he began to clear mud away from the right rear wheel of the wagon. Judging that he'd scooped out enough of the gooey, clay-laden muck, Ranyl and Tad stuffed some dried wood into place in front of the wheel.

Standing shoulder to shoulder, Ranyl, Tad, and the barrel-chested smith, Fyrgus Clyde, shoved from behind, while Fyrgus's youngest boy, Thad, whipped up the horses. Only twelve, Thad was lean as a whippet. The boy took after Emma, his mother, Fyrgus claimed, with blond hair and blues eyes. Young Thad could handle a team all right enough. At his urging, the horses threw their weight into the harness, and the wagon lurched forward. The sudden movement deposited both Tad and Ranyl face down in the mud. Sturdy Fyrgus Clyde managed to keep his feet.

Tuan Marques's laugh rang infectious, lilting, and unguarded. Ranyl and Tad exchanged glances and climbed to their feet to find Fyrgus grinning at the two of them like an oversized imp. "I can't bear to watch any longer," Tuan managed between bouts of mirth, "not with these ribs."

"Lucky for you," Ranyl growled, "Tad and I are too well mannered to thrash an invalid."

Emma Clyde stepped up, careful not to drag her skirts in the mud, to place a small leather bucket filled with fresh water on dry ground near the edge of the roadbed. Straightening, she offered Ranyl and Tad each a clean towel.

"Scouts comin' in," Emerson Hart hollered from up toward the front of the wagon train. Dressing quickly, Ranyl strapped on his sword belt and hurried forward. When he arrived, Ranyl saw that Luke Holt and his four companions had already dismounted. A quick glance confirmed they'd recovered the missing sorrel and, it appeared, a pair of would-be horse thieves.

The first was a young lad—Ranyl estimated he was around fourteen or fifteen years of age—with dark hair and very blue eyes. Though his wrists had been bound behind his back, the youth's chin-up stance fairly radiated defiance. At his side stood a young woman, a couple of years older, Ranyl guessed. The girl had the same raven-black hair and striking blue eyes as the lad. The two were obviously related, likely brother and sister.

The young man was dressed in typical Kylgahran garb, a grey cotton shirt and woolen trousers of a similar color. A pair of battered calf-length leather boots covered his feet. He was bareheaded. Though of good quality, the youth's clothes looked travel-worn and stained. The young woman's dress, a light-blue long-sleeved cotton frock, wasn't in much better shape. Her hair, fashioned into a simple braid, fell to the tops of her hips, and the slender girl carried herself with an air of quiet dignity. A belly mound showed through the folds of her dress, just pronounced enough to make clear her pregnancy.

"Caught 'em plain as day, milord," Luke Holt stated without preamble. Since the visit to Selkyrk, his rangers had taken to addressing him as Lord Ranyl and such. Ranyl had grown tired of correcting them. Once he was married, he supposed the title would be warranted, if not well suited. "They claim to be of the Ard Kenyon clan but won't give their names," Holt continued. "The lad was armed with a bow and a dirk. He had but two arrows left and no string for the stave. The lass had naught but a belt knife and a haversack full of spare clothes and such." Reaching into his shirt, the tall ranger extracted a small velvet purse. "The girl was carrying this. Some jewelry, rings and such, but no coin. They're pretty well played out, sir, the both of 'em."

Ranyl nodded. "Who are you?" His question roused nothing but silence. Ranyl shrugged. "It will be less trouble to hang you than feed you. Give me your names, and I'll promise not to stretch your necks until after you've eaten."

"You'd hang a woman?" the youth asked, outraged.

"That is the usual punishment for horse thieves, is it not?" Ranyl inquired mildly.

"I stole your bloody nag. She had naught to do with it," the boy exclaimed.

The little sorrel was a filly, well formed and lively, with perked-up ears and alert brown eyes.

"Ginger is hardly a nag," Ranyl commented. "You've a good eye for horseflesh, I'll give you that." He looked to the young woman. "Are you any more sensible than he is?"

"My name is Soriel Morgan of Clan Ard Kenyon," the girl replied with quiet dignity. "He is my brother Syngen."

Watt Quigley, who had been riding point at the head of the train, came pounding up. Reining his mount to a halt nearby, the young ranger glanced at Soriel Morgan, took a second look, and then called out to Ranyl, "Riders approaching from the north, milord, a dozen of 'em. Well mounted, they are, and armed like a war band. Riding along bold as brass, acting like they owned the place."

"Did you see a sigil?" Ranyl asked.

"No, sir," Watt replied. "They ain't carryin' a flag er nothin'." The scout's keen green eyes drifted back to Soriel Morgan. He ventured a smile. The young pregnant woman ignored him. Watt's smile stretched to a grin, and he touched his hat brim in salute.

"We should say hullo, I reckon," Ranyl decided. "Keep an eye on these two," he ordered Watt. Catching Mae's attention, Ranyl said, "See they are fed, and ask Tuan to examine the lass." Mae nodded.

Ranyl and twelve of his men formed two loose ranks, spanning the breadth of the Long Reach Road at the head of the train. Ranyl took a position near the left end of the second rank. Eight of Ranyl's men stood armed with swords and targes. Ranyl himself declined a targe but took his place with his broadsword and Meggie's knife belted at his waist. His four additional retainers, all standing in the second rank, held doubly curved horse bows at the ready, broad-headed arrows knocked.

The remainder of his men, ten of them in number, counting Fyrgus, his two eldest sons, and young Tad, kept a close watch on the rear of the caravan and their two prisoners. Ranyl saw the horsemen approaching. They rode in a compact column of fours. As they neared, he counted twelve of them altogether, ten men and two women. The two women rode in the middle of the formation. A trio of pack horses on lead ropes trailed the last group of four.

The male riders were clad in boiled leather cuirasses and armed with baelrycs. Each had targes and quivers of throwing darts strapped to their saddles and wore broad-brimmed trail hats of a uniform dark green. The women wore no armor but like the men were clad in brown woolen trousers and knee-high leather boots.

Young, the women looked to be, and both were dressed in close-fitting, cream-colored cotton blouses that left no doubt as to their sex. One was blond, and while Ranyl couldn't be certain as they sat astride horses of somewhat different size, she appeared slightly shorter and fuller bosomed than her companion, a slender, dark-haired girl who rode with a natural grace, as if she and her mount were one.

Ranyl's eyes settled on the dark-haired lass as if drawn by some irresistible force. She couldn't have been more than eighteen years of age. A rich, deep brown, her long tresses were, bound in a thick single braid. Her body was supplely made, long legged and slim hipped. She wore a tartyn knotted loosely about her throat. The sigil embroidered into the silk of the tartyn showed that of a banded war hammer, the Ard Ryan clan mark. The riders reined to a halt a few paces short of Ranyl's first line. Ranyl could clearly see the brunette's face, a finely shaped oval with a daintily sculpted nose and a generous, full-lipped mouth, dominated by large brown eyes. She had a dimple in her chin.

Realization dawned. Ranyl knew without question he gazed upon the countenance of his betrothed. *"Pleasing enough."* Ranyl finally understood his father's sly smile. Tessymir Ryan was the most beautiful girl he had ever seen.

22

Like a Solstice Hog

A tall redheaded man at the head of the column of Clan Ard Ryan horsemen called out, "Is this the party of Ranyl Emyrt, Esquire?"

"Who is it what asks?" Luke Holt replied. Beneath the brim of his black-felt trail hat, the tall ranger's blue-eyed gaze swept over the riders arrayed before him.

"It is impolite," the dark-haired girl said in a smooth, pleasing contralto, "to answer question with question."

"No more so, milady, than to approach under arms without offering identification," Luke replied calmly, looking steadily up at the lass.

The girl smiled, her eyes crinkling with amusement. Her expression revealed very white, evenly spaced teeth and somehow seemed to emphasize the cleft in her chin. "I am Tessymir Ryan of Clan Ard Ryan." She nodded at the rider up front. "The tall fellow with the bad manners is Davis Killoe, first sword of Clan Ard Ryan."

"I meant no offense, Squire Emyrt," Killoe directed his remark to Luke Holt. The Ard Ryan retainer was easily as tall and well muscled as Holt and even wider through the shoulders.

"If you had offended me, First Sword," Ranyl said quietly, "you'd know it."

Tessymir Ryan's gaze shifted from Luke Holt to Ranyl. The young squire felt the weight of her regard. The laird apparent to Clan Ard Ryan had expressive eyes, a rich cinnamon brown. Swirling within those luminous depths, Ranyl saw a flicker of emotion. In an instant Ranyl knew he'd been measured and found wanting. Disappointment registered, dimming the light in those beautiful orbs. A moment only and it was gone, replaced by wary neutrality.

For Ranyl, it was as if he'd been slapped. Despite his vow to begin anew in the North Country and to set aside his past, he felt an old bitterness rise in his chest like bile. Without thought, his left hand curled about the hilt of his broadsword.

Filled with an icy rage he knew ranged beyond reason, Ranyl forced himself to meet Tessymir Ryan's gaze. "As we are making our manners the now, my lady"—even to his own ears, Ranyl's voice sounded cold and distant—"may I offer you and yours the hospitality of our camp?"

Taken aback, Tessymir Ryan straightened in her saddle. Anger glinted in the maple-colored recesses of her eyes. Her delicately cleft chin rose. "Your van is still astride the road, *Squire* Emyrt." The girl placed a frosty emphasis on Ranyl's lesser title. "We would not wish to delay or inconvenience you."

With his left hand still firmly gripping his sword hilt, Ranyl removed his hat with his right and sketched a bow suitable for greeting an innkeeper. "Halting the now is no inconvenience, my lady," Ranyl said evenly. Standing upright, Ranyl tugged his hat back into place. "We have some business to attend to, and I'm in no particular hurry."

His implication rang clear. The sparks of anger dancing in Tessymir's umber-hued eyes flared to open flame. "If it offers an excuse to climb down off this bloody horse"—the blonde's voice was pitched only slightly higher than the laird apparent's and every bit as musical—"I am more than willing to inconvenience you."

Ranyl judged the blonde to be a few years older than Tessymir, perhaps his own age or thereabouts. Her eyes were Highland Blue, a clear light green about her pupils banded by a darker shade of grey around the edge of her irises. She had a small rosebud mouth, and as she was smiling, Ranyl saw that her teeth were as fine and white as those of her dark-haired companion.

"As no one saw fit to introduce me, my name is Alyair Murfrey of Clan Ard Ryan, first cousin to her ladyship, here." She thrust a pertly rounded chin toward Tessymir Ryan. In anyone else's company, Ranyl thought, Alyair would have been truly lovely. Sitting beside Tessymir, she appeared merely pretty.

Despite himself, Ranyl couldn't keep the smile from his face. Sweeping his hat from his head, Ranyl executed a very correct bow, one that would have pleased even his grandmother. "You are more than welcome, my lady."

"You are covered in mud, sir," Alyair observed.

Glancing down, Ranyl could see that her charge was valid. Mud, dried grey and clinging, caked his boots and the front of his trousers. "Yes," he allowed, "there seems to be rather a lot of the stuff up here. Our wagons have developed a particular affinity for it. Extricating them has become nearly a full-time job."

"Is that the business to which you referred earlier?" Tessymir's voice sounded slightly less glacial.

Meeting Tessymir's eyes once again, Ranyl shook his head. "No, we're about done shoving on wagons for the time being, my lady. What remains is a small matter of horse theft."

Ranyl led the way toward the rear of the wagon train. The Ard Ryan entourage dismounted. Handing their reins to a pair of nearby retainers, the two women followed close behind him. As Ranyl neared the middle of the van, Mae Hoskins hurried toward him.

"My lord," she called, "a moment, if you please."

"Squire, please, Mae, if you will," Ranyl corrected her. "We're minding our manners this afternoon."

Mae paused half a step away and looked briefly at the strangers arrayed behind Ranyl. Her blue-green eyes widened at the sight of the two women. She bobbed a brief curtsey. "They are half starved, the poor darlings," she told Ranyl. "Tuan says the girl and her babe are both well. I convinced her to take some food for her baby's sake. The boy won't touch a bite." Mae stepped in close, laying a small hand on his forearm to whisper for his ears alone. "The two of them are running from something, that's certain. They're so young, Ranyl, scarcely more than children. You won't be too hard on them?"

Laying his hand atop hers, Ranyl murmured, "You and Tuan take the girl to the rear of the train, as far out of earshot as you can. I don't want to frighten her. I do intend to scare the piss out of that stubborn little brother of hers. Do ya ken?"

Mae smiled, bright and warm, her relief evident. "As we are minding our manners, I don't suppose it would be proper for me ta kiss ya?"

"I reckon not." Ranyl tugged at an ear, a rueful expression on his face. "Dammit." Mae laughed. "Have Emerson bring the lad to me here," he ordered firmly.

"Right you are, sir." Mae curtsied again and rushed off to comply.

Turning to Luke Holt, Ranyl instructed, "Fetch a rope." Without a word, Holt nodded and slipped away.

Emerson Hart appeared shortly, escorting a stoic-looking Syngen Morgan. Flanked by Watt Quigley, the young horse thief's wrists remained bound behind his back. The youth strode along with his shoulders square and his head up.

"I understand you refused to eat," Ranyl greeted him.

The boy shrugged, blue eyes glinting. "Seemed like a waste of food."

"Or a demonstration of pride," Ranyl said mildly. "False pride, in your case, as any man who would stoop to theft is without honor."

"Soriel wanted to buy a horse and some food from you, offering a portion of her jewelry as payment." Syngen looked Ranyl straight in the eye. "I dissuaded her."

"Why did you?" Ranyl queried.

Luke Holt stepped up quietly, a long coil of rope held loosely in his big hands. Syngen glanced briefly at the oiled hemp and then returned his gaze to Ranyl. "I had no way of stopping you from taking all her jewelry, or anything else you wanted. She's been hurt enough."

"You admit to stealing the horse?" Ranyl's question was quietly stated.

"I do," Syngen replied in a similar tone.

Ranyl's voice hardened. "We hang horse thieves."

The boy paled. "What happens to my sister?"

"Is it true you hail from Clan Ard Kenyon?" Ranyl inquired. Syngen nodded. "We'll see her safely to Ard Kenyon holdings, give her a plaid and some food, and wish her good luck."

"What of her jewelry?" Syngen pressed. "It is all she has left."

"She'll have it when she leaves our company," Ranyl promised. "You have my word."

Syngen nodded once more. "All right enough."

Ranyl turned to Emerson Hart. "String him up," he directed. "Do it proper, like a solstice hog."

Emerson Hart was a few years Ranyl's elder, a bit wider across the shoulders, and slightly thicker through the chest. He had ginger-colored hair and earnest grey eyes and was a lot smarter than he looked, with a fine eye and ear for detail. In the Midlands, where both Ranyl and Emerson were reared, the custom was to hang a solstice hog by its heels. Emerson was also the best hazard player Ranyl ever saw. You could read nothing from Hart's expression.

"Bind his ankles," Hart commanded curtly. Judging from their faces, Ranyl saw a number of his rangers, less able to school their expressions, had caught the significance of his instructions as well. Watt Quigley was grinning openly. Ranyl hoped the bloody fools didn't give him away.

"Squire," Tessymir exclaimed, taking a step toward Ranyl, "he is only a boy."

"He's a horse thief, my lady," Ranyl informed her calmly. "I can't let a horse thief off." Emerson tossed a length of rope over a sturdy bough from a nearby oak.

"I'll buy his life from you," Tessymir offered. Ranyl raised his hand, and his rangers halted. His ankles tied, young Syngen swayed a little. Luke Holt laid a strong hand on the lad's shoulder to steady him.

"At what price?" Ranyl inquired.

"Seven hundred silver," Tessymir fairly spat at him.

Ranyl looked at her carefully. "That's a generous offer."

"I felt certain," Tessymir purred in a voice low pitched for a woman and cold enough to freeze a pot of ale, "the son of Stephyn Emyrt would understand the value of money, if nothing else."

"I can't claim my father's acumen," Ranyl replied matter-of-factly, "but as you are to be my bride, would not accepting equate to paying myself out of mine own purse?"

Brown eyes flashed. *Light,* Ranyl thought. *Even when angry, she is beautiful.* Tessymir seethed. "I'll pay you from my dowry." In Kylgahra, a bride's dowry was *hers* and would remain so throughout her marriage.

Though he knew it was hard on Syngen, Ranyl was beginning to enjoy himself. He rubbed his chin, as if in thought. "Tempting, but I think not. Once we're wed, you are likely to need your dowry coin for tableclothes and pewter and such." Squaring his shoulders, Ranyl pronounced, "Today, justice shall be served."

Tessymir looked as if she was ready to spit fire at him. Davis Killoe took half a step forward. Tessymir stopped him with a quick jerk of her head. She glared at Ranyl as if he'd just slithered out from under a rock.

Turning once again to Emerson Hart, Ranyl barked, "Get on with it."

Kneeling, Emerson quickly looped and tied one end of the rope around the bindings securing Syngen's feet. "Haul away," Emerson cried. Four rangers pulled as one. The rope drew taut, and Syngen's feet were snatched out from under him.

Emerson grabbed a double handful of the boy's shirt back to keep his face from striking the ground. Emerson held on, holding the lad's head and shoulders a couple of span above the leaf-strewn grass beneath the spreading branches of the oak until his heels had been raised high enough to clear. Emerson released him as the rangers tied off the rope. Young Syngen hung suspended, up-side down, swaying gently from the rope end secured to his ankle bindings.

"Ten of the strop, Emerson," Ranyl ordered. "Lay to with a will, if you please." Luke Holt silently passed a length of harness strap on to Emerson Hart. Setting his feet, Emerson swung his arm back and brought the strap down across Syngen Morgan's backside. Harry Hart had a strong right arm. Syngen endured the first three blows in silence. He whimpered as the fourth was struck and cried out at the fifth. By the tenth he was howling right proper.

"That's ten, milord sheriff," Emerson Hart announced, coiling the harness strap in his hand. All Kylgahran sheriffs were original-ly scions of the nobility. Over time, the practice changed, more than one wit noting that, after all, sheriffs had to work for a living. These days, most sheriffs' postings went to esquires or outright com-moners. Despite this, for whatever reason, the lordly appellation remained in use. As his sheriff's term had ended, the title no longer applied in Ranyl's case. Judging from the look in his eyes, Ranyl knew Emerson had misspoke on purpose.

"Thank you, Harry," Ranyl said quietly. Raising his voice, Ranyl addressed the rest of his men standing close to hand. "And thank you, gentlemen; that will be all."

"All right, boys, clear off," Hart rumbled, leading Ranyl's contin-gent of rangers toward the wagons.

Tessymir stood with her arms folded beneath what Ranyl had to admit was an absolutely splendid bosom. Standing at her cousin's side, a wry smile tugged at the corners of Alyair Murfrey's delecta-ble little mouth. Davis Killoe loomed just behind, looking ... well, dangerous.

Stepping close, Ranyl lowered his voice. "Excuse me, ladies." Ranyl jerked his head in the direction of young Syngen Morgan, still dangling inverted at rope's end. "His pride will be stinging worse than his bum. What's to follow is best done in private."

"I suppose you think you are very clever," Tessymir said tartly.

Ranyl grinned at her. It might have been wishful thinking on his part, but he thought he saw her eyes soften just a bit in response.

"You'll find wine and shade at my wagon. Emerson can direct you." Catching Alyair's eye, he went on. "Seven hundred silver. Is she always so free with coin?"

Matching his expression, Alyair replied, "She's a terrible spendthrift, milord sheriff. You'll need to watch her like a hawk."

"Generous of spirit, though." Ranyl cast an appraising glance at Tessymir Ryan, scratching his whiskered chin. "Not the worst of faults." With a nod, he sauntered over to take a seat beside Syngen Morgan. Rolling her eyes at her cousin, Tessymir strode off in the direction of the wagons.

"You know you were squealing like a girl there towards the end," Ranyl said conversationally to Syngen.

"You're a right bastard, you are," Syngen spat. "I'll carve your guts for this someday."

"Handy with a sword, are you?" Ranyl queried.

"I said someday," Syngen allowed.

"I could teach you." Ranyl opened the bargaining. "The sword, I mean."

"Why would you do that?" Syngen asked.

"You were more worried about your sister's hide than your own," Ranyl answered. "You never begged, and you didn't really start caterwauling until the fifth stripe. I'd have been bellering at two."

"You don't think I mean it, do you?" Syngen challenged.

"If I didn't think you meant it, I wouldn't have offered," Ranyl said seriously. "On the day I think you are good enough or your nineteenth birthday, whichever comes first, I'll give you a go if you still want to. You win, and you get your freedom, my sword, and any horse you want from my stable."

"I won't get far without some money," Syngen commented.

"That's your worry," Ranyl told him.

"What about my sister?" Syngen wanted to know.

"That could get complicated," Ranyl mused. "I can't make any promises until I know her story."

"Cut me down," Syngen offered, "and I'll tell you."

Rising to his feet, Ranyl slipped Meggie's knife into his right hand and sliced through the bonds tying Syngen's wrists. Once he was sure the lad's arms were free, Ranyl warned, "Mind your noggin." He slashed the ropes binding Syngen's ankles. The boy squawked as he tumbled into the grass at the base of the oak.

The outraged youth glared, staring up at Ranyl from his knees. "You could have broken my neck."

Ranyl shrugged. "If your reactions were that slow, you'd never make a swordsman by any road."

Syngen shook his dark-haired head and then straightened his shoulders. "Soriel was married to Rafe Balliard of Clan Ard Fraiser nigh on to two years ago. The Balliards are esquires. Their holdings lie southwest of here. Our parents are dead. 'Twas an uncle of ours what arranged the marriage. Rafe's got a temper. He hit her some right off, but Soriel is smart and pretty, and it weren't too bad, she says. Not long after Soriel married him, Rafe's left shoulder was mangled in a Guilley raid. Never did heal. The Balliards brought in a healer who delved him and claimed she couldn't do much; too long after the injury she said. She left some syrupy stuff for the pain. Rafe prefers wysoi."

Syngen rocked backwards and sat down, crossing his legs in front of him. Ranyl took a seat at the lad's right side. "Rafe gets mean when he drinks. A couple of weeks back, he got real drunk. I heard Soriel cry out. When I went into their room, she was lying on the floor, arms and legs curled round her belly. He was standing over her with a piece of firewood in his hand. I told him to quit. He took a swipe at me, lost his balance, and fell. He cracked his head on the mantel of the fireplace and died."

Syngen looked Ranyl in the eye. "I never meant to kill him. Soriel said we had to clear out, right then, the two of us."

"Why, if it was an accident like you say?" Ranyl wondered.

"We're commoners," Syngen answered. "My father was a merchant, a successful one. The Balliards offered for Soriel because of her portion. They never really took a fancy to her, and as for me"— the boy shook his head—"I was barely tolerated. With one of their own dead and only the two of us to tell of it, Soriel reckoned they'd hang me and marry her off to Jeptha. He is the only Balliard brother left unwed. At least Rafe had an excuse for being ornery. Jeptha, well, he's just naturally mean. We grabbed a few things, slipped out for an afternoon ride, and just kept going. We figured on meeting up with a cousin of ours, Tyrell Morgan of Clan Ard Kenyon, up north of here a-ways. Soriel thought he would offer us shelter until we could decide what to do."

"You are certain Rafe is dead?" Ranyl inquired.

Syngen nodded.

"Soriel is a widow, then," Ranyl concluded.

Syngen nodded again. "Four days ago, Soriel and I stopped beside a little brook. I tied the horses off but left them saddled. The water was cool and sweet, and there was shade. We must have dozed off. When we woke up, the horses were gone. They'd left me my bow but cut the string, showing off, I reckon."

"You're lucky your bowstring was all they cut," Ranyl observed.

Syngen made no argument. "I tried tying it, but the cord snapped the first time I loosed from a full draw. We had nothing but the clothes we stood up in and a small bag Soriel was using for a pillow. We tried stopping at a farm two days ago, but they ran us off. By the time we came across your wagon train ... well, we were awful hungry and a little desperate."

"Stealing that horse was pretty damn stupid," Ranyl asserted. "Not to mention dishonorable."

"How was I to know you were once a sheriff and your retainers a bunch of ex-rangers?" Syngen countered. "And speaking of dishonorable, when was the last time you were lost, alone, and four days hungry?"

Choosing to ignore that last bit, Ranyl proposed, "I reckon Soriel can shelter with us also; that is, at least until you and I are squared away. While you train, you'll be in my service. I'll pay you ten silver talents a month and all the food you can eat. Tell Soriel I'll pay her twelve. You'll earn it, the both of you."

"How come she gets twelve silver a month and I only ten?" Syngen sounded indignant.

"She's a lot prettier than you are, for one thing, and easier to get along with to boot. Besides, even with the baby coming, I expect she won't eat but half what you do. Have we got a deal?"

"What if my nineteenth birthday comes, and I'm still not good enough to have a go at you?" Syngen inquired.

"If you aren't good enough by then, you never will be," Ranyl said evenly. They regarded one another, steadily, for a long moment.

"I give you my word," Syngen vowed, gravely extending his right hand.

Ranyl clasped the boy's hand in his own. "Let's see about getting you something to eat. You have some firewood to cut before nightfall."

23

Small Successes

"He's insufferable," Tessymir Ryan exclaimed. The laird apparent to Clan Ard Ryan sat upon what she had to acknowledge was a very clever folding chair with a collapsible canvas seat and back and a wooden frame that pivoted about a pair of sturdy steel bolts. Her cousin, Alyair perched upon a similar device at her side. They were located in the lee of a wagon Emerson Hart said belonged to the sheriff. Mae Hoskins, the buxom little blonde who Tessymir had seen clinging to Ranyl Emyrt's arm earlier, tended to a large cook pot on the far side of the wagon. Two blond-haired boys with the same blue-green eyes as the Hoskins woman clambered into the wagon to fetch a game board. She saw them climb down. One was carrying a Stones board, the other a bag that presumably held stones—small, round, highly polished black and white pebbles. *His wagon, indeed,* Tessymir fumed.

Alyair took a sip of her wine, an entirely passable white, and smiled. "He has a mischievous grin, rather boyish, actually."

"Like a pugnacious tree stump," Tessymir avowed. "Milord mud finch, he is, with a scraggly beard."

"Sym," Alyair admonished gently, "how many lordlings do you know would put their shoulder to the wheel of a stuck wagon? He has not plied a razor for a couple of days, I'll grant you, but then how could he know today was the day he'd meet his intended?"

"You are defending him?" Sym flared, aghast. She couldn't stand being called Tess. All her close friends and relations referred to her as Sym. Alyair was like a sister to her.

Sym's lovely blond-haired cousin smiled into her wine cup. "I'm surprised he didn't pitch you into that creek yonder, the way you were ogling that tall dark-haired ranger."

"I never," Sym protested but then lowered her voice. "It is just that he looked so much like Rowyn. They could be brothers, don't you think?"

"I prefer redheads myself, with wide shoulders and well-muscled thighs," Alyair said mildly, ignoring Sym's query. "You know what they say about men with muscular thighs, don't you?"

Judging by her blush, Alyair saw her younger cousin knew very well what the goodwives had to say about men with strong thighs. "You think he noticed?" Sym frowned, a thoughtful crease forming between two perfectly arched eyebrows. "The sheriff, I mean."

"Oh, Sym." Alyair laughed softly. "You should stay far away from hazard tables." Hazard was a card game popular in Kylgahra.

Sym jerked a thumb in the direction of the wagon. "I wonder if all sheriffs' wagons come equipped with little blond-haired women," she whispered furiously, "with blue-green eyes and large"—Sym hesitated—"pots."

Alyair laughed. "The well-rounded individual to whom you refer is a widow, or the next thing to it, I suppose, as rangers in service are not allowed to marry. Her ranger was killed at Ranyl's side—his best friend, apparently. Ranyl agreed to take his friend's two sons into his service when they come of age. Their mother wanted to come north, seeking a new start. Ranyl obliged her."

"I'll bet," Sym growled, only partly mollified. "How is it you know this?"

"The same way I learned he's been sleeping under the wagon

while the blonde and her boys slumber comfortably inside," Alyair replied coyly. "I asked."

That was kind of him and loyal, Sym admitted, if only to herself, *but still.* "He was rude," Sym declared righteously.

"The good sheriff didn't fall all over himself upon first sight of you, as men are wont to do, I'll grant you," Alyair conceded. "How boorish of him."

Sym stuck her tongue out at Alyair. After a moment of reflection, her cinnamon-colored eyes clouded, and she tossed her head in vexation. "I lost my temper."

"Very prettily, I might add," Alyair said encouragingly. "It's a pure wonder he didn't melt right then and there into the tops of his muddy boots."

"I've made a muck of it, haven't I?" Sym said ruefully.

Sym is as honest as the day is long, Alyair thought lovingly, *without a jot of guile in her, the poor girl.* "Oh, I don't know about that." Alyair's slender shoulders rose and fell. "You are beautiful, any fool could see that, and I'll wager our sturdy sheriff is anything but foolish. You've a bit of a temper. I reckon the sooner he learns about it the better. You are spirited with a kind heart, too. I think he took note of that as well. I suspect he is not entirely disinterested."

Seated on an overturned barrel beside a nearby supply wagon, Ranyl fidgeted.

"Goaded her a purpose, did you?" Tuan asked as he deftly applied a pearl-handled razor to Ranyl's jaw. Ranyl had washed and changed into a clean dark-green cotton shirt and brown woolen trousers. He'd also put on his best pair of well-tooled brown-leather boots.

"Aye," Ranyl acknowledged sourly. "I think she hates me."

"You do have a flair for making terrible first impressions," Tuan informed him, meticulously scraping away. "I positively loathed you for an hour or two after our first meeting." Setting aside the razor, Tuan reached out and gently tugged Ranyl's ear. "Aside from your abominable taste in wine, I find you almost entirely tolerable the now." Taking up a damp towel, the youthful healer wiped the last vestiges of shaving soap from Ranyl's face and leaned slightly away. "There," Tuan enthused, "you really are quite handsome."

"If you like redheaded tree stumps," Ranyl remarked.

"Stop that," Tuan scolded, sounding miffed. "Stop feeling sorry for yourself, and stop treating her like some unwashed uncle who has overstayed his solstice visit. You can be quite charming when you try. Believe me, I know." Turning sharply away, Tuan folded his arms. The slender little healer was wearing snug-fitting leather trousers and a long-sleeved cream-colored silk shirt with lace at the cuffs.

Rising from the barrel, Ranyl stepped close and fingered the frill at the end of Tuan's left sleeve. "Lace, in the middle of a wilderness. A bit overstated, don't you think?"

"A little style is never out of place," Tuan responded stiffly. "Besides, it is about all I have left that is clean. You really don't like it?"

"It looks good on you," Ranyl assured him. "For the record, I think you are barely intolerable yourself."

Tuan turned to face him, green eyes glinting. "You know," Tuan said in a soft, sultry tone, "I specialize in seducing married men."

"I'll have something to look forward to, then," Ranyl noted, smiling. He sighed, his smile fading. "Wish me luck."

Tuan closed both fists and pressed them to his bosom. "All the best."

Ranyl and Tessymir were almost wincingly polite to one another during supper. Mae and Kate served, and after the meal, Tuan sang. The youth had a light voice, but one that was also pitch perfect and evocative. He was good, and he knew it and appeared genuinely thrilled at the applause he received as he finished.

Following the meal, Tessymir and Ranyl had a few moments alone, seated side by side near the fire. "Would you care for some more wine?" Ranyl asked to break the silence that seemed to be rising about them like a malevolent fog.

"No, thank you," Sym answered. "The meal was very fine."

Ranyl nodded. "Between the two of them, Kate and Mae keep us well fed."

Conversation lapsed once more. A little desperate, Ranyl recounted Syngen's story. As he finished, Ranyl found himself gazing into the umber depths of Sym's eyes.

"Do you believe him?" Sym asked.

Ranyl smiled. "I do. Young Syngen has his quirks, but dissembling isn't among them."

Sym matched Ranyl's smile with one of her own. "The Balliards do have a certain reputation." Sym tossed her head, her expression sobered. "Bad blood has existed between the Kenyons and the Fraisers for generations. My father has often been caught in the middle. I suspect Soriel's dowry received a warmer welcome than the lass herself."

"An unfortunate circumstance," Ranyl agreed. There was no mistaking the wry twist to his voice.

Of a sudden no longer able to meet his eyes, Sym lowered hers. "Your healer," Sym said evasively, "has a minstrel's skill."

"A jongleur, if you please, my lady," Ranyl corrected her, smiling once more. "Tuan is a little sensitive."

"He seems somewhat ..." Sym paused, searching for a suitable description of Tuan Marques.

"He's flaming Odd," Ranyl supplied, "and determined to care not a whit who knows it."

"That is liable to land him in terrible trouble one day," Sym remarked.

"He's among friends," Ranyl said firmly. Ranyl's gaze again met Tessymir's, and his voice gentled. "I owe him a life." Ranyl shrugged. "He has a banner man's courage, that one, and a kind heart, and he's awfully young."

"You like him," Sym declared with a smile.

By the Fates, Ranyl thought, *she is lovely in the firelight.* "I do," Ranyl conceded. "He likes you, by the way."

"I'm glad someone does," Sym said tartly. Ranyl found he had nothing to say in response. "I hear you rescued him from a mob in Selkyrk," Sym continued.

"It wasn't much of a mob," Ranyl demurred, "and healers can be mighty useful, even ones who are a trifle"—Ranyl smiled—"high strung."

"I understand the young horse thief and his sister have also been added to your retinue," Sym noted.

"I couldn't very well leave them wandering about out here," Ranyl hedged.

"Evidently not." Sym smiled once again. "How many are there in your company, good squire?"

"Forty-six," Ranyl replied, "including the recent additions, not counting myself or the wee bairns still on the way."

"Forty-six!" Sym exclaimed. "My lord sheriff, are you leading a wedding party or an invasion?"

"They are good people, all," Ranyl began with some heat, until he noticed the glint in her wide-set brown eyes. "Is that going to be a problem?" he asked in a softer tone.

"My father will have final say, of course"—Sym's smile broadened—"but I should think not."

"That's good to hear. Thank you." Ranyl smiled, making no attempt to hide his relief. It seemed to Sym as if his guard dropped and with it, any vestige of a barrier between them. *He does look like a boy*, she thought, and for the first time that day, Sym realized how young he was, only a few years older than herself, really. The realization stirred a nervous flutter in the pit of her stomach.

"Are you in the habit of collecting strays, sheriff?" Sym inquired.

"If you treat them right," Ranyl proclaimed, "strays often prove to be the most loyal of companions."

"That has been my experience as well." Sym stood, her expression softened. "It appears we agree on something."

Ranyl took to his feet and raised his cup in salute. "To small successes."

Sym lifted her cup in response. They each took a sip. "Good night to you, Squire Ranyl."

"And to you, Lady Tessymir."

Ranyl watched as she turned and strode gracefully into the darkness.

24

To Begin Again

They made good progress the next morning, starting under a clear blue sky. Heavy-laden grey clouds began to roll in around noon, and the soft afternoon rain that followed grew to a torrent as soon as the wagon train stopped for the night. After a cold supper, the entire contingent spent the evening huddled under the canvas tops of the wagons. Tessymir's outriders pitched their tents on a slight rise at the edge of the wagon park. At Ranyl's insistence, Tessymir and Lady Alyair took shelter in Ranyl's wagon, sharing the space with Mae and her two sons. Ranyl and young Tad bedded down with Watt in one of the supply wagons.

As the mixed company of ex-rangers and Ard Ryan retainers broke camp the following morning, Fyrgus Clyde's wagon bogged down before reaching the rain-sodden surface of the road. Ranyl, aided by the smith and Lukas Holt, had just begun the usual practice of digging out the left rear wheel when Davis Killoe, accompanied by three Ard Ryan clansmen, stepped up.

"Excuse me, milord sheriff," Killoe proffered. "You might want to be tryin' this." The man standing to the tall first sword's right had a long pine bough about as thick as Ranyl's calf, cut and shaped, slung over his right shoulder. Ranyl noticed that while most of the smaller branches had been cut away entirely, a few stubs near the base of the main bough remained trimmed only to within a hand's width or so of the spar. "If you'll allow us to demonstrate, we'll give it a go."

Ranyl nodded, and Killoe turned to a stocky-looking Highlander on his left. "All right, Conor," Killoe directed. The Ard Ryan retainer stepped forward to place a sturdy-looking log just in front of the stuck wheel. The man with the bough then carefully positioned the butt end atop the log while fitting one of the regularly spaced stubs against the wheel axle. "We lift, you push," Killoe explained.

"You heard the man," Ranyl said. Ranyl and his rangers positioned themselves.

"On the count of three," Killoe ordered. As the three count rang out, young Thad Clyde, perched alone atop the driver's seat, urged the horses forward. Ranyl, Fyrgus, and Luke Holt shoved at the rear of the wagon, while Killoe and his three heaved upwards on the pine bough. With the wheel weight off loaded, the wagon lurched ahead, clearing the rut, and then trundled onto the packed surface of the roadway.

Ranyl congratulated Davis Killoe. "I've a feeling you've done this before."

For the first time since their meeting, the big Highlander actually smiled. "We're long on mud up here, Sheriff." Killoe waved a ham-sized fist at the cut bough. "Lady Tessymir had us fashion this last night afore we tucked up."

"Be sure to convey my thanks to Lady Tessymir," Ranyl responded. Shrugging back into his plaid, Ranyl clapped his trail hat firmly into place.

"Forgive me, milord sheriff," a musical feminine voice called out, "but wouldn't your cause be better served by rendering such thanks in person."

Ranyl turned to see Lady Alyair Murfrey of Clan Ard Ryan swathed in a fine grey winnowed-wool cloak standing nearby. Ranyl tugged politely at the brim of his hat. "That would require conversing with Lady Tessymir," Ranyl noted. "Doing so has thus far proven to be ... precarious."

A puckish glow lighted Alyair's Highland Blue eyes. "Are you so easily discouraged, milord sheriff?"

"I am that," Ranyl acknowledged with a smile, "but rarely dissuaded."

Alyair flashed an answering smile. "Will you lend me your arm, sir?"

Stepping to her side, Ranyl complied. Alyair wrapped both slim-fingered hands about his left arm at the crook in his elbow. Tucked neatly at his side, as if she belonged nowhere else, Alyair strolled easily, guiding him toward the rear of the train. "Sym is still at breakfast," Alyair informed him.

"I've already eaten," Ranyl protested.

Alyair sighed and peered up at him from beneath long, tawny eyelashes. "You really are hopeless, aren't you."

Ranyl's smile returned. "Apparently."

"If you can refrain from spilling porridge in her lap," Alyair instructed, "you'll find Sym easy enough to get along with."

"She's easy enough to look at, that's for certain," Ranyl allowed. He glanced down at Alyair and continued in a conspiratorial whisper, "As are you, my lady."

Alyair stopped in her tracks and glared up at him. "You are being kind, Ranyl Emyrt. Keep that up, and I'll kick you in the knee."

Ranyl chuckled. "I'll resort to conniving; how'd that be?"

Tugging firmly on his arm, Alyair resumed her progress. "Beauty is a blessing and a burden, Ranyl," Alyair explained softly. "Beauty attracts men, but for most, it is all they see."

Ranyl pressed his right hand down atop both of hers and squeezed gently. "Most men are bloody fools."

Alyair looked at him. She smiled. "Well then, my lord sheriff, you must take care to stand not among them."

Tessymir Ryan, clad in a dove-grey cloak fashioned of winnowed wool with what appeared to be a woolen riding dress of a slightly darker hue beneath, greeted the pair of them with a smile. "You're too late for breakfast, but there is a bit of bread left, and the tea is still hot."

Alyair released Ranyl's arm and curtsied. "I finished breakfast half an hour ago, Lady Sym, thank you very much. However, I am certain this sturdy fellow"—she cast an appreciative glance Ranyl's way—"could do with a bite of bread. If you will excuse me, I'll leave you to it." She turned and slipped away.

"You'll have to forgive Alyair." Tessymir spoke in that throaty contralto of hers, the sound of which never failed to set Ranyl's scalp to tingling. "She insists on being ... colorful."

"She's good company," Ranyl averred, "and I could do with a bite of bread."

"Please sit," Sym invited, indicating an empty folding chair placed on the opposite side of the small campfire beside which she sat.

Ranyl did so and accepted the cup of tea she proffered. "I wanted to thank you," Ranyl stated. "We've already made good use of the pine-bough lever you provisioned for last night."

"We've some experience with stuck wagons up here, Squire Ranyl," Sym noted, while handing him a generous chunk of white bread rimmed by a golden-brown crust.

Ranyl heard no barb in her use of his proper title. "Master Killoe said much the same."

"The soil is not so rich here in the North as in the Midlands," Sym explained, "but the land itself—the woods, the hills, and the moors—have a beauty like no other." Sym's tone conveyed the certainty only an eighteen-year-old could muster.

"So long as you don't mind the damp." Ranyl took a bite of his bread to keep from twitting her further.

Still, there was no mistaking the sparks suddenly crackling in her maple-brown eyes. "We are a hearty folk and proud," Sym declared. "You would do well to remember that."

"The bread's good," Ranyl allowed, holding the bit remaining aloft.

I'm glad you approve of something, Sym thought. Biting her tongue at the last moment, she said, "A baker there is in the village at Grey-mark with a fine hand. I stop by as often as I can."

Luke Holt appeared in the next moment, striding purposefully to Ranyl's side. "The van is assembled, milord. We are ready to roll."

"Let's get going, then," Ranyl directed. "Have Watt take the point." Ranyl set aside the tea cup and climbed to his feet. He turned to Sym. "Thank you for the hospitality, my lady. If you will excuse me." Ranyl popped the last of the bread into his mouth.

Sym smiled with as much grace as she could manage. She said nothing as Ranyl and the tall Highlander at his side walked away. Sym could not help but notice the broad sweep of Ranyl's shoulders and the way his torso tapered to his waist. He moved easily, if not gracefully, with a well-controlled muscularity.

Sym rose to her feet and called to a retainer standing patiently nearby, "Time to go."

The train had been on the road only a couple of hours when Watt galloped back with word of a dozen riders approaching. "They're riding under an Ard Fraiser banner, milord," the lean young scout informed Ranyl.

Ranyl drew rein, bringing Stepper to a halt. "Ard Fraiser, is it?" His charcoal-grey eyes darkened with thought. "We'd better get Soriel and Syngen under cover."

Watt nodded. "I'll see to it, milord."

Ranyl made his way forward, stopping alongside the lead wagon driven by Fyrgus Clyde. The big smith thrust his chin toward a group of exactly twelve riders approaching at a steady trot. "Ornery-looking bunch," Fyrgus noted.

Ranyl's left hand caressed the long hilt of the broadsword at his side. "I doubt they're out sightseeing," he concurred.

The horsemen halted a few paces short of Clyde's wagon. A thick-set man at their front, wearing a battered black-felt trail hat and an Ard Fraiser plaid over a chain mail hauberk, called out, "Who is in charge here?"

Ranyl eased Stepper ahead, closing the distance with the man in the black hat to only a couple of paces. "Squire Ranyl Emyrt of Clan Ard Mourne is my name," Ranyl responded. "The wagon train is mine. We are escorted by Laird Apparent Tessymir Ryan of Clan Ard Ryan and a few of her retainers."

"So you're that Emyrt, are ye?" The sturdy fellow up front thumbed his broad-brimmed hat a little further back above his forehead, revealing a shock of medium-blond hair—greying at the temples, Ranyl saw—and amid the two-day stubble mantling his cheeks and jaw. Without waiting for an answer to his query, the stranger continued. "I am Sheriff Eustus Treymore of Clan Ard Fraiser. We're looking for a pair of fugitives. Wanted for murder, they are. A brother, fourteen, and sister, aged seventeen; the girl is pregnant. They are likely headed for Ard Kenyon territory. Have you seen anyone that might fit their description?"

"We've encountered no criminals during our travels thus far, Sheriff," Ranyl said evenly.

Eustus Treymore had flinty grey eyes. They narrowed slightly. "That's an interesting answer, Squire."

"It is the truth," Ranyl told him.

The sheriff swung down from his saddle, as did Ranyl. "I hear you were a sheriff once yourself," Treymore remarked. "You'll be familiar with this, then." Reaching into his plaid, the sheriff extracted a folded sheet of heavy vellum and passed it to Ranyl. The vellum sheet contained the warrant of arrest for both Syngen Morgan of Clan Ard Kenyon and Soriel Balliard of Clan Ard Fraiser. "You'll notice," Treymore pointed out, "the warrant is signed by Laird Fraiser and endorsed by Laird Ryan, young Tessymir's father."

"All looks to be in order, Sheriff," Ranyl acknowledged, returning the warrant.

"This warrant gives me the authority to search your wagons, Squire," Treymore declared. "Do you have any objections?"

Ranyl shook his head. "Not so long as your lot mind their manners and their muddy boots."

"Haggerty, with me," Treymore ordered a tall, dark-haired retainer sitting his horse near to hand, holding the Ard Fraiser banner. "Sylas, you and Dunstan stay with the horses. The rest of ye, two to a wagon." The sheriff pointed to Clyde's vehicle. "Start with this 'un. Be careful of the crockery, but look close."

As Sheriff Treymore's men dismounted to begin their search, Watt trotted up to Ranyl's side. "They are nowhere to be found, milord," the young scout whispered. "And Mae says she can't find Lady Tessymir either."

Ranyl nodded but said nothing. He had no reason to doubt the legality of Treymore's warrant. Even without Laird Owain Ryan's endorsement, Ranyl was not about to spill blood over it. If Treymore's search located Syngen and Soriel, Ranyl could do little enough about it except to hope that Tessymir's presence might mitigate any culpability on his part for not handing them over in the first place.

Ranyl and Watt stayed close to Treymore as the sheriff and his men worked their way down the train. About two-thirds of the way along, the sheriff turned to Ranyl. "You wouldn't happen to have any wysoi about, would ye?"

"Not for someone rifling through our wagons, no," Ranyl replied.

Treymore spat onto the muddy ground at his feet. "It's a little early in the day anyhow." He raised his voice, hollering to his men. "Hurry it up, there." Treymore shook his head. "This is taking too bloody long," he muttered. Finally, he signaled to Haggerty. "C'mon, we'll take this one ourselves."

Treymore strode purposefully to the rear of one of the supply wagons. Haggerty stood to the sheriff's left side, with Ranyl and Watt just behind. Like most of the wagons in the train, the supply vehicle came equipped with a canvas cover. The rear opening was closed, sealed by a canvas sheet tied into place at the bottom by a pair of leather thongs attached to each corner. Without ceremony, Sheriff Treymore tugged loose the lower right-hand slip knot and swept the covering aside.

Looking over the sheriff's shoulder, Ranyl saw Tessymir Ryan, naked to the waist, bent over a washbasin, a keg of plain soap in one hand, a damp washcloth in the other. At the rustling sound of the canvas cover being pulled to one side, Sym straightened, folding both arms demurely across the front of her torso. Sym's long brown hair had been woven into an elaborate single braid that tumbled to the small of her back. The creamy skin of her upper body seemed to glow within the dim interior of the wagon. Turning slightly away, she peered calmly back at Sheriff Treymore. Ranyl saw something dangerous in that regal gaze, very like the look a robin might cast toward an unfamiliar insect.

"Custom in the Highlands, sir"—Sym's sultry voice fairly dripped scorn—"requires a gentleman to announce his presence before entering a private space."

Treymore let go of the covering in his hand as quickly as if the cloth had suddenly burst into flame. "Yes, ma'am; beg pardon, ma'am," the sheriff stammered. "Treymore is my name, ma'am, Sheriff Treymore. We need to search the wagon." Whipping his head about, Treymore cast a harried glance Ranyl's way. "Sweet Light, is that—"

"Lady Tessymir Ryan," Ranyl supplied with a smile. "Laird Apparent to Clan Ard Ryan, in the flesh"—Ranyl's smile stretched—"literally."

"I heard that, Squire Ranyl," Sym called crisply from inside the wagon. "I'll be with you directly."

Moments later, Sym emerged from the wagon, clad in a grey woolen riding dress complete with divided skirts. She stepped adroitly, unassisted, down from the vehicle.

"Sorry for the intrusion, Lady Ryan," Treymore apologized. "We are searching for a pair of murderers." Reaching again into his plaid, Treymore handed over the warrant. Sym wordlessly accepted the document and began to read.

"My apologies as well, my lady," Ranyl put in, "although in truth I'm hard-pressed to work up any genuine regret."

Sym's cinnamon-colored eyes rose from the vellum sheet in her hands long enough to peer into Ranyl's own. "I hope you *gentlemen* found your inspection worthwhile."

"Yes, ma'am," Sheriff Treymore enthused. In response to the icy glare Sym next directed his way, Treymore gulped as if he'd just swallowed a potato bug. "That is," the burly sheriff improvised, "no offense was intended, ma'am."

Sym sniffed.

"You'll note, milady," Sheriff Treymore continued hastily, "that your father himself has endorsed the warrant."

"His having done so, milord sheriff," Sym said coolly, "do you think it likely to find your *alleged* murder suspects hiding behind my skirts?"

"I was just doing my duty, milady," Sheriff Treymore protested.

"Rest assured, Sheriff," Sym purred, "I shall be certain to apprise my father of the zealous means by which you do so."

"Ah, yes, ma'am," the sheriff replied. "Thank you, ma'am."

Sym returned the warrant to Treymore. "Are we finished here, Sheriff?" she inquired pointedly.

Straightening, Treymore looked about. "That's the last of 'em, sheriff," one of his retainers reported.

"I reckon we are, then," Sheriff Treymore allowed. "Good day to you all." Striding toward the front of the train, Treymore yelled, "All right, you lot, let's get a move on."

Sym waited in silence until the sheriff and his men swept past, riding south. Only when they'd disappeared round a bend in the road did she step back to the rear of the supply wagon. "It is all right," she called softly, "they've gone. You can come out the now."

Ranyl watched as Syngen and Soriel emerged from the supply wagon. Watt Quigley darted forward to hand the pregnant Soriel down. The girl hesitated for a moment, but then took the young Highlander's hand and allowed him to assist her.

"Well played, my lady," Ranyl complimented Sym.

For some reason, the normally self-assured Lady Tessymir seemed discomfited by his observation. "Perhaps we should see them moved to a wagon that has been thoroughly searched. Just in case Sheriff Treymore should ..."

"Begin to wonder," Ranyl supplied, "why the Laird Apparent to Clan Ard Ryan would be performing her morning ablutions in the back of a supply wagon?"

Sym said nothing, but Ranyl saw the blush bloom in her cheeks.

"A prudent suggestion," Ranyl conceded, "but hardly necessary, I think, as the good sheriff was well and truly routed." He smiled. "Your methods may be a little unorthodox, my lady, but highly effective."

Sym's delicately cleft chin rose as he spoke, and her eyes tightened at the teasing tone of his voice. "I hope you don't think ... that is, the situation was rather desperate."

Ranyl swept the trail hat from his head and bowed deeply, formally. "Thank you, my lady."

Sym blinked as if startled, and her blush deepened. "It was nothing."

"Bold action born of quick thinking in a tight spot is not nothing, my lady," Ranyl insisted. His tone deepened slightly. "I am in-
debted to you."

The weather remained clear for the rest of the day. Kate and
Mae put on extra helpings of stew and fresh-baked biscuits for supper. Ranyl and Sym sat side by side on folding chairs placed near
one of the campfires. Tuan sang for them, his selection light and
airy. Once the young healer put away his harp, the group that had
gathered fireside dispersed. Ranyl once again found himself alone
with his intended.

He took a sip of his wine. "From time to time, I've heard your
cousin call you Sym."

Sym nodded. "I am named for my grandmother. Her name was
the only thing about her I didn't love. I can't abide Tess." She hesitated a moment, glancing down into the wine cup in her hands. "I
have an aunt everyone calls Tess, and she's ... difficult."

Ranyl laughed softly. "We all have one of those. Mine is an uncle." He took a breath. "May I call you Sym?"

Sym looked up. Ranyl saw the smile that followed begin in the
depths of her eyes. "Only if I may call you Ranyl."

Ranyl smiled back at her and felt his pulse quicken. "I am sorry
for the way I behaved earlier, at our first meeting especially."

As well you should be, Sym thought immediately but managed to
hold her tongue. "You didn't exactly go out of your way to charm,"
she allowed.

"According to Tuan, I'm terrible at first impressions," Ranyl
confessed. "You were not what I expected." He sounded bemused.

"I am sorry if I disappointed you," Sym said a little defensively.

"It is not my disappointment that is of concern, my lady," Ranyl
intoned, his smile fading.

Sym took his meaning and was glad of the campfire's soft glow, for it hid the blush she felt mounting her cheeks. "I don't suppose we could start again."

"I reckon not," Ranyl acknowledged, "but we can go on from here." Ranyl's smile returned. "Hullo, Sym, it's nice to meet you, despite that hole in your chin." He stuck out his hand.

He saw Sym's cleft chin rise, her cinnamon-brown eyes flashing. She drew a breath, and her expression transitioned into a mischievous smile. "Hullo yourself, Ranyl." She took his hand, "Has anyone ever told you that you look like nothing so much as a tree stump?"

Ranyl's smile widened. "You're the third person today, actually."

Sym laughed, the sound of it unguarded, happy. His fingers, calloused and strong, closed gently about hers, and their touch sparked something bright to life within her heart. For the first time since her father had informed her she was to wed for the benefit of her clan, Sym felt a stirring of hope. Hope that duty and happiness might twain. *Sweet Fates*, she prayed, *let it be so.*

25

Family Ties

Most of the drovers headed back west, leaving Cos the morning after Jyn and Aeryk's return from the Greenwood estate. Some were still a little squinty eyed and hungover from a few days' worth of trail-end celebration, but all had full wallets, thanks to Sam's foresight. Estyr traveled with them. Predictably, she had not been best pleased by the notion. Aeryk had found her sitting on the bed in his room the night before.

"I don't see why I can't ride along with you and Mr. Sam," Estyr greeted him without preamble.

"You will be safer and more comfortable going with Cable and the boys," Aeryk proffered. "It'll be more fun, too. You and Cable can swap fibs for hours on end. Caleb will show you how to ride like a drover, and Daymen Reed can teach you to play the lyre."

"Daymen Reed thinks too much of himself," Estyr opined.

Aeryk took a seat on the bed beside Estyr and put his arm around her. "That's my girl," he said fondly. "You best keep an eye out for smooth-talkers like Daymen."

"I wouldn't slow you down none," Estyr sallied.

Aeryk sighed. "You're going with Cable, and that's the last of it."

Estyr shot to her feet and turned on him. "You're not my papa," she said furiously. "You got no right to tell me what to do."

"I'm not your papa," Aeryk agreed gently. "I am, however, a fair bit larger and stronger than you are, Bones. I'll sit on you if I have to until the wheels are turning, but come tomorrow morning, you'll be sharing a wagon seat with Cable Dowd."

"That isn't fair," Estyr cried. Vexed, she folded her arms beneath her breasts.

Kneeling at her feet, Aeryk looked up into Estyr's stormy emerald eyes. "Maybe not," he allowed, "but it *is safer*, ya ken?"

Estyr took a half step back. Aeryk never took his eyes from hers. "Stop it," she exclaimed, lowering her hands to her sides. "You look like a whipped pup."

Climbing to his feet, Aeryk smiled. "Is it working?"

Estyr actually stamped her foot. "I don't want to."

"I know." Aeryk embraced her. "So I won't twit you for stamping your foot just the now like some wee rascal." After a moment, he felt her arms steal up around his waist.

"You will be careful," she entreated, relenting.

"I will," he vowed.

"You'll hurry," she admonished.

"Aye," Aeryk promised, "that, too."

Estyr's voice softened to a childlike whisper. "It won't feel like home 'til you come."

As the noon hour drew near, Sam and Aeryk approached the Elven villa for the purpose of attending a midday meeting with the Elven mercenary captain, Aya-Bal-Mar. Elven sentries sketched brief informal bows and waved them through the front gate. Much to Aeryk's disappointment, Jyn was not there to greet them. Over tea and biscuits, they continued planning for the trip north next summer. For what seemed like the fifth time, they went over the logistics of the planned trek beyond the Torean Mountains.

Aeryk had begun to suspect the planning sessions were as much an excuse for Sam and Aya to spend time together as anything else. They did agree on a list of trade goods to carry with them into Anduyin territory. Aeryk was pleased that most of his suggestions made it onto the list. Aya directed Aeryk to find Jyn and pass the final version of the trade goods list on to her.

Aeryk brightened at the prospect until Aya said, "Aeryk, there is something you should know before seeking out Jyn-Ael-Tor this afternoon." In response to his questioning look, Aya explained, "Jyn's elder sister arrived in Cos yesterday. Her name is Pak-Dyn-Tor. Pak is traveling with a mate, also of the vyldeen, named Kul-Cah-Zul."

Aeryk nodded but said nothing.

"Jyn-Ael-Tor was showing the pair of them the grounds earlier," Aya informed him. "They should be returning to the main portico soon. Do be careful, Aeryk Emyrt." A blind man could have seen the warning emanating from Aya's sapphire gaze.

"Thank you, Aya-Bal-Mar, for the biscuits," Aeryk said, hesitating only a little, "and for the advice." He picked up the trade goods list and walked out of the room.

Aeryk caught sight of Jyn standing on the landing fronting the main annex with two Elves he had not seen before. The first, an Elfin, was about Jyn's height and shared her silver-blond hair and honey-colored skin. He assumed she must be Pak-Dyn-Tor. The third elf, clearly an Elfan, stood perhaps three finger widths taller, with medium-blond hair and skin a couple of shades darker.

Jyn and her sister were similarly attired in white silk blouses and close-fitting brown-leather breeches. The Elfan wore a silk shirt of cornflower blue and what looked to be grey silk trousers. All three were dressed in finely worked knee-length calfskin boots. Each had a johten belted at the waist and one of those long, slim-bladed daggers Elves seemed to prefer.

As he approached, he could hear the Elfan saying something about horses. *Syac*, which meant horse, happened to be one of the few Ilyrian words Aeryk understood. Aeryk halted a couple of paces away and stood quietly, waiting. He knew Jyn had seen him walk up; their eyes met briefly, but the elf did nothing to acknowledge his presence.

When the Elfan stopped talking, Aeryk spoke in Aylitic. "Excuse me, Jyn-Ael-Tor." Three pairs of large, almond-shaped Elven eyes swung toward him. Jyn's were the by-now-familiar amber; Pak-Dyn-Tor's eyes showed grey. The third elf's glinted a deep blue. Bowing, in what he hoped amounted to a suitably respectful manner, Aeryk went on to say, "Captain Aya-Bal-Mar said to pass this along." He handed the paper with the trade goods list on it to Jyn.

Jyn nodded her head in greeting and accepted the folded vellum sheet. Glancing at it, Jyn said in Aylitic, "Thank you, Aeryk Emyrt." Jyn's tone sounded strictly neutral. She might as well have been thanking a stranger for passing the salt.

"Are your servants in the habit of interrupting, Jyn-Ael-Tor?" the Elfan asked, speaking slightly accented Aylitic as well. His voice conveyed a studied blend of disinterest and annoyance.

"Aeryk is no servant, Kul-Cah-Zul," Jyn responded. "He is a Kylgahran scout. I know him to be both brave and resourceful."

"Still, Jyn," Pak-Dyn-Tor chided, "a hireling must be taught some manners, surely."

Aeryk could not help but notice the intent look Jyn's sibling cast his way.

"I make allowances for Aeryk, elder," Jyn said steadily, "as I owe him my life." Jyn met her sister's gaze without defiance but without flinching either. After a moment, Jyn looked first to Kul-Cah-Zul and then to Pak-Dyn-Tor. "If thee will excuse me?" Pak-Dyn-Tor nodded, and the trio of Elves exchanged bows. Jyn turned to Aeryk. "A word, if I may, Aeryk?" Without waiting for a reply, Jyn walked by him.

Aeryk turned and fell into step with Jyn-Ael-Tor as the young elf made her way further down the portico.

"Have I blundered yet again?" Aeryk asked when she halted.

"Not in any way that matters," Jyn replied. Her eyes searched his. "I am sorry if that was ... uncomfortable."

Aeryk glanced over his shoulder to be certain they were out of earshot. "The manner in which your sister spoke the word 'hireling' did manage to imply something one would not want to touch with one's bare hands."

"Pak is somewhat reserved," Jyn acknowledged. The corners of her mouth ticked upwards.

Aeryk tossed his head. "For an elf, that's going some."

Jyn arched an eyebrow. "Shall I apologize a second time?"

"No, dymena." Aeryk smiled. "How long will your relations be around?"

"I don't know." Jyn shrugged. "Indefinitely, perhaps."

Aeryk grimaced. "Sam has decided to ride along with Captain Aya when the duke's goods arrive. He and I will head west once they're back. Maybe I should say my good-byes the now and stay out of your way thereafter."

"I do not wish to say good-bye to thee, Aeryk Emyrt, only farewell," Jyn told him. "We shall meet again in the spring."

"Thee, is it?" Aeryk's smile returned. "Still friends, then."

"Of course," Jyn said evenly. Aeryk saw Jyn's answering smile bloom first in the depths of her eyes. "Farewell, Aeryk Emyrt."

Aeryk bowed. "And you, Jyn-Ael-Tor."

Jyn returned his bow in the brief, informal manner reserved for friends and close relations and watched as Aeryk turned on his heel and strode away.

26

A Visit to Barber Street

The Altairan brooded, absently drumming his fingers on the polished surface of the writing table before him. A tall, well-made man of middle years with a full head of dark hair, deep-set brown eyes, very white teeth, and a luxuriant mustache, Tierza feared and hated him with every fiber of her being. They met, as was usually the case, in a room at the back of his clothing store.

"Anduyin horses?" The Altairan, whose name was Lykas Greytower, hardly sounded interested. "It does not seem probable, does it?"

"No," Tierza acknowledged, "but I heard much the same from some of the others before they left." Greytower's disinterest surprised her. He'd been much more intent a couple of days ago. Something else must be in the wind. *Either that, or some new woman has fallen into his grasp.* Tierza didn't know if Lykas Greytower actually hailed from Altair, one of the old kingdoms located along the northeastern shore of the Middle Sea between the realms of Kios and Myrl. A common Syrdisian surname, Greytower, but the given name Lykas was not.

"It is fortunate that you were able to single out the young one, this Aeryk," Greytower remarked. "How did you accomplish that, exactly?"

"Pure chance," Tierza responded. "Your instructions were only to make contact with one of the drovers, as they are called. Aeryk just happened to be the first one I met."

"Do you think he is lying?" Greytower speculated. He was seated in a padded leather chair. Between them stood his writing table, a sturdy design made of walnut. Pens and paper were nowhere in sight. She'd never seen him write anything.

"It is possible. But his manner is open-handed, and he does not seem very sophisticated," Tierza said. "If there is a lie in him, I have not yet seen it."

"He is, however, in the employ of Elves, who are notoriously sophisticated. It is entirely possible that they are lying to him." Greytower leaned back in his chair and placed both hands behind his head, stretching the fabric of his richly tailored linen shirt. The Altairan was muscular and proud of it. "A consignment of household goods, was it, to the master of the Greenwood estate or one of his relations, transported by Elves?"

"That is what he said," Tierza affirmed.

"Felix Clearview is a nithing," Lykas Greytower asserted, "a weakling and a fool." He paused, leaning forward once more; his eyes narrowed. "His cousin, on the other hand, Duke Martyn, is not, and as for household goods, I wonder."

Tierza kept silent. The Altairan liked the sound of his own voice. He had proven to be less tolerant of others.

"Spend some time with him, the young one," Greytower decided, "preferably in his bed. If he knows anything, I do not doubt you will be able to discover it." He glanced out of the window. *Gauging the time*, Tierza thought. "You may go."

Trying not to let her relief show, Tierza exited the room and made her way down the hall as quickly and quietly as she could. Sometimes, she hated having to use a crutch, especially in this place, where any weakness was ruthlessly exploited. She saw Greygor Gullwatch, one of the Altairan's cutthroats, standing at the end of the hall. Gullwatch was one of the Altairan's favorites, a rich man in his own right, if the rumors were true.

Greygor was tall and lean. He rarely washed, and his lank sand-colored hair and pockmarked skin had a perpetually oily cast. His eyes were a dull, dead grey—unless he was hurting someone; then they glittered, hot and carnal. He smiled at her. She'd had to spend the night with Greygor once, one of the Altairan's object lessons in obedience. She ducked her head as he would expect her to and kept moving. Greygor did nothing to impede her progress. He knew the Altairan found her useful. They both understood this meant she was safe from him until the Altairan found her otherwise. Outside, the sun was shining. It was not far to Barber Street. She had plenty of time.

Aeryk had no difficulty finding Barber Street. He still gawped at the size of the city and the throngs of people who lived and worked there. As he and Wyli threaded their way through traffic, approaching what he hoped was Tierza's shop, or at least the shop where Tierza worked, he realized that he'd seen more people in the short distance between Copper and Barber Streets in Cos than he'd meet in a year back home. The barbershop turned out to be a framed wooden building, as were most of the structures lining Barber Street.

Struck by what to his eyes seemed a discordant array of bright colors with which the buildings were painted, Aeryk could only shake his head. The shop where he'd been told he could find Tierza showed a startling shade of yellow. A buxom woman, aged, he reckoned, somewhere in her thirties, stood in the doorway. Clad in a sleeveless blue cotton dress, covered by a large white apron, she was redheaded, green eyed, and fair skinned. She could have been a Kylgahran.

She smiled in a manner as friendly as it appeared genuine. "Can I help you, sir?"

"I need to see Tierza," Aeryk replied with an answering smile. "Please tell her it's about my horse."

"Wyli," Tierza's unmistakable, sultry soprano voice emanated from within the shop. "Is that you?"

The redhead stepped aside, and Tierza made her way out on to the porch. She too wore a simple cotton frock, pale green in color, and an apron. Leaning on her crutch, she pulled a large red apple from the pocket of her apron. Looking up at Aeryk, she said, "This is for Wyli. May I?"

"Sure," Aeryk invited her, "just hold it in the palm of your hand. He won't bite."

Stepping close, Tierza extended her hand, holding the apple in it as he'd instructed. Wyli was soon munching happily away. The gelding made short work of the fruit, and then stood shaking his head side to side. "What does that mean?" Tierza inquired.

"He likes you," Aeryk responded.

Tierza's silky raven hair was bound up in a strip of cotton cloth the same color as her dress. She brushed a stray wisp from across her forehead and smiled. Her large light-brown eyes seemed to come alive when she smiled.

"Mind if I step down?" Aeryk asked.

"We won't do much business if you don't," Tierza observed dryly. As he dismounted, Tierza took his arm and hugged it. She looked across the boarded walk to the woman in the doorway. "Myra York," Tierza announced, "this is Aeryk Emyrt of Clan Ard Mourne, a wild Highlander from the far west country. You can tell by the whacking great sword he carries and the steely glint in his eye."

"It is a pleasure to meet you, Aeryk," Myra York said kindly, "and this famous horse of yours. Don't pay too much heed to everything Tierza says. She talks a lot of blather much of the time, but her heart is in the right place."

Tierza had earlier told Aeryk that Myra was Thatch's woman and the mother of his child. "His wife, you mean?" Aeryk had asked.

"No woman in Cos who has sold herself for money can wed," Tierza informed him. "Thatch is slow to anger, Aeryk, but be careful what you say about Myra in his presence."

Aeryk wondered if Tierza could marry in Cos but had not voiced the question.

"Thank you, Mistress York," Aeryk said, meaning it, pleased to see the discomfited expression on Tierza's face.

Recovering quickly, Tierza released his arm and told him, "You can tie Wyli up in back; there's water there. I'll let you in through the rear door."

The rear of the building faced into a wide alleyway. Aeryk was surprised to see vegetables of various types growing in a series of large earthenware pots that lined both sides of the alley. Some wash hung on a clothesline, waving gently in a light breeze. He tied Wyli's reins to a wooden railing at the edge of a narrow back porch, positioning the Morgyn so he couldn't get into the vegetables. A large bucket of water stood nearby. Placing it within easy reach for Wyli, he stood scratching the gelding's ears. The back door swung open, and Tierza leaned across the threshold to beckon him inside.

He followed her down a short hallway to a chamber of about the same dimensions as his room at the Rising Star. A good-sized oak bathtub stood filled, with steam gently rising, in the center of the room. A padded leather couch placed along one of the walls looked comfortable, if a bit well worn. An open cupboard containing a neatly folded array of white cotton towels and a collection of bottles and ceramic jars stood against the third wall. The fourth wall, opposite the door, was dominated by a window, the panes of which were made from some sort of frosted glass. While he could not see through the window, sunlight from without flooded in and filled the room with a warm glow. Two sturdy wooden stools sat one on each side of the door. A polished brass mirror about the size of a Kylgahran targe hung upon the wall, just above the right-hand stool.

"This is our private bathing room," Tierza commented with a touch of pride.

"Impressive," Aeryk said. "It looks expensive," he added a little apprehensively.

"Not for special guests." Tierza's smile again lit her eyes. "Put anything you want washed or mended on this stool." She pointed to the one without the mirror over it. "When you've bathed, pull this cord"—she indicated a cotton rope hanging alongside the door and threading through the wall above it—"and I'll be back to see about your haircut. There is soap and a towel on the tray by the tub."

The bathwater was fine, and the soap smelled ... well, like soap, for which Aeryk was grateful. He had feared Tierza's special guests or customers or whoever might prefer something flowery. Explaining to Sam why he suddenly smelled of lilacs or some such would have been awkward. Maybe it was Aya-Bal-Mar's influence, but Sam had become a little too adept at arching eyebrows himself lately to suit Aeryk.

Wrapped in a towel after his bath, Aeryk tugged on the cord and took a seat on the stool in front of the mirror. A few moments later, Tierza stepped into the room, closing and then latching the door behind her. She wore a floor-length grey cotton robe, not a dress. Her crutch she had tucked under her left arm. Over her right shoulder, slung by a narrow strap, she carried a small leather case. Her hair flowed freely down her back, long, gleaming, and black as night. Despite her crutch, Tierza moved gracefully to his side and breathed in deeply, delicate nostrils flaring slightly.

"You smell better than Wyli for a change," she proclaimed.

"I've been bathing pretty regularly lately," Aeryk pointed out. "Practically civilized, I'm getting to be."

Laying the leather case on a small shelf under the mirror, she opened it and took out a pair of scissors and a comb that looked as if it had been carved from ivory. "Don't become too civilized, Aeryk. I'm afraid you'll lose some part of yourself in the process. That would be a shame." Extending the scissors and comb to him, she asked, "Hold on to these for me?"

Aeryk complied and sat waiting as Tierza slipped the robe down off her shoulders and let it fall to the floor. Beneath, she wore only a light cotton shift. White in color and without sleeves, the garment reached to about her calves. It was belted about the waist with a strip of cotton cloth but otherwise hung open down the front. The thin fabric clung to the lush contours of her breasts.

Aware he was blushing, Aeryk said, "Sorry, I didn't mean to stare."

Hobbling close so she could run her fingers through his hair, Tierza spoke softly. "I wore this for you. I hoped you would look and see something other than my crutch."

"It takes only a few moments in your company, Tierza, for me to forget all about your crutch," Aeryk replied.

Tierza said nothing but pressed close, setting aside the implement in question. He could feel the warmth of her skin through the thin fabric of her shift. She reclaimed the scissors and comb. "When cutting hair, I normally use a high stool," Tierza informed him, "but if you will allow me to lean on you"—she eased even closer, and he could feel the zephyr-soft caress of her breath on the nape of his neck—"to steady me, we'll get on with this."

Tierza maintained a soft silence while she cut his hair, deftly applying scissors and comb. Through the cloth of her shift, the flesh of her hips and waist felt warm to the touch. Her body remained continually in contact with his, thigh to thigh, breast to arm, her belly against his back, as she eased her way behind him. She finished standing in front of him, between his legs.

"There," she said, leaning back slightly to look him over, thrusting her hips gently against his groin. "How handsome you are."

Almost painfully aroused, Aeryk pulled her close to him. Her mouth came up against his, warm, sweet, and seeking. Her lips parted, and he could feel the subtle probing of her tongue. He heard the clatter of scissors and comb as they hit the waxed wooden floor. Her hands urgently tugged at the towel about his waist, freeing him. Tierza climbed into his lap, pulling aside the folds of her shift. She gasped as his organ pressed into the warm, moist inner core of her loins. She enveloped him, moving slowly at first and then with ever-increasing urgency. Her slender body arched sensually onto his, a wanton blend of wet heat and longing. Crying out, he crushed her to him, his sex throbbing and pulsing into hers.

He held her close and then leaned back so he could see into her eyes. They were warm and soft, like sunlight on molasses. "Did I hurt you?" he asked. She shook her head and then kissed him. She started to lift herself free, but his grip tightened, holding her in place. "Don't go," he pleaded.

She relaxed against him. He was still inside her. Reaching to her waist, he loosened the cloth strip holding her shift in place. Pulling the garment down off her shoulders, he took gentle grasp of her upper arms, arching her back away from him.

"What are you doing?" she asked breathlessly.

"Looking at you," he responded intently. Instinctively, her hands moved to cover herself, but he stayed her, saying, "How beautiful you are." Dipping his head, Aeryk placed his mouth over her left breast. She moaned softly at his touch. Running his tongue over a rose-colored nipple, he could feel it budding. His manhood stiffened again, and he began to move inside her. Tierza flung her arms about his neck, clinging to him as to life itself. He slid his hands down, cupping her buttocks. They strained together, moving as one. She cried out; her body writhed and shuddered against him. He could contain himself no longer and climaxed a second time.

Later, they lay atop some towels placed to cover the couch. Aeryk reclined against a padded leather arm, while Tierza pressed close to his side, one slim thigh tossed over his. Her hair she'd flung over her right shoulder. It tumbled across his chest like a gossamer-soft ebony waterfall.

"It's near dark," Aeryk said.

Tierza stretched, arching her back like a kitten, and then settled down, snuggling close. "I have a room," she told him, "at the other end of the building—in the cellar actually, but it has a little window, just at the top of the wall. It's small. There is a bed. We could spend the night together, if you like."

"Myra won't mind?" Aeryk asked, touched and pleased by the invitation.

"No. By now she's probably closed the shop and gone home." Tierza kissed his shoulder. "I have some bread and some cheese."

"Is it the same smoky-flavored cheese as from the other night at the Rising Star?" he asked hopefully. Aeryk really liked that cheese.

Tierza smiled. "Yes, it is, and some sharp cheddar as well, and some wine."

"Uh-oh," Aeryk's inner voice chimed, *"I hope it isn't more of that syrupy stuff."* He asked, "Is it that same dark, sweet wine as well?"

Tierza flared up at his question. "Aeryk Emyrt, do you think I'm made of money?"

"No," he said quietly. "I think you are made of moonbeams and fairy dust, bright tomorrows, and song."

"Fool," she chided, hugging him fiercely. "It is a perfectly serviceable wine, a little too dry, maybe."

Fates be praised, Aeryk thought, *I might actually like it.*

Tierza ran her fingers across his chest, stopping when she touched the medallion. "What is this?" she asked, idly.

"A gift from my father," Aeryk said. "It is supposed to be a charm against evil, magic, that sort of thing."

"Does it work?" Tierza sounded intrigued.

"So far," Aeryk observed.

Digging her knuckles into his ribs until he winced, Tierza then lifted the medal from his chest and continued her inquiry. "Isn't this a rune symbol? Do you know what it represents?"

"It is the rune symbol Fey," Aeryk affirmed. "According to my father, it stands for the dignity and freedom of the human spirit."

Placing the medal lightly back on his chest, Tierza asked, "Do you believe there is such a thing?"

"I doubt mine is particularly dignified," Aeryk mused. "But I believe each of us does have a spirit, a soul, if you will, of our own. I think perhaps it is the only thing we possess that is truly ours."

Tierza lay back against him, saying nothing.

Running his fingers along her spine, Aeryk asked, "Will you tell me why, Tierza?"

"Why what?" She sounded sleepy.

"Why us? Why now, here?" Aeryk wanted to know. "I'm going to be leaving in a few days. I've told you I'm not certain when or even if I'll be back."

"Well," Tierza said in that smoky voice of hers, "to begin with, you are devastatingly handsome."

It was his turn to dig his knuckles into her ribs, making her squeal. "You are the one who is beautiful." Aeryk spoke with his lips pressed into the lush mass of her hair. "And that is no answer."

"I said to begin with," she scolded him. "I decided I liked being rescued. More particularly, I liked the way you rescued me, lifting me into your saddle so easily and so carefully. And you are more attentive of my bosom than my limp. I like that, too."

Fates forefend, he was really going to have to be more careful about where his eyes went.

Folding her hands upon his chest and resting her chin atop them, she thought a bit. "Also, I knew that you had never been with a woman, and I wanted to be your first."

"How did you know that?" he asked, astounded and a little worried. *How clumsy had he been?*

"Mistress Canty," Tierza responded.

Light! Danyl had warned him women would talk about anything.

"She pulled me aside and gave me quite a talking to. She was concerned about"—Tierza paused for a moment—"about my intentions. She is very fond of you, you know."

"Oh, well," Aeryk said, mildly astonished. "That's good to know."

"Some women of all ages, shapes, and types can be harpies, Aeryk," Tierza said, sounding indignant. "Hard-hearted. If one of those gets her claws into a good man, especially one who is young and inexperienced ... well, Mistress Canty and I were determined not to let that happen to you."

"I'm grateful to Mistress Canty and especially to you." Aeryk ran his fingers down her back to fit his hand gently around her left buttock, giving it a little squeeze. He marveled at how human flesh could be so soft and firm all at the same time.

"I knew you would be gentle." Tierza's voice took on a husky tone. "I hoped you would be thorough." At his look, she smiled, kissing him briefly on the lips. "You were both gentle and very thorough. In future, you should remember that, Aeryk; it matters to a woman."

"Yes, ma'am," Aeryk promised.

"Mostly," Tierza concluded, "I wanted someone like you to remember me. You will remember me, won't you, Aeryk?"

"All my life long." Aeryk knew he'd never said a truer thing.

That night in her room, after seeing to Wyli and eating some bread and cheese and drinking a little wine that wasn't too bad and making love again, he pulled Tierza, naked, into his arms, holding her across his lap. She was such a tiny little thing.

Hugging her close, he said, "Tierza, if you'd like to get out of Cos, I'll take you. Anywhere you want to go, provided we can get there by horseback."

"Anywhere," she teased, "even Taggert's Landing?"

He grinned. "You'd like it there. And we could sure use a good tailor. A seamstress is pretty much the same thing, isn't it?"

She hesitated only a moment, and then said, "I can't, Aeryk. I have obligations." Her voice sounded burdened, as if weighed down. "Thank you for asking, Aeryk. All my life long, I will remember that you asked."

She had only a little difficulty seeing Aeryk off the next morning. *Associating with young men*—Tierza smiled, warming at the thought—*can sometimes be very gratifying.* After his departure, Tierza washed herself carefully. The Altairan might want her, and he was particular about some things.

27
Arrival

Swinging down from the saddle, Ranyl led Stepper to the crest. Sym walked at his side, leading her mount, a long-legged gelding she called Dart. As he topped the ridgeline, Ranyl caught first sight of Greymark, the hold of Owain Ryan, laird of Clan Ard Ryan. The sun shone high in the sky; early afternoon, it was, on the fourth day since Sym's party had met Ranyl's wagon train. Taking her reins and his, he tied them securely to a nearby gorse bush. Together, they stood side by side, overlooking the ancestral home of Clan Ard Ryan.

In Kylgahra a *hold* referred to the fortified dwelling of a clan laird. Other clan properties—farms, mills, and even entire villages— were designated as tithings. Most holds comprised a manor or Long House, surrounded by some type of palisade. A few great holds, such as Clan Ard Erryn's fortress South Watch, were mighty castles, ringed by towering battlements of stone that enclosed entire villages. Some border holds were little more than wooden palisades built to protect manors that looked more like farmhouses than great keeps.

Greymark, the Ard Ryan hold, sat astride a set of bluffs over-looking the River Alder. The hold stood protected by a wall of stone quarried from the cliffs near to hand. Greymark had grown over time, and its curtain walls were irregularly shaped but obviously well maintained. The Long House looked to be a two-story affair built of the same blue-grey stone that formed the outer walls. The walls of Greymark encompassed a middling-sized village.

Basking in the soft light of a late autumn afternoon, the Ryan hold appeared solid, prosperous, and secure, if perhaps a little old-fashioned and picturesque, with the Tylcairn Mountains rising just beyond. Ranyl could see people moving about, some entering or exiting through open gates in the walls. White smoke swirled busily from a dozen chimney tops. The stone-walled hold looked as if it belonged, as if it were part of this land, not merely resident upon it. Sym had not said how significant Ranyl's portion weighed in terms of righting Clan Ard Ryan's finances. They both knew his father's coin was the reason for the marriage contract binding them.

"Greymark looks as if it has always been," Ranyl said.

"Aye," the slim-hipped lass standing beside him said on a breath. Greymark was more than home to Sym; it formed the center of her world, the place where everything and everyone she loved resided—well, almost everyone. Sym pointed to a large plot of open ground a short distance outside the walls. "That field is fallow. It should serve well enough as a wagon park until we can arrange for more permanent accommodations."

The field, like the hold itself, was located on the southern bank of the Alder River. The Alder wound its way south and then west from its point of origin in the Tylcairn Mountains, across the north-ern reaches of Kylgahra, emptying into the Maeryc Ocean near the coastal city of Warwyck. Though not suitable for large ocean-going ships, the Alder did serve as a useful conduit of travel and trade for smaller craft and an array of river barges.

"More than adequate," Ranyl agreed, "especially as I reckon most of the folks will be fair giddy just to stay in one place for more than a night at a time."

"Are you certain you won't stay over?" Sym asked for the third time that day. "You really should meet my father, you know."

"I need to learn the lay of the land," Ranyl replied patiently. "We've arrived well ahead of schedule. I can put the next few days to good use, scouting, and at the same time spare your father the strain of first impression until you've had a chance to fortify him against it." Ranyl wore a blue cotton shirt, a plain tartyn of blue silk, and brown woolen trousers. Ranyl's grey-felt trail hat canted across his forehead and, as ever, his broadsword and Meggie's long-bladed knife were belted at his waist.

"My father is a remarkably sturdy fellow," Sym replied with a clear smile in her eyes. "I think just a few hours will be enough to get over the upset, and you'll have a lifetime to get to know Ard Ryan holdings."

"The sooner the better," Ranyl contended, undeterred. "Beside which," he added, speaking in a more private tone, "I've already met the Ryan I'm most interested in knowing."

She looked into his eyes. They were as grey as thunderclouds and warm enough to start a blush rising in her cheeks. "Do you know that is the closest you've come to talking prettily to me in nigh on to four days?" Sym teased. She'd found the past few days enlightening. Still, this man who was to be her husband remained something of an enigma. No fool, of that she stood certain. Ranyl bore the burden of command with the ease of long practice.

His men were fighters. Her own eyes told her that, even without Davis's quiet assurance. They had confidence in him. He was no craven, then. They questioned more than her father would have tolerated, and he answered simply, without haughtiness. In return, his rangers showed respect with no wariness. Ranyl was approachable but apart. He was so with them and with her as well.

Still present was the barrier that he'd flung into place between them upon first meeting. She knew because every now and then, for a moment or two, he would lower the thing and let her through. Intelligent, endowed with a sardonic sense of humor that was, Sym suspected, far more sophisticated than her own, Ranyl saw the world differently than she. He and Alyair appeared to understand one another without trying. For some reason, Sym found that to be equal parts intriguing and infuriating. Ranyl clearly liked Alyair. With Sym, he seemed to be reserving judgment.

"Talking prettily comes naturally to some men," Ranyl stated a little ruefully. "When I try, well, *trying* is exactly what it sounds like."

Sym regarded him steadily, her large brown eyes twinkling. "Maybe a little practice is all that is wanting."

"You could come along," Ranyl suggested. "I'll promise to practice mightily."

Sym hesitated a moment, considering, and then shook her head—reluctantly, it seemed to Ranyl. *Wishful thinking, that,* the voice in his head scoffed.

"I can't," Sym lamented. "Lairds Kenyon and Fraiser are to visit tomorrow or the next day, in separate parties, no doubt. Some fence-mending is in order. My father will want me by his side." Turning her head slightly away, she pinned him with a slantwise look. "You should be there, too."

"We are not married yet, my sweet laird apparent." Ranyl smiled a little too gleefully to suit Sym. "I've a short while still free of the harness."

"What a thing to say," Sym groused, brown eyes flashing.

He'd made no demands of her physically. She'd worried some about that and had steeled herself against the possibility. Some men, she was well aware, once formally betrothed, would have viewed bedding her straightaway as a right well earned or at least well and truly paid for by the weight of his portion. He'd made no attempt even to kiss her. She'd experienced only the occasional touch of his hand.

"Aye, well," Ranyl allowed, "if soon or late I have to step into harness with somebody, it might as well be you." Stuffing his hands into his belt, Ranyl hunched his thick shoulders. "Could do worse, I reckon."

"You're awful," Sym declared with some heat. But Ranyl noted a slight upward quirk at the corners of her mouth.

In some ways Sym was easy to read. She made no attempt to hide her emotions. Discerning her intent, however, proved not so easy. Well spoken, smarter than he, Ranyl reckoned, Sym had been born and bred to stand at the head of her clan. She appeared to him as hard to know as she was easy to be with. He wished for the hundredth time that she was not quite so beautiful. *Why would a man want his wife to be less attractive to his eyes?* The question sounded ridiculous in his own mind until he considered the answer. *So that he might appear more so in hers.*

"I come from a long line of awfuls," Ranyl acknowledged freely. "You've met my father?" In response, Sym shared with him a brief knowing glance and a wry smile. "If you think my father is something, wait until you meet my uncle, Bryghton. When it comes to Emyrts, girl, you've a bargain in me."

"So says you while ye ride away, leaving me to come home alone," Sym decried.

"You are hardly returning empty-handed," Ranyl noted reasonably, jerking a thumb in the direction of the wagon train spread out on the road behind them.

Sym ducked her head, looking anything but mollified. Ranyl stepped close, near enough to catch her scent, a delicate touch of strawberry. "When first I saw you," he said earnestly, "I thought you were the most beautiful girl I'd ever seen. I knew it, the same way I know the sun will rise tomorrow. What I could not grasp was why." Sym raised her eyes to his. "I have it the now," Ranyl continued. "Somehow you are aglow from within. Yours is an inside-out kind of beauty, the type what lasts and lasts. You'll be lovely when you're eighty." The barrier separating them tottered; she could feel it weakening.

Sym saw that his eyes were very serious and as steady as the sun shining overhead. She smiled a little tremulously and demurred. "You mean despite the hole in my chin."

"I see no defect." Very gently Ranyl laid the thumb of his right hand into the slight indentation in her chin. "But you don't need to be perfect to be beautiful, Sym." He murmured with a quiet intensity, "You possess a beauty all your own, like no other."

Ranyl took her right hand in his left. At his touch, Sym felt her heart jump. She lowered her eyes and smiled joyously. "You talk prettily enough when you put your mind to it," she observed.

"I don't know what the custom is here in the north," Ranyl told her, "but where I come from, a man is expected to gift his betrothed with a token long held and dear to him, so as to honor her." Ranyl pulled something from his shirt pocket. Sym could see that it was a ring, finely wrought of gold, crowned by a black pearl. "This belonged to my grandmother. An Emyrt she was to her toes but one who somehow managed not to be awful. I hope you will accept this."

"Oh, Ranyl," Sym exclaimed, "it is beautiful."

The barrier came crashing down, banished, she hoped, for good and all.

"My grandmother was a tiny little thing. Her fingers were like a child's," Ranyl warned, looking abashed. "It is likely not to fit. I was thinking ..."

"Try here." Sym held up the little finger of her left hand. Ranyl slipped the ring into place. The fit was perfect. "There," Sym cried triumphantly, "it is as if it were made for me."

"That isn't your ring finger," Ranyl pointed out.

Sym tisked. "What matters is that it was *her* ring. And now it is mine, and I shall wear it as she did, always."

Ranyl tugged the hat from his head and let it fall to his feet. He placed his right hand in the hollow of Sym's hip, where it narrowed to join her waist. Sym could feel the strength in his hands, though Ranyl's grip was gentle, his fingers warm and sure. Sym's breath caught. Slowly he pulled her to him and pressed his lips to hers.

A first kiss, Sym had always been told, embodied a moment of magic, where anything was possible. She'd known heady passion before, in the arms of another. Sym thought Ranyl's kiss was meant to stir something else. A greeting, his gentle touch was, a meeting between equals, a beginning. A surge of relief swept through her. He would not ask more than she could give. Sym's body softened, molding to his. Her lips parted, and Ranyl's mouth moved subtly on hers.

Ranyl broke off the kiss, pulling his head away slightly to gather her in his arms. "That could get to be a habit," he whispered. She could feel the trickle of his breath brush her ear as he exhaled.

They were nearly the same height. Bending her head forward, Sym discovered she could rest it comfortably at the base of his neck.

"Pretty speech and stolen kisses." She smiled. "Of a sudden, Ranyl Emyrt, you are beginning to worry me." She could feel his arms tighten about her.

"I'll take nothing from you, Sym, not ever, my word on it." There was a throb of some pent-up emotion in his voice. This mattered to him, but she knew not how or why.

Leaning back so she could see into his eyes, Sym placed the fingers of her right hand on his cheek. "Promise only to share, as we have just shared, and I'll be content."

"You deserve some happiness," Ranyl intoned.

Sym heard the sincerity in his voice and knew his concern was genuine. He held her in some regard. The knowledge sent a surge of warmth spreading through her belly. Sym tucked her head again into place at the side of his neck. "If I was unhappy, Kylgahran, you'd nay doubt it."

Sym felt his body relax, the tension easing. She could also feel a chuckle rise from somewhere deep within him. "All right enough," he said finally, her betrothed, "a bargain fair, my bonnie."

Sym laughed and hugged him. It was like embracing an oak tree. That is, if an oak were made of living flesh, warm and strong and smelling slightly of leather and wool, plain soap, and man. "Thanks for that," she replied, "and for this." She held up her ring, admiring how it glittered in the sunlight.

"That ring is one of three my grandmother had struck," Ranyl informed her. "One she kept; the second she gave to her daughter, my father's sister, Joslyn; and the third went to my mother. When Grandmother died, her ring passed on to me."

"You've never mentioned your aunt," Sym prompted.

"Aunt Joslyn died some twenty years ago," Ranyl replied, "in the Lywgahra, struck down by a Cymbri war arrow. I must have met her, but I can't recall."

"What was she doing out east?" Sym wondered.

"Word was she eloped with a sorcerer's apprentice." Ranyl smiled. "At least that's what I overheard Cook saying early one solstice morning. My father will say only that she died a bonnie. I don't know what the real truth is, but in my entire life I've heard my father speak kindly of only three people, all of whom wore one of grandmother's rings." Ranyl's smile broadened. "I think he likes you, by the way. He said I would find you 'pleasing enough.'"

"Did he?" Sym replied tartly. "That was big of him." Though she'd only met him the once, Sym did not care much for Stephyn Emyrt.

"My father is hard to know. Some would say that's a good thing." Ranyl's smile faded. "Come on," Ranyl said, his reluctance evident. "We'd best get back." Retrieving his hat, he led her to her horse.

Sym had assigned Jemy Dudgin of Clan Ard Ryan to ride along with Ranyl and the six rangers he'd chosen to accompany him. Jemy, a leanly built towhead with keen green eyes, was one of Sym's retainers, a steady young man a year or two Ranyl's junior, who knew the Ryan lands like the back of his hand.

"Listen to Jemy," she said softly in parting shortly thereafter, speaking for his ears alone. "It would not do for you to get lost or go blundering into a scrape that need not be."

"Your faith in me is inspiring," Ranyl responded wryly in a tone no louder than her own.

"This is not only borderland, my lord sheriff," Sym told him. "*'Tis the north*, and you know naught of it. I would not want to see you damaged."

"I should have given you Nanna's ring three days ago," Ranyl surmised. He smiled as he spoke.

"More fool you," Sym declared and then reached out to clasp his hand. "Do be careful."

More touched by her small display than he was willing to admit, Ranyl replied, "I'll only be a few days. If Jemy hollers, I'll jump; I promise."

Ard Ryan tithings were average size for a Kylgahran clan, forming overall a roughly square-shaped region about three days' ride across in any primary direction. The hold, Greymark, was located in the southwest quadrant. The principal village, York, situated two days' ride further north, sat also along the banks of the River Alder. In addition to Jemy Dudgin, the six rangers Ranyl selected to ride with him included Emerson Hart, as well as Lukas Holt and Watt Quigley.

In particular, Ranyl wanted Hart's and Holt's counsel with respect to how the Ard Ryan assets were being utilized. Hart had been a farmer and a soldier before joining the ranks of the Wyteridge Rangers, and Lukas Holt a lumberman. Ranyl had asked Lester Wylson of Clan Ard Cullen to join his scouting party as well. Wylson was a miller's son and would most likely have followed his father's trade, had not a scrap over a comely thatcher's daughter led to a stabbing. The magistrate ruled that while the fight appeared to be fair enough, any lad so eager to wield a blade might as well do so as a ranger in defense of Ard Mourne holdings.

Wylson had turned out to be a good man—a good ranger, anyway. Like Watt Quigley, Wylson was one of those who had taken to the bow. About the same height as Watt, the auburn-haired, grey-eyed Wylson stood some thicker through the shoulders. Ranyl figured, with all the water and timber covering Ard Ryan lands, a miller's eye might come in handy.

Timber and water there were in plenty on the ride north. The River Alder was the main watercourse but by no means the only one. A number of creeks and large, fast-flowing rills crisscrossed the Ard Ryan lands. Holt especially was impressed by the woods. "These are ancient stands, milord," the tall, usually laconic ranger observed. "Good white oak and cedar in addition to pine and even some golden yew. Unusual, it is, to find golden yew this far north. Seasoned oak is always in demand, and good cedar, why, that's near worth its weight in silver."

Ranyl spotted a goodly stream, deep and swift, flowing near the edge of a large stand of timber and pulled Lester Wylson aside. "How would this be for a mill site?"

"Don't come much better, sir," Wylson drawled. "You could run a dam up yonder." Lester thrust his chin upstream. "A far piece it is from any of the fields, but just about perfect if you was thinkin' of a sawmill. Of course, if you don't mind my sayin', sheriff"—Wylson squinted at him—"ya might be better off laying the mill further downstream, where this rill joins with the Alder. The water don't run sa swift, but you could cut a side channel to control the flow simple enough, and it'd be easier to haul cut wood off from down there, either by wagon or straight on to a barge."

Hart was less enthusiastic about the quality of the farmland. "Too far north, I reckon, milord; it'll never be better than fair."

Jemy guided them around more than one bog and straight through a large moor. They rode for hours in water never less than ankle deep on the horses. Watt reckoned the bogs could be drained. Emerson agreed, saying the land uncovered would likely be more fertile than most of what the Ryans had under cultivation the now. Per Ranyl's direction, they rode in a wide circle, bypassing York, returning to the rise overlooking Greymark on the morning of the sixth day.

"Welcome home, sir," Jemy announced, gazing down upon the grey-walled enclosure.

"Aye." Ranyl grinned. "Safe and sound and, by my reckoning, only lost twice."

Jemy grinned back. "I wouldn't say lost, exactly, sir, just misplaced a little, maybe."

Ranyl extended his hand. "Thanks. We'd have been lost proper without you."

Jemy seemed caught a little off guard by the gesture but clasped Ranyl's hand willingly enough. Their return met with no fanfare whatever. Tall, rawboned Davis Killoe informed Ranyl that both the laird and the laird apparent were in the fields and would not return until the evening meal. This gave the young Kylgahran plenty of time to wash and dress and stew in anticipation of his first meeting with Owain Ryan, laird of Clan Ard Ryan and soon to be both Ranyl's overlord and father-in-law.

A widower, Owain Ryan had Sym's walnut-brown hair, though greying some at the temples. His eyes, set deep in a tanned, leathery countenance, were blue. Ranyl could see no cleft in his chin. The man's features were regular, but Ranyl felt certain Sym's beauty must have been a gift bestowed by her mother. Sym had said very little about her mother, only that she died years ago, and her father had never remarried. She'd told him even less about an older brother, whose death just under a year gone had made her laird apparent.

Dressed simply in a grey woolen shirt and trousers, Laird Ryan wore no sword at his belt, only a plain hilted Highland dirk. Not yet fifty, Owain stood tall and lean and looked fit, despite a slight limp. Ranyl noticed the man favored his left leg. *Perhaps Tuan might be able to do something.* Ranyl filed the thought away. Owain greeted Ranyl politely, and they talked small for a while until Sym came down to dinner, her hair dressed in an elaborate single braid, wearing a green cotton frock with a slightly daring neckline.

"Sorry to have taken so long," Sym murmured as she joined him at table.

Ranyl smiled appreciatively. "Worth the wait, by any road."

Sym colored slightly in response to his compliment, "How are you and Father getting along?"

"Compared to our first encounter"–Ranyl's smile stretched to a grin–"splendidly."

"That's not very reassuring." Sym's lively brown eyes glinted in response. "Blood feuds have started over less."

In Ranyl's estimation, his first evening with Laird Owain went smoothly enough. Sym sat between them and did most of the talking.

After the meal, Owain Ryan leaned forward in his chair at the head of the table and idly swirled the wine left in his cup. "My man Jemy says you're fair wild about water mills."

"We found a good site, where Cutter's Rill spills into the Alder," Ranyl recounted in reply. "Fyrgus Clyde can fashion a saw and the gears. Lester Wylson will know what's needed for the wheel works. Lukas Holt says the timber growing all along the rill is fine. With a sawmill in place, we can load the lumber into barges and ferry planks and posts all the way to Warwyck, if needs be, to find a market."

"And should there be a glut of good lumber in Warwyck? What then?" Owain queried.

"Luke Holt says fine oak is always in demand, and tall pine for masts and spars, especially in a large seaport such as Warwyck, and he was fair giddy over the cedar," Ranyl responded.

"Your man Holt knows what he is about, does he?" Owain wondered.

"Luke Holt is not a man given to idle talk," Ranyl said confidently. "Emerson Hart says the same about the timber. The two together are like coin in yer poke."

"Hart's the fella what wants to drain the bogs?" the laird of Clan Ard Ryan asked next.

"I don't imagine he'd mind some help in the doing." Ranyl smiled. "He is confident it can be done, and the bottom land so revealed will clear more than three quadrants of arable in less than one season." A quadrant was a section of land equal in extent to one square kylo.

"You appear to have seen a great deal in a short time," Owain commented.

"Perhaps," Sym suggested, "a new perspective reveals much, Father."

"More likely it's naught but wishful thinking," Laird Owain muttered but with a thoughtful cast to his blue eyes.

At her father's request, later that same evening, Sym met privately with him in Laird Owain's sitting room.

Owain opened their conversation with a query. "Since your return, you've said next to nothing about young Emyrt. What do you think of him?"

Sym took a seat in front of the hearth and gazed for a moment into the flames. "I trust him," she offered finally.

Owain grunted. "That's not what I expected to hear."

"He isn't what I expected, either," Sym allowed.

"What did you expect?" Owain asked.

"A younger version of his father," Sym replied succinctly.

Owain laughed shortly. "Thank the Fates for small favors." Stepping to the fireplace, Owain laid a hand upon the mantel and turned his head to gaze steadily at his daughter. "You sound hopeful."

Sym smiled. "I am."

"Have the two of you talked about setting a date for the wedding?" Laird Owain inquired.

"No." Sym hesitated a moment. "At least, not exactly."

"Good." Owain nodded. "We'll stage the formal betrothal for the first of next month, with the wedding to follow two weeks hence."

"But Papa," Sym protested, "that's more than five weeks away."

"Anxious, are ye, daughter?" Owain queried. Even in the soft glow of the fire and the two oil lamps illuminating the room, Owain saw the blush suddenly blooming on Sym's cheeks.

"With a marriage contract signed, and the groom come so far, such delay is unseemly, Father," Sym argued, "and well ye know it." Her chin lifted. "What is your reasoning?"

"The day after you left to meet your betrothed," Owain explained, "Syrilla paid us a visit." Syrilla was what Highlanders referred to as a Wise One—a witch, in other words. A healer of great renown, Syrilla had also been blessed with the power of foresight. She could see the future, bits and pieces of it, at any rate.

"A foretelling," Sym prompted.

Owain turned away from the hearth and placed both hands in the small of his back. "Only sorrow will follow should Tessymir Ryan of Clan Ard Ryan not wed during the month of the waning moons." Owain frowned. "Her words exactly. Syrilla would nay say more, claiming no good would come of it." In Kylgahra the month of the waning moons marked the last of the year.

"Syrilla told me once that a foretelling was hard to interpret," Sym mused, "as often a curse as a blessing. I wonder what it was exactly that she saw."

"Syrilla rode through storm and gale to deliver her warning," Owain said gravely. "Whatever the origin, I think it would be unwise to ignore it."

"I must tell Ranyl," Sym began.

"That you must not do, Sym," Owain cut her off. "Syrilla was adamant on that point. She intended to speak only with you. Syrilla was more than a little put off at having to confide in me. She had pressing business elsewhere, apparently, and could not wait for your return."

"Ranyl may see this delay as a slight," Sym observed. "What can I tell him?"

"That you are complying with your father's wishes," Owain proffered, "in accordance with an old Ryan family custom. If he's well and truly vexed, you may tell him that as a marriage contract has indeed been signed, I have no objection should the bedding commence some afore the wedding."

"Papa!" Sym exclaimed.

"You did ask, daughter." A wry twist framed Owain Ryan's smile. "One of the first lessons a laird must learn is that if ye cannot stand the answer, do not put the question."

28

Sparring

The day following his visit to Barber Street, Aeryk wanted no part of another planning session with Aya-Bal-Mar and Samwell Austyn. Sam didn't seem to mind, so instead of accompanying him to the captain's quarters in the Elven compound, he wandered down toward the drill ground. The villa, as the Elves referred to it, served, for all intents and purposes, as a fortress. An outer wall made of sandstone blocks about twelve span in height enclosed the rectangular compound. Three gates provided access to a large inner courtyard. The main gate opened on to the street fronting the villa. Secondary gates were built into the adjacent walls. The back wall of the compound, opposite the main entrance, stood gateless.

In addition to the primary building, three stories tall, which housed the officers' quarters, a main dining hall, a library, and various meeting rooms, the compound also included separate kitchens, stables, a blacksmith's shop, barracks for the syrs, and other outbuildings, including a small hospital. The villa was designed to accommodate a permanent garrison of two full companies of Elven cavalry, about two hundred syrs, with additional rooms for visiting officers, cooks, smiths, and other specialists. The internal courtyard provided space for gardens, each centered upon a fountain and a practice area for the syrs to drill. Having never been to the drill ground, Aeryk thought he'd take a look.

According to Sam, about half of the Elves, one full company under Aya-Bal-Mar's command, were going to escort the belated consignment of goods to Duke Highgarden's new estate, Balmuir. The plan was for the escort to leave in the morning tomorrow, returning by sundown three days later. Sam thought he'd ride along. The day after the escort party returned, Sam intended that he and Aeryk would leave Cos and head home to Lywgahra.

Aeryk needed to find a proper way of saying good-bye to Tierza. A gift of some kind seemed right, something a musician would like, maybe, but he was at a loss as to what that something might be. He reckoned he should have a talk with Mistress Canty. The innkeeper seemed to know all about the two of them anyway. Tierza acted as if their relationship embodied little more than play—"a pleasant afternoon that became a very pleasant evening" was how she described it.

Aeryk found himself standing alongside the Elven drill ground. The practice space, or arena, as the Elves called it, appeared square in shape—essentially, a leveled piece of ground covered with sand. The perimeter of the practice area was lined with a series of thick posts, taller than a typical elf. These posts, Aeryk knew, were used as part of standard Elven sword drill. The Elves employed a wooden practice sword that reminded him of the stryath used back home. The Elven practice sword was shaped like a johten, a gracefully curved, tightly wrapped bundle of reeds or sticks. He spotted a number of Elves whacking away at the posts while two pairs of syrs squared off against each other in the center of the sand-laden arena.

"Greetings, Aeryk Emyrt," Tyk-Ban-Gyl called out, walking up to Aeryk with a brief, informal bow that Aeryk recognized as a sign of acceptance.

Returning the bow, Aeryk said, "I see you, Tyk." *That's probably pushing things some,* Aeryk thought. He liked Tyk. The Elfan acted less reserved than most. Tyk smiled in response, apparently not offended by Aeryk's offhand greeting.

"I have not seen you here before." Tyk's raised eyebrow indicated that his statement was actually a question.

"My first visit," Aeryk confirmed.

"You are not required?" Tyk nodded in the direction of the main building.

"No," Aeryk said. "The value of my strategic input seems to have been exhausted."

Tyk's grin indicated the syr-sah found Aeryk's observation vastly amusing. "You are wiser than you look, Aeryk." Turning on his heel, Tyk looked back over his shoulder. "Come with me, and I'll show you around."

Tyk-Ban-Gyl led him into one of the outbuildings next to the drill ground. Upon entering, Aeryk saw that the shed contained an array of practice equipment, including padded arming jackets such as the one Tyk was wearing, a rack full of quarter staves, another of the wooden johtens, and, much to his surprise, a small barrel of what appeared to be stryaths. His interest piqued, Aeryk walked over to the barrel for a closer look. A couple of the practice swords were simply carved pieces of ash wood, shaped to resemble a Kylgahran baelryc. The majority of the Elven stryaths, however, appeared to be of a proper bound design, constructed from ironwood strips lashed together. Selecting one of the latter, Aeryk pulled it from the barrel to test its feel. In his hands, the practice sword felt a little light, but the balance was perfect.

Holding the stryath aloft, Aeryk turned to Tyk and asked, "Know your enemy—is that it, Tyk-Ban-Gyl?"

Bowing a little more formally than he had when greeting Aeryk, Tyk responded. "A complication that goes along with mercenary service, Aeryk Emyrt, is that one never knows who one's adversaries are going to be."

As *usual*, Aeryk thought, *I don't know if I'm being complimented or insulted. Bloody Elves.*

"Would you care for a practice bout?" Tyk asked. Aeryk shook his head, but Tyk pressed. "Just a little sparring with me. The first to two touches wins, and the loser will buy two cups of very bad wine? You would honor me by accepting."

Aeryk figured that last bit probably meant something. He didn't want to offend Tyk. It wasn't as if he had anything better to do, and the worst that could happen was that he'd get thumped a couple of times and have an excuse to buy the elf a decent cup of wine. "It would be my pleasure," he said.

Tyk smiled. "We shall see about that, Kylgahran."

Wondering if he'd made yet another error in judgment, Aeryk slung the stryath over his shoulder and followed Tyk out into the sunlit arena.

Tyk walked up to a young syr, an Elfin, exercising with a practice johten at one of the posts. "Hoi, Pyp," Tyk called. The young elf stopped and turned toward the syr-sah. Coming to attention, Pyp saluted smartly, pointing the wooden johten toward the ground while holding the hilt just under her chin and shouting, "Syr-sah."

"You'll have to forgive Pyp-Dun-Dee, Aeryk," Tyk said, as if explaining something that should no longer need explanation. "Having arrived only recently, young Pyp, here, is trying very hard to appear soldierly."

Pyp looked at Aeryk. "Just trying to make a good impression, syr-sah." Pyp's eyes, Aeryk saw, were a misty grey, and her tawny hair, long and curly, was doing its best to escape from the hastily tied leather thong attempting to hold it into a ponytail. Aeryk guessed Pyp must be the youngest elf he'd so far met, a couple of years, at least, shy of his own age. Pyp was light skinned—lighter by a shade than Jyn—and slender, even by Elven standards. She stood a full hand's width shorter than Tyk. Pyp's features were pleasing. Aeryk noticed a smattering of freckles splayed across a slightly upturned nose.

Bowing, Aeryk gave his name and said, "It is a pleasure to meet you, Pyp-Dun-Dee."

Judging by the raised eyebrow, something about Aeryk's greeting surprised Pyp. The young Elfin returned his bow, saying, "The honor is mine, Aeryk Emyrt."

"Until recently," Tyk explained, "Pyp, here, had embarked upon a promising career as a scribe. She is determined the now to throw it all away and swing a sword."

"I'm better with a bow," Pyp put in quickly, looking first to Tyk and then to Aeryk. The young elf lowered her head and kicked the sand of the arena with a booted toe. "My mother is a scribe, and her mother before. It is a fine profession. It is just that, well, scribing is so ... boring."

"An education should not be wasted." Tyk said, sounding serious. Pyp looked miserable.

Uncertain if he should, Aeryk plunged ahead anyway, saying what he felt. "There is nothing wasted in honorable service, Tyk. And it is Pyp's decision to make, yes?"

"You really are a barbarian, you know that?" Tyk observed.

"Here in Cos city, I am reminded of it on a daily basis," Aeryk said dryly. "Have I said anything untrue?"

Pyp's light grey eyes fairly beamed gratitude.

Shaking his head, Tyk jerked a thumb at Pyp and said. "She will act as your second and explain the rules." Tyk looked at Pyp. "A standard sparring match to two touches. I'll be right back." Tyk sauntered over to a group of four Elves idling in the shade of another outbuilding, presumably in search of a second for himself.

"Rules," Aeryk muttered, more to himself than to Pyp. "Of course there must be rules." Turning to the young elf at his side, he asked, "Are there a great many rules, Pyp?"

Turned out, there weren't too many. As a practice bout, Pyp explained, no strikes to the head or face were allowed. Any contact of the practice sword with any other part of an opponent's body would count as a touch. The touched combatant was honor bound to call out the contact as soon as it was felt. A touch would end a sparring round. Either participant could request a short rest period between rounds. The first to achieve two touches would win the sparring match. The function of the seconds was to monitor the match to make certain no illegal blows were struck and to settle if necessary any disputed touches.

Unbuckling his sword belt, Aeryk handed the sheathed baelryc and dirk to Pyp and inquired, "How much trouble am I in here?"

"Tyk is very skilled," Pyp said without hesitation. "I've not used one much, but this baelryc of yours seems unwieldy. It is like swinging a log. You will never match the speed of a johten strike. I think it is highly likely that you are in for a good thumping."

"Tyk might have been right in one respect, Pyp," Aeryk pointed out. "You're a little too honest for soldiering."

"No offense was intended, Aeryk Emyrt." Pyp sounded sincere.

"None taken," Aeryk responded, swinging his arms to loosen his shoulders.

Tyk returned in a few moments. With him was an Elfan Aeryk had seen before on sentry duty at the main gate. Tyk introduced the new arrival, named Das-Poh-Dyn, as his second. Das-Poh-Dyn quickly offered to wager Pyp the cost of a midday meal on the outcome of the sparring match. Pyp readily accepted. This surprised Aeryk, considering Pyp's assessment of his chances. As Tyk and Das made their way out on to the arena floor, Aeryk raised the question.

Pyp answered, as if explaining to a very young child the danger of touching a hot skillet, "I am honored to be your second."

Shaking his head, Aeryk took up a position opposite Tyk. Pyp had won the coin toss between seconds and so would call the start of the match.

Pyp called, "Ready." Aeryk assumed what was called the mid-guard stance in Kylgahra. The baelryc could be used in both one- and two-handed grips. The mid-guard stance incorporated a single-handed grip, with the swordsman's body turned at right angles to his opponent and the sword arm extended. As he was right-handed, Aeryk's right foot was placed in front, his left well behind, with both knees flexed. The mid-guard stance could be employed both with and without a targe and could be used either to attack or defend.

For his part, Tyk took a two-handed grip, holding the practice sword at chest height. The elf's shoulders faced Aeryk squarely, and his feet were about shoulder width apart, with his right foot positioned slightly ahead of his left.

Pyp cried, "Begin!" Aeryk remained on the defensive, awaiting Tyk's opening strike.

Aeryk soon realized the accuracy of Pyp's assessment of Tyk's abilities. The Elfan was both fast and decisive. Tyk's wooden johten seemed to blur in a series of fluid slashes. Giving ground, Aeryk narrowly avoided taking a hit on the very first exchange. Tyk pursued, launching strike after strike. Finally, sidestepping to his right, Aeryk feinted left and lunged. Tyk's upper body pivoted with cat like grace, his johten swept up, parried smartly, and then flashed downward to slash across Aeryk's right thigh just above the knee.

"Touch," Aeryk acknowledged, stepping back and lowering his stryath.

Breathing deeply, Tyk smiled and bowed. "Would you like to take a moment between rounds?" he offered politely.

"Aye," Aeryk said with an answering bow, "I would." Aeryk walked back to where Pyp was standing with a towel and a water flask.

"What say you, Pyp?" Aeryk asked the young elf.

"I think it is a long time until breakfast," Pyp answered a little mournfully. "Is Tyk so fast you cannot counter at all?"

"Out west, young Pyp, there is a very wise man named Basyl," Aeryk said, enjoying himself. "Basyl says that in all things, you should first seek to understand."

Perplexed, Pyp asked, "What does that mean?"

"You won't miss any meals, Pyp," Aeryk replied. "My word on it."

Aeryk again took up the mid-guard position. Tyk's opening stance was also the same as for the first round. At Pyp's call to begin the second round, Aeryk attacked, using the length and weight of his stryath to full advantage. Though fast and well schooled, Tyk struggled to counter the sheer power of the baelryc. On the second exchange, Aeryk managed to beat his way inside Tyk's guard and drive his stryath home, striking the elf just below the heart. In actual combat, it would have been a killing blow.

"Touch," Tyk called, lowering his practice sword. Aeryk bowed, and asked if Tyk would care for a rest between rounds. At Tyk's nod, Aeryk returned to Pyp's side.

Accepting the water flask from Pyp, Aeryk took a quick swallow and asked, "You really bet the last of your meal money?"

Pyp nodded. "I usually have some left over, but I spent most of my wages this month on a book I found in one of the street markets, a novel written a century ago by a Tieran noblewoman." Pyp lowered her voice to a whisper. "Parts of it are really lurid. You are welcome to borrow it if you like."

"I'll look forward to it," Aeryk said, smiling.

"This Basyl," Pyp inquired, "he is your teacher?"

"One of them." Aeryk nodded. "My father he is, also."

"I should like to meet him," Pyp stated.

"I hope you can one day, Pyp," Aeryk said. "I know Basyl would enjoy meeting you." This comment seemed to both please and embarrass the young Elfin, as Pyp ducked her amber-haired head in response.

Looking up after a moment with a serious cast to her eyes, Pyp implored, "You won't be too hard on old Tyk, will you, Aeryk? He's a good egg."

"My word on that, too," Aeryk assured Pyp as he stepped back into the arena.

The third round went pretty much the same as the second. In response to a blow Aeryk succeeded in landing to Tyk's side, Tyk called, "Touch."

After exchanging bows, Aeryk stepped forward and held out his right hand. Uncertain as to a proper response, Tyk tentatively mimicked Aeryk's gesture and seemed a little startled when Aeryk clasped his hand, saying, "Well done. That was closely fought."

"Thank you, Aeryk," Tyk said a little ruefully, releasing his hand. "I think we both know I was badly overmatched. Perhaps you could—"

"That was a poor showing, syr-sah." Kul-Cah-Zul's voice contained a carefully measured degree of disdain. The Elven noble had stepped onto the sand of the arena and stood only a few span away. Clad in a flowing silk shirt of royal green, tight dark-leather breeches, and the seemingly ever-present knee-high calfskin boots, Kul-Cah-Zul wore a johten in a belt scabbard above his left hip. A long-bladed dagger in a plain leather sheath hung at his right side, attached to the green silk sash twined about his waist. "Perhaps, Aeryk Emyrt, you will indulge me with a proper sparring match, one that employs bared steel."

"No, thank you," Aeryk demurred as politely as he knew how.

"You do not care to partake of the blade dance, Kylgahran?" Kul-Cah-Zul's tone was as cold as a winter night. The emphasis he placed on the name of Aeryk's homeland managed to sound equal parts aloof and insulting.

"Steel is sharp," Aeryk replied. "Accidents happen, even while dancing." He did his best to mimic Kul-Cah-Zul's emphasis and tone when he spoke the last word.

"To refuse a sparring match is a grave insult," Kul-Cah-Zul informed him, his cobalt gaze heating. "Even a barbarian should understand this."

Aeryk could not think of the proper honorific for addressing someone of Kul-Cah-Zul's station. Instead of getting it wrong and sounding the complete fool, Aeryk decided to forego title altogether.

"If your intention is to demonstrate superior skill, Kul-Cah-Zul, a practice sword should suffice," Aeryk said evenly. "If you intend otherwise, you will first need to explain what offense I've brought against you."

Kul-Cah-Zul stiffened as if Aeryk had spit on his boots and took a white-knuckled grip on the dagger at his right side, blue eyes blazing. "The wooden sword will do," Kul-Cah-Zul said finally, stiffly. Pivoting to his right, Kul-Cah-Zul looked to an Elfan whom Aeryk had never seen before. "Vyldeenter Byl-Bin-Dar, will you stand second for me?"

"It will be my honor to do so, Vyldeen Kul-Cah-Zul," Byl-Bin-Dar responded.

Vyldeen was apparently the honorific he'd been searching for, Aeryk realized. If memory served, *vyldeenter* designated some sort of lesser noble. He had no idea exactly what the distinction was. Kul-Cah-Zul handed his johten and sword belt to the vyldeenter, and took up a wooden practice sword. Aeryk noticed the Elven noble did not relinquish the dagger fastened to the sash encircling his waist.

"Pyp-Dun-Dee," Aeryk called, "will you honor me by standing second?"

Pyp bowed deeply in affirmation but said nothing. A few moments later, as they stood together at the edge of the arena, Pyp commented, "That was clever."

"You think so?" Aeryk responded noncommittally.

Nodding, Pyp enthused, "After what you said, Vyldeen Kul-Cah-Zul could not insist upon meeting you with bared steel without first giving offense. Brilliant."

As if that makes any bloody sense, Aeryk thought.

"But of course, you knew that," Pyp continued. "Who are you, Aeryk Emyrt, to address nobles as you do?" Pyp could not hide her amazement.

"Just a cowhand in over his bloody head, Pyp," Aeryk growled.

Startled, Pyp could not suppress a brief laugh.

"If I give this asshole a proper bashing, what bad could happen?"

"With nobles involved, it is hard to say," Pyp stated, "especially under the eyes of his mate." Pyp pointed to the other side of the arena. Aeryk saw Pak-Dyn-Tor looking on. Standing at her side was Jyn-Ael-Tor.

"Bloody Elves." Aeryk sighed and then looked at Pyp, adding, "No offense."

"None taken," Pyp said promptly. Shrugging in the elegant fashion only an elf seemed able to achieve, Pyp went on, "When in doubt, bash away, I'd say."

Uncertain, Aeryk took a mid-guard stance. Pyp had once again won the coin toss. At the command to begin, Aeryk slid to his right and allowed Kul-Cah-Zul the opening move. The Elven noble proved to be quick enough, but, in Aeryk's estimation, was neither as strong nor as skilled as Tyk. After two brief exchanges, Aeryk's stryath slipped past the noble's guard to strike the elf on his right forearm. The strike was not a heavy blow, but Aeryk clearly felt it. While he started to disengage, Kul-Cah-Zul rolled his wrists, pushed Aeryk's practice sword aside, and struck him sharply, just above the right wrist.

"Foul!" Pyp cried, as if unable to fully credit what she had just witnessed. "Aeryk Emyrt scored first touch. The vyldeen's response was illegal."

"I claim first touch," Kul-Cah-Zul said calmly. "The Kylgahran's second"—the vyldeen leveled a disparaging look at Pyp—"disputes. What say you, Byl-Bin-Dar?"

"I say Vyldeen Kul-Cah-Zul has garnered first touch," Byl-Bin-Dar said after only a slight hesitation.

Pyp didn't bat an eye. "Not so. The vyldeen fouled."

"Our seconds are in dispute, Kylgahran." Kul-Cah-Zul seemed pleased. "Unresolved, this is a matter of bared steel, raised in challenge between them. What say you?"

"The touch is yours, Vyldeen Kul-Cah-Zul," Aeryk said evenly, "and the lesson mine." Bowing, he requested, "May I have a moment with my second?"

"Of course," Kul-Cah-Zul said graciously.

He had to practically drag the furious Pyp to the side of the arena. "They cheat. There is no honor in them," Pyp hissed, glaring daggers at the vyldeen and his second.

"Take it easy, Slim. It's only the first touch," Aeryk advised. *Slim* seemed to be a good nickname for his youthful second.

Pyp's grey eyes softened, but she refused to look away. "It is still not right, Aeryk Emyrt, and thee knows it."

The *thee* both startled and pleased him, but Aeryk wanted to make sure his point got home. "The first rule of soldiering, Slim," he said gravely, "is never to stick your neck out. Butting heads with those two could cost you. More than you can afford. It isn't worth it." Pyp took a breath, but Aeryk forestalled her. "Let it go, for my sake, please."

The *please* must have done the trick. Pyp nodded.

For the second round, Aeryk took the high-guard stance. This involved a two-handed grip on his stryath, his feet shoulder-width apart, facing his opponent. The practice sword was held aloft above his right shoulder, with his right hand placed slightly above his left on the hilt. High-guard featured an aggressive posture, designed to initiate an attack. The first blow would always be a sweeping downward strike. The timing of the first blow was critical. If executed to perfection, the initial strike from high-guard would be the only blow necessary. It took Aeryk three blows to beat through Kul-Cah-Zul's guard and deliver a reverse thrust to his midsection, hard enough to stagger the elf. Kul-Cah-Zul dropped to his knees, gasping for breath.

"I claim the touch," Aeryk said, loudly enough for all those standing around the arena—there seemed to be quite a few the now—to hear. Looking at Byl-Bin-Dar, Aeryk challenged, "Do you dispute it, vyldeenter?" He spat out the honorific as if it had a bad taste.

Byl-Bin-Dar's right hand slid instinctively toward his sword hilt. Controlling himself with an effort, the Elfan growled back, "The touch is yours."

"What was it thee said about the butting of heads?" Pyp asked mildly as he returned to her side.

"Pay no attention to me, Slim," he said. "I'm three ways a fool."

"A fool with a Guidon's courage," Pyp said approvingly. Aeryk had no idea what a Guidon was, but he liked the way Pyp said it. "Why do thou call me Slim?" Pyp asked.

"It's a nickname," Aeryk explained. "An expression of ... well, that is, of approval and acceptance where I come from."

Pyp cocked her head slightly to one side. Her eyes were suddenly as opaque as sea fog, unreadable.

Giving up, Aeryk said, "If you find the term offensive or in any way inappropriate, I apologize."

"If it pleases thee, I am glad of it," the Elfin said gravely. Thinking he had crossed into territory that perhaps he should not have, Aeryk stepped once more on to the sand of the arena. Kul-Cah-Zul again soon fell prey to a pressed attack Aeryk initiated from the high-guard position. Aeryk thwacked the vyldeen none too gently across the left shoulder and stepped quickly back without lowering his guard.

"Touch," Kul-Cah-Zul barked, "for all the good it will do you." Cobalt eyes ablaze, Kul-Cah-Zul grasped the hilt of his dagger with his right hand, staring intently at Aeryk. For a moment, Aeryk thought the Elfan was about to draw the blade, but though Kul-Cah-Zul's grip tightened, the weapon remained sheathed.

Suddenly, Aeryk felt as if the medallion about his neck had turned to ice, and a chill ran briefly down his spine. The feeling passed as quickly as it came. Shrugging it off, Aeryk grounded his stryath and laid both hands across its pommel. Kul-Cah-Zul snatched his hand away from the dagger as if its touch had become painful. What a moment before had been rage in his deep-blue eyes winked out, replaced in an instant by confusion. Slamming the practice sword in his hand down to the arena floor, Kul-Cah-Zul turned on his heel and stalked away.

Aeryk looked across the arena to discover Jyn-Ael-Tor's amber eyed gaze fixed upon him. Jyn's elder sister, Pak, had slipped away through the crowd, apparently following after Kul-Cah-Zul. Squaring his shoulders, Aeryk nodded.

Acknowledging his nod with one of her own, Jyn turned away. He could not read her expression. Neither could he suppress the feeling of finality that gripped him, as if he'd just witnessed a door being latched shut.

29

Secrets

Tierza found the Altairan, Lykas Greytower, in one of his quiet moods. This made him more difficult to read, which made her nervous. He was capable not only of violence but remarkable cruelty. A wrong word could cost her dearly. As he sat behind the writing table in his private quarters, she stood before him, leaning on her crutch, and recounted Aeryk's tale of a plan to lead a group of Elves out west in search of Anduyin horses.

"They could never make such a journey before winter closes in on them," Greytower commented. The long fingers of his hands formed a steeple in front of his face.

"The Kylgahran are returning to their homes in the west country for the winter. They'll be leaving in a few days. I don't think the young one knows exactly when." Tierza repeated what Aeryk had told her. "They will meet the Elven party next spring, somewhere around Bennet." Home to a small but colorful collection of merchants and frontiersmen, Bennet served as a trading post in open territory on the Sayx River, north of Cos.

"And Aya-Bal-Mar will be leading this party of Elves?" the Altairan asked.

"Yes," Tierza said, hoping he'd come to the last of his questions. He had not. He went on for some time, covering the ground again. Finally, he fell silent.

Rising, Lykas Greytower walked round the table and ran the back of the fingers of his right hand down her left cheek. He had large hands, and strong. "This is all you know? After a night in his bed?"

How had he known that? Or was he guessing? She said nothing.

"I could have made better use of you by loaning you out to Tryon Velt." Velt, a wealthy merchant, new to Cos, liked to bugger young boys and small women—after cutting off their hair, that is. She'd heard whispers the merchant was willing to pay well for the privilege of doing other, less savory things.

"Aeryk has in his possession a pendant," she heard herself saying. "A charm, he says it is, against magic."

"Barbarian claptrap," Lykas said, the menace now clear in his voice.

"The medallion is ancient." Tierza spoke as calmly as she could. "Forged, not cast, and made of pellinwahr. It is fashioned into the Elven rune symbol Fey." An Elven word *pellinwahr* meant black iron. Less dense than wrought iron, pellinwahr must have been some form of alloy. The secret of its making had long been lost; at least, that was her understanding. Many smaller talismans of old were made of pellinwahr.

"You are certain?" Greytower's tone now showed genuine interest.

"That the medallion is made of pellinwahr, yes," Tierza confirmed. "As to whether or not it is a talisman, I cannot say."

"Come back this afternoon, at the start of the fourth hour. I will have instructions for you," Greytower directed, dismissing her.

As she stepped outside into the soft, late morning sunlight of a fine autumn day, Tierza felt soiled and, worse, craven. She had mentioned the medallion only to distract the Altairan, to save herself, knowing that by doing so she would place Aeryk in danger. Tierza knew well how far most people would go, how low they would crawl, just to stay alive. Survival mattered, after all, like nothing else. Tierza thought of herself as beyond shame; she'd been wrong. Sagging against the cracked blue paint covering the outside wall of the Altairan's shop in the alley at the rear of the building, she wept.

A short time later, Tierza encountered her older brother, Ramon, as she made her way back to Barber Street. Knowing Mother, Ramon was probably only her half brother, but he remained the closest thing to family that she had. Ramon looked as if he had been drinking, which he did pretty regularly. He looked happy, which meant the dice had been kind to him. He was always dicing and lost more often than he won.

Ramon's gambling debts—or, more specifically, his inability to pay them—had provided the Altairan with the means of enlisting her services. As Greytower put it, "Spread your legs, or bury what's left of your brother."

She loved her brother. He'd been kind to her as a child. But he had grown into a fool and was fast becoming a drunken fool in the bargain.

"Hello, Songbird," Ramon said cheerfully. "Shall I buy you some breakfast?"

He always called her Songbird. "It is nearly noon, you fool," Tierza said, not unkindly.

"All the better people never have breakfast before noon," Ramon said grandly. "Or perhaps you'd rather I told you a secret." His voice dropped to a whisper. "A secret concerning the Grim One." The Grim One was what Ramon called the Altairan.

Pulling Ramon aside, she guided him into the shade of a nearby alley adjacent to a bakery shop. Tierza asked quietly, "What secret?"

"They are going to raid the Elven villa and cut a few fancy throats in the process," Ramon whispered excitedly. "Tomorrow night, maybe."

"Who told you this?" Tierza whispered back.

"No one told me," Ramon averred a little blearily. "I overheard Greygor Gullwatch talking with Devon Longshanks." Both men were in the employ of the Altairan. Gullwatch, she knew better than she wanted to; the other, by name only.

"Do they have any idea you were eavesdropping?" Tierza made no attempt to hide the worry in her voice.

"If they had any such idea, they'd have given me a second smile." Ramon dragged his forefinger across the base of his throat. "There's more," he went on. "A couple of particular Elves, it seems, need to get dead. Someone named Kul-Cah-Zul and at least one other, Jyn-Ael-Tor, I think it was. Elves have such stupid names. Gullwatch is not happy." Ramon belched. "Apparently, he isn't going to get to do the throat cutting. They're bringing in someone special."

"Have you spoken of this to anyone, anyone at all?" Tierza asked urgently.

"Do you think I'm a complete fool?" Ramon held up his right hand, palm outward to forestall any comment from Tierza. "You're the first person I've talked to about this."

"You need to get out of Cos, brother." Tierza spoke firmly. "You have a little money?"

"A little," Ramon said guardedly. "They didn't see me, Tierza. There is no danger. I swear it."

"None you are aware of, you mean." Tierza spoke more harshly than she'd intended. Ramon had a stubborn streak. It would not do to push too hard. "Buy passage on the first packet boat headed downriver that you can. It makes no difference where it's going; just get out of the city. Do it today." Tierza looked into his eyes, pleading.

Ramon smiled. His eyes were the same color as hers, but his hair showed light brown, not black. He'd been a handsome boy. Though still young, his face seemed to sag the now. Whether from a lack of sleep, or the drink, or the loss of hope, Tierza did not know. "Little Songbird, you worry too much."

And you, brother, worry not enough, until it is too late, Tierza thought. She said, "Come with me to the barbershop, and I'll make you some dinner. And then we'll talk some more about packet boats headed downriver."

30
Agents of the Golden Hand

Siersay Grier, sorcerer of the Golden Hand, ran her brush vigorously through her hair. One hundred strokes a day, her guide Pepina Meadows had advised her, was necessary for it to shine properly. Siersay's hair glistened, a rich walnut brown. Her eyes were brown as well, a typical combination for a Syrdisian. The Golden Hand represented the oldest Syrdisian society of sorcerers, dedicated to preserve and defend the Leopard Throne of Syrdis.

Literally, she supposed that meant she was sworn to give her life, if necessary, to serve and protect a piece of furniture. She smiled into the polished brass mirror suspended from a wall in front of the chair, in which she sat at the thought. Her smile revealed even white teeth. She was careful with her teeth. Siersay knew, of course, that the throne represented but a symbol of the sovereignty and the people of Syrdis. *How best to serve them the now and, through that service, advance her own cause?* She wondered.

Pepina had described Siersay as pleasant-faced. Pepina was a hag, but in this regard, Siersay sighed, her mentor stood correct. Siersay looked like the peasant's daughter she was. Her eyes weren't bad, she thought, but her face appeared a little too round, the rest of her features a little too blunt to be beautiful. Her body, on the other hand, pleased her. At twenty-eight, she was a woman in her prime. Her bosom was full, high, and firm, and her waist and hips as slim as hard work and an iron will could make them. She was very careful with what she ate and drank. The Sircassian, her most recent lover, seemed suitably appreciative.

To serve Syrdis and advance her own interests, she was going to have to kill some people. The elf, Kul-Cah-Zul, headed the list of three who were to die. One of the others, an Elven scholar who labored as a scribe at the Castellan villa in Cos, went by the name of Mik-Tad-Low. The third and least important target was a young Elven noble named—what was it?—Jyn-Ael-Tor.

Most important of all, Siersay needed to recover the objects, a pair of them. The first object was a talisman of considerable potency. In return for a substantial sum of money, Kul-Cah-Zul had agreed to first pilfer the talisman and then deliver it to the Golden Hand in Avrys. After accepting a large payment in advance, the elf had apparently been successful in obtaining the item but then refused to hand it over. Instead, Kul-Cah-Zul had fled north, journeying with his lover, Pak-Dyn-Tor, to Cos.

The second object was a book, an obscure history of the ancient city-state of Mayne. Singled out to die, this Mik-Tad-Low, because of what she knew about the content of the book. Mayne flourished nearly a millennium in the past, a beacon of learning and civilization, before falling suddenly into ruin. Little knowledge of the lost city survived in modern times, not even its exact location.

Just why the Golden Hand had determined murder and theft were necessary fell beyond Siersay's grasp. Treachery, she supposed, must not go unpunished. Kul-Cah-Zul's offense warranted death. As for Mik-Tad-Low, well, knowledge in the wrong hands constituted a dangerous thing. Siersay felt some sympathy for the young Elven noble Jyn-Ael-Tor. Apparently intended merely as a ruse, the elf's death would serve only to disguise the nature of their true mission and obfuscate any connection between the murders and the objects in question.

Much depended on intelligence provided by the Golden Hand's agent in Cos, an Altairan called Lykas Greytower. The Sircassian—her Sircassian—a man named Rodrik Bowe, loathed Greytower. Bowe hailed from Bandehar in the east and was a member of the Sircassian League, a highly trained, superbly skilled band of assassins. Bowe served as but one of six Sircassians currently at her disposal—a relatively large group and not inexpensive, but then again, her task was formidable.

Despite being an exquisite killer, Bowe was not an instinctively violent man. He detested bullies of any stripe. Greytower was a brute, of that Siersay had no doubt. She'd learned long ago that to succeed, one had to make use of the tools available, however crude. The question that pertained concerned Greytower's competence more than his methods. So far, his information, that which she could independently verify, had been accurate. If the Altairan's most recent findings were also correct, the time to strike was nigh, or more specifically, tomorrow night at moons' set.

Objects, indeed. Siersay tossed her head and continued to wield her brush. Her superiors, elders within the society of the Golden Hand, were fond of the indirect, insisting, it seemed to her, upon never calling a thing what it actually was.

Siersay kept any such thoughts closely held. However arcane and convoluted their methods, the members of the Golden Hand's inner circle, the Ring Bearers, as they were known, had access to knowledge and power beyond her ken. Somehow, the Ring Bearers had known the objects she sought, and the trio of Elves targeted would all be in Cos city in time to dispatch her and her Sircassians. This Kul-Cah-Zul had only just arrived. She and her team had been in place for three days. *How had they known?* Siersay well knew the only means of discovering an answer to that query required first finding ways to succeed where others failed.

Siersay also knew her task would be further complicated by the ongoing alliance between Syrdis and the Elven nation of Ilyria. The Golden Hand's interests, of course, reached beyond national boundaries. Knowledge formed the true source of sorcerers' power, and the need to acquire and safeguard it could not be hampered by barriers so flimsy and changeable. Still, murdering Elves without incurring the wrath of the Ilyrian government would require a deft touch.

Siersay herself perceived no obvious association between Kul-Cah-Zul, the talisman in his possession, and the scholar with her dusty tome concerning the legendary city that had fallen so long ago, all of which ranged well beside the point. Her instructions were clear. How best to comply with them was Siersay's only concern. Failure, she knew, would bring dire consequences and not for her alone. An image of her younger sister, Solay, an initiate of the Golden Hand and a true beauty, sprung briefly, unbidden, into her mind.

Success demanded that they infiltrate the Elven villa in Cos and murder three Elves, two of whom were nobles and would likely be guarded. They would have to steal the objects in the process, ideally in a manner that left the theft undetected or at least obscured by other actions. If the Altairan's information proved accurate, much of the Elven garrison would soon be away from the villa, escorting a consignment of goods to a Syrdisian noble at a newly acquired estate northwest of the city. They were to leave Cos tomorrow and not return for days. Siersay could see no reason for delay.

At the sound of the knock on her door, Siersay put down her brush, rose to her feet, and grasped her sorcerer's stave. Precisely five span in length, crafted of white ash, varnished and highly polished, her staff gleamed. Only a little thicker than the base of her thumb, the stave radiated power—literally, to those few with the ability to invoke the Yir, and, perhaps as important, figuratively, to everyone else. A carving of a voluptuous mermaid decorated the top of her stave. Siersay had always found the endpiece appealing. She stood clad only in a silk dressing gown of pale blue. With her stave in her hand, however, Siersay would have felt at ease even naked.

"Come in," she called.

The door opened partially, enough for Rodrik Bowe to peer into the room. The assassin scanned the chamber automatically, thoroughly, and then allowed his gaze to rest approvingly on her.

"Greytower is here," he announced. *Here* was a private residence, located in the affluent southeastern portion of Cos, overlooking the Sayx River. A two-story affair made of wood and red brick, the home served the young sorcerer and her subordinates as a headquarters of sorts. Siersay's rooms occupied much of the second floor.

"He was not to come to this place," Siersay stated quietly.

Bowe kept his expression carefully neutral. He'd already asked permission to kill Greytower. Siersay was not a woman to be pushed. "He says it is important."

"Show him in, then," Siersay directed, hiding her displeasure. She never gave instructions merely to demonstrate her authority. She did not like having them ignored.

Moments later, the door swung fully open, and Lykas Greytower stepped into the room. Bowe followed, positioning himself so that he could step between Siersay and Greytower, should it be necessary. The Altairan entered, armed with a large knife in a belt sheath on his left side. She knew Bowe did not like this, but disarming Greytower would have made plain her distrust. Perhaps later, if time permitted, she would find a way to make it up to Rodrik Bowe.

She found the contrast between the two men remarkable. Both were tall and well formed, although she much preferred Rodrik Bowe's sleek, catlike build to Greytower's heavier, more rounded muscles.

The look in both men's eyes made her very aware she was female. Bowe's warmed her, while Greytower's made her skin crawl. She did not fear the Altairan, not with so deadly a weapon as her sorcerer's stave in her hand. Without it, though, *if she were ever drugged or otherwise unable to access the Yir and stood helpless before him*—she pushed the thought aside and waited to meet his eyes. The Altairan's gaze swept over her with a studied insolence until he finally looked into her eyes. Bowing, Lykas Greytower glanced away briefly. Siersay did not return or even acknowledge his gesture.

"Forgive the intrusion, sorcerer," he said. "I believe one of the Kylgahran scouts, the young one, has in his possession a talisman."

A talisman represented a rare find. Most were innocuous enough, but every now and then, something truly remarkable would surface. "Go on," Siersay replied.

The Altairan described the medallion Tierza had discovered belonging to Aeryk Emyrt.

"Your operative is certain the medal is made of forged pellinwahr?" Siersay asked.

"Tierza is a reluctant whore," Greytower said. "She struggles with the concept of obedience, but the information she provides is always accurate."

"Amid the book of known talismans is a series of Fey amulets. Some are reputed to be very potent as a ward against adverse magic of all kinds," Siersay summarized, as much for Bowe's benefit as for Greytower's. "The description matches well. If the Kylgahran's medallion is a Fey amulet, the Golden Hand will wish to acquire it." Siersay paused, and then went on, her voice hardening. "Why was it necessary for you to come here, just the now, to discuss this?"

"Tierza does not think the Kylgahran will willingly be separated from his trinket. It is constantly on his person. The simplest way of obtaining the medallion will be to remove it from his corpse," Greytower explained. "This young Kylgahran, along with the black-haired warrior, have visited the Elves on a daily basis for much of the past week. I do not know how the Elves will respond to his murder. In light of your ... other plans, I thought it best to secure your approval before going ahead."

"I see," Siersay responded. "Do you have the proper resources to obtain this trinket, as you call it?"

"If you are asking whether or not I need help killing the Kylgahran, the answer is no. Tierza will do it. It will not be the first time she has dispatched someone for me." Greytower smiled as if recalling a fond memory. "Poison will be the method. This Fey amulet is no proof against poison, is it?"

"No," Siersay confirmed. "It is not." Siersay thought a moment. As much as she shared Rodrik Bowe's dislike of the Altairan, she could not fault his judgment in this matter. "Would it be possible for your agent"—Siersay did not care for Greytower's use of the word whore—"to carry out this action tomorrow evening?"

"I think that can be arranged," the Altairan said, "if the price is right."

"Eighty crowyns, gold," Siersay offered without hesitation. "The reward stands only if the item is indeed a Fey amulet talisman." A gold crowyn was worth about fifty times that of the more common silver talent. A merchant in Cos whose yearly income topped eighty gold crowyns would be considered wealthy.

"And if it is not?" Greytower asked.

Siersay's shapely shoulders rose and fell eloquently.

"Surely the death of the Kylgahran is worth something, if only for the aggravation it will cause our Elven friends," Lykas Greytower said, bargaining.

"You do not know that, Master Greytower." Siersay's voice brooked no argument. "And you are being handsomely compensated for your help with regard to our Elven *allies*."

"As you say, sorcerer," Lykas Greytower acquiesced. "The Kylgahran will be dead and his medallion in our possession by moons' rise tomorrow night, well before your other endeavors are initiated. Do you wish confirmation of our success before you begin?"

Siersay shook her head. "I will leave the matter to you, Master Greytower. Just be certain you are successful. Deliver the medallion to me here, the morning after."

Upon the Altairan's departure, Rodrik Bowe closed the chamber door and stalked to her side. *He moves like a leopard*, she thought; her loins stirred just watching him.

"I intend never to disobey you, sorcerer," the Sircassian vowed, "but before we leave Cos, I shall kill that creature for the way he looks upon you. This I swear. Should my own life be forfeit for doing so, then so be it."

Setting aside her stave, Siersay stepped into his arms, kissing him as thoroughly as she knew how.

"How can I deny such a request?" Siersay said huskily.

With a satisfied smile, Bowe lifted her effortlessly into his arms and carried her toward her bedroom. It seemed she was going to have to make time for him after all.

31
Tierza's Choice

Greygor Gullwatch showed Tierza into the Altairan's office before the start of the fourth hour after noon. Telling her to sit at a small chair placed in front of the tall racketeer's writing table, the cutthroat left the room, closing the door quietly behind him. She had arrived early. The Altairan frowned on tardiness. Tierza did not have to wait long.

"They are convinced the Kylgahran's bauble is a talisman. You are to take it from him," the Altairan said as he walked into the room.

He carried a leather satchel with him. Sitting behind his writing table, Lykas Greytower extracted a pair of darts from the case that looked like somewhat larger versions of those used for gaming at the Rising Star and numerous other inns and saloons throughout Cos. Each dart was encased in a small but sturdy leather sheath.

"You remember these?" Greytower asked.

"Yes," Tierza said, her voice barely audible.

Once before, she had made use of those very implements or ones exactly like them. The point of each dart was made of blued steel—a small groove cut in a serpentine pattern around the shaft, running back from the point. The oblong body of the dart was fashioned of rosewood; three fins crafted from stiffened leather fit glued into channels carved at the rear of the handle. The darts could be thrown accurately over a surprising distance or plunged into flesh like a dagger. Tierza's initial reluctance to make use of them had led to her spending a night in the hands of Greygor Gullwatch.

"The poison is the same—cerdyth," Greytower commented.

Cerdyth was based upon the venom of a viper, known throughout the Middle Sea region simply as the brown snake. A concentrated dose of the type smeared on to the tips of the darts the Altairan placed atop the writing table caused almost instantaneous paralysis of the extremities. Death followed a short while later.

Greytower ordered, "The young Kylgahran, this Aeryk Emyrt, is to die by moons' rise tomorrow night. Remove the talisman from his body and return it to me here."

"Is it really necessary to—" Tierza never finished asking her question. The Altairan's slap left her ears ringing.

"You will do exactly as you are told." Lykas Greytower spoke softly, almost gently. "If you fail, we will find some other means of dispatching the Kylgahran, and you will die, and your brother will die. Your dying will not be pleasant. Do you understand?"

"I understand," Tierza replied.

"If you succeed, a golden crowyn will be yours," Greytower promised, "to do with as you please."

"I will place a candle in the window of his room when I'm done with him." Tierza's voice, usually so evocative, sounded flat and emotionless. "Less effort that way for your watcher."

The Altairan refrained from striking her yet again. After tomorrow tonight, one way or the other, something would have to be done about Tierza. He would decide on the morrow.

That evening, Aeryk found Tierza seated on a chair in front of the window in his room at the Rising Star. He noted that she'd taken off her sandals. Her bare feet did not reach the floor but swung idly back and forth. Wearing one of the simple frocks bound at the waist by a sash, so popular among the women of Cos, Tierza had tossed her wrap of scarlet wool on to the bed. Her crutch leaned against the wall, near to hand. She sat gazing out the window, apparently deep in thought.

As he entered the room and pitched his hat onto a table near the door, she looked up and smiled. "Thatch let me in. I hope you don't mind."

"Not so long as you can refrain from tidying the place up." Aeryk returned her smile. Removing his belt and laying both baelryc and dirk on the table as well, Aeryk crossed the room to kneel before her. The chair stood tall enough so that as he knelt, the top of his head came just to her chin.

"What have you been up to?" Tierza asked, reaching out to run her fingers though his hair.

"Sword practice, mostly," he responded. "I sparred some with Elves. It was ... educational."

She teased, "Sharp lessons being the best ones, eh?"

Laying his head against her breasts, Aeryk slipped his arms around her. "Wooden swords," he said, glad for the feel of her and her warm, clean scent. "No danger, except to my pride."

She hugged him. "What is wrong?" Tierza murmured.

"We'll be leaving, Sam and I, in three or four days," Aeryk ground out, surprised at how hard it was to actually say the words.

"Then we should have tonight and the whole of tomorrow and two days more." Tierza's smoky voice seemed to swirl about him. "That is more time than you thought, is it not?"

"It is," Aeryk concurred.

"So what is really wrong?" Tierza pressed gently.

"I miss you," Aeryk said simply, meaning every word.

Tierza tilted his head back and leaned forward to kiss him. Her raven-black hair flowed unbound and cascaded toward Aeryk, shrouding both their faces.

"You are sweet," she told him, "but if you keep talking like that, I will cry, and I don't want to cry, Aeryk, not the now. There will be time for that later. Tonight ..." She ran a finger lightly alongside his face, tracing the line of his jaw. "Tonight is for other things." She kissed him again, more deeply this time. He lifted her from the chair to lay her gently upon the bed.

Some while later, Aeryk lay on his back beneath a single blanket with Tierza pressed close to his side. He marveled once again at the silky-smooth texture of her skin. The room had grown dark. He thought she might be asleep until she rose up to kiss him on the ear.

"You are good company," she whispered.

Looking about the room, he remarked, "We may have missed supper."

"I brought some apples and cheese, the smoky kind," she added to forestall any questions from him, "and some of those little sausages you liked so much at breakfast yesterday."

"Good and all," Aeryk said fondly, squeezing Tierza just hard enough to make her grunt. "After we eat, would you like to go anywhere?"

Tierza tossed her head in the negative and lay back against him. "I am exactly where I want to be."

"Will you be angry if I ask you again to come with me?" Aeryk didn't know if it was right to ask or even if he really wanted Tierza to come, but he knew if she wanted to go with him, he would not leave without her, not the now.

For one long, luscious moment, Tierza allowed herself to think she might accept. It was impossible, of course. If they made it out of the city—no easy task with the Altairan's cronies watching—and into the wilderness, maybe Aeryk's frontier skills would see them through to the west country. The Altairan knew where they were going, though. He knew about Aeryk's home in Taggert's Landing. Would he pursue? With the talisman undoubtedly worth a small fortune, Tierza felt certain he would.

Even if, by some chance, Lykas Greytower decided the talisman was not worth the effort, he could still seek vengeance. To ruin any chance she would have at happiness with Aeryk, all the Altairan would need to do was send a messenger to the Kylgahran's little village, armed with nothing but the truth. Once word got out as to who and what she was and what she'd done, Aeryk would have nothing to do with her. It might be possible to travel somewhere else for a while, but she knew how badly Aeryk wanted to go home. He would not stay away forever, and the truth about her would be waiting whenever they arrived.

If she really loved Aeryk, would any of this matter? A moot question, as she was not in love with him. There remained too much boy in Aeryk. Still, he had shown her more kindness, more consideration, and more regard in the short while spent in his company than she had known from anyone, save her brother Ramon, in a lifetime. She felt joy in his presence and genuine passion at his touch, but that did not amount to love. Perhaps in time, but they had no time.

There was her brother to consider also. Leaving him behind would be the same as consigning him to death. She had committed murder once already to stay alive and to keep Ramon alive. No, she had decided. She could not leave Cos with Aeryk. The Altairan held all the cards. For her and her brother to survive, she must kill again.

"I thank you again for asking, Aeryk," she said as gently as she could, "and I will never forget that you did. Your wilderness is not for me. Not even with you to ease the way. I do not think Cos or any city like it is for you. What we've shared, even for such a little while, is ours forever, but our time together must end. In your heart, you know it is so."

"I reckon," Aeryk said just as gently. He was happy for the darkness that cloaked them, which hid his face and eyes and his embarrassment at the relief he felt as she spoke. She would not try to hold him, and in his truest heart, he was glad of it.

Aeryk awoke in the dawn to find Tierza already dressed, sitting at the edge of the bed, watching him. In the soft light of the room, her eyes shone, warm and golden brown.

"I must spend the day with my brother, Aeryk. I told you about him, remember?" At his nod, she continued. "I will meet you here this evening, in the hour before moons' rise."

Tierza hurried to the small apartment her brother maintained on Barber Street. Together, they set out toward the river. Greygor

Gullwatch maintained a set of rooms above a warehouse overlooking the city docks. The Altairan owned the warehouse. Gullwatch's choice of residence allowed him to keep a close eye on his employer's property while providing the cutthroat more privacy and more living space than most, especially among those who began life by growing up in Cos's poorest section, known as Dogtown.

As she made her way up the warehouse stairs in the second hour past dawn, Tierza knew Gullwatch was to take no part in the raid planned against the Elven compound at moons' set of the coming night. She adjusted her shawl. She wore the scarlet wool today over a dress she'd selected especially for the occasion. The blue frock featured long sleeves and a low-cut neckline. Early morning constituted an awkward time to visit, but she had little choice. If he was not alone, the situation might well become complicated.

Taking a deep, calming breath, she knocked at his door.

"Who is it?" he called from within.

Recalling his blank, nearly lifeless eyes, Tierza thought even his voice seemed to lack animation. A useful trait, she supposed, for a murderer. "Tierza," she answered simply. "I am alone."

The door cracked open, and Gullwatch peered out. "What do you want?" he asked in a neutral tone. He always spoke in a near monotone, even while deep inside her, rutting and asking if she liked being ridden that way.

"I need to speak with you," she said quietly, "in private."

Looking past her carefully, Gullwatch nodded and stepped back, opening the door. He stood aside to watch her walk by. Tierza artfully leaned a little more heavily on the crutch under her left arm than necessary. Making her way into the room, she turned in time to see Gullwatch slide a long heavy-bladed knife back into a sheath he had affixed to a hook embedded in the door.

The room was sparsely furnished. An unmade bed occupied a spot against the far wall, a plain wooden table near the door. Two chairs sat beneath a small window on the wall adjacent to it. In the middle of the opposite wall, a second door leading to an adjoining room stood closed. A small chest of drawers stood next to the bed, and an array of weapons, including a pair of crossbows, hung from hooks and pegs throughout the room. Rumor put Gullwatch in possession of a cache of coins, worth a considerable amount, somewhere.

The Altairan's henchman swung 'round to face her. He lifted a thumb back over his right shoulder, pointing at the knife. "A Three Rivers Hawken," he said conversationally, "best knife ever made for gutting a man." His flat grey eyes rested upon her, waiting.

"I have come upon a way of making some money in a manner that will not interfere with the Altairan's trade. I can't do it alone," she told him. "I need your help."

"Don't seem likely, you coming to me." His eyes continued to gaze steadily at her. "Considerin'."

"You were doing the Altairan's bidding." She met his flat-eyed gaze without flinching. "I don't hold it against you." To Tierza, the lie seemed to echo through the small room.

"Why me?" His eyes told her nothing. She hadn't expected them to. His question said he was alone. That was good.

"You are capable, smarter than you look." Tierza spoke matter-of-factly. "And the Altairan does not seem to begrudge you a little extra profit, so long as his trade is not hurt."

"He may not be so generous with you involved," Gullwatch said, which was true enough.

"He doesn't need to know." Tierza looked him in the eyes and lowered her shawl. "Help me earn enough to get out of Cos, and I'll find a way to make it worth your while."

His eyes still said nothing, but she noted easily enough where they were looking. "What is to keep me from telling him about your visit and your purpose here?" he asked. "Doing so might earn me a taste of what you're offering without the risk."

She smiled at him. "I'll deny it, and then the Altairan will have a decision to make."

"You think he'll believe you?" For the first time, Gullwatch actually seemed interested in their conversation.

Tierza shrugged, making certain she used the gesture to full effect. "I'm valuable to him. After tonight, I will have proven myself very valuable. And he likes planting himself between my legs." She laid her shawl upon the bed and leaned her crutch against it.

"Can't blame him for that," Gullwatch admitted, watching her. Stepping close, he said, "I'll have that taste, girl, before I hear you out."

Folding her hands together over her breasts to form a feeble barrier between her and the tall cutthroat, Tierza looked helplessly up into his eyes as he drew near. She nudged her crutch with her crippled left foot. The stick toppled, clattering to the floor. His eyes flicked to it. His head turned slightly away as they did so. She slipped the poisoned dart from the sheath in her left sleeve with her right hand and plunged it into his abdomen. Gullwatch's eyes, just for an instant, registered surprise. His right hand shot out, clasping her throat, but there was no power in his grip. His knees buckled, and she guided him to the floor. Gullwatch sat with his back resting against the side of the bed.

"The poison is a new form of cerdyth," Tierza told him, withdrawing the dart and laying it carefully aside. Slipping a small glass vial from the sash about her waist, she continued. "This is the antidote." She held the vial up where he could see it. "You will soon feel a numbness rising up from your legs. When it reaches here"—she touched his chest—"it will be too late. Tell me where your cache is located and all you know about the raid planned against the Elven villa tonight. Talk fast, Gullwatch. You do not have much time."

Tierza had to credit Gullwatch. He had a flair for brevity. He told her what she needed most to know in a few short sentences. Removing the stopper from the vial, she trickled the contents, a little rosewater, between his lips. He swallowed eagerly, convulsively. The rosewater would do nothing to counteract the poison, but Tierza believed that no one, not even a cruel, black-hearted, raping piece of shit like Greygor Gullwatch, should die with no hope whatsoever.

Precisely as he'd indicated, they found Gullwatch's cache in a compartment under a floor board in the warehouse below. A heavy crate labeled "farming tools" rested atop it. Tierza needed Ramon's help to move the thing out of the way. The cache turned out to be more valuable than Tierza had dared hope, nearly eighteen hundred talents of silver and thirty gold crowyns. She and Ramon went carefully through the cutthroat's rooms. In addition to weapons, they found a wallet filled with small coins, a few extra blankets that were reasonably clean, a good store of utensils, pots and pans, and some food, including beans, flour, and dried fruit that would travel well and several bottles of surprisingly good wine.

As the warehouse stood quiet, devoid of people at the time of Greygor Gullwatch's demise, they dragged his body out into the storage area and hid it under a tarpaulin. The corpse wouldn't remain hidden long, but they didn't need much time, and at least it would not be discovered by a cursory search of Gullwatch's rooms. Ramon helped Tierza load their plunder onto a handcart they'd rented, and together, brother and sister, left the warehouse and made their way back to Barber Street. Tierza managed not to sick up until they reached the alleyway just behind Myra's shop. She vomited there, into one of the vegetable pots, and crumpled beside it, shaking, while Ramon ran to fetch Myra.

The day dragged slowly by for Aeryk. Sam had departed earlier that day on his way to escort the Elves heading to the Balmuir estate. Aeryk ate breakfast alone, exchanging small talk briefly with Mistress Canty. He didn't ask about a gift for Tierza. Sam wasn't due back until sundown three days hence. That left plenty of time to take Tierza shopping. He figured they'd wander about some. When her eyes lit up, he'd know what to buy. If worse came to worse, he'd come right out and ask her.

Aeryk spent some time looking after Wyli. The gelding frisked a little, in good shape, more than ready to start the trip home. He took a bath and had a nap. With a wet stone Aeryk carefully went over the edges of his baelryc and then his dirk. When Tierza pushed open the door of his room, she found him juggling walnuts by candlelight. Aeryk could keep three in the air pretty readily, but four at a time ranged still a little beyond him. Upon entering, Tierza looked at him, smiled, and shook her head but said nothing.

"You're late," Aeryk remarked, snatching the walnuts out of the air. "It is long after moons' rise."

Slipping out of her familiar scarlet shawl, Aeryk noted she wore the same green dress she'd had on the night she'd spent singing at the Rising Star a few days ago.

"Please don't scold me." Tierza spoke softly. "I've had a hard day."

When he put his arms around her, she clung to him, not with passion but with what seemed more like sadness or relief. "What's wrong?" Aeryk asked after a time.

"I miss you," she replied simply, sounding as if she meant every word.

Knowing he had no solution to that problem, he kissed her gently and tried to change the subject. "How is your brother?"

"He is gainfully employed for a change," Tierza replied, thinking: *If Ramon even looks at a gaming table this night, I will have his liver on a plate.* "Are you hungry?"

"I am," Aeryk acknowledged.

"There is a little place, just down the street, that serves a very good beef steak," Tierza informed him.

"Sounds good," Aeryk enthused.

"First, I'm wondering if you would fetch us some mulled wine. There is a chill in the air tonight, and the Rising Star is known for its mulled wine. Very warming, it is."

Tierza's request sounded more like an order to Aeryk's ears, but he'd never had a cup of mulled wine and thought it might be worth a try.

"Do I go see Thatch?" Aeryk inquired.

"I don't think Thatch is working tonight," Tierza responded. "Whoever is tending bar should be able to help you. You'll have to wait. When you get back, I'll have a surprise for you."

"Sounds even better," Aeryk commented on his way out of the room.

After Aeryk had closed the door behind him, Tierza pulled the curtains to his window together and then slipped a lit candle between them, waving it slowly back and forth three times. She then placed two folded pieces of paper in plain sight on the foot of the bed, returned the lit candle to the table, and gathered up her shawl. With her crutch under her left arm, she cautiously opened the door and looked up and down the hallway. Seeing no one, she slipped out of Aeryk's room and made her way, as quickly and quietly as she could, to a door leading to the back stairs.

32
Duel in the Dark

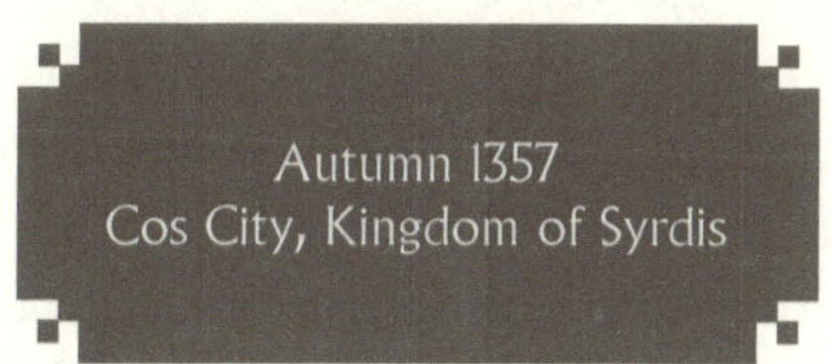

Upon returning to his room bearing two cups of hot mulled wine that smelled faintly of cinnamon, Aeryk found Tierza had gone. *A surprise, all right enough,* Aeryk thought but nothing like what he'd hoped. He saw the notes lying on the bed.

The first read:

Aeryk,

I must go. We will not meet again.

I will remember and cherish every moment we spent together.

Leave Cos as quickly as you can.

There are those who seek the talisman you wear and would kill to obtain it.

Farewell.

Tierza

Tierza's gone—the thought lanced home. Aeryk knew they were soon to part but had not expected this or the sense of loss that suddenly opened like a void in his heart. *"There are those who seek the talisman you wear."* Who? Why? He'd told no one in Cos about the Fey talisman—except Tierza. *Tierza, what have you done?*

The second note was neither addressed nor signed, but the handwriting was unmistakably the same as the first:

The Elven villa in Cos is to be raided tonight by moons' set.

Three Elves are targeted for death, Kul-Cah-Zul, Mik-Tad-Low, and Jyn-Ael-Tor.

When Tierza set out to surprise, she didn't muck about. Hurrying to the door, he flung it open and looked into the hallway. He saw no one in either direction. He didn't call out Tierza's name, knowing that doing so would be a waste of breath. Strapping on his sword and dirk, Aeryk thrust the second note into his belt, grabbed his hat, and bolted through the door.

Aeryk raced down the stairs of the Rising Star and out a side door to the stables. As he entered, Aeryk noted no attendant was present. A pair of oil lamps suspended from hooks on either side of the door illuminated the stable's interior. A third cast its light from a table set near the front of the long double row of horse stalls. Not bothering with a saddle, Aeryk looped a soft cotton lead rope 'round Wyli's neck and clambered aboard. Fetching one of the oil lamps from its hook alongside the door as he rode by, Aeryk pushed the gelding hard, covering the distance between the inn and the Elven villa in as little time as possible.

Swinging down, he showed the note to the pair of sentries at the front gate. The Fates were with him as Tyk-Ban-Gyl was one of the two on duty. Neither Tyk nor the other sentry knew Kul-Cah-Zul's or Jyn's whereabouts. The third elf on the list was apparently some sort of librarian. Tyk felt certain she would be found in her quarters just off the library.

Tyk collared a pair of syrs passing by and sent one running to rouse the company. Tyk assigned the second to escort Aeryk to Jyn's rooms in the main annex. Tyk himself would check on the librarian and then go to Kul-Cah-Zul's chambers, which were located in a different section of the villa's main building. The Elfan assigned to accompany Aeryk bore the name Rit-Ban-Day. Rit wore no armor but was armed with johten and dagger. Before leaving the central gate, Rit snatched up a torch and set it alight, using one of the two already illuminating the entryway. Aeryk still carried the lamp he'd brought with him from the stable at the inn.

Rit-Ban-Day led the way. As they dashed across the courtyard, Aeryk glanced upward. The stars shone brightly in the chill autumn night, scattered across a sky as black as death. Both Trasceran moons had set.

Jyn's lodgings were on the second floor of the compound's main building. As they rounded the corner of the corridor leading to her rooms, they nearly stumbled over the body of an Elfan that lay crumpled against the wall, his throat neatly slit. Some distance down the hall, a second Elfan sprawled facedown on the marble floor in a still-spreading pool of blood.

"Ware Elves!" Aeryk shouted. "Intruders, ware Elves!"

They'd taken only a couple of steps further down the hall when the elf at his side grunted. A dagger hilt blossomed suddenly from Rit-Ban-Day's chest. The Elfan collapsed, his drawn sword clanging on the stone floor. The torch Rit carried dropped as well, skidding a short distance forward, casting an eerie light into the chamber. Swinging his own blade into the mid-guard position, Aeryk caught sight of a figure emerging from the shadows that cloaked the far end of the hallway. Too tall for an elf and dressed all in black, the stranger advanced, flourishing a gracefully curved sword in his right hand. Aeryk had never seen the like of the blade the man displayed. No johten, the weapon's design featured a single-handed grip and an elaborate cagelike handguard.

Aeryk feinted to his right and then shifted left and delivered a thrust aimed at his opponent's throat. His adversary countered easily, altering stance and position with fluid grace. Their swords met; sparks danced along the blades. By the Fates, the bastard was fast. Seemingly without effort, his ghostly silent enemy parried Aeryk's every strike. A lightning-fast riposte nearly took Aeryk in the eye. At the last instant, the young Kylgahran managed to jerk his head out of the way. The tip of his assailant's blade still scored Aeryk's cheek under his left eye socket. Aeryk stepped quickly back, opening some space between him and his adversary. The man before him stood hooded and wore a mask over the lower portion of his face. In the light of the lamp, Aeryk saw the stranger's eyes were blue and showed a still, quiet calm.

Aeryk flung the oil lamp at the fellow's head and pressed forward. As Aeryk closed the distance separating them, the man ducked under the lamp, which smashed against the far wall of the chamber. Knowing he was overmatched, Aeryk lunged, a seemingly reckless move, but it was as if he could hear Danyl's voice in his head, urging, "At him, lad." Expecting to feel the bite of the tall man's steel at any moment, Aeryk pushed closer, seeking to crowd the bugger. Aeryk's opponent suddenly slipped, his foot skidding in the life's blood of the Elfan lying on his face in the hall.

Though the slip caused only a moment's hesitation, it was enough. Aeryk stepped in, ripping upward with the rugged cross guard of his baelryc. The sturdy iron boss struck the black-clad swordsman under his jaw, snapping his head back. Lowering his shoulder, Aeryk smashed into the man in black. The fellow stumbled, losing his balance, and Aeryk brought his baelryc flashing down in a vicious draw cut that nearly severed his foeman's head.

Stepping over the still twitching form at his feet, Aeryk cried, "Jyn! Ware Jyn!"

An arched doorway loomed just ahead. Snatching up the still burning torch, Aeryk leapt through the aperture, dodging left to right and tossing the torch ahead of him as he did so. The doorway opened onto a wider entry hall. On the other side of the room stood another black-clad warrior, curved sword drawn. Advancing, Aeryk saw movement beneath the shadowed arch across the chamber. Anticipating another dagger, Aeryk again assumed the mid-guard stance.

Instead of steel, a bright blue light emanated from the shadows. A brief flash pulsed only for an instant but incredibly intense. Aeryk felt a sudden chill run through his body, radiating outward from the medallion around his neck. The light, bright as it was, should have blinded him in the dimly lit room, but it did not.

Ignoring whatever threat remained in the archway beyond, Aeryk closed on the second swordsman. The man seemed startled, as if surprised to see Aeryk still on his feet. His sword swept up, and he managed to ward off Aeryk's first strike, but only just. Caught off guard and slightly off-balance, the second foe's counterstrike went wide, and Aeryk slipped his blade past his enemy's sword, planting a hand's span of watermarked steel into his chest, just below the heart. The man dropped like a stone. His heart hammering, Aeryk pressed his back to the wall and paused a few moments to catch his breath.

Jyn's rooms, Aeryk knew, lay just beyond the entryway chamber and were fronted by a small courtyard open to the sky. Aeryk entered to find a third warrior garbed in black, standing near the far wall. Like the first two, the man wore a stygian tunic made of silk and trousers of the same color and material. His feet were encased in some sort of soft-soled shoes, with leggings wrapped about his calves. Hooded, a black scarf masked his face also. Only his eyes showed above the mask. While it was too dark for Aeryk to determine the eye color, there was no mistaking their intensity.

"You have been lucky this night." The man's tone sounded pleasant, conversational. He spoke Aylitic with a subtle accent Aeryk could not place. "Toss me that bauble you wear about your neck, and live a while longer."

"I'll sell it to you," Aeryk said. "Here's my price." He raised his sword, settling this time into the high-guard position.

"Fool," the masked warrior spat contemptuously. Gliding forward, the curved blade in his hand swept upward. Aeryk felt a sense of calm wash over him. It was as if he could feel Basyl and Danyl standing with him in that small garden as the stars shone overhead. If he had only moments left, he determined to live them as a Kylgahran should—with courage, so the Fates would call his name as his soul crossed over to the spirit realm; with honor, so he could look his father's shade in the eye and embrace his mother's without shame.

As his foe drew near, Aeryk struck first. His baelryc swept down. Using the two-handed high-guard grip, Aeryk slashed at his adversary. The baelryc was heavy. No matter the quality of his antagonist's steel or his skill, the relentless sweep of the Kylgahran broad sword demanded respect. Aeryk struck again and again. Thrown on to the defensive, Aeryk's long-limbed opponent gave ground, artfully warding every blow. Sidestepping with uncanny ability, the tall man whirled, driving a slim-bladed knife into Aeryk's thigh.

The masked swordsman stepped nimbly back out of reach and cried, "Now die, Kylgahran."

Aeryk felt hardly any pain at all. Instead, a chill numbness spread from the wound in his leg, radiating outward. He knew instinctively that the blade must have been poisoned. Pulling the knife free of his thigh, Aeryk slid down on one knee. As he did so, his foe raised his arms to shoulder height, spreading them outward in exultation.

Now who is the fool, Aeryk thought. He shifted his grip on the baelryc in his hands and then did something both Basyl and Danyl had absolutely forbade him ever to do in combat. Whipping his arm forward, he hurled his baelryc at his enemy like a spear. The Kylgahran blade struck Aeryk's foeman in the stomach, imbedding deep. The man fell, dropping his own weapon to clutch at the broadsword protruding from his gut. Aeryk had drawn his dirk in anticipation of a second toss, but he could see there was no need.

"You first," Aeryk growled back.

Climbing to his feet took considerable effort. Feeling dizzy, with numbness spreading implacably throughout his lower extremities, Aeryk willed himself forward. Standing over his prostrate adversary, he grasped the hilt of his baelryc with both hands. Summoning the last of his strength, Aeryk wrenched the blade free. The downed man screamed, his hands grasping futilely at the gaping wound in his belly.

"Take your time," Aeryk told him.

Staggering back a few steps, Aeryk fought to hold on to consciousness and the sword that had been his father's—his true father, Danyl had told him when he first pressed the blade into Aeryk's hands. Aeryk had no one to pass the sword on to, but Sam would see the baelryc returned safely home. *All right enough*, he thought. He slipped to his knees. Grounding the point, he reversed his grip on the hilt of his gore-splattered baelryc and clung to it with both hands. He leaned into the weapon, determined not to die on his back—except that is where he found himself moments later, staring up at the stars.

Above him, spoiling his view, a stranger's face appeared. Framed by a tousled mass of snow-white hair, the stranger peered into his eyes. The stranger's eyes seemed enormous, almond shaped. He could not tell what color, but they radiated calm and a kindness that was palpable. An Elfin, Aeryk thought the stranger must be, but there was something odd, different.

The Elfin laid her hands on both sides of his head, and he felt a tingling, strange and deep, stir somewhere in his chest. The tingling sensation grew in intensity and seemed to battle with the numbness that permeated his body. No pain, really, but his reaction still startled him. *Burn me*—his last conscious thought echoed between his ears—*I've wet myself.*

33

A Lesson Learned

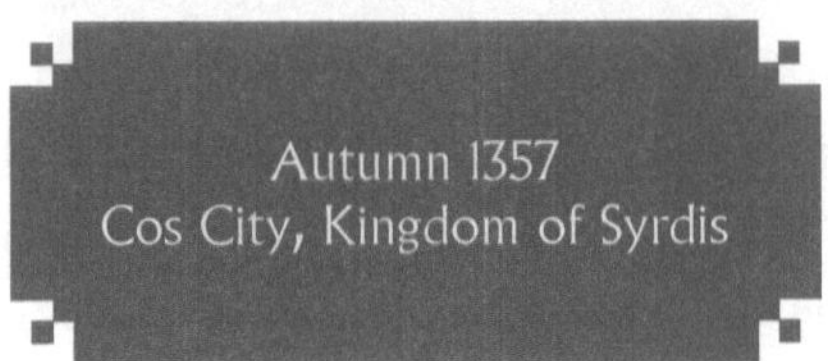

Upon returning to the two-story home she had rented, Siersay Grier went immediately to her rooms. Removing her cloak and setting aside her stave, the sorcerer sat at her writing table and tried to comprehend what had just occurred. At first, everything had gone well, almost too well. She and five of her Sircassians, led by Rodrik Bowe, had successfully infiltrated the Elven villa. The sixth Sircassian, a man named Hasan Real, had remained at the residence to guard the place in their absence.

As planned, two of the assassins silently scaled the wall near one of the ancillary gates. The pair quickly dispatched the lone Elven sentry and opened the gate for the rest. They split into two teams, Rodrik leading one and she the other. The Altairan's description of the inner compound—and in particular, the main annex—proved accurate. Rodrik and a second Sircassian went to the first-floor library in search of the book.

Siersay had provided a questing charm crafted from a page once torn from the very tome they sought. Rodrik had no difficulty finding the book or killing the hapless historian, Mik-Tad-Low, as she sat reading in a tiny alcove adjacent to her quarters. Siersay and two others went in search of Kul-Cah-Zul. The fifth Sircassian stayed with the horses just outside the compound's outer wall.

Siersay herself felled Kul-Cah-Zul. Invoking the Yir and drawing upon the amplifying power of her stave, she unleashed a finger-slim beam of balefire into the Elfan's chest before he could reach the dagger talisman that lay upon a dresser at his bedside. Balefire manifested as a bright blue light. It consumed life as fire burned wood. The elf collapsed without a sound.

Siersay briefly examined the talisman. The dagger was of ancient origin, the blade forged of pressed steel in the Tieran fashion, the cross guard plain brass, the wooden handle wrapped in leather. Though ordinary in appearance, the talisman was potent, capable both of deflecting magic directed against it and inflicting disabling pain at an intended target. Siersay did not think the Yir force unleashed by the dagger would kill, but the pain would be intense, sufficient to incapacitate its victim perhaps to the point of unconsciousness. Of course, Siersay knew these were secondary attributes, ascribed, she thought, to mask the talisman's primary function, perhaps.

Rodrik and his accomplice rejoined Siersay and the two Sircassians with her as they headed for Jyn-Ael-Tor's quarters. Rodrik and his companion had found it necessary to slay a pair of Elves in the hall leading to Jyn-Ael-Tor's rooms on their way to the vyldeen's lodgings. Jyn-Ael-Tor was nowhere to be found. At that point, Siersay could have called a halt to the mission. Both objects were in her possession, and the two primary targets had been eliminated. She wanted to secure complete success.

As an aide to Aya-Bal-Mar, Jyn-Ael-Tor reportedly spent much time in the captain's quarters on the third floor. Siersay decided to take Rodrik and one other Sircassian with her to the third floor. If the young elf they sought was not in the commander's quarters, perhaps a quick search would reveal something else of value. She directed the remaining two Sircassians to the second-floor landing.

"Stand guard there," she told them. "We'll meet you as quickly as we can." The pair saluted and slipped silently away.

Rodrik went ahead to scout the way to the third floor; turning left he glided across the courtyard and entered the hall. She and the remaining Sircassian, a young man named Balin Karr, followed. It was then they heard someone from further down the hall, shouting in Aylitic, "Ware Elves! Intruders, ware Elves!"

Glancing through the archway at the end of the next section of hallway, Rodrik held up two fingers, indicating two adversaries were attempting to raise the alarm. He then closed his fist twice, signaling that he would deal with both of them. Rodrik possessed impeccable skill, acquired through years of training and experience. Astonished, Siersay gaped when shortly thereafter a swordsman she'd never before seen darted through the arch. The young man wore a broad-brimmed hat. His face was bloody, and so too was the broadsword in his right hand. Siersay knew that if Rodrik lived, the stranger would never have gotten by him. Shock, grief, and rage roiled within her.

"He's mine," she told Balin. The young Sircassian nodded.

Stepping a little further back into the shadows, she opened herself to the Yir. Focusing the power through the talisman stave she bore, she loosed a second bolt of balefire even more powerful than the one that killed Kul-Cah-Zul. The balefire struck home, smashing into the chest of the unknown swordsman. Nothing happened. The man should have died instantly. Instead, he never even flinched and closed rapidly, with lethal grace, on Balin Karr.

Dismayed, Siersay turned and fled back through the hall to the courtyard beyond. There she encountered the two Sircassians she'd sent to the second-floor landing. They'd heard the shout as well and were returning to provide support. The senior of the pair was a man named Rigel Trew. Rodrik trusted him. It was then that the identity of the unknown swordsman occurred to her. His clothes, his accent and the broadsword he carried all indicated he was a Kylgahran. A Kylgahran that stood immune to balefire. He must be the one who wore the Fey talisman. The one Lykas Greytower was supposed to have had murdered by moons' rise.

She doubted young Balin would be able to stop him if Rodrik could not. Siersay laid a hand on Rigel's arm. "A Kylgahran is going to enter the courtyard presently. He will be wearing a talisman, an amulet about his neck. Kill him, and take the talisman. Use this, if needs be. The blade is coated with ampercin." She handed him the sheathed poisoned knife she usually kept with her. Ampercin was deadly, nearly as fast-acting as cerdyth and even more certain.

In the company of her remaining Sircassian, she watched from the doorway at the far end of the courtyard as Rigel dueled with the Kylgahran. They were interrupted by a pair of Elves dashing up the stairs from below. By the time they had dealt with them, Rigel was down, and the courtyard had filled with Elves; most carried bows with arrows at the ready. One of the Elves knelt beside the Kylgahran. Even from where she stood, Siersay could feel the power of the healing flow coursing from the elf into the prostrate barbarian. At that point, she could do nothing but flee. The last of the four Sircassians who had accompanied her into the villa lowered Siersay to the ground beyond the outer wall from the second-floor landing, using a rope, and then followed, clambering down with catlike ease.

Her sitting room was lit by a single candle set atop a dressing table against the far wall. It flickered, casting shadows. The silence coiled about her and was stifling. Their return from the Elven villa had gone without incident. On the surface, her mission remained a success. Placed upon the table in front of her lay the dagger talisman and the history book the Golden Hand had sent her to Cos to obtain. The dagger talisman, potent and rare, represented a remarkable find. Its ancillary properties could be invoked by thought alone, with no ability to invoke the Yir required.

The talisman's primary purpose, however, could be utilized only by deft application of the power of the Yir. The principal function of the dagger talisman was to act as a key. That much Siersay knew. *A key to what?* She would have given much to know the answer to that question. Why had Kul-Cah-Zul kept the talisman and fled? Could it be that he had been seduced by the power of the talisman? Surely the elf would have known the Golden Hand would not tolerate such a betrayal.

Kul-Cah-Zul had paid for his treachery, and the scholar, too, lay dead. But the cost had been dear. *Rodrik, oh Light, Rodrik,* she thought. She had not seen his body. The hope was a fleeting one. Alive, he would not have allowed the Kylgahran to pass. Elves had flooded into the open-air courtyard from the hallway that led past his location. He would not have allowed himself to be taken while still living, not under any circumstances. No, Rodrik was dead and two others as well. Three Sircassians lost in one night. Jyn-Ael-Tor still lived. Siersay's mission had become only a partial success at a bitter price.

That cursed Kylgahran had corroded her victory. The knowledge that he must have paid for it with his life brought no solace. Very few healers could ward against a lethal dose of ampercin. Siersay had seen for herself the knife bedded deep in the young barbarian's thigh. Though his death was a near certainty, the Kylgahran should never have lived long enough to interfere in the first place. He had trumpeted Lykas Greytower's failure. The Altairan would, without doubt, place the blame upon his operative, the whore Tierza. Siersay's hand closed unbidden about the haft of her stave, becoming a white-knuckled grip. Knowing the Altairan, Siersay suspected this Tierza would not live to see the dawn. She vowed Greytower would not live to look upon the morrow's sunset.

Sleep eluded her. In the morning Siersay donned a black silk gown. Sleeveless, the dress gathered at the waist by use of a broad black-leather belt. The neckline was almost modest. It hinted more than it revealed. In her homeland, black served as the color of mourning. Siersay decided it would do for vengeance-taking as well. The knock on her door startled her. She had not expected anything to happen so early. Taking up her stave, she turned to face the door. "Enter," she said.

Hasan Real stepped into the room. She did not know the Sircassian well. He had been the last to join her troop, arriving only after she the others had already reached Cos. Like most Sircassians, he stood tall, sleekly muscled, and blond. His eyes were blue, so like Rodrik's. The thought pained her. She suppressed it ruthlessly. "Lykas Greytower is here," Hasan said. "He begs an audience with you, sorcerer."

"Show him in, then Hasan Real." Siersay noted some surprise at how calm her voice sounded. *Beg, he will,* Siersay promised herself, *for all the good it will do him.* The Altairan appeared, clad in essentially the same manner as on his previous visit. He was armed only with the large belt knife. He had wrapped a grey woolen blanket about his broad shoulders. Autumn had deepened in Cos, and the morning air rippled with cold. Hasan followed him into the room, taking a position slightly behind her and a few steps to her right. It didn't really matter. She intended to deal with the Altairan herself.

Bowing, Lykas Greytower said, "The city is abuzz with news of your exploits last night, sorcerer. I trust you were successful."

"We were, Greytower." Siersay's voice made the autumn chill seem warm by comparison. "Have you come to deliver the Fey talisman as promised?"

"I cannot, sorcerer." The regret in Greytower's voice sounded genuine. "My operative failed in her mission. She has disappeared. I know not why. My people search for her the now, and if she lives, she will be found and will reveal all before she dies. That I promise you."

"Your promises do not seem to count for much," Siersay observed, hefting the stave in her hands.

"Nothing is certain until it is done and seen done," Greytower responded. "I offered you confirmation. You declined."

"You seek to shift blame for your failure on to me?" Siersay's rage nearly matched her astonishment at the man's sheer gall.

"I own my failures, sorcerer," Lykas Greytower said evenly. "And I have learned to compensate for them—a lesson, I fear, that will come to you too late." He raised his left hand. Siersay felt a pin prick in her right arm. A glance revealed a small dart protruding from her upper arm, near the shoulder joint. Looking to Hasan Real, she saw him slipping what must have been a miniature blowgun about the size of a flute back into his tunic. The Sircassian's face was expressionless. Grasping her staff with her right hand, she plucked the dart from her arm with her left. She felt no pain once the dart was withdrawn. Perhaps there existed a slight numbness in the vicinity of the tiny puncture wound itself.

Instinctively, she reached out to the Yir. Nothing happened. Instead of the usual sweet rush of feeling, she sensed only emptiness. "That will be all, Hasan," Greytower directed the assassin. "See that we are not disturbed."

The Sircassian nodded and left the room.

"Gold knows many masters," Greytower commented. "You have not been poisoned, Siersay," he continued reassuringly. "The drug is called camadyl, after the shrub whose root is its main ingredient. It was invented by an apothecary right here in Cos. He sought to develop a medicine that would relieve toothache. The drug's effect on those who can invoke the Yir was unexpected. Some mistakes are truly remarkable, are they not?"

Desperate, Siersay tried again and again to access the Hidden Source. She could not.

"The effects of the drug are only temporary," Greytower explained. "The dose now coursing through your veins should wear off in four or five hours. However accurate, I suspect that knowledge will be of little use to you."

In her panic, Siersay forgot about the dagger talisman resting atop her writing table and swung her stave like a club in an attempt to smash the Altairan's face. He snatched the stave in midair. Rolling his wrists, he sent her tumbling to the floor in the middle of the room while wresting the ash wood staff from her in the process, as if she was a child.

Lykas Greytower smiled. Siersay began to scream even before he touched her. Her screams continued for a long while. Occasionally, the Altairan would pause to ask questions. She answered as best she could, knowing her responses would avail her nothing. Siersay was correct. When he had finished with her, the room knew only quiet, the timeless silence of death.

34
Betrothal Challenge

Ranyl Emyrt of Clan Ard Mourne dreamed. He knew it, somehow, and yet the awareness did nothing to weaken the grip of the sleep-born images. Meggie stood before him, young and lithe and free of hurt or pain, an impish smile on her face. She beckoned for him to follow and turned away. He'd taken only a step or two when a cry rang out from behind. He whirled about to see Sym running toward him. To her rear, Ranyl saw dark shadows rise amid a swirling grey mist. Ranyl reached for the sword at his side. Meggie screamed.

Ranyl awoke to find dawn's first light tumbling through the window of his bedchamber. The dream troubled him. He'd dreamed it once before, the night Sym told him of her father's intent to hold their wedding during the month of the waning moons, a couple of weeks prior to the start of the winter solstice celebrations, whose end would mark the beginning of the new year.

She'd taken his hand and asked that Ranyl accede to her father's wishes in the matter. Ranyl fancied he could still feel her hand in his and see the soft look in her eyes. She'd never before asked him for anything. In that moment, Ranyl reckoned he could have denied her nothing. The ensuing weeks had flown by.

"Dreams reflect more our fears than our futures," a typically sanguine Tieran saying went. True enough, Ranyl reckoned, but still, something about that particular dream haunted him. At noon this day, the first of the month, a betrothal ceremony for Sym and Ranyl was planned. A bit old-fashioned, the betrothal pronouncement, merely a formality actually, given the signed marriage contract.

A knock sounded at his door. Before Ranyl could reply, the portal swung open just wide enough for Tuan Marques to stick his head into the room. "Good," the youthful healer announced, "you're awake. With some luck and sufficient elbow grease, we should be able to render you presentable by noon, with a little time left over for a bite to eat."

Dabner Rhymes, a priest of Tal, would preside over the betrothal ceremony. Rhymes stood a bean pole of a man, with long gangly arms and legs. Of middle years and balding, the priest retained only a horseshoe-shaped iron-grey fringe of curly hair looped about his head, just above his ears. The man had a prominent nose and an even more pronounced Adam's apple that bobbed dutifully whenever he talked. He spoke in a rich and evocative voice, however, suitable for his calling, and Sym clearly adored him.

The ceremony was to be staged in the central courtyard of Greymark hold, a large square that fronted the manor. Flanked by Tuan and Emerson Hart, Ranyl preceded his betrothed into the square and stood before the priest. Escorted by her father, Sym entered the courtyard clad in a dark-green cotton dress, long sleeved, with a snug-fitting bodice. Her hair hung loose and flowed in silken waves about her shoulders. Ranyl had never seen her with her hair down.

"Stop gaping at the poor girl like some upcountry clodhopper," Tuan hissed, elbowing Ranyl sharply in the ribs. "You are about to become a nobleman, officially. The least you can do is act the part."

Resplendent in a cream-colored silk shirt with the inevitable lace ruffles lining the cuffs and matching waistcoat, the young healer looked every bit of him a scion of noble rank.

Ranyl owned only one silk shirt and waistcoat. He was saving those for his wedding. For the betrothal ceremony, he wore a matching dark-blue woolen waistcoat and trousers over a white cotton shirt and his best pair of boots. A wide leather belt wound round his middle, supporting sword and knife. He was bareheaded.

"Easy enough for you to say," Ranyl growled softly. "She's far too fine for the likes of me."

"She is luckier than she knows," the young healer pronounced. Ranyl glanced down to find Tuan's forest-green eyes steady on his. "Stand up straight, the now," Tuan instructed, "and smile, for pity's sake."

With Sym's umber eyes upon him, warm and beckoning, Ranyl found he had no trouble smiling. She returned the expression.

"What is it?" Sym asked as he approached.

"I've never seen you with your hair down," Ranyl answered.

"Tradition, here in the north, for such as this," Sym informed him. "It is a little unruly, I know." She took his arm.

"It is lovely," Ranyl proclaimed. "I think we should pass a law prohibiting braids."

Sym's eyes crinkled. "Exactly the sort of wool-headed thing a man would conjure up."

"Take a close look in the mirror," Ranyl retorted, "and I'll rest my case."

Sym's eyes softened, growing serious. "It occurs to me there remains much we do not know of one another." She looked as if she was about to say more but had no chance as the priest's sonorous voice called the gathering to attention.

The courtyard was crowded; all of Ranyl's people were present and dozens more Ard Ryan retainers and clan members filled the square. In a brief preamble, Rhymes opened with a couple of jokes at Ranyl's expense. The crowd laughed good-naturedly, and somewhat to his surprise, Ranyl felt himself relaxing a bit. Rhymes closed his introduction by teasing Sym just enough to make her blush.

The formal part of the ceremony required only a few lines. Just at the end, Dabner Rhymes asked of the crowd if anyone present had cause to object. From his perfunctory tone, it seemed clear the priest expected no response. Before Rhymes could continue, a firm, clear voice called out, "I object."

Across the square, Ranyl saw a tall young man step out from amid the press to stand a few paces in front of the crowd. For an instant, Ranyl thought he was looking at Lukas Holt. The man had the ranger's height and wide-shouldered, rawboned build. Dressed in a plain brown woolen shirt and trousers with a black, broad-brimmed felt trail hat atop his head, the stranger stood armed with baelryc and dirk. Like Holt, the fellow was brown haired and blue eyed. A few years younger, Ranyl estimated; this intruder could have passed for the ex-ranger's kid brother, undeniably handsome right down to the cleft in his chin. *This is all I need,* Ranyl found himself thinking, *another tall, handsome son of a bitch with a dent in his chin.*

"Who objects?" the priest challenged.

"Rowyn Cutter of Clan Ard Ryan," the young man responded evenly, in a voice set to carry easily across the square.

"On what grounds do you object?" Dabner Rhymes inquired.

Rowyn Cutter's gaze settled steadily on the young woman standing at Ranyl's side. "I object on the grounds that Tessymir Ryan and I are already betrothed." A murmur rippled through the people jammed into the square at the sound of the young man's words. Ranyl's stomach churned. *Not this, not the now.*

"What say you, Tessymir Ryan?" Dabner Rhymes's deep, resonant voice rang out.

Dread coiled with icy fingers about his heart as Ranyl looked at Sym. Her large brown eyes were fixed upon the tall, young Kylgahran standing at the edge of the square. Sym stood erect, her shoulders back, and pronounced in a calm, clear tone, "I am not the now nor have I ever been betrothed to Rowyn Cutter."

"Your claim is disputed, Rowyn Cutter," Dabner stated. "Will you withdraw the charge you make?"

"I will not," Cutter vowed.

"Have you any proof to offer?" Dabner inquired.

"I do, in the form of this token," Rowyn replied, "given to me by her as a pledge of love and troth." Rowyn reached into his shirt and extracted a straight pin fashioned of brass and topped by what appeared to Ranyl's eyes to be a piece of carved jade. A collective gasp emanated from the crowd at the sight. Ranyl had seen number of Ryan men wearing similar devices in the lapels of their coats. He knew nothing of the significance of such, but the effect on the northerners gathered was obvious.

"A gift freely given," Sym acknowledged in the same, cool steady tone, "of the heart but not as a promise of marriage."

The tall Kylgahran took two long strides toward the center of the square, drawing nearer to Sym. "Will you publicly deny our love?" Rowyn asked, his voice a raw mix of hurt and anger.

"Whatever we once shared is over the now and done." Sym's voice was gentle and sad and as final as a grave.

Rowyn Cutter shifted his gaze to Ranyl. With grim certainty, Ranyl knew what was coming. His left hand curled about the hilt of the broadsword at his belt. He felt a warm surge of exultation course through his body. "What of you, Midlander?" Cutter placed a sneering emphasis on Ranyl's place of origin. "You stand silent. Will you deny my claim?"

"It matters not." Ranyl pitched his voice to carry throughout the courtyard. "Lady Tessymir has denied your charge. That is enough."

"A coward's answer," Rowyn proclaimed. His eyes roamed over the gathering, searching for some sign of support. "I say she is rightfully mine to wed. If you are to claim her with honor, you must first meet my challenge."

"No," Sym cried. For the first time her smooth contralto quavered slightly. "I will not see blood spilled because a boy"—she looked directly at Rowyn Cutter—"refuses to accept what a man must."

Sym looked to Ranyl. She could see in his eyes the barrier between them had returned with an icy intensity. Ranyl's left hand tightened on the hilt of his sword; she saw his knuckles going white.

"No violence, please," Sym entreated.

After a moment, Ranyl nodded and spoke to Rowyn Cutter. "Withdraw the charge of cowardice, and there will be no quarrel between us."

Cutter's blue eyes locked on to Ranyl's. "I will not."

Ranyl smiled. Sym, standing close, could see the bitter twist to his mouth, not so the crowd further away or young Rowyn either.

To the larger assembly, it seemed as if Ranyl savored Cutter's insistence. "So be it. Noon tomorrow. Swords."

"Done," Cutter agreed. Without further word, the young Kylgahran turned on his heels and shouldered his way back through the crowd.

"Are we finished?" Ranyl asked of a subdued Dabner Rhymes.

The priest raised his hands to shoulder height, palms extended. "A betrothal challenge is offered and is to be settled by contest of arms at noon tomorrow. This ceremony is ended. Go the now, all of you, in peace."

Ranyl's eyes settled on Sym's. He saw anguish in the burnished maple depths but could not interpret its meaning. His jaw clenched. "I would like to speak with you and your father, the now, in private."

She half reached out to him with her right hand and then seemed to catch herself. "We can meet in his sitting room, as soon as may be." She turned away.

Ranyl watched her go, feeling as if a chasm was growing wider between them with each step she took. He called his retainers together and asked young Tad to fetch his satchel. The dark-haired groom dashed off to comply.

"I'll need two witnesses," Ranyl stated. "Emerson, if you would, and Tuan, I think." Hart and the slim little healer both nodded. "Lukas," Ranyl ordered quietly, "get our people together. Use the wagon park. Stay there, and keep a close watch. I want no trouble if we can avoid it."

"Aye, lord," Lukas Holt replied and then tugged his hat brim. "A couple more of us should stay with you, sir, just in case." Ranyl was not disposed to argue and merely nodded. Tad returned shortly from Ranyl's quarters in the Long House, satchel in hand. Ranyl, accompanied by two veteran rangers, in addition to Emerson Hart and Tuan Marques, made his way to Laird Owain's sitting room. The chamber was relatively small, dominated by a large reading table, a handful of ornately carved wooden chairs, and a large, well-stocked bookshelf.

Sym and her father had preceded them and rose to their feet as Ranyl, Emerson, and Tuan stepped into the room.

"Emerson and Tuan will serve as my witnesses," Ranyl said without preamble as he entered the room.

Sym stiffened, her expressive brown eyes widening. Ranyl saw no change of expression on her father's lean visage. Owain Ryan simply nodded and stepped to the door, speaking softly to someone without. They waited in tense silence until Davis Killoe, accompanied by a short, slight man Ranyl recognized as Benjamyn Lowell, Owain Ryan's steward, walked into the room.

Once the door was closed, Ranyl turned to Sym. "Tell me about Rowyn Cutter."

"He is an Ard Ryan retainer. Until slain fending off a Sueve raid, Rowyn's father preceded Davis as first sword," Sym replied promptly and then continued without hesitation. "Rowyn and I were lovers, but I never promised to marry him."

The ice rimming the charcoal depths of Ranyl's eyes congealed. He said nothing in response but withdrew a heavy sheet of vellum from the leather satchel in his hands.

"This is a copy of the marriage contract signed between us," Ranyl said, speaking to Owain Ryan. "It reads, in part, 'shall bind in marriage Ranyl Emyrt of Clan Ard Mourne, Esquire, and the maiden Tessymir Ryan of Clan Ard Ryan, Laird Apparent.'" Ranyl placed the sheet of vellum down on the writing table. "It would appear the contract, as written, stands breached."

From the corner of his eye, Ranyl saw Sym straighten, her face paling. Davis Killoe shifted his feet, and he laid a big hand on the hilt of his baelryc. Owain Ryan's blue eyes went cold as winter snow.

"Do you seek to have it voided?" Laird Ryan spoke softly, but his voice was as hard as any blade.

Ranyl shook his head. "Amended, rather." Taking a seat at the table, he extracted a pen and a small ink bottle from a special pouch within the satchel. He wrote swiftly and briefly at the bottom of the contract page and then slid the modified document across the table to Owain Ryan.

"This," Ranyl announced, pulling a second piece of paper from the brown leather satchel, "is the attachment referenced."

Owain scanned the words Ranyl had added to the bottom of the contract. "This amendment states that upon completion of the wedding ceremony, the persons named in the attachment are to be formally incorporated as retainers of Clan Ard Ryan and endowed with all rights and privileges thereto."

The laird of Clan Ard Ryan fingered the attachment. "The people designated are those who journeyed here among your wedding van?" Ranyl nodded. Ryan's gaze settled on the broad-shouldered young squire from Wyteridge. "I would have done so in any case."

"Then the modification is one you should be able to readily accept," Ranyl surmised quietly. "I have one additional request."

Owain's eyes narrowed. "Go on."

Ranyl looked at Sym. She met his gaze, her wide-set brown eyes suddenly implacable. "I propose we be married today, this afternoon." He hesitated, looking uncomfortable. "It will not be necessary to consummate the marriage until after the events of tomorrow play out."

Sym lowered her eyes.

"My lord," Benjamyn Lowell observed, speaking to Owain Ryan, "the wedding is planned for First Day, two weeks hence. Formal notices have been dispatched."

"If he is killed tomorrow," Tessymir Ryan interjected, "Squire Ranyl wishes to have put our wedding behind him, so as to ensure the status of his people here."

"Completing the wedding ceremony today has the added benefit," Ranyl expounded, "of securing my portion for use by Clan Ard Ryan, regardless of what transpires tomorrow."

"Your father may not see it that way," Laird Owain asserted.

"A contract is a contract, my lord," Ranyl stated. "My father understands that. He also knows that not every investment returns a profit."

Laird Owain's eyes settled upon those of his daughter. "A wedding today, the first day of the month of the waning moons, is acceptable."

Sym nodded. "I should like to change into my wedding gown," she announced into the brief silence that ensued.

Sym looked at her betrothed. The ice was gone from his eyes. He remained distant, the barrier firmly in place. Upon hearing her request, he appeared embarrassed.

"Of course," Ranyl concurred.

"A private ceremony, I think, Father," Sym suggested, "in the main dining hall. Just enough guests to ensure there is no doubt as to the validity of the proceedings."

"Dabner Rhymes is staying over," Owain replied. "I'm sure he will be willing to perform the wedding. Shall we say the second hour before sunset?"

Sym nodded and then took a seat beside Ranyl at the table. "May I have a word with you alone?"

"Yes," Ranyl answered before turning to Emerson Hart. "Rangers, wives and"—Ranyl smiled—"healers only. Be sure Mae knows she is welcome to attend as well. We'll need some volunteers to look after the children."

"Yes, sir," Hart responded.

"Congratulations," Tuan exclaimed, bowing formally to the couple sitting at table. Tuan and Harry Hart left the room together. At a nod from Laird Owain, Davis Killoe and Benjamyn Lowell were next to leave.

"Obligations are ponderous things," Laird Owain said after his retainers had departed. He looked carefully at the two young people seated before him, "but if the heart is willing, they need not stand in the way of happiness." Without waiting for a response, he stepped quietly from the room.

Once they were alone, Sym saw no point in delay. "I was sixteen and very much in love, or at least I thought I was."

"Love is a heady thing," Ranyl conceded, "all-consuming even." He paused a moment. "Your brother's death and the need for you to marry outside Clan Ard Ryan pulled the two of you apart?"

Sym shook her head. "That served as a good excuse, one I made use of, but that was not the reason. Rowyn and I were coming apart before then. Do you believe me?"

Somewhat to his surprise, Ranyl found that he did and said as much. Sym looked away. "You need not fight. I will speak to my father, to Rowyn, something ..."

"It is too late for that, Sym," Ranyl interrupted, firmly but gently. "Rowyn laid a charge of cowardice at my feet today and did so publicly. Having done such, he cannot turn away with honor, and I cannot without playing the craven. As your consort, I suppose I could be many things; a coward is not one of them. Your father will tell you the same."

Sym's eyes, wide and soft, peered into his. "Rowyn is very skilled with a blade."

Ranyl smiled. "Perhaps he will be overconfident then." Gauging the pained expression on his intended's face, Ranyl sobered. "The contest between us tomorrow need not be to the death. I will make the offer."

Sym lowered her eyes. "Worth the try, I suppose." She did not sound hopeful.

"From the moment he stepped into the courtyard this day, Rowyn intended to challenge me. Nothing you could have said or done would have prevented that," Ranyl said quietly. "I am not of your people. Sooner or later, such a test was inevitable. Only the manner of the thing remained to be determined." Ranyl's smile returned. "I would rather have left it a while longer, mind, but there was never a chance of avoiding it all together. None of this is your fault." As he spoke the words, Ranyl wondered if he believed them. A better man would, Ranyl knew, but he found that he did not.

"You are being kind." Sym raised her eyes to his once more. "I would have preferred honesty."

"You may be the reason for Rowyn's challenge," Ranyl acknowledged, his expression suddenly as serious as his voice, "but if it had not been him, here, today, the test would still have come in some other fashion, somewhere, sometime soon."

"Is there nothing I can do?" Sym asked.

Ranyl took her hand; his eyes searched hers. "When we are wed this afternoon, leave your hair down."

35

A Morning After

Aeryk awoke, lying on a bed in a chamber not known to him. Across the room from the foot of the bed, a window graced the wall. Through the window a soft light shone. Seated in the window frame, he saw Jyn-Ael-Tor. The Elfin was clad in a dark-blue sulsah. The silk tunic clung to the sleek contours of Jyn's slender form. Her legs were bare from mid-thigh, and she wore a pair of leather sandals on her feet. Jyn had dressed her pale blond hair in a single, shimmering braid, falling to the small of her back. In her slim, four-fingered hands, the young elf held a strand of large beads, each about the size of a hazel nut. Her finely wrought features seemed drawn and weary. Even so, Jyn's beauty reached out to him, more compelling than ever.

"Is it morning?" Aeryk asked. His voice sounded strange in his own ears, as if it were stretched thin. His head hurt a thick, dull ache. His mouth and throat were dry and, upon swallowing, tasted like something old and sick had taken up residence within.

Upon hearing him, Jyn seemed to sag briefly against the window sill. After a moment, the elf looked out and responded. "The dawn is just coming. It is beautiful."

Watching Jyn framed in the window by the gentle light of dawn, Aeryk said, "You should see it from here." The elf took his meaning. He could tell by the subtle tilting of her head and the ghost of a smile that flickered across her face so briefly he might have imagined it. But he knew that he had not.

"What are those?" Aeryk asked, nodding at the beads in her hands. Even that small movement caused his head to throb.

"These are prayer beads," Jyn answered him.

"That can't be good," Aeryk commented.

The toss of Jyn's head was more pronounced this time, and her smile lingered. "You have been very near death," Jyn said, laying the beads on a table near the wall and crossing the room to sit on the edge of the bed at his side.

Aeryk was suddenly keenly aware that he lay naked under the thin blanket that covered him. Jyn took his right hand in her left and reached across the bed to place the fingers of her other hand lightly upon his forehead. "The fever has gone at last, thank Providence." He could not say which pleasured him more—the sound of relief in Jyn's voice or the gentle touch of her hand. "How is your leg?"

My leg. Aeryk had to think a moment. *The knife wound.* Gingerly, he flexed his leg beneath the covers. "My leg feels fine," Aeryk reported. "It's my bloody noggin what hurts."

"The aftereffects of the poison, I suspect," Jyn remarked. "Are thee thirsty?"

"Aye, I'm dry as chalk," Aeryk allowed.

Jyn rose from the bed and returned to the table to fill a ceramic mug with water from a pitcher standing there. He struggled to sit up, startled by the effort it took even to lift his head.

"Hush, be still," Jyn said. Slipping quickly back on to the bed, she slid her left hand and arm under his back and, using her left leg as well, levered him up enough to drink from the cup in her right hand. The water tasted cold and sweet.

When he'd drunk his fill, Jyn eased him back down and again rose from the bed. Placing the mug back on the table, she said, "I shall fetch the healer."

He'd made it all the way into a sitting position, saying, "No, Jyn, don't go," when the pain that suddenly seemed to be splitting his head in two caused him to gasp. The room began to swirl. Jyn darted back to the bed. Clasping one hand on each of his shoulders, the elf pushed him back down on to the pillows.

"Fool, boy," Jyn hissed. "Lie still."

"Be happy to," he said after a moment, grateful that the pain in his head was already ebbing. "Just please don't go. I ... that is"—he hesitated, looking up into her eyes of amber gold—"I've missed you—thee, I mean."

"And I have missed thee, Aeryk." He heard the catch in Jyn's voice, but the elf recovered quickly, saying more briskly, "I will not leave thee. But thee must promise to lie still."

Aeryk closed his eyes and smiled as Jyn took his right hand and cradled it in both of hers. Squeezing gently, he said, "You'll need to explain again about the *thee* business. What was it about four in a row?"

Jyn squeezed his hand in return, laughing softly. She touched his left cheek. "I'm afraid there will be a scar."

"That's all right," Aeryk responded. "I wasn't all that pretty to begin with."

Jyn then laid her hand upon his chest. "Strong Heart," she murmured.

Aeryk grinned. "Thick head sounds closer to the mark."

"Strong Heart is what the syrs have been calling thee," Jyn informed him. "Thee managed to down three Sircassians, Aeryk. It takes a strong heart, indeed, to do that."

"Sircassians." Aeryk had never heard the term. "The tall fellas in black?"

Jyn nodded. "The Sircassians are highly trained, remarkably skilled assassins, Aeryk. Defeating one of them in single combat is considered a feat of arms; besting three is an act of true heroism."

Taken aback, Aeryk quickly described the sequence of events in the hall passages of the Elven villa. He told Jyn how the first Sircassian would have done for him almost certainly if the assassin hadn't slipped in a pool of some poor elf's blood. The second just stood there, as if Aeryk posed no threat until too late. He told Jyn about the flash of blue light, though he still did not understand what it meant.

"The third one would have finished me if the healer hadn't come along," Aeryk summarized. "I don't remember doing anything heroic, Jyn." He concluded, a little desperately, "Those bastards just kept coming at me."

Jyn sat gazing at him, her almond-shaped eyes aglow. "Closer to the truth, Aeryk Emyrt, is that thou would not stop coming at them." The elf slipped a piece of paper from her sash. It was the second of Tierza's notes. She held it up in front of his eyes and then pressed it down on his chest. "I think that thou are the worst of liars"—Jyn's voice throbbed—"and the best of friends."

Embarrassed, he knew not what to say. A few moments passed and then a few more. "How long have I been laid up?" Aeryk asked finally to break the silence and, with any luck, change the subject.

"This is the morning of the fourth day," Jyn answered.

"That long?" Aeryk said, stunned. "Has someone been looking after my horse?"

Jyn smiled, nodding her head. "Pyp-Dun-Dee has been spoiling Wyli shamelessly."

"That's good." Aeryk felt relieved. "Sam's going to be pissed. If the snows catch us, crossing the Syga Plain won't be much fun."

"Sam has visited twice since his return," Jyn assured him. "If he is wroth with thee, I've seen no sign of it. The captain visits as well, as do Pyp and Tyk."

"And what of thee, Jyn-Ael-Tor?"

Jyn tucked her head, as Elves tend to do when embarrassed, and stayed silent.

"Have you seen the outside of this room in three days and a night, elf?" Aeryk asked pointedly.

"Thou were so hurt, and then so sick," Jyn said, sounding as discomfited as she appeared. "And when I held thy hand, thee did seem to rest more easily. The healer said I was of some help to thee, although I think she said it more for my benefit than for thine."

"Thank you," Aeryk told her.

"It was no great sacrifice, truly." Jyn smiled. "Unconscious, thou are not nearly so aggravating."

Clasping Jyn's hand firmly in his, Aeryk relaxed, lying back on the pillows. He closed his eyes. It felt good all at once, just to be alive. He wondered, then, what fate had befallen Tierza. *How had she known of the raid? Was she in danger?* Her first note implied she was leaving. He'd ask Sam to check on her whereabouts.

"Kul-Cah-Zul is dead," Jyn announced.

Opening one eye, he looked up at her. "Aye, well, that's a shame."

At the tone of his voice, Jyn shook her head. "Killed, the healer says, by a blast of balefire." Jyn paused to let that sink in. "Balefire is a construct of the Yir, sorcerer's magic that manifests as a bolt of bright blue light. Deadly, it is."

The significance of what the young elf just told him took root. "Shite." He touched the amulet about his neck with the fingers of his left hand. "I reckon Basyl was in earnest." He told Jyn about the Fey talisman, all he knew anyhow.

"Why would a sorcerer want to kill Kul-Cah-Zul in that manner?" Aeryk wondered.

Jyn shrugged gracefully. "That is a question my elder and captain Aya-Bal-Mar would give much to have answered." The timbre of Jyn's voice changed. "Six others perished as well, Aeryk. The healers were able to save one syr felled on the stairs, leading to the second-floor landing."

"I am sorry to hear that," Aeryk said sincerely.

"Among them was a scholar, marked for death upon that list of thine, a historian by training, serving here as our chief scribe. Mik-Tad-Low was slain in her quarters on the first floor." Jyn sounded perplexed. "As gentle a soul as ever I've met; her death and the raid itself make no sense. Nothing of consequence, it seems, was taken."

Aeryk steeled himself. "Do you know why your name was on that list, Jyn?"

"No," the elf answered simply. "Perhaps as many as six Sircassians and at least one sorcerer capable of balefire—the cost of staging such a strike would be considerable." Jyn shifted her position on the bed. He caught her scent. She smelled of soap and a subtle musk he could not place that still managed to quicken his pulse. "Kul-Cah-Zul was the type to have enemies, but the truth is neither he nor I are or were all that important. And as for Mik-Tad-Low ..." Jyn tossed her head and fell silent.

"No connection exists between the three of you?" Aeryk asked.

"Aside from being here, in this place, at the same time, no," Jyn responded.

"I'm just grateful thee escaped." Aeryk sighed, relief evident in his tone. "How did you?"

"I was not here, in my quarters, as they expected." Jyn raised a hand, indicating the room about them. "Instead I was away from the compound."

"Away?" Aeryk echoed. "Doing what, exactly?"

"My duty," Jyn spoke cryptically.

"Duty." Aeryk tossed his head and then winced. "You Elves and your bloody secrets."

"We all have them," Jyn continued crisply, "even thee, Aeryk Emyrt." Her voice softened. "Thou should not have risked thy life for mine."

"It is what friends do," Aeryk contended. His eyes found hers.

Jyn's eyes shone, wide and soft. "I wish thee would not do that." She looked away.

"If that were true Jyn-Ael-Tor, you would not have said *thee*," Aeryk asserted.

"Are thee calling me a liar?" Jyn inquired. She would not look at him.

"Not I," Aeryk answered. "It is your eyes that betray thee."

"I cannot look back at thee." Jyn's eyes found his once more, though, even as she spoke. "We cannot be, Aeryk Emyrt. There can be nothing between us."

"Except you have looked back at me, Jyn," Aeryk said. "I see thee. *We are*, and there has been something between us since the moment we met." Taking her by the arms, Aeryk gently pulled Jyn toward him until their mouths touched. Soft as rose petals, her lips felt warm and beckoning.

Jyn broke off the kiss, lifting her head just far enough to peer once more into his eyes. She lay the fingers of the left hand lightly against his cheek and slowly shook her head. But her eyes clung to his.

The door to Jyn's sleeping quarters opened, and through it stepped a white-haired Elfin clad in a simple cotton tunic. Jyn leapt to her feet.

"Not exactly the decorum expected of a sick room." The Elfin's gaze swept from Jyn to Aeryk. Her smile took any sting out of the words. "You must be feeling some better," she said to Aeryk.

Jyn's bow appeared a trifle rushed, not nearly as elegant as usual. "Greetings, Healer," Jyn said. "May I present Aeryk Emyrt of Clan Ard Mourne?" Turning to look back at Aeryk, Jyn completed the introduction by adding, "Aeryk, this is Wyt-Can-Sue, sorcerer."

"We've met, I think," Aeryk remarked.

Small for an elf, a full hand's width shorter than Jyn, and slightly built, Wyt-Can-Sue's hair, dressed in a simple ponytail, showed snow white. Though free of wrinkles, there seemed to be an aged aspect to the healer's features. Her skin was a shade darker than Jyn's, her eyes silver grey. Wyt-Can-Sue nodded, her smile softening. "You were very brave."

Aeryk returned her smile. "I seem to recall wetting myself."

Wyt-Can-Sue's expression took on a mischievous cast. "Perhaps your bladder is not quite as courageous as the rest of you."

"It is good to see you again, Healer," Aeryk proffered. "I hope you will forgive my manners or rather, the lack of them. Thanks for saving my hide."

Taking Jyn's place on the bedside, Wyt-Can-Sue clasped his wrist with one hand and placed the other on his forehead.

"Well," Wyt-Can-Sue announced after a moment, "the fever has abated; that's encouraging. With your permission, Aeryk, I need to examine you a bit more carefully. The process is called delving. It involves use of the Yir. It will not take long and should cause you no pain. May I begin?"

"As long as it is quick, go ahead." Aeryk thrust his chin at Jyn. "We had only just begun to argue."

Jyn tossed her head but said nothing.

Wyt's smile returned. "Yours appears to be an unusual form of discord." Leaning forward to lay a hand on either side of his head, Wyt closed her eyes. Aeryk felt a rush of warmth spread through his body, as if he was blushing from head to toe. This was followed by a slight tingling that began in his chest and seemed to radiate outward to his extremities. After a moment or two, Wyt straightened.

"He is out of danger," the healer spoke over her shoulder, directing her comment to Jyn-Ael-Tor. Looking back at him, Wyt shook her head. "You have the constitution of a mountain lion, Aeryk Emyrt."

"A mountain goat is more likely." Aeryk had decided he liked this healer.

Wyt twisted her upper body around to face Jyn. "Captain Aya-Bal-Mar wishes to see you, Jyn-Ael-Tor."

"Just the now?" Jyn asked in the most polite tone of voice imaginable. "Sorcerer, are you certain?"

"The captain was quite specific, so there is no use dissembling." Wyt actually chuckled. "Worry not; this Kylgahran won't go anywhere, I promise you that." With a last, long look at Aeryk, Jyn walked quickly through the door, closing it quietly behind her.

Folding her arms beneath her breasts, Wyt gazed intently at Aeryk.

Aeryk nodded towards the door. "You disapprove," he surmised.

"It is not my place to approve or disapprove," Wyt replied. "Jyn-Ael-Tor cares for you; that much is obvious."

"Not according to her," Aeryk countered.

"Liaisons between Elves and tersyans are not uncommon. Differences are exotic, after all, and the exotic attracts," Wyt observed, as if recounting some lecture on the topic. "Lasting relationships, on the other hand, are rare indeed."

"Worth taking a chance for then, wouldn't you say?" Aeryk responded.

"Perhaps," Wyt conceded. "The point being if what you really want is a woman to love, you should not go chasing after an Elfin, especially one who is of the vyldeen *and* Order Castellan."

"Sounds like good advice," Aeryk acknowledged with a rueful

grin. "The problem therein, old Danyl says, is that good advice is like cheap liquor—easy to get but hard to swallow."

Wyt smiled briefly, tossing her head in the elegant way only Elves could. "Speaking of which, I've something here for you." The healer stepped to a cabinet on the far side of the room. "Who is old Danyl, by the way?"

"Danyl Trask of Clan Ard Drew is a wily old badger of a Highland swordsman." Aeryk smiled fondly upon speaking his mentor's name aloud. "And a bachelor he is, too," Aeryk appended.

"I shall look forward to an introduction," Wyt said wryly. She extracted a leather case from the cabinet, opened it, and removed a ceramic jar. "What you need most the now is a deep, healing sleep. This potion will help you to it."

"I've been asleep for over three days," Aeryk exclaimed.

"Mostly, you have been unconscious. There is a difference." As the healer busied herself with mixing powder from the jar and water into the mug he'd used earlier, she commented, "That's quite a piece of finery you have chained about your neck. You were poisoned by a large dose of ampercin. Alone, I doubt I could have done much to help you, Aeryk. But aided by the power of that amulet, I could have dueled with Father Death himself. It is a talisman of great antiquity and even greater potency. The fewer who know you are in possession of it, the better, I think."

Walking back to his bed, the healer sat again. Wyt handed him the mug. "Drink this down," she said briskly. "May you dream of a certain amber-eyed Elfin and improbable outcomes."

As medicines went, the stuff didn't taste too bad, and in Aeryk's weakened state, sleep took him almost immediately.

36
New Beginnings

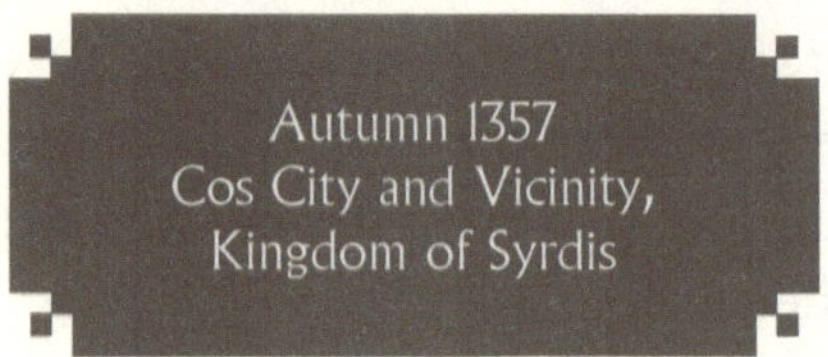

Dawn, five days after their departure from Cos, found Tierza in the company of her brother, Ramon; Thatch, the barman; his woman, Myra; and their daughter, Sylva. The small group camped alongside a dirt road that wound its way north out of Cos. The road led eventually to the border of the Tieran province of Quistyn del Aurus. A small fire burned cheerfully, offering some protection against the damp morning chill of late autumn. Thatch said he could smell rain in the air. Myra had some bacon frying and was reheating a pot of beans from the night before. Ramon sliced some flatbread to round out the meal, while Tierza sang softly to little Sylva, nine years of age.

Upon hearing Tierza's account of Gullwatch's death, Myra quickly concluded that she, Thatch, and little Sylva needed to get out of Cos in a hurry. They couldn't be certain the Altairan would take action against them, but the threat seemed very real. Greytower could not tolerate betrayal of the type Tierza and Ramon had instigated without appearing weak. He would strike back. If Tierza and Ramon slipped his grasp, their closest associates would likely emerge as the next best targets. The barbershop was rented space, so once they decided to go, preparations took only a little time.

At the edge of camp, three horses stood patiently, hobbled and tethered to a line of rope running between two sturdy iron pegs driven into the ground. The horses were not the best, but they hauled away readily enough at the day wagon and the light buggy Ramon had purchased with a portion of Gullwatch's cache. Thatch bought the horses, using some money he and Myra had managed to put aside. The day wagon was large enough to hold most of their household goods. Two horses serviced the wagon as a team. They kept some extra supplies in the buggy, and their third animal pulled it. Normally, Tierza and Ramon rode in the buggy, while Thatch's family occupied the day wagon.

The trip north out of Cos had so far proved uneventful. They were far enough outside the city the now that Tierza had begun to relax a little. She still carried a crossbow, loaded and drawn within easy reach, while they traveled. The pair of sheathed poison darts and a slim-bladed dagger, Tierza also kept always in her possession. Thatch maintained the second crossbow, also cocked and ready, with him in the day wagon. Both he and Ramon were armed with heavy bladed knives and long-handled, iron-knobbed cudgels. One look at Thatch's broad chest and heavily muscled arms generally proved sufficient to ensure any strangers they met remained cordial and polite.

Tierza and her companions made their way out of the city in the deep of night. Cos had grown steadily in recent times, and traffic in and out of its precincts at all hours was no longer anything unusual. They passed through the city gates and into open country without incident. Most of Gullwatch's loot remained carefully hidden, lashed in a waxed canvas bag to the underside of the day wagon. Tierza had offered to share the money with Thatch and his family.

Heading north overland had been Ramon's idea. His reasoning took into account that the Altairan's main strength concentrated along the docks. Why risk booking passage downriver, something the Altairan might well expect, when they had the resources to simply ride away from the city going the opposite way? Ramon seemed a changed man since he and Tierza had killed and robbed Greygor Gullwatch. Tierza had not seen him take a drink, and he appeared quieter and more thoughtful than usual. How great a crime was murdering a murderer? Tierza decided the question was moot. She would have killed Gullwatch a dozen times over, whatever the cost to her soul, and deemed it a small price to pay for Aeryk's life and her freedom.

Except that if what Ramon had heard at Beacher's Bend turned out to be true, Aeryk's life had not been spared. Beacher's Bend was a small trading post on the Sayx, three days travel north of Cos. Ramon had gone alone to the post to purchase some additional supplies for their journey. Word had already reached the traders via one of the packet boats concerning the raid on the Elven villa in Cos. A number of Elves had been killed, and word had it some wild young Kylgahran hacked three Sircassian assassins to bloody gibbets before being struck down himself. Of course, Aeryk couldn't simply do the reasonable thing and pass along word of the pending raid and then stay out of the way. He would have to charge in, sword swinging, and get himself killed. *Three Sircassians—oh, Aeryk,* she thought. She'd wept at the news. She was through crying the now.

Just where they were going and what they would do when they got there, Tierza knew, were decisions that would be left to her. Quistyn del Aurus, she had decided, already was to be their immediate destination. Somewhere in the border region, where life was still wild and no one asked too many questions. They'd heard rumors of a silver strike at the base of the Shyre Hill country near a town called Lanyr. Where silver was being mined in any significant quantity, there would also be other opportunities to make money.

Their old lives would have to be left behind, as dead to them as the brave young Kylgahran. In her case, casting aside her old life left her with nothing to mourn. The life she'd led to that point had done little, except to teach a few bitter lessons. She would gladly walk away from it if she could. If their new start was to be paid for with blood money, so be it. Adamant in her determination, Tierza resolved they would survive and prosper, one way or the other.

Two hours past midnight the following morning, Lykas Greytower glared at the blood splattered remains of Hasan Real. Enough moons' light dripped into the alley for Greytower to make out the Sircassian's lean features. Even taken unawares, the tall blond son of a bitch had cost Greytower two of his best men. Removing his neck cloth, Lykas pressed it against the long, shallow gash that scored his left side. A dagger, hidden in Real's boot, had cut cleanly through Greytower's leather jacket and the richly embroidered linen shirt beneath. Both garments would have to be replaced. Stepping forward, Greytower launched a kick that struck Real's body squarely in the groin.

"Feel better, do ya?" Nigyl Ringworth, last of the three henchmen originally accompanying Lykas this evening, inquired, flashing a gap-toothed grin from the doorway of the apartment house a few steps away, in which he'd suddenly reappeared. Nigyl had big yellow teeth, generally consistent with a lean, horsey countenance.

"Did you find the coin?" Lykas growled. Greytower had paid Real two thousand talents silver—payment to keep the Sircassian's mouth shut regarding events surrounding the death of sorcerer Siersay Grier. Real had passed the money on to an accomplice, a young prostitute named Zenia Damore. The Sircassian then asked for more, observing how precious a commodity silence was.

"Aye," Greytower's lanky companion, universally known as Ringworm, affirmed, holding aloft a small leather satchel, "the whore, too." The cutthroat slouched down the short flight of steps to join Greytower in the alleyway.

"She told you where it was?" Greytower asked.

Ringworm grinned again. "Eventually."

Greytower's dark eyes swept up and down the alley. Shadows cloaked the passage. He saw and heard nothing. "Took you long enough," Lykas chided.

"Ah, well, ya see, she were quite a looker," Ringworm explained, "and after, she weren't in no shape to complain, nor charge me neither. I, uh, took my ease, ya might say."

"What a ghoul you are," Greytower told him. Ringworm apparently felt no response to that observation on his part was required and said nothing. "You're certain she's dead?" Greytower queried.

"I slit her throat on the way out," Ringworm assured, "just to make sure." He shook his head. "People are funny, ya know? A whore will spread her legs fer hundreds of men, rob, cheat, and steal from the lot of them while she's about it, without so much as batting an eye. And then along comes a fella she takes a shine to, and just like that, she's as loyal as a sheepdog."

"I don't much like dogs." Greytower took possession of the satchel. "Let's go," he ordered.

"What about Hap and old Roe?" Ringworm wondered, thrusting his chin at the bodies of Greytower's other two henchmen as they lay sprawled on either side of Hasan Real's corpse.

"They should have been more careful," Greytower said shortly. He led the way back up the alley, leaving the three bodies where they lay. *Loose ends*, Greytower thought sourly. Greytower's purpose this evening had been to tidy things up a bit. Hap and Roe were known associates. *Not a good thing.* They were also notorious thieves with a violent streak, just stupid enough to take on a Sircassian. *It might be all right.*

As for Hasan's accomplice, the murdered Zenia Damore, well, whores had a way of winding up that way here at the edge of Dogtown. At least they'd recovered his coin. *You'll stay quiet the now, Real*, Greytower thought, *and your whore, too.* Walking briskly down darkened streets, Greytower knew it was only a matter of time before agents of the Golden Hand came calling. He had a decision to make.

37

Home

Upon waking, Aeryk found Jyn-Ael-Tor seated beside his bed. Bare-headed, her hair woven into a pragmatic-looking single braid, Jyn otherwise appeared in full field kit, surcoat, and chain mail, with sword and dagger belted at her waist. Her left hand rested atop the coverlet on the bed.

"When I said we had only begun to argue," Aeryk observed, "I did not think you would take me quite so seriously."

The corners of Jyn's mouth curled upwards. "I am about to leave—a patrol north of the city. I was beginning to fear thee would not wake in time."

Aeryk glanced at the window. Dawn, or thereabouts. "Truth to tell, I really don't feel much like arguing."

Jyn's ghost of a smile faded, and she dipped her chin. "I don't think there is much point to it."

"Improbable outcomes," Aeryk acknowledged. "I've heard the tapestry of history is woven of none but such." Extending his hand, he closed his fingers about hers.

Jyn lifted her head and smiled at him. "My people say the difference between the improbable and the impossible, however small it may appear, is as vast as all creation."

"Aye, well." Aeryk smiled in return. "Your people talk a lot of blather. The impossible happens every day." A spark swirled in the tawny recesses of her eyes, and Jyn's expression softened. She shook her head but remained silent. "How long on patrol?" he asked.

"Ten days, at least," Jyn answered. "Our route will take us along the northern border."

Ten days was too long. Sam would want to be gone before then. "Then this is the last time I shall see you," Aeryk began tentatively.

"Until our rendezvous in the spring," Jyn finished firmly.

"Jyn," Aeryk queried, "what about the threat to your life?"

"Precautions are being taken," Jyn stated cryptically.

"Precautions?" Aeryk parroted. "What kind of precautions?"

"Thee must trust me," Jyn insisted. "All will be well."

Aeryk's jaw tightened upon hearing that, but he merely nodded. "The spring," Aeryk opined, "seems like a long time away."

"And tersyans are notorious for having short memories," Jyn teased with a smile. "Likely thee will forget all about me."

"I could more easily forget how to breathe," Aeryk said, "than the memory of an afternoon spent along a riverbank in the company of a silver-haired Elfin." Jyn's eyes never left his. "I've never known anyone so beautiful or brave," Aeryk continued, "or so susceptible to hiccups." Jyn's smile brightened. "I cannot help but wonder what happened to her?" Aeryk murmured.

Jyn sobered. "Perhaps she was nothing more than an illusion."

"Never that," Aeryk averred, and then said in a softer tone, "A dream, maybe."

Without releasing Jyn's hand, Aeryk sat up and leaned across the bed to kiss her. Jyn returned his kiss; her lips tasted honey sweet beneath his. He gently pulled away. "If you are about to tell me I shouldn't have done that, you can save your breath," Aeryk murmured.

"No good will come of it." Jyn tossed her head slightly. "And yet I am glad that thee did." She reached out and touched his cheek. "I must go."

"You will take care out there," Aeryk urged.

"And thee," Jyn whispered. "Farewell, Aeryk Emyrt." Jyn brushed her lips once more against his, rose smoothly from the chair, and left the room.

Aeryk lay back and stared at the closed door. Sleep beckoned, but Aeryk fought it, determined to fix every moment since his last waking in his mind, so he would know it for truth, not merely the wishful conjuring of his heart.

When Aeryk next awoke, he saw Pyp-Dun-Dee, clad in a simple oatmeal-colored cotton tunic, seated cross-legged at the foot of his bed, darning a sock. Lifting his right leg, he gently nudged Pyp on the hip with his toe. "Hullo, Slim," he said.

"Aeryk," Pyp cried happily. Slipping off the bed, the young elf bowed. "Joyful I am to see thee."

"There is no need for you to bow, Pyp," Aeryk grumbled, tired of the Elves' endless devotion to proper decorum.

Cocking her head, Pyp set aside sock, needle, and thread and observed, "Thou have no regard, Aeryk Emyrt."

"I know," Aeryk concurred, "my manners are atrocious." Looking Pyp in the eye, he continued, "You and me—that is, me and thee are friends, aye?"

"Aye, honored I am to be thy friend, Aeryk." Pyp's wide-set grey eyes twinkled. "Thee is aware that thy grammar is even worse than thy etiquette?"

"Bugger your grammar, Slim, and your bloody manners, too." Aeryk couldn't keep the smile from his face. "Bow away, if it pleases thee. Just don't expect me to bow back."

"Barbarian," Pyp scoffed. Sitting on the bed at his side, she took his right hand in both of hers. "Thee gave us quite a fright, Aeryk Emyrt."

"I managed to scare myself pretty thoroughly, too," Aeryk admitted.

"Three Sircassians—what were thee thinking?" Pyp inquired, wide eyed.

"I wasn't, as usual," Aeryk said. "Thinking, that is."

"That is a very bad habit, Aeryk," Pyp observed.

Aeryk went on to describe the sequence of events that transpired the night of the raid on the Elven villa. "I'm cured, Slim," Aeryk concluded fervently. "From here on, I intend to be the thinking-est critter thee ever saw."

Pyp tossed her head and laughed. "I'll believe that, Aeryk Emyrt, when I see it."

As if summoned by the sound of Pyp's laughter, the door to the sleeping chamber where Aeryk lay swung open to admit the healer, Wyt-Can-Sue. "Good morning," Wyt said with a brief, informal bow. "How do you feel?"

"Hungry," Aeryk responded immediately. He was actually very hungry, famished as a matter of fact.

"That is always a good sign," Wyt remarked, smiling. After a brief examination, Wyt declared that she would bring some breakfast before Aeryk started gnawing on the furniture.

While he worked away on a second bowl of porridge, Samwell Austyn stopped by. Sam seemed genuinely glad to see him. After a brief exchange of greetings, Sam exclaimed, "Three Sircassians—what in the name of all the Fates were you bloody thinking, boy?"

Pyp nearly fell out of her chair laughing. This earned the young Elfin a glare from both Kylgahran. Aeryk once again launched into an account of the events surrounding the attack on the Elven villa. Pyp stood, saying that as she had heard the story once before and had to take a turn at watch this evening, she was off to get some sleep.

Bowing first to Sam, Pyp said, "Farwell, Samwell Austyn." Turning to Aeryk, the slender elf bowed a bit less formally and smiled. "I see thee, Aeryk."

"I think that youngster has taken a shine to you, Aeryk," Sam observed after Pyp had gone.

"I hope I didn't start something there I can't finish," Aeryk pondered out loud. "Sam, do you recall that young singer at the Rising Star? She was small, pretty, with a crippled left foot."

"I recollect." Sam arched one eyebrow in a decidedly Elvish manner. "Did you start something there as well?"

"Reckon I did. Come to think of it, Tierza—that's her name—did most of the starting and what finishing there was, too." Catching Sam's eye, Aeryk went on. "She is the one who left me the note warning of the attack on the Elven compound. I got the impression that she planned to leave the city. I'm wondering if she did, or if she might be in trouble." He described the barbershop and its location, mentioning her connection to Thatch the barman and his woman, Myra.

"I know Thatch hasn't been seen for days," Sam told him. "Mistress Canty is some put out. I'll ask around."

"Do it careful, Sam," Aeryk warned. "Those Sircassian bastards are tricksome. And Jyn is convinced there is a sorcerer involved, too."

Wyt stepped back into the room a moment later with a bowl of fruit and a basket of bread so fresh it still steamed.

"Greetings, Healer." Sam bowed respectfully.

He sure does that better than I do, Aeryk thought.

"How soon can this rascal travel?" Sam asked.

"He needs at least another good night's rest," Wyt said, speaking to Sam.

Why is it, Aeryk wondered, *that healers talk about sick or hurt folks as if they weren't there?*

"I'd like to see his bowels move. The way he is putting food away, I suspect that shouldn't take too long. He may be able to travel as soon as the day after tomorrow." Sam thanked the healer and then made his way out.

"I don't think anyone has ever expressed an interest in my bowels before," Aeryk stated, "moving or otherwise."

Laying the food on his bed within easy reach, Wyt smiled. "Never underestimate the importance of proper pooping, young man."

Aeryk got out of bed around noon and dressed. He spent much of that afternoon wandering about the second floor of the villa. Aeryk ate an enormous supper, consisting of two meat pies, a plate of steamed vegetables, and three tall mugs of fresh milk. He woke in the middle of the night with an urgent need to move his bowels, which he did, apparently to Wyt-Can-Sue's satisfaction; at least the healer seemed satisfied after examining him the following morning.

Once he finished breakfast, Aeryk made his way down to the stables, where he'd been told he could find Pyp.

"Hullo, Slim," he said, walking up to the slender young Elfin as she groomed Wyli in the gelding's stall, running a curry comb over the glossy flank of the Morgyn. "And how are you, old fella?" Aeryk asked, giving Wyli a good scratch between the ears.

"I see thee, Aeryk," Pyp said, smiling, no bow this time.

"Did you get into any trouble, standing second for me that day on the drill ground?" Aeryk inquired, afraid the direct question would likely offend the young elf, but he couldn't see any other way around, and he needed to know.

"No," Pyp answered. Her expressive mist-grey eyes stayed steady on him as she responded.

"You wouldn't fib to me about a thing like that, would you?" Aeryk pressed.

"I might," Pyp said without hesitation. "Because honored I am to have been thy second. But there is no need." Her grey-eyed gaze never wavered.

Pyp stepped into his arms. Aeryk embraced her. Uncertain what to say, he joked, "You are a rare friend, Pyp, one to ride the river with, but sometimes I worry about your judgment. I purely do."

"Friends," Pyp echoed softly.

"Aye, so long as thee will have me." Aeryk gathered the slender young elf close.

After a moment or two, Pyp leaned slightly away, looked into his eyes for a long moment, and then nodded. Sliding both arms up around his neck, Pyp kissed him. The pliant warmth of her lips against his and the supple press of her body stirred him deeply.

Pyp broke off the kiss, turning her head slightly away. "A remembrance," she murmured.

Stunned by her kiss and his reaction, Aeryk managed, "As if I could ever forget thee."

Pyp rested her head upon his shoulder. "We choose our friends. My mother says no other decision so defines us. I am glad of thee, Aeryk Emyrt."

"As I am of thee," Aeryk told her.

Pyp hugged him tightly for a moment longer and then stepped back. "We will meet again. I know it. Fare thee well until then."

After a brief examination the following morning, Wyt-Can-Sue pronounced Aeryk fit to travel. A storm brewed up that night, heavy winds and rain. For three days the storm raged, only to be followed by another.

At Captain Aya's invitation, Sam and Aeryk waited out the weather in guest quarters on the grounds of the Elven villa. "There was no word of Tierza at all?" Aeryk asked for what must have been the third time on the day he and Sam moved to the villa.

Patiently, Sam explained once again that there had been no sign of Tierza, Thatch, or his woman. "Aya and her people will keep an eye out," Sam assured him, "but no one on Barber Street we've talked to has seen them in days."

Aeryk nodded, hoping the three of them had at least made it safely out of the city.

Leaden skies finally cleared a week later. Sam and Aeryk left Cos, headed west that day. Sam was mounted on his graceful bay stallion, while Aeryk rode Wyli. Each Kylgahran led a packhorse loaded with supplies, including winter clothes and some extra blankets. Sam intended to travel fast. They camped the first night a little over forty kylos from the city.

"Are you feeling all right?" Sam asked as they settled around their campfire, with the horses tethered nearby.

"How do you know when you've done the right thing?" Aeryk inquired in response.

"Ask Wyli." Sam laughed softly. "I've got no notion." A moment's pause, and Sam continued more seriously. "Usually, it isn't too hard to figure when you've done wrong. If I were you, I'd give myself the benefit of the doubt."

They made good time, better than Aeryk thought possible. Wyatt met up with them about three-quarters of the way back. The wiry Tuchyck appeared, ghosting up to their campsite as they were putting a kettle on the fire. Aeryk was glad to see the leather-skinned, blond-haired scout, especially since Wyatt carried four letters for him, one each from Basyl, Lara, Danyl, and Estyr.

Lara's letter spoke briefly of Estyr's arrival and of the joy her presence had brung. Estyr's note was even shorter, a nearly indecipherable scrawl, urging him to hurry home and "not get into no truble." Danyl's missive brimmed with local goings-on, while Basyl's ranged further afield, noting in particular that they'd heard the civil war, the so-called War of Houses, which had wracked the Tieran Empire for the better part of four decades, had finally come to an end. Just what that might entail for the other peoples of the Middle Sea stood anyone's guess. Tier resurgent posed a threat like no other to any independent realm in the region. Aeryk quickly set the thought aside. The Kylgahran Highlands and even the Lywgahra, out east, were located far from any Tieran border.

Wyatt brought more good news. The rest of the drovers had all made it home safely, and already talk swirled of another drive, planned for late summer next year. After supper, Wyatt spoke briefly to Sam in the Tuchyck tribal tongue. Aeryk could not follow the exchange.

Sam smiled and looked over at Aeryk. "Wyatt says something has made a man of you, Aeryk. He wants to know if it was a sword or a woman."

"Tell him he's seeing things." Aeryk glowered, which made Sam laugh. After a moment or two of reflection, Aeryk relented, admitting somewhat ruefully, "I reckon it was some of both, that and a cat-eyed elf."

It snowed hard on them only once, and by then, they were nearing the end of their trek. For days they had been able to see the Tylcairn Mountains girding the western horizon. Finally, they topped a familiar rise, and there before them lay the Elkhorn Valley and Bright Water Creek, shimmering in the crystal chill of a late-autumn afternoon. Wyli whickered, tossing his head, as a white mist rose from his nostrils. Looking out across the valley dusted with snow, Aeryk felt his heart swell, for home they were.

38

A Beautiful Dream

Tessymir Ryan had always envisioned being married in the Brynnai temple that stood atop Wylde's Hill near the center of York. All the Ryans wed there. Instead, her wedding took place in the main dining room of the Long House, a place for solstice dinners or supping with visiting lairds. The room was not filled to capacity. About three score people attended. She'd seen more than that gathered to haggle over the price of grain.

Her wedding gown was white, the traditional color for such in Kylgahra. The skirts were fashioned of silk; the scoop-necked bodice of linen, lined with pearls. The pearls had been taken from a necklace once owned by her great-grandmother. Ranyl wore a grey silk waistcoat with a matching shirt, also of silk, and dark-grey woolen trousers. Wide shouldered, her groom, he looked solid and solemn.

As she approached, escorted by her father, Ranyl's reserve cracked a bit, and he smiled. She'd left her hair down. A trifle scandalous, that, but she could see that it pleased him. The ceremony was brief. Dabner Rhymes, presiding, proved nothing if not proficient. They recited their wedding vows, pledges of fidelity, truth, and kindness, to bind them their whole lives long. No mention there was of love. Kylgahran viewed marriage as a practical matter. After exchanging their wedding promises, Dabner Rhymes pronounced them wed. In accordance with tradition, the ceremony closed with a kiss.

They shared a kiss, brief and gentle enough to border upon being chaste, but neither was it cold or distant. A marriage reel followed. Not quite the elaborate affair originally planned. Food and drink were available in abundance; a serving of roast beef comprised the main course. Ranyl said little, hardly speaking at all, really, except to ask if she would allow him to slice her meat. Sym felt a little embarrassed by that. She was perfectly capable of cutting her own food, after all. He went about it so earnestly, though, that she couldn't help feeling touched by the gesture.

The band, a hastily assembled group, comprised three fiddlers, a pair of flutists, and a harpist—young Tuan from Ranyl's party. The tunes they played were simple but familiar, and Sym thought them charming. Sym and Ranyl opened the reel. She danced next with her father. Davis Killoe was her third partner and then some of Ranyl's closest retainers, the last being Emerson Hart, Ranyl's head ranger, who appeared to Sym even thicker through the chest and shoulders than her husband.

My husband—the thought seemed alien to her—*for how long?* She'd tried to warn Ranyl of Rowyn's skill with a sword. Looking over the top of Emerson's shoulder in the direction of the head table, she caught a brief view of Ranyl and her father with their heads together. They seemed to be deep in conversation.

Sym lost track of partners thereafter. The reel had begun before sundown. A couple of hours it was before midnight when her father called for a close. Ranyl appeared at her side and the three of them— Ranyl, her father, and her—walked to the sitting room where they had met earlier. Lukas Holt and a ranger whose name she could not recall took up stations at the sitting room door, along with a pair of Ard Ryan retainers.

Upon entering, Ranyl and her father sat immediately at table and resumed the conversation that had apparently consumed them for most of the evening. Sym said little, feeling Ranyl's sense of urgency. The discussion focused on further developing Ard Ryan resources, timber in particular, a sawmill, and even a boatyard.

"You can trust Emerson's judgment," Ranyl concluded.

Owain Ryan nodded and rose to his feet and offered his hand. "Good luck on the morrow. Don't underestimate Cutter. He's knacky with a blade."

"I never underestimate a man with a sword in his hand," Ranyl said quietly.

Sym stood also. Her father took her hand. "Never have the Highlands seen a lovelier bride." His blue eyes warmed as he smiled. He leaned close. "Except once, maybe," he whispered, "the night I married your mother."

Impulsively, Sym hugged him close. Releasing her, Owain turned to face the young married couple.

"May the Fates watch kindly over you both. Good night." Without another word, Owain Ryan strode from the room, his limp hardly noticeable. The four retainers followed silently on his heels.

Sym stood alone with her husband for the first time.

"You look good in white," Ranyl observed quietly.

"Grey suits you," Sym replied.

Ranyl glanced down at himself. "I look like someone took the trouble to drape a perfectly nice set of clothes over an anvil."

"Very distinguished, you are," Sym soothed.

Ranyl winced. "That was just plain mean."

Sym laughed and stepped close to take his hand. "I find I've developed a fondness for anvils and tree stumps and things of that sort. I can't think why."

"I hope the ceremony was all right," Ranyl said, his concern evident.

"It was fine," Sym assured him. "Father was overjoyed. He saved a fortune."

"I keep telling you," Ranyl asserted, "your father is not the Ryan who concerns me."

"It was still fine." Sym smiled. "Not what I expected, but then, neither are you."

"Some of your relatives will be miffed," Ranyl pointed out, uncertain what to make of her assertion.

Without thinking, Sym proffered. "We'll stage a reel next month and invite the lot. With any luck, they'll bring wedding presents."

"With any luck," Ranyl echoed, his expression bleak enough to frighten her.

"Are you all right?" Sym asked, unable to keep a quiver of anxiety from her voice.

"I'm scared." Ranyl smiled wryly and patted her hand. "I always am before battle. The night before is the worst of it."

"Would you like me to stay with you?" Sym asked, not knowing quite what she would do if he said yes.

Ranyl's smile warmed, but he shook his head. "Best not." Squeezing her hand with one of his, he gently reached out to touch her cheek with the other. "There will be other nights. I promise."

"I shall look forward to them," Sym declared. Their parting kiss was as brief as that they shared to seal the vows of marriage, but tender for all that. "Good night," Sym said on a breath.

"Good night," Ranyl responded.

They separated upon exiting the sitting room. His room was in the guest quarters at the opposite end of the hall with respect to hers. Sym walked directly to her room and changed out of her wedding dress. She donned a pale-blue gown of silk, sleeveless, with a plunging neckline. Rowyn had always favored it.

About her waist Tessymir carefully wound a satin sash of a slightly darker hue. She slid a razor-sharp, double-edged dagger with a blade exactly the same length as her middle finger into the sash at the small of her back. The ivory handle of the dagger faced down. Amid the satin folds she could scarcely feel the presence of the diminutive weapon, even knowing of its presence.

Finally, she coiled a thin woolen wrap about her shoulders and slipped back into the hall. Davis Killoe had informed her that Rowyn Cutter would be staying the night in the apartment his father once occupied. The rooms were located at the end of an outbuilding adjacent to the Long House.

Following his father's death, Rowyn had served as an Ard Ryan retainer. Sym's elder brother Dohnar had died in a fall from his horse while hunting, his neck broken. *Such a waste and a tragedy,* Sym thought. Rowyn had returned to his family farm as soon as her father began marriage negotiations. She had not seen or heard from him in months prior to her betrothal ceremony.

Striding across the courtyard, Sym took no notice of the moons' light glinting off dew-slicked cobblestones. Almost full they both were, the moons, and the light that shone from them was bright enough to cast shadows. Rowyn answered her knock almost immediately. He opened the door and stood warily, bare to the waist, a long-bladed dirk held firmly in his right hand. The glow of a single candle lit dimly the room's interior.

"May I come in?" Sym asked quietly.

"I don't think that is a good idea," Rowyn replied sotto voce.

"Bloody necessary it is, though," Sym enjoined. She could not see the color of his eyes. Backlit as they were by the single candle, they appeared as black pools. "Please."

Silently, he stepped aside. "I was half expecting Davis and a couple of his finest."

Stepping past him, Sym removed her wrap, tossing it across the back of a wooden chair. "Do you think we'd resort to murder?

"Confident, is he?" Rowyn speculated, ignoring her question. "This husband of yours."

"He's killed men in battle," Sym contended.

Rowyn shrugged. "As have I. Any fool can kill." Rowyn paused. "Does he know about us?"

Sym nodded. "I told him today, after what you did in the courtyard. How could you?"

"How could I not?" Rowyn countered. "I am in love with you. Nothing will ever change that." Rowyn shook his head. "Married you anyway, he did. I suppose that makes sense, if it is a title he's after. He was a fool to do it, though."

"How so?" Sym asked softly. Rowyn reasoned no further than his personal feelings carried him. Not so bad as faults went, really, but completely unacceptable in one who sought to stand at the head of a clan.

Rowyn smiled. Sym knew well the expression. How her heart had raced the first time Rowyn had directed that expression towards her, as if smiling only for her. She'd been twelve at the time, Rowyn but a year older. "When I kill him on the morrow, your father can still claim his portion, and I will be free to claim you."

"Kill him tomorrow, and you'll have no part of me," Sym vowed. Rowyn peered carefully into her eyes. Wide and lovely as ever they were, he saw; steady, too, and determined.

"I can't just walk away," Rowyn said. Sym thought she heard a tinge of regret in his voice.

"Of course you can," Sym urged. "Do so, and I'll come to you, in a year and a day, and we can be together always thereafter. I'll go with you anywhere you choose."

"A year and a day," Rowyn mused. In Kylgahra, custom held that if no child was conceived a year and a day after being wed, a Kylgahran couple could dissolve their marriage. In fact, either man or wife could have the marriage annulled, whether or not the other agreed. The custom was little used but as valid as any law passed down from the Council of Lairds. "You would stay free of his bed?"

"No," Sym acknowledged.

"Then how can you be certain to remain without child?" Rowyn inquired.

"I am well schooled," Sym asserted confidently, "and Alyair is a skilled midwife."

"You would kill his child in your womb?" Rowyn sounded shocked.

Sweet Fates, forgive me. "If necessary," Sym promised. "I don't think it will come to that."

"And what am I to do, for a year and a day?" Rowyn wondered.

"Bring in a good harvest or two," Sym told him acerbically. "We'll need the coin."

"You would abdicate lairdship of the clan?" Rowyn's disbelief was fairly palpable.

"Yes," Sym declared simply, "to save it."

"Save it how?" Rowyn challenged.

"The Emyrts understand commerce," Sym explained. "Ranyl

has seen, in a few weeks, ways and means that lay hidden right in front of our eyes for generations."

"A bloody merchant, he is," Rowyn swore, "no true warrior."

"To survive," Sym flared, "we Ryans must make more of what we have. He has the knack of it."

"There is the warrior's way," Rowyn retorted. "We can take what we need from our enemies."

"And make more of them in the bargain?" Sym snapped. "We are too few, and they too many as it is. Don't be a fool."

Rowyn's voice lowered. "I am foolish only about my feelings for you." He stepped close and slipped his arms about her. His kiss was gentle at first and then passionate. Sym tore her mouth away and pressed her face into his chest, breathing heavily. "Tell me you no longer love me," Rowyn demanded.

I loved the possibility of you. "I no longer love you." Sym had to force the words past the lump in her throat. Killing a dream, even one she had relinquished, squeezing the life out of it forever and all, was, she found, no easy thing.

"Then why are you here in my arms on your wedding night?" Rowyn pressed.

"Clan Ard Ryan needs Ranyl Emyrt more than it does me, more than it does us." Sym spoke evenly, as if she were speculating on the likelihood of rain the next day.

Rowyn scoured her eyes with his. "If that is so, then all we've shared was a lie."

Sym shook her head slowly, her eyes wide and beseeching. "What we shared was a dream, a beautiful dream, from which we the now both must wake."

"That can nay be true," Rowyn growled. He kissed her again, hungrily, his lips warm and seeking. "My favorite dress," he murmured, shifting his mouth from hers to caress the slender column of her throat with lips that seemed to burn.

His hand closed briefly on her left breast. Sliding it higher he slipped his fingers underneath the fold of the gown to guide the cloth down off her shoulder. Sym felt his hand, so strong and so familiar and once so welcome, grip firmly the velvety flesh of her bare breast. His left arm tightened about her. He was a good bit taller than she. His groin fit tightly against her abdomen. Sym felt her pulse racing. Rowyn ran the thumb and forefinger of his right hand over her exposed nipple. She could feel the bud rise, taut beneath his touch.

With her right hand, Sym slid her dagger slowly from within the sash at the small of her back. Deeply impassioned, Rowyn's lips found hers once again. Lifting her right hand, Sym pressed the blade to his throat. Though small, the weapon was fashioned of fine steel, razor sharp. A twist of her wrist would open his throat. Rowyn froze, going completely still. He could feel the blade pressing against the soft flesh at the base of his neck, just hard enough to draw a fine trickle of blood. He made no move to back away or to prevent her. He simply stood there, holding her as gently as if she was a child.

"If that is your true purpose in coming here, you'd best get on with it," Rowyn said evenly. "There will be a lot of blood. You'll likely ruin your dress."

Sym lowered her blade. "I can't," she whispered.

"Why not?" Rowyn asked, his voice grating. "I know you are not squeamish."

"Because"—Sym's voice broke—"ours *was* a beautiful dream." She let the dagger slip from her fingers. It clattered briefly on the wooden floor.

"I could take you the now." Rowyn's voice was harsh, strained, as if he was in pain.

"You can take nothing from me." Sym's low-pitched voice, usually so full of warmth, sounded as cold and distant to Rowyn's ears as stars aloft in a wintry night. "Not the now and not ever again if it is your intent to kill Ranyl Emyrt on the morrow."

"So I am to abandon you or my honor," Rowyn ground out. "That is the choice you bring?"

"Walk away from this fight," Sym implored. "I will know why, and I will honor you for it my life long. I will keep my promise."

Lowering his arms, Rowyn stepped back. "You'd better go before you are missed."

39
Honor Served

Tuan Marques could not sleep. The steward had offered him lodgings in partial payment for the performance he'd rendered earlier that evening. Tuan had enjoyed the music. Rustic and simple, but there was something mournful and wise about the sound the fiddlers wrought. Melodies born of Kylgahra, that spoke of narrow valleys with tree-lined ridges, tumbling rills, mountain mists, and longing. *Longing for what?* Tuan wondered. *These people are of my blood, yet I do not understand them.*

On the morrow, Ranyl Emyrt would duel unto death. *He is my only friend.* Tuan knew full well Ranyl stood his protector as well. *If he falls, what happens to me?* The thought shamed him. Tuan's room was one of many reserved for guests visiting the Ard Ryan hold. More specifically, Tuan corrected himself, for retainers of visiting guests. True guests, those whose social standing equaled that of the laird and his family, would find lodgings within the Long House itself. Tuan discovered he didn't mind. Clean and snug his room and the roof overhead was—well, not made of canvas.

Located adjacent to the Long House, in a long narrow outbuilding, Tuan's was one in a series of such rooms. A cluster of privies stood a short way outside, shared by the visiting retainers. Dressed only in a long white cotton shirt, the blond-haired youth turned restlessly on to his side and discovered his bladder was full. He could have made use of the chamber pot stored in a small cabinet against the far wall but ultimately decided a breath of night air would do him good.

Wrapping an Ard Mourne plaid about his shoulders, Tuan eased open the door and stepped outside. The night air did feel good, clean and chill. Winter stirred, and this far north its grasp closed quickly. The moons' light flooded the courtyard. He couldn't quite make out the green of the junipers lining the long porch that fronted the guests' quarters. Ahead, at the very end of the outbuilding, he saw a door swing open. A young woman stepped through. She appeared tall and slim, with long dark hair worn loose. Tuan paused, almost in midstride, and then sidled up close to a nearby wooden pillar with a juniper growing beside it.

Tuan recognized Tessymir Ryan; it could be no other. In the bright moons' glow, the pale beauty of her face showed unmistakably. She adjusted her dress, tugging it into place, as if she were still in the process of donning the garment. She looked back into the room she'd just exited. Framed in the doorway, a tall young man stood naked to the waist. The pair exchanged words briefly, and then she strode away, headed back toward the Long House. After voiding his bladder, Tuan returned to his room. Sleep escaped him for the remainder of the night. A brief inquiry in the morning confirmed what he already suspected—the two-room apartment at the end of the adjacent outbuilding had belonged, for the previous night, to Rowyn Cutter.

Morning dragged by slowly for the young healer. Tuan found he had little appetite. A number of people complimented him for how well he'd played yesterday. Normally such praise would have warmed him. Not today, though; today felt different. Rarely plagued by indecision, Tuan fretted, not knowing what to do.

He spotted Emerson Hart striding across the courtyard in the direction of the Long House and flagged him down. Tuan knew Ranyl trusted the barrel-chested ranger implicitly. Tuan told Emerson what he'd seen in the wee hours of the morning. The slab-shouldered ranger's features darkened with the telling. "You must speak of this with Ranyl," Emerson decided when Tuan finished. "He should know of it."

"What if the knowledge does him more harm than good?" Tuan worried.

"Ranyl faces death this noon," Emerson declared. "A man has the right to know what he's fighting for—and against."

Ranyl Emyrt sat in his room on the second floor of the Ard Ryan Long House. With the window pushed open, a fresh, chill breeze flowed through. The young Kylgahran wore a pair of loose-fitting, grey woolen trousers. His feet were encased by thick woolen socks and his most comfortable boots. A grey cotton shirt, one that buttoned all the way down, covered his torso. He'd left the shirt unbuttoned. The duel required Ranyl and his opponent to fight bare to the waist, without armor or targes. Skill with a blade alone would determine the outcome. He would finish dressing by wrapping a wide, thick, bull-hide belt about his waist. The belt would provide some protection for his lower abdomen.

In addition to his sword, he would be allowed to carry a secondary weapon. Ranyl had selected Meggie's knife. Fyrgus had carefully honed Meggie's blade the night before. The big smith had taken a look at Ranyl's broadsword as well. Fyrgus returned the weapon, saying he'd oiled it but could find no flaw in the edge whatever. Shaking his craggy, salt-and-pepper-haired head, Fyrgus observed, "The bloody thing would get no sharper if I were to apply a whetstone from here 'til the next turn of creation."

The bull-hide belt with broadsword and Meggie's knife, both sheathed, rested atop a writing table close to hand. Ranyl sat in a rocking chair placed alongside. He'd slept some, a few hours before the dawn. He'd eaten sparingly at breakfast that morning, good white bread and some musk melon. Ranyl looked up at the knock upon his door. He thought it a little early for Emerson Hart to return. The two had talked earlier, just after dawn. Ranyl went over, once again, the plans they'd made while surveying the Ard Ryan holdings. Emerson knew what he was about. The ideas were sound. If only the Ryans would listen. "Come in," Ranyl called.

Tuan Marques and Emerson Hart stepped quietly into the room. Ranyl's second was clad in a white cotton shirt, brown woolen trousers, and boots. Bareheaded, he had a plaid woven in the distinctive blue and green cross-hatched pattern and embroidered in white silk with the crossed swords of Clan Ard Mourne. Baelryc and dirk were both suspended in leather sheathes from the wide belt at his waist. The little healer wore a cream-colored silk shirt, minus the lace at the cuffs, and the snug-fitting brown-leather breeches he seemed to prefer. His two retainers halted a couple of paces away and stood side by side, their expressions solemn.

"No lace this morning, Tuan?" Ranyl observed with a smile. "Aren't you feeling well?"

"You'll have to forgive me," Tuan replied tautly. "I seem to lack the Kylgahran's zest for bloodshed."

Emerson cast a disparaging glance toward the slender youth at his side, "Tuan stumbled across something last night, *milord*," Ranyl felt certain the emphasis upon his newly acquired title was for Tuan's sake. "We felt you should know of it."

Tuan recounted what he'd seen. Ranyl's face tightened as he heard the young healer out in silence. To Tuan, it seemed as if the Kylgahran's eyes had been transformed into dark-grey ice that burned as if lit from within. "You are certain it was her?" Ranyl asked when Tuan finished.

"I am, my lord," Tuan replied gently, "and sorry I am for it."

"Tuan was not certain he should speak of this," Emerson put in gravely. "I told him a man has the right to know what he's fighting for."

Ranyl looked at his friend. Emerson's grey eyes had darkened with concern and with anger. Sym had no way of knowing it, but in slow talking, ginger-haired Emerson Hart, she had taken on an implacable enemy. He had no time to worry about that the now. If battle taught any lessons at all, it was first things first.

Climbing to his feet, Ranyl said quietly, "Harry, we both know what I'm fighting for this day, and it has naught to do with Tessymir

Ryan." Hart appeared relieved, Tuan only sad. "Thank you both." Ranyl directed his gaze to Emerson Hart. "I would just as soon wait here. Will you fetch me when it is time?"

Hart promised to do so, and he and the young healer vacated the room. Ranyl walked slowly about the chamber. Hurt and rage welled within him. Sym's actions made no sense. Why would she go to Cutter? She'd offered to spend the night with Ranyl. Was that just a stratagem, a ruse put forth because she knew he would decline? What did she hope to gain—a final tryst with her beloved? *Perhaps she'd gone there to dissuade Rowyn Cutter.* The thought gave him pause. *Damned hopeful,* the bugger between his ears scoffed. *Likely damned foolish,* Ranyl conceded, but if true, she'd risked everything to help him.

Ranyl drifted back to the table and idly rested his hand upon the hilt of his broadsword. He thought he heard someone cry out, a high keening, full of pride and encouragement, somewhere distant. Ranyl whirled about, searching the room, looking toward the open window. Only silence greeted him, and he saw nothing. *Am I losing my mind as well as my wife?* Returning to the table, Ranyl picked up Meggie's knife, resting in its sturdy leather scabbard. He sat, holding the sheathed blade in his hands. He could see Meggie's face, as clear as those of the moons at night. Fine, wide grey eyes and an impish smile, *I might cross over this day. If I do, Meggie will be waiting.* Ranyl felt his anger melt away. His breathing slowed. Reverently, he kissed the hilt of the weapon.

Rising, he lifted the wide leather belt from the table and buckled it about his waist, carefully attaching the sheath holding Meggie's knife just above his right hip. He turned to the window, his eyes drawn to the graceful sway of the pine tops on a ridge nearby beneath the bright blue sky of a pleasant day, warm for this time of year. Ranyl stood there, not thinking, letting the soft breeze and time itself wash over him. In what later seemed like only moments, a knock sounded at the door. Emerson Hart pushed the portal open. "It is time, my lord."

Ranyl's heart thudded heavily in his chest. He grasped the hilt of his broadsword and felt, once again, a rush of feeling pass through his body, just as it had the first time he'd ever touched the boar-hide grip standing amid the dust motes swirling in that lonely looted tomb. As it had then, a sense of calm stirred within. Fear, still present, seemed to step back a pace. Ranyl strode purposefully to the door where Harry waited and then followed his retainer into the hallway beyond.

Upon arriving, Ranyl saw the courtyard fronting the Ard Ryan Long House brimmed with people ringing the square. There was but little noise, only a soft murmuring that ebbed and flowed between those gathered. Harry had led him out a side door on the first floor. Two chairs had been placed on the portico of the house at the head of the short flight of stairs leading up from the stone-lined floor of the courtyard. Tessymir Ryan sat in one, while her father, Owain, occupied the other. At the foot of the stairs, already stripped to the waist, baelryc in hand, stood Rowyn Cutter. Dressed in a manner similar to Ranyl, the tall, young Kylgahran appeared calm and fit. Rowyn's gaze rested unabashedly upon Tessymir Ryan. Ranyl's wife stared straight ahead, her face a pale oval, her expression tense but unreadable.

Looking about the square, Ranyl saw a few familiar faces. Young Syngen Morgan stood with his arm wound about his sister, Soriel. Emerson Hart's wife, Kate, and Mae Hoskins held each other's hands, fairly radiating anxiety. Lukas Holt leaned against the side of one of the outbuildings, his sky-blue eyes watchful. Dark-haired Tad Gyllis smiled encouragement. Whipcord-lean Watt Quigley, also standing near Soriel, held aloft a clenched fist. Tuan Marques slipped free of the crowd, appearing as if conjured at Ranyl's side. "Good luck," the slender young healer whispered.

The smile Ranyl found upon his face surprised him. He paused and laid a firm hand on the youth's shoulder. "I hope you find what you seek and someone worthy of you to share it with."

Tuan nodded, swallowing hard, and stepped back.

Ranyl walked across the square and took up a position facing Rowyn. Without a word, he handed his broadsword to Harry and removed his shirt, passing that along to his retainer as well. Hart extended the sword, hilt first, toward Ranyl, holding the leather sheath firmly in his left hand as he did so. Ranyl wrapped the fingers of his right hand about the grip and slid the broadsword free from the scabbard Fyrgus Clyde had fashioned for him. The weapon felt feather-light in his hand; blue-grey steel gleamed as if eager to begin.

Owain Ryan rose to his feet. The laird of Clan Ard Ryan stood clad in a white silk shirt, a dark-blue woolen waistcoat, and matching trousers. He surveyed the crowd; silence fell.

"Challenge has been made and accepted. Before coming to blows I offer each combatant one last opportunity to set aside violence." Owain raised his left hand, indicating Rowyn Cutter. "Will you withdraw your charge?"

"My cause is just," Rowyn called in a firm, clear voice. "My challenge stands."

Owain lowered his left hand and raised his right. He asked of Ranyl, "Will you turn away?"

Ranyl raised his eyes. In doing so he could see Tessymir sitting to her father's left. She wore a light-blue cotton frock, long sleeved, with a scoop-necked bodice. Her rich walnut-brown hair flowed loosely about her shoulders, bound only by a strip of silk cloth Ranyl recognized as a tartyn, cross-hatched in the distinct blue-and-green pattern and bearing the crossed swords of Clan Ard Mourne. Sym's wide-set brown eyes reached out to him.

Knowing he might be playing the fool, Ranyl briefly raised his sword in salute to her. "Can't," he declared simply.

"A formal challenge has been affirmed between you. Custom calls for a duel to the death," Laird Owain stated. His right hand remained aloft. "Do you wish to alter the terms?"

"I do," Ranyl replied, "to first blood." The crowd murmured.

Laird Owain's right hand fell and his left rose. "Will you accept a contest to first blood?"

"I cannot," Rowyn Cutter called without hesitation. Another murmur flitted through those assembled.

Raising his right hand once more, Owain looked to Ranyl. "The challenge stands a duel to the death. Will you accept?"

Ranyl's gaze settled on Rowyn Cutter. "I must."

"Stand to your marks," Laird Owain directed. A pair of white chalk lines, facing each other two paces apart, had been drawn upon the flagstones near the center of the courtyard. Ranyl Emyrt and Rowyn Cutter stepped up to them.

Watching, her heart racing, Tessymir Ryan was struck by the differences between the two men. Several years older, Ranyl stood nearly a head shorter but just as wide across the shoulders and thicker through the chest. Rowyn moved with an easy natural grace. He looked like a predator stalking his prey, exuding confidence. Rowyn's greater height and the length of his arms and legs would be a real advantage. Ranyl's stride seemed purposeful, like a man with a job of work to do. Ranyl's arms and legs might not be as long as Rowyn's, but they were more heavily muscled.

"Wait for my signal," Owain commanded. As he stood to his mark, Rowyn assumed what Sym recognized as a high-guard stance, an aggressive, two-handed posture that clearly indicated he intended to attack. Ranyl stood in a mid-guard stance. Commonly used in conjunction with a targe, the mid-guard position was more versatile and could be used either offensively or defensively, but it featured a one-handed grip. To Sym, it appeared as if Ranyl had blundered before the duel even began. A powerful two-handed strike would be difficult to ward off with a one-handed grip.

"Begin!" Owain Ryan shouted.

Instead of waiting for Rowyn to come to him, Ranyl darted forward the instant the cry to begin sounded. Feinting to his left, Ranyl stepped right as he came within range and launched a straight-armed thrust at Rowyn's throat. His timing disrupted, Rowyn was thrown on to the defensive. His weapon swept down, blocking Ranyl's sword, and he initiated a counterstrike of his own.

Ranyl appeared to have anticipated him. The heavy broadsword in his hand brushed that of Rowyn Cutter's baelryc. The blades met in a whisper, not a clang. Then Ranyl's sword slipped past Rowyn's in a movement so subtle and quick Sym could not truly say she saw it, even though she was staring with rapt, tortuous attention at the two combatants. Rowyn's reflexes saved him. He managed to twist his body aside. Even so, Ranyl's blade scored the taller warrior's upper left arm just below the shoulder joint.

Rowyn danced away, ignoring the cut, and attacked from high guard. Ranyl shifted his stance, placing both hands on the long haft of his sword. The two swords met again, ringing this time like temple bells. A series of swift slashes were exchanged, and it was Ranyl who disengaged, blood trickling down his torso from a gash above his left breast. The two adversaries circled one another briefly before Rowyn moved again to the attack.

Ranyl met him, and once more the heavy blades whirred, steel ringing on steel. Ranyl seemed to stumble. Sym felt a cry rise in her throat. Rowyn's blade swept down, but Ranyl side-stepped. Though not as graceful as his younger opponent, Ranyl was quick and strong. His riposte took Rowyn in the right thigh. With a cry of rage, Rowyn whirled, lashing out aggressively. Ranyl beat off his assault but appeared to be tiring.

Sweat-drenched, their bodies glistening, both swordsmen switched to single-handed grips, their right legs well in advance of their left, bent loosely at the knees, blade arms extended. Rowyn thrust. Ranyl parried. A flurry of blows followed, blending into nearly continuous motion like a dance. The taller warrior's blade struck home, taking Ranyl in the side.

Rowyn recovered and immediately aimed an overhand cut at Ranyl's left shoulder, intending to finish the duel. Ranyl, wounded but still cat quick, warded the blow from beneath and leapt close, slamming the hilt of his broadsword into Rowyn's jaw. The blow staggered the dark-haired youth. Ranyl pressed his advantage, tripping his taller adversary and sending him sprawling with a powerful shove. As Cutter fell, Ranyl darted forward and stabbed him high in the chest. Not a fatal blow, at least not instantaneously, but one that left Rowyn seriously wounded.

Rowyn's baelryc slipped from his hand. Kicking it away, Ranyl stood above him, broadsword poised to strike. The blade in Ranyl's hands seemed to quiver, to hunger. A simple downward thrust would finish it. From somewhere, Ranyl thought he heard a faint cry of warning—Meggie's voice, calling out to him as if across some great distance.

Ranyl hesitated. "Yield," he cried. "Yield and live."

Cutter's blue eyes met his, radiating nothing but calm. Slowly, the Ard Ryan retainer shook his head, "I cannot."

Ranyl felt a wave of exultation, hot with triumph, surge through his body. He had license the now to strike to end this, to take vengeance for—*for what?* Meggie's voice came to him once more, just at the edge of perception, even fainter than before, filled with unspeakable anguish. He would not be the cause of further pain, not to her.

"I claim the victory," he called in a voice pitched to carry throughout the courtyard. Never taking his eyes from his downed adversary, Ranyl shouted, "Does anyone here dispute it?" An uneasy, restless sound rippled through the crowd. This was against all custom.

"No," Cutter exclaimed, struggling to rise. Ranyl lashed out with his right foot, kicking Rowyn in the side of his head.

Rowyn slumped, and Ranyl raised his voice. "Anyone besides this idiot?" Silence reigned, as if those watching were holding their breath.

"You entered, warrior, knowingly, into a duel to the death." Owain Ryan's calm baritone reverberated across the square. "How is honor served by this display?"

"I did not come here to kill Ryans," Ranyl replied savagely. Lowering his sword, he stepped back and turned to face the laird of Clan Ard Ryan. "And there is something to be said for courage."

Owain fixed his gaze upon Ranyl for a long moment and nodded. "I see no victory here," he called, "but no shortage of courage either. I will not dispute you."

Ranyl swallowed, his throat painfully dry. He glanced at Sym. She was looking at him, not Rowyn. *Well, that is something, maybe.* Ranyl's knees nearly buckled. He doubted he could lift the sword in his right hand again if his life depended on it. Nodding respectfully to Laird Owain, Ranyl pivoted and walked back in the direction of the side door through which he'd entered the courtyard.

Tuan intercepted him. "If you are quite finished," the young healer said furiously, "come sit over here before you fall down." Tuan guided him to a small wooden bench.

Emerson Hart stood to one side, a wide grin on his usually stoic face. Lukas Holt was standing on the other.

As Ranyl drew near, the tall, dark-haired ranger muttered, "Balls over brains, a bad habit that, sir." Ranyl couldn't argue, not without admitting he had a dead girl's voice in his head.

"Once is my limit," Ranyl rasped softly. "Does anyone have anything to drink?" He took a seat upon the bench. Tad Gyllis appeared by his side, wineskin in hand.

"Not yet," Tuan snapped.

Wearily, Ranyl passed his sword over to Emerson. The blade, once light as a moonbeam in his hands, seemed the now impossibly heavy. Hart took the broadsword, carefully wiping the shimmering steel free of blood, and sheathed the weapon. Ranyl felt its absence with mingled relief and regret.

Tuan reached around to place one hand at the back of Ranyl's neck while placing the other just below the wound in his side. "Ready?" Without waiting for Ranyl to respond, the blond-haired youth closed his eyes. Ranyl felt the familiar tingling he associated with a healer's touch stir in his breast. He'd experienced Anharyd's healing flows more than once. Young Tuan's was much more powerful. The tingling surged rapidly to the edge of pain. Ranyl gritted his teeth; sweat poured out of him. His chest burned. "Done," Tuan said shortly, lowering his hands.

"Was it necessary to do that quite so enthusiastically?" Ranyl inquired mildly.

"Think of it as a small lesson in probity," Tuan smiled unabashedly. "Was it not you who chided me for indulging in ... heroics, I believe you said?"

"I don't recall," Ranyl lied half-heartedly.

"Would you like me to see what I can do for that other hero?" Tuan jerked his head in the direction of the courtyard.

"Yes, please," Ranyl replied, "and thank you, Healer."

For some reason, Ranyl's expression of thanks seemed to embarrass Tuan. "Wash the blood off him," Tuan directed crisply. "Dry him carefully and keep him warm. He will need immediate rest and food." The young healer looked to Tad Gyllis. "A little wine won't hurt him any." Without another word, Tuan turned away.

Accepting the wineskin from Tad, Ranyl looked over his shoulder at Lukas Holt. "Go with him. Keep the little bugger out of trouble, if you can."

The laconic ranger shook his head. "I'll do my best." He moved, following quickly on the heels of Tuan Marques.

The wine was well watered but still burned as he swallowed. Victory was his, whether Laird Owain acknowledged it as such or not. Ranyl could feel yet the weight of Tessymir's stare, her umber eyes wide, her expression tense but otherwise unknowable. *A victory, all right enough,* Ranyl thought wearily, *but what have I won?*

Over his objections, Harry and Tad washed Ranyl's upper body free of blood and sweat, dried him thoroughly, and helped him back into his shirt. Ranyl's legs and arms felt as if they were fashioned of lead that somehow managed to ache like fire. The climb up the stairs to the second floor of the Long House nearly undid him. He had to pause at the head of the stairway, his ears ringing, while his heart hammered in protest.

"My lord husband." Sym appeared before him, looking as lovely and serene as a still mountain lake. "Would you indulge me and sit awhile, just here?" She pointed to an open door across the hall.

"Of course," Ranyl acceded. Ignoring a hard look from Harry Hart, Sym took Ranyl's left arm and guided him to the far side of the hall and through the open doorway. Ranyl stepped into a small sitting room equipped with a pair of overstuffed cloth-backed chairs placed before a double door that fronted a large balcony. The doors had been flung wide, and he could see a finely wrought stone balustrade lining the far side of the balcony. A small settle rested near a brick-lined fireplace, and an oval-shaped writing table occupied the middle of the room. Ranyl slumped gratefully into one of the chairs. Sym took a seat beside him.

"If you please, gentlemen," Sym addressed Emerson Hart and Tad Gyllis, who had accompanied Ranyl up from the courtyard, and a trio of her own retainers, including, Ranyl saw, the steward of Clan Ard Ryan, Benjamyn Lowell. "I would like a few moments alone with my consort."

Harry looked to Ranyl. At Ranyl's nod, Hart gestured to Tad, and the two of them walked from the room. The Ard Ryan retainers followed. As soon as they were alone, Sym turned to Ranyl. "You look awful," she exclaimed.

Ranyl smiled. "You should see the other fellow."

"I mean it," Sym pressed, the concern on her face evident, "you are pale and wan as if exhausted. Are you certain that young healer of yours knows his business?"

"Well enough," Ranyl assured her. "All I need is some rest and food." Ranyl's expression sobered. "Why did you go to him last night?" He had not meant to ask; the words just slipped free as if of their own accord.

If Sym was surprised by his question, she showed no sign of it. No need there was for her to ask of whom he spoke. Her eyes, a luminous maple brown, settled upon his. "I hoped I could dissuade Rowyn, convince him to walk away from the duel you fought today. Why do you ask?"

"One of my people saw you leaving Cutter's room in the small hours last night"—Ranyl paused a moment—"still fastening your dress as you walked away."

"I see," Sym said very softly. "Were you spying on me, my lord?"

"On our wedding night." Ranyl almost smiled. "No, I'm not that prescient. He was headed to the privy and came upon you by accident."

"And so you think I spent our wedding night in the arms of Rowyn Cutter." Sym lowered her eyes.

"I was four years a sheriff." Ranyl's voice sounded quietly neutral. "I've learned that what people suspect often has more to do with what they fear than what they know. Will you speak of it?"

"I've seen Rowyn fight." Sym raised her eyes to his once more. "I did not think you could win today. I should have had more faith, I know, but I felt certain you could not prevail."

"He's impressive, a real looker," Ranyl said sardonically. "I'll give him that."

Sym's eyes flashed angrily. "It is not that, you fool. I know him. He's brave and fierce and determined. His father was first sword. Rowyn was raised with a blade in his hand. I've seen him kill." Her voice quavered slightly. "I don't know you, not really, not that way. I did not want to be responsible for your death."

"So you went to him, a man who was once your lover, on the night of our wedding," Ranyl summarized wryly, "and offered—what, in exchange for my life?"

Sym spoke softly. "I told him, if he would retract his challenge, I would go away with him, anyplace he wanted, in a year and a day."

Sym saw something flicker in the charcoal depths of his eyes, and she knew he, too, recognized the significance of what she'd just said. "You planned to stay free of my bed?"

Sym smiled.. *How could men be so simple in some ways and so impossibly complex in others?* "I am well schooled and very regular," she explained. "We have an excellent midwife in the family. You are kind and patient." Suddenly, she found it very hard to look at him and instead found herself staring at her toes. "With a little effort, I think I could remain free of child a year and a day from the now."

"Upon which time you would annul our marriage and abdicate?" Ranyl surmised.

"Yes." Sym raised her delicately dimpled chin. "By then your ideas would have taken root. My father would have seen the value in them. I have a number of cousins of marriageable age. My father could adopt one of your choosing. That would bypass any difficulty over inheritance."

"Very neat." Ranyl looked away. He couldn't keep bitterness from his voice. "Clan Ard Ryan secures some new sources of income. You get to run off with the man you love. I have my pick of a bevy of Ryan heiresses. Everyone gets what they want. It would appear you have a flair for politics."

"I never said it is what I wanted," Sym replied. "I told you I am not in love with Rowyn Cutter. I have not lied to you."

Ranyl forced himself to look again into her eyes. "What if you miscalculated and found yourself pregnant. What then?"

Sym's wide-set brown eyes reached out to him, tears welling. "I don't know. I swore to Rowyn I would do whatever was necessary, but I don't know if I could do that."

"You promised to relinquish the Ard Ryan lairdship," Ranyl recounted grimly, "to kill our unborn child, if necessary, and spend your life with a man you say you do not love, to save my life?"

Tears spilled onto Sym's finely formed cheeks. Her eyes bored into his, beautiful and terrible. "No, husband, not for your life; for the good of my clan."

She's telling the truth. Ranyl felt the bite of it like a knife in his belly. He could not look away. "He refused you."

Sym nodded. "He said that to do as I asked would make a lie of everything we'd shared." Sym's eyes probed his, beseeching. He'd seen that look once before, in Helyn Chambers's eyes the day he broke off their betrothal. "Rowyn kissed me. He slid his hand into my dress, tugging it down. I slipped a small dagger from my sash and held it to his throat, just hard enough to break the skin. He simply stood there, waiting." Sym's throaty contralto faltered, and she swallowed hard. "I couldn't. I dropped the knife. He said it was time for me to go. I left. It was then your man must have seen me."

A memory flashed into Ranyl's mind. As he stood over Rowyn Cutter, sword poised to strike, he'd seen a narrow red cut mark at the base of his foeman's throat. Ranyl remembered a thought flitting through his brain at the sight that—if the wound had been a finger width deeper, the problem that was Rowyn Cutter would have been solved forever. Ranyl shook his head.

"You don't believe me?" Sym inquired softly.

Reaching out, Ranyl gently brushed away a tear as it glimmered beneath her left eye. "It isn't that. I was just thinking, sometimes women *are complicated.*"

Sym slipped from her seat to kneel gracefully before him. "Then you do believe me?"

"Aye, that I do," Ranyl acknowledged. "I saw the cut at the base of his throat." The corners of Sym's mouth curved upwards, and a smile blossomed until she noted his head shake again, sadly this time. "A man fancies one day being first in the heart of the woman he weds. Comes to that, I don't suppose I stand much of a chance with you, do I?"

Her budding smile fled, and a helpless look flooded Sym's cinnamon-colored eyes. Ranyl clasped her hand.

"No need to fash yourself," Ranyl soothed. "I'm bound to be a wee bit jealous from time to time is all. If you'll allow me that, we'll get on well enough."

"Today, in the courtyard"–Sym's low-pitched voice throbbed–"I'd never been so frightened, and it had naught to do with any thought of my clan."

"Aye, well." Ranyl smiled, grey eyes warming. "That's hopeful."

Sym returned his smile, a little tremulously. "Where do we go from here?"

"I don't know about you, wife, but I'm bound for my room," Ranyl replied evenly. "If you'll have some food sent up, I'll share a bit of it with you, and then I intend to sleep for a week. When I wake, if I find you've been up to any more mischief, I'll tan your bottom and follow my nose from there."

"Mischief!" Sym flared, umber eyes flashing once again. "It was not I who went gallivanting all over the countryside, leaving me to return here alone and explain your absence, or accepted a challenge from one of my clansmen without so much as a second thought, or went off half believing I would be unfaithful before we even–"

Ranyl succeeded in stemming the torrent by kissing her. Sym stiffened for a moment and then relaxed against him, her mouth molding sweetly to his. Sliding her arms about his neck, she returned his kiss. At his touch, Sym felt a warmth begin to spread within her belly as a small ripple of joy coursed through her heart. For Sym realized in that moment her husband trusted her and that despite everything, she and Ranyl had managed to make a beginning.

40

Alone in the Dark

Stephyn Emyrt of Clan Ard Mourne sat stock still in his favorite chair beside a well-worn writing table in his office—his counting house, his wife, Ellah, had called it. Through an open window set into the opposing wall, he could see the courtyard below, awash in moons' light. A single oil lamp affixed to a wall-mounted stanchion beside the door cast its golden glow into the room.

A heavyset, wide-shouldered man of middle years with reddish brown hair and eyes the same shade of grey as those of his two sons, Stephyn stirred, finally, glancing down at the sheet of paper that lay atop the battered surface of the table before him. The courier who delivered the letter had given his name as Cable Dowd of Clan Ard Cullen.

In the soft light of the lamp, Stephyn read once more the neatly penned script. No heading graced the letter, no greeting at all; it began:

You can trust the bearer, a balding, blue-eyed, gapped-toothed fellow who was a sailor in his youth.

The last time I wrote you it was with sad tidings concerning the death of a young woman we both loved. Enclosed is a token so that you will know this letter is genuine. By rights, I should have sent it to you long ago. I refrained from doing so against the needs of this day. I ask your forgiveness.

Stephyn slowly opened the fingers of his left hand. Resting in his broad palm lay a ring, Joslyn's ring, his sister's, one of a set of three identically crafted. Ellah wore hers until the day she died. His fingers curled once more, coiling into a clenched fist. Beloved Joslyn, so beautiful and so kind, gone too soon. The letter continued:

Before she died, the young woman we loved gave birth to a boy child, sired out of wedlock by a man to whom we two swore undying loyalty, a man we served each in our own way, in victory and in defeat. The great tree under which we gave our oaths lives still. It is too soon to say where this path will lead, but the time has come for me to ask. Where will you stand?

By any road, old friend, Godspeed.

The letter remained unsigned, but Stephyn harbored no doubt as to its author. Basyl Conroy of Clan Ard Owen had written, nearly twenty years ago the now, with word of Joslyn's death. The man, the father of her child, could be no other than Evahn Eldyr of Clan Ard Eldyr, to whom both Basyl and Stephyn had given their oaths of retainer. Killed in battle perhaps a year and a half before Joslyn's passing, Evahn had inherited lairdship of Clan Ard Eldyr just prior to his death. The Ard Eldyr clan mark was a rugged oak—*the great tree lives still.* Basyl's meaning showed clear. In accordance with clan law, Joslyn's bastard son, the only living child of Evahn Eldyr, stood, by right of birth, laird of Clan Ard Eldyr. *What might it mean, Stephyn* wondered, *to be laird of a broken clan?* Stephyn took a long, deep breath. *I can think of but one way to find out.*

Stephyn extracted a fresh sheet of vellum from a shelf beneath the table. Pressing it down upon a leather writing pad, he dipped a quill into an inkwell and wrote quickly but with care:

Enclosed is the token you sent. I return it for the same reason you gave. I'll be wanting it back.

You will forgive me, old friend, for responding to your question with one of my own. How best may I serve?

Say hullo to my nephew for me.

Godspeed, indeed.

Glossary of Terms

Term	Sounds Like	Definition
All Father	All Fa-ther	Deity worshipped by those of the Penitent faith; the primary religion of the Tieran Empire and the kingdoms of Ayle, Syrdis, and Wystros
Altair	Al-tare	Kingdom located on the northeastern shore of the Middle Sea
Antium	An-tee-um	Capital city of the Kingdom of Ayle; located on the eastern flank of the Donn Narrows (see Myr Sea)
Ayle	Ail	Kingdom located on the north-central shore of the Middle Sea; also adjacent to the northeastern shore of the Myr Sea. The Ayle are long term allies of the Tieran Empire
Aylitic	A-lih-tick	Primary language of the Ayle; also one of the most prominent tongues used for trade and commerce throughout the Middle Sea region, especially in lands north and west of the Middle Sea
Almyr	Al-mir	Deity also known as the Mother Goddess or the Trascera Mother: worshipped by the Elsacians
altyrn	all-tern	Tieran junior officer rank; typically a company commander

Term	Sounds Like	Definition
Askante	ah-skhan-tee	Specialized light infantry raised by the Gracci faction during the War of Houses. Askante carry a clutch of javelins (throwing spears) a round, bronze faced shield for defense, and the kante, a long bladed, short hafted thrusting spear. Well conditioned and highly mobile, they have a reputation as tough fighters
axton	axe-tun	Title given to a senior priest within the Penitent faith
baelryc	bail-rick	Hand-and-a-half hilted bastard sword preferred by Kylgahran Highlanders: Typically two and a half span in blade length, for most men about the same distance as from shoulder joint to fingertip with their hand and arm fully extended. A straight bladed weapon, the tip of the baelryc is formed into a symmetric, double edged point. The leading edge of the sword is razor sharp over its full length. About a span from the point, the back side of the baelryc blade gradually thickens to a blunt, rounded edge that extends back to the hilt. Most hilts feature a simple iron cross-guard. The blade itself is made of water marked steel, called so because the repeated hammered folding and quenching of the base iron mixed with charcoal during the forging of the blade leaves ripples in the finished steel that resemble a water mark

Term	Sounds Like	Definition
Bandehar	Ban-dee-har	Kingdom located at the southeastern extreme of the Middle Sea region along the shores of the Olyth Ocean to the east and the Saeryc Ocean to the south
Beagle	bee-gul	Slang term Tieran Marines, seagoing heavy infantry, use in reference to their regular infantry counterparts
Briny	bri-nee	Slang term Tieran Regulars, heavy infantry, use in reference to their marine counterparts
Brynnai	brin-eye	Of or pertaining to the Brynnai faith: primary religion of the Kylgahran and their forebears, the Sea Isle folk; the Brynnai believe in a Creator, the One God, and the Four Fates who act as intermediaries (see Four Fates)
caestor	kay-stor	Mid level Tieran bureaucrat; an administrator; duties vary; sometimes assigned as a school supervisor
Cartsys	kart-sis	Mainland north of the Middle Sea; an Aylitic word that means homeland; bordered on the west by the Maeryc Ocean and on the east by the Olyth Ocean; the northern extremes of the Cartsys encompass the Lands of Snow, north of the Torean Mountains, a vast hinterland about which little is known

Term	Sounds Like	Definition
Chieftain of Lairds	Chief-tan of Lehrdz	Principal executive of the Kylgahran Council of Lairds; elected by vote of the council members to a term of six years, the Chieftain is primarily a battle leader
compaglium	com-pag-lee-um	Tieran word for a temporary fortified encampment usually surrounded by a combination of trench and staked, wooden palisade
Confederation of Clans	Con-fed-er-a-shun of klanz	Governmental structure of the Kylgahran clans; an association of clans ruled by the Kylgahran Council of Lairds headed by the Chieftain of Lairds
Confederation of Sorcerers	Con-fed-er-a-shun of sor-ser-erz	Organization of sorcerers within the Tieran empire; most large cities have a corresponding confederation, the Confederation of Tyne (capital of the Tieran province of Quistyn del Aurus) is an example
Cos	Koss	Syrdisian city located on the banks of the River Sayx in the northwestern reaches of the kingdom

Term	Sounds Like	Definition
croix	kroy	Primary weapon of Tieran regular infantry and marines: a thrusting spear, the croix measures eight span in length, about the distance the average soldier can reach up to standing flat footed with one arm fully extended over his head. A croix spearhead is one and one quarter span long, triangular in shape with a pyramidal cross section made of pressed steel. Affixed to an ash wood shaft, the spear point is counter weighted by a steel spike one third of a span in length riveted to the butt of the weapon. The croix can be thrown effectively, but is intended almost exclusively for use in close combat
cutter	kuh-ter	A fast, mid-sized sailing ship; typically features a two mast hermaphrodite sail configuration utilizing a mix of both square and lateen rigged courses; cutters are highly prized by merchantmen and smugglers alike for their speed and maneuverability
Danos	Da-nos	Island nation south of the Morro peninsula. The Danoans often serve as mercenaries and are among the favored auxiliaries of the Tieran Empire. The Danoans are famed archers and the fearsome Danoan longbow is dreaded on battlefields throughout the Middle Sea

Term	Sounds Like	Definition
Drach Orckens	Drak Or-kenz	An order of Penitent monks; a warrior society the Drach Orckens provide armed escort to pilgrims and church officials traveling between religious sites. Renowned for their skill as metal workers and vintners the Drach Orckens also lend money. The Penitent faith frowns on usury but the Drach Orckens charter specifically allows the practice. The Drach Orckens are a close knit, secretive society, supposedly in control of vast wealth and rumors abound concerning them. Sorcerers are said to be amongst their ranks and it is whispered, witches, too. Their sigil is the rune symbol throi, also known as the death's head
dymena	deh-min-ah	Proper form of address for a female Elven noble
dymenu	deh-min-ooh	Proper form of address for a male Elven noble
Elfan	El-fan	Male elf
Elfin	El-feen	Female elf
Elsacian	el-say-she-un	Ethnic minority within the Kingdom of Ayle, living principally in the major cities such as the capital, Antium: Elsacians hail originally from the portion of the Basyr Peninsula now known as the Tieran province of Quistyn del Tagus. Elsacians tend to be fair skinned and blond haired with a distinctive cast or tilt to their eyes

Term	Sounds Like	Definition
Enduyi	En-doo-ee	A breed of horses favored by the Elves of Ilyria; famed for their speed and agility. Typical coloring varies from black to brown including roan with manes usually of black or brown
Esquire	Es-quire	A class of lesser Kylgahran nobles; landowners who can claim at least four quires or one quadrant of land or the equivalent in property (see quadrant)
Fey Amulet	Fey Am-u-let	Magic talisman in the form of a circular disk crafted of pellinwahr (an iron alloy) characterized by the rune symbol Fey emblazoned on the surface of the medallion. Fey talismans are reputed to ward against all forms of adverse magic that is intended to do the wearer harm
Four Fates	Four Fates	According to the Brynnai faith, the Four Fates are immortal servants of the Creator. They see done His will. There are two brothers, Ryx, who stands for courage and Tal who champions justice, and two sisters, Eym who represents liberty and Lyn who embodies the spirit of love

Term	Sounds Like	Definition
Glavius	Gla-vee-us	Tieran infantry sword; double edged, blade length of two span with a symmetrically shaped triangular point. Forged of pressed steel, the Glavius is a heavy short sword nearly three fingers in width at the base of the blade. The Glavius will cut readily enough but it is principally a stabbing weapon
Glaylic	Glay-lick	Native language of the Kylgahran and their antecedents, the Sea People (People of the Sea Isles)
Greymark	Grey-mark	Ancestral Hold of Clan Ard Ryan (see Hold)
Greystock	Grey-stalk	Village nestled round Deben Bay on the northwestern coast of the Myr Sea in the Tieran Territory of the Three Rivers
Gyft	gift	Name given to the ability to invoke (utilize) the power of the Yir (that is the ability to do magic)
Gyft Ryll	gift rill	Special schools within the boundaries of the Tieran Empire and the Kingdom of Ayle devoted to developing the ability to use the power of the Yir; in addition to instruction in working directly with the Yir, Gyft Rylls offer a wide range of education in subjects including history, medicine, language, and mathematics

Term	Sounds Like	Definition
heartstone	hart-stone	A grey, glassy stone capable of being knapped like flint into various tools and weapons, arrowheads, spear points and such. Heartstone possesses a peculiar property in that no sorcerer or witch can use magic to ward against it as a weapon
hacker	haa-kur	Slang term Highland sailors have ascribed to the Kylgahran cutlass or sea sword; basically a pared down version of the Kylgahran baelryc adapted for close quarter fighting including a "caged" or "basket" hand guard in lieu of the simple cross bar guard of the full-sized baelryc
Henfyrd	Hen-feared	Large town in the Tieran Province of Quistyn del Aurus; located on the east bank of the River Wyst at its juncture with the Middle Sea
Highlands	Hi-landz	Traditional home of the Kylgahran (see Kylgahra) Clans, the term refers to the rugged combination of hills and narrow ridge-topped valleys that lie between the Tylcairn Mountains and the Cartsys west coast of the Maeryc Ocean
Hold	Hold	Kylgahran term referring to the principal residence of a Clan Laird; typically a fortified dwelling
Housecarls	Hous-karlz	Designation given to a class of warriors within the Kingdom of Syrdis; the housecarls are traditionally heavy cavalry; the most vaunted arm of the Syrdisian military

Term	Sounds Like	Definition
Ilyria	Ill-ir-ee-ah	Island homeland of the Elves; a chain of islands in the Maeryc Ocean south and west of the Cartsys mainland
Ilyrian	Ill-ir-ee-ahn	Language of the Elves; an ancient tongue widely spoken throughout especially the southern portion of the Middle Sea region
invoking the Yir	in-vo-king	Process by which a sorcerer accesses the power of the Yir, the source of sorcerer's magic. Invoking the Yir by a sorcerer corresponds to a witch's summoning of the One (see summon)
jaltryn	jall-trin	Padded leather arming jacket worn by Tieran soldiers, infantry and cavalry alike, beneath their chain-mail armor
keppi	keh-pee	An Elsacian dress featuring a snug fitting bodice and a full skirt
kernyl	ker-nel	Tieran army officer rank ascribed to each regimental commander
Kios	Kee-os	Kingdom located just north of the Basyr Peninsula. Eastern neighbor and long standing foe of the Kingdom of Ayle
Kylgahra	Kill-gar-ah	Traditional home of the Kylgahran (see Highlands) Clans, the region encompasses the rugged combination of hills and narrow ridge-topped valleys that lie between the Tylcairn Mountains and the Cartsys west coast of the Maeryc Ocean; a Glaylic word meaning Highlands

Term	Sounds Like	Definition
Kylgahran	Kill-gar-ahn	Of or pertaining to the people of Kylgahra
Kylgahran Clans	Kill-gar-ahn Klanz	Familial groupings of the Kylgahran people; the government of Kylgahra is based on the clan structure; each Clan is ruled by a Laird (see Laird)
kylo	kee-low	Standard Tieran measure of distance; one kylo is composed of sixteen hundred paces (see pace, span)
kyrobi	ky-roh-bee	A broad, brocaded belt of waxed linen worn by women in lands all around the Middle Sea
Laird	Lehrd	Ruler of a Kylgahran Clan; the equivalent of an individual Clan Chieftain; lairds are not absolute monarchs, the extent of their authority is shaped by years of precedent and tradition; no clan will tolerate a tyrant; lairdship of a clan is inherited, passed down to the eldest child of the current laird regardless of sex; about half of the Kylgahran lairds are therefore female; each laird automatically ascends to a seat on the Council of Lairds the ruling body of the Kylgahran Confederation (see Confederation of Clans)
Lands of Snow	Landz of Snow	A great wilderness extending north of the Torean Mountains; home to a number of tribal folk who in the past have sometimes moved south to raid or even invade the lands surrounding the Middle Sea

Term	Sounds Like	Definition
legio	leh-gee-oh	A Tieran term referring to an army barracks, typically associated with a permanent military installation (see puglium or stadia)
Lynium	leh-nee-um	Primary language of the Tieran Empire; spoken in all provinces and territories of the empire. Also one of the most prominent tongues used for trade and commerce throughout the Middle Sea region
Maeryc Ocean	Mair-ick O-shun	The great ocean extending west of the Cartsys mainland
Mayne	Main	Legendary city state, once the jewel of civilization in the Middle Sea region, long fallen into ruin. The exact location of the once renowned city state is unknown. The prevailing view is that Mayne was most likely located somewhere in the northeastern portion of the Morro Peninsula. A minority view contends the site must have been much further north
Middle Sea	Mih-del See	Large body of salt water bordered by the Cartsys mainland on the north and the east and by the Morro Peninsula to the south. The Middle Sea opens into the vast Maeryc Ocean to the west

Term	Sounds Like	Definition
Morgyn	Mor-gin (hard g)	Breed of horse favored by Kylgahran clansmen. Mountain bred, the Morgyns are medium sized, swift and sure footed. Not as fast as the elegant Enduyi horses favored by the Elves of Ilyria or as powerful as the Panyir chargers of Roi, the Morgyns combine a good turn of speed with incredible endurance. They make excellent cow horses. Typical coloring varies from brown to grey, often dappled with manes usually of black or gold
Morro Peninsula	Mor-oh	Territorial heartland of the Tieran Empire; a large peninsula that lines the southern shore of the Middle Sea
Myr Sea	Mihr See	Also known as the Inland Sea; a body of salt water shaped roughly like a giant thumb angling mostly north and west; the base of the thumb, the southeastern terminus, connects with the much larger Middle Sea through a channel known as the Donn Narrows. The Myr Sea is bordered along its northwestern coast by the Tieran Territory of the Three Rivers, the Tieran Province of Quistyn del Aurus occupies most of its southwestern shoreline while a portion of the Kingdom of Ayle lies along the eastern shore of the sea south of the river Poe
Myrl	Mehrl	Kingdom located on the eastern flank of the Middle Sea bordered by Relwyn to the south and Altair to the north

Term	Sounds Like	Definition
nithing	nih-thing	A Tieran term meaning *of no consequence*
Olyth Ocean	Oh-lith O-shun	The ocean extending east of the Cartsys mainland
pace	pace	Standard Tieran measure of distance; one pace is composed of three span; corresponds to the approximate length of an average man's full stride (see kylo, span)
pallester	pah-les-ter	Tieran term for a parade ground located within a military installation such as a puglium or a compaglium.
pellinwahr	pe-lin-wahr	An Elven word referring to a metallic alloy of iron; looks like black iron but is less dense. Pellinwahr is a material often used in the manufacture of magic talismans
Penitent Faith	Pe-neh-tent Faith	Dominant religion throughout the Tieran Empire and the kingdoms of Syrdis, Ayle, and Wystros. Penitents worship a deity known as the All Father, the Creator and bringer of Light and Life (see All Father)
pressed steel	prest steel	Steel composed of charcoal laced iron formed by repeated folding and hammering of the base metal during forging; pressed steel is the standard for Tieran military grade weaponry; also called layered steel

Term	Sounds Like	Definition
puglium	puh-glee-um	A permanent Tieran military installation typically including, barracks, stables, a hospital, baths, various workshops and storage facilities. Also known as a military campus.
quadrant	kwah-drant	A Kylgahran term pertaining to a property holding equivalent in size to four quires (see quire)
questing charm	qwe-sting charm	A magic talisman capable of guiding a bearer to the person for whom the charm was conjured. No ability to invoke the Yir is necessary to make use of a questing charm. Questing charms may be fashioned from most objects, especially those that have been in close personal contact with the individual sought. Questing charms usually work only on sentient beings, although a form of questing charm can be fashioned from a part of a thing, a page torn from a book or a sliver shaved from a wooden item for example. Inanimate objects may be enchanted to emit a telepathic beacon, but only someone with the ability to invoke the Yir would be able to detect the telepathic transmission. Iron will not serve as a questing charm, and neither will some gemstones (see also seeking charm)
quire	kwy-er	A Kylgahran term denoting a square plot of ground measuring four hundred paces on a side

Term	Sounds Like	Definition
Quistyn	Kweh-sten	A word in Lynium, the language of Tier meaning an imperial holding. The formal designation for all Tieran provinces begins with the words, Quistyn del
regenerative talisman	re-gen-er-a-tive tal-is-man	Subset of magic talismans (see talisman) with the capacity to regenerate. If placed in close proximity to a mundane object with matching physical properties, a regenerative talisman will transfer its magical properties while retaining its own. The time required varies, but regenerative talismans all have the capability to replicate provided the target mundane object is a close enough physical match to the talisman. Sorcerer's staves and seeking charms are examples of regenerative talismans
regent	ree-gent	Tieran army officer rank above altyrn and below kernyl. A regent typically commands two companies. Five regents are usually assigned to each regular army regiment. Of the five, one is normally a senior regent (regent, senior), typically the regiment's second in command
regent, senior	ree-gent, sen-ee-or	Tieran army officer rank just below that of kernyl. A senior regent is usually second in command of a regular army regiment

Term	Sounds Like	Definition
regiment	reh-jah-ment	Principal Tieran army operational unit composed of ten companies of one hundred soldiers, not including officers for a total of one thousand troops. Each regular army regiment is designated by both a name and a number ranging between zero and one hundred; examples are the 5th Minoa, 6th Gemina, 10th Accer, and 33rd Regulus. The combination of name and number are unique although both name and number are reused; examples include the 12th Minoa, 6th Accer, and 5th Regulus
regular	reh-gu-lahr	Designation given to professional Tieran soldiers. Regulars enlist for a period of twenty years. At the end of their twenty-year enlistment they have an opportunity to either retire or to re-enlist for an additional five years. The five-year re-enlistment bonus is substantial, a single lump sum payment equivalent to three years pay. Tieran regulars are heavy infantry. Their principal weapon is a thrusting spear called the croix (see croix)
Relwyn	Rel-win	Kingdom composed of a confederation of tribes located northeast of Roi. The Relwyn are fierce warriors and perennial foes of the Roi. While no formal alliance exists, the Relwyn have long served as mercenary auxiliaries in the armed forces of Tier

Term	Sounds Like	Definition
Roi	Roy	Kingdom occupying the lands just east of the Tieran Empire on the Morro peninsula. The warlike Roi are the most venerated and powerful foes of the Tieran Empire
Saeryc Ocean	Sair-ick O-shun	The southern ocean, extending south of the Morro Peninsula
sajar	say-jar	Tieran non-commissioned officer rank. In Lynium, the language of Tier, sajar literally means the leader of twenty. In a regular army regiment composed of ten, one hundred man companies, five sajars are assigned to each company. The senior sajar in each company has the rank of Sajar First
scralyng	scray-ling	A Kylgahran term denoting a person of low regard and questionable heritage
Sea Isles	See Eyelz	Island Kingdom located in the Maeryc Ocean to the west of the Cartsys mainland; ancestral home of the Kylgahran
seeking charm	see-king charm	Regenerative magic talisman (see regenerative talisman) capable of identifying individuals with the ability to invoke the Yir. Held in the hand of someone capable of invoking the Yir, seeking charms emit a soft blue light. Seeking charms may be fashioned from a wide variety of materials. Iron objects and some gemstones will not serve. See also questing charm

Term	Sounds Like	Definition
Sircassian League	Sir-cas-see-an	Originating in the kingdom of Bandehar, the Sircassian League is a highly trained, superbly skilled band of assassins, available for hire to anyone with the will and the coin necessary to make use of their unique services. Sircassians also serve as bodyguards and spies and thief takers
spada	spay-dah	Tieran cavalry sword; single edged, blade length of nearly three span with a symmetric leaf shaped point. Forged of pressed steel the straight bladed spada is primarily a slashing weapon designed for use on horseback
span	span	Standard Tieran measure of distance; one span represents the distance from the crease in an average sized man's elbow to the base of his middle finger (roughly equal to one English foot). Three span comprise a pace (see pace, kylo)
stadia	stay-dee-ah	A Tieran school for officer training, more common than a military academy
stone	stone	Standard Tieran measure of weight (roughly equal to four English pounds)
Suffolk Islands	Su-folk Eye-landz	Island nation located in the Maeryc Ocean north and west of the Cartsys mainland

Term	Sounds Like	Definition
Summoning the One	Suh-mon-ing the One	To summon the One is the Wcyken's version of invoking the Yir (see invoking the Yir). The One or the Power of the One is the source of magic utilized by practitioners of witchcraft (thought by many to be the same source as the Yir)
Syrdis	Sir-dis	Kingdom occupying and extending north from the Cambrian peninsula located at the north-west terminus of the Middle Sea. Syrdis is one of the old kingdoms, often at odds with indigenous tribal peoples to the north and northwest and an on again off again adversary of the Kylgahran
talisman	tal-is-man	Magic device capable of utilizing the Yir to perform one or more various functions. Some talismans are capable of amplifying greatly the power of the Yir fed into them, enhancing the ward cast through their use. Sorcerer's staves are one example of such. In modern times, few retain the knowledge to produce talismans. Those with such knowledge tend to guard their secrets closely. Over time, talismans have become increasingly rare and arcane
telemosis	teh-le-mo-sis	One of the four basic forms of magic that comprise the Yir; involves the transformation of energy from one type to another. Telemosis is used to generate sorcerer's fire and for the truly skilled, the more sinister and deadly balefire

Term	Sounds Like	Definition
telestasis	teh-le-stay-sus	The most exotic of the four basic forms of magic that comprise the Yir and the most controversial. Telestasis pertains to altering the properties of matter, or more specifically, infusing the power of the Yir into matter, changing its nature or condition. Perhaps the most basic application of telestasis is the transformation of water into ice. It is widely believed that in earlier times, during periods of High Magic, telestasis served as the principle form used for the manufacture of talismans. Some think telestasis, the so-called fourth state of magic, is not a form at all but rather a catalyst, a necessary element in the use of all three of the other basic forms, but not a separate form in its own right. After all, employing telemosis to extract heat from water also produces ice. The argument is that no proof currently exists of a purely telestatic application. A few believe telestasis is actually a conduit to the realm of Spirit, a means of bridging the gap between the material world and the ethereal plane. This, of course, is heresy, at least per the tenets of the Penitent faith
Tensys	Ten-sis	Syrdisian city; located on the west bank of the River Wyst at its juncture with the Middle Sea

Term	Sounds Like	Definition
Three Rivers	Three Reh-verz	A territory of the Tieran Empire located along the northwestern coast of the Myr Sea, bounded by the Escalon Plateau to the north, the Syrus River to the west and the Poe River to the east
Tyne	Tine	Capital of the Tieran Province of Quistyn del Aurus, located on the western flank of the Donn Narrows (see Myr Sea)
vyldeen	vil-deen	A member of the Elven nobility
Vyrland	Veer-land	Large Island nation in the Maeryc Ocean north of the Sea Isles; populated by fierce, warlike seafarers who regularly raid all along the west coast of the Cartsys mainland as well as the Suffolk Islands and the Sea Isles
Wycken	Wih-ken	Of or representing the community of witches. It is said that becoming a witch is to be of the Wycken
wysoi	wih-soy	Liquor distilled from fermented wort (as that obtained from corn mash); a favored beverage of the Kylgahran
Wystros	Wis-tros	Kingdom occupying the Hynde peninsula which extends westward into the Maeryc Ocean just west of the Middle Sea. Wystros is one of the old kingdoms, a traditional foe of the Syrdisians and a long time ally and trading partner of the Kylgahran, especially the Southern Clans

Term	Sounds Like	Definition
Yir	Year	The source of sorcerer's magic on Trascera. The power of the Yir also known as the Hidden Source is divided into four basic states or forms, Telepathy, Telekinetics, Telemosis, and Telestasis. Some believe the power of the Yir and the magic used in the practice of witchcraft known as the Power of the One are indistinguishable, both drawn from the same Hidden Source. Others believe that the differences though subtle are distinct and that the two forms of magic are separate both in substance as well as in practice (see Summoning the One)

Acknowledgments

I would like to express heartfelt thanks to the following:

1. George Haire and to the memory of Don Dargo, a pair of high school teachers who saw *something*. Sorry it took so long

2. Lori Bradford, for helping the seed to grow

3. Mom and Dad, because

4. The staff at Wheatmark, Inc. whose insight, professionalism, and patience helped me get out of my own way

5. Rebecca, my wife, my soft rock, who never wavers

And to all who give of their time to read the thing

Until next time,

Randy Ellena
Fresno, CA